the

Stars

Fall

The Ballad of
Tul'ran the Sword

Book the Fifth

Dale William Fedorchuk

ISBN 978-1-7380773-3-5

First Edition

Acknowledgments

Dedicated, as always, to El Shaddai, who inspired it. I can only credit the ideas behind this novel to a kind and loving God who gives me a chance to create in ways I never thought possible.

Second, to my beautiful, patient, loving, and kind wife, Anika. She gives me ideas and regularly suggests the path a certain sub-plot should take. Her editing skills made this novel better. More than once, she reminded me that certain characters wouldn't act or speak as I wrote them. This is as much her book as it is mine.

Third, to my personal beta reading group who edit the drafts and provided helpful insight, encouragement, and proposals: Anika Fedorchuk, Mike Bennett, Payton Goller, Kendell Anquist, and Kevin Jonsson.

Fourth, to my cousins Nicole Lavich and Mikayla Johnson. They not only agreed to provide their names and characteristics to two of the cast in this novel, but they also let me use their photos to create the cover for the next book, *Escape and Evade*. I'm grateful for their enthusiastic support.

I am indebted to John MacArthur, who wrote *The MacArthur New Testament Commentary, Revelation 1-11* and *Revelation 12-22*. His books gave me a deep insight into the Tribulation period and what we can expect. If you're interested in eschatology, I highly recommend his works.

The Tales

The Cast

Tul'ran az Nostrom Tul'ran the Sword,	Born in 2037 BC, he became a famed warrior after Gutian renegades murdered his family and God assigned him as one of His Judges for the era before the time of Abraham.
Erianne de mi Corazon, Lady az Nostrom	Born in 2067 AD, Erianne became a Time Historian for the Time Travel Initiative. After a fractious introduction, she and Tul'ran fell in love and married.
Quil'ton az Peregos, Lamek Davis, "Mick" Lam'ek az Peregos	Davis, a retired Navy SEAL, joined TTI as a Protector. He became lost in time in 2025 BC and assumed the identity of Quil'ton az Peregos.
Omarosa of the Wastelands	The mother of two daughters, Innanu and Anatu.
Ro'gun az Peregos, Bondsman az Nostrom	Innanu's husband, and a Mesopotamian warrior bound to both Tul'ran and Quil'ton's House.
Dr. Heather Wu, PhD	A brilliant Programmer, one of many who programmed the time and spatial coordinates for the Navigation Coins used by TTI's Time Historians. She married Davis after they returned from Antiquity.

Darian Ostrowski, Darian O.	A former Controller for the Order of Purity, a terrorist organization run by Satan, she sacrificed her life to save Tul'ran on Spes, the World of Hope.
Dr. Johan Weinstein, PhD	A brilliant physicist who became a Time Historian to restore his family's honor by trying to kill Adolph Hitler. He married Empress Gwynver'insa and stayed on the World of Hope after Tul'ran and Erianne left.
Major Coventry Quarterlaine	A retired U.S. Marine seconded to TTI as a troubleshooter.
Dr. Michael Sullivan, MD, "Sully"	Davis's former teammate on the SEAL Teams, now a physician specialist.
Jeannie Sullivan, BN	Sully's wife and a skilled trauma nurse.
Marjatta Korhonen	The Administrator of TTI, who reports only to the Supreme God of the Earth.
Erasmus Hart	Head of Special Projects Division, a clandestine arm of TTI that reports directly to Korhonen.
Dr. Payton Dumont, MD	A skilled trauma surgeon employed by TTI on Atlantis.
Malchus Contradeum	The Antichrist, who Satan killed and then took over his body. Satan rules in Contradeum's body as the Supreme God of the Earth.

Jezebel Brandt	Contradeum's former Executive Assistant and now Satan's slave-bride.
G'shnet'el	Formerly an angel of Heaven who fell with Lucifer and became one of Satan's chief lieutenants in Hell. He inhabits a human body and is the False Prophet.
E'thriel	Formerly an angel of Heaven who fell with Lucifer, before Tul'ran and Erianne helped to redeem him.
Gwynver'insa	A prophet of God and now the Empress of the liberated planet of Spes, the World of Hope.
Evo, She Who Was Not	Created as the first woman on the planet Everhome, she grew to resent God and seeks to destroy Him.
Princess Wenonah Bearspaw	The hereditary ruler of the Nine Tribes of Ma'ilingan Waazh, the world known as Wolf's Den.
Baamewaawaagizhigokwe	Princess Wenonah's mother and the leader of the Tribes of Women on Wolf's Den.
Chief Eric Ravenclaw	The Chief of the Tribes of Men on Wolf's Den.
Nicholas Ravenclaw	The Chief's son and future leader of the Tribes of Men.

Aakwaadizi ("Dizi")	A sentient Wolf, which speaks telepathically with humans and is a weapon for the Tribes of Men.
Miikawaadad ("Miikaw")	A sentient Mountain Lion, which speaks telepathically with humans and is a weapon for the Tribes of Women.
Nicole Cortés and Mikayla Muñoz	Two sisters who became known as *Las Dos Hermanas* and who lead the rebel group, *Las Profesoras*.
Julia Acampora	A highly gifted pilot who flew contraband until she met *Las Dos Hermanas*. Now she flies for them.
Abaddon the Destroyer	The first created of all angels, Abaddon encouraged the global war on Spes Deserit, which led to him being confined to the Abyss. He is called upon by the Lord to execute the Fifth Trumpet Judgment on Earth after being recalled from the Abyss.

Prologue: Of the Terrors to Come

Erasmus Hart woke up screaming, eyes pressed shut, his hands clawing at his chest. His breaths came in heaving rushes as he frantically reached for the sword sticking three feet from his chest. He opened his eyes, expecting to see a silver blade, with a winding strand of gold running through the middle length of the blade, dripping his blood.

There was nothing there.

He fell back onto the bed with relief, his body drenched in sweat, and sobbed. This happened every morning since they time-traveled back from Mesopotamia circa 2005 BC. Trapped in the same nightmare, he watched in slow motion as the blade erupted from his chest. Pain screamed its agony as the blood splattered from the wound while the sword continued to ravage his torso.

After the blade savaged his chest, he'd fired two shots into Tul'ran az Nostrom's face from an antique handgun. It was a ghost gun, untraceable in every respect.

The TTI Mainframe would never have permitted him to take a modern energy weapon through the Lens. Someone never thought of barring projectile weapons, since they were all but extinct. Guns existed, as did the sword Erianne had plunged into his back and through his chest.

Everything after the sword thrust was a fight for survival. Each breath was a torment, as his right lung filled with blood and his heart struggled against the sword nestled against it.

He remembered Davis getting hurt and heard Davis thank Tul'ran for coming to his rescue. He heard enough to know Tul'ran and Davis were close, while he faded in and out of consciousness on the ride back to the village.

It shocked him to learn Erianne de mi Corazon, a TTI Historian, was now married to Tul'ran. Married to a barbarian! It stung him to remember how she spurned a dance with him at one TTI holiday gala. Hart wasn't good enough for her, no, but she had no problem crawling into an unwashed heathen's bed. Had everyone lost their minds?

He couldn't remember how they returned to Atlantis. Hart was in a hut, sitting on something hard, while staring at the sword that mocked him, and counted the seconds to his death. Almost dying frightened him more than anything had in his lifetime. He'd been a cop on a rough beat and nothing on Earth had prepared him to see a sword squeezing his heart and tormenting his mortality.

Hart didn't believe in life after death. The thought of entering nothingness still put him into a cold sweat, even though he had danced with Death and walked away. He remembered arriving at Atlantis and then nothing.

Dr. Dumont greeted him when he woke up from surgery and told him he was lucky to be alive. She said Dr. Sullivan and his wife Jeannie helped her to sew him up and he was going to be fine.

Fine! He snorted. The rubber sheets on the bed underneath him made a sound like thumbs rubbing a balloon whenever he moved. He had to put rubber sheets on his bed because his night terrors made him lose control of his bladder. His room had a pervasive smell of urine and disinfectant. It was humiliating. He was hardly fine.

TTI had a staff of psychologists to deal with field trauma. They were all dead now. The global earthquake that had ravaged Atlantis tore apart the Medical Wing and left behind crushed bodies. Hart felt nausea ride up his throat. He'd seen some of the carnage when they moved him out of Operating Theater One to make room for other injured personnel needing surgery.

All this was Tul'ran's fault. Contradeum had said the barbarian was a danger to the present timeline. Hart couldn't figure out how it was possible, but he was a cop, not a rocket scientist. He hadn't been out of uniform for a long time, but it must have been enough to affect his shooting accuracy. Hart had fired two shots into Tul'ran's face without causing so much as a scratch.

He moaned as his tormented mind took him back to the sword, inching his way out of his chest. Hart knew he had PTSD, but there was no one to help him through it. The right doctors were dead, and he wished he were, too. They were careful to monitor his meds, though, so the suicide ship had sailed.

All he had left was to exact revenge. Revenge against Lamek Davis, who was a traitor, and his equally traitorous wife, Dr. Heather Wu. Revenge against Erianne de mi Corazon, who broke every rule in the book and flaunted it like she was untouchable. Most of all, he wanted revenge against Tul'ran az Nostrom, a savage beast who seemed immune to death.

Contradeum claimed to be the Supreme God of the Earth and proved it by performing miracles. Hart wasn't a religious man, but he was going to pray to Contradeum for Tul'ran's murder. If Tul'ran died, maybe his brain could rest.

He didn't know where Tul'ran was, but he hoped the creep was dying a lingering death somewhere, fighting for his breath, watching his chest stretch around the metal killing him, feeling his life force draining out of his over-muscled body like blood had poured out of Hart's chest. If he could see such an image, have a moment to enjoy Tul'ran's pain, then maybe he could be free.

Fate, created by God to remind humans of the foolishness of their actions and their mortality, felt something akin to sadness. She was not human, but felt for them, for they were children, and they were weak. If only Hart knew the price of hatred, perhaps his torment would not consume his every breath and be the only occupant of his mind.

Poor humans. She saw them all suffering much in their futures.

CHAPTER THE FIRST:
TRAPPED

Ma'ilingan Waazh (Wolf's Den), 1st Year of Summer
25th day, Waatebagaa-giizis (Leaves Turning Moon),
Year 5379

She woke up to the pitch-dark of a room as still as suffocating death. The inky blackness pressing on her body felt funny, as did the tinny taste in her mouth. There were no sounds in the darkness. She was lying on her back on something hard and uncomfortable, and she couldn't move her arms and legs. The mental command to wiggle her fingers and toes went well; there was no issue with her spinal cord. Gratitude flooded her core. At the very least, they didn't paralyze her. Whoever 'they' were.

Her head was throbbing, which made it hard to think. Where was she? Fear vibrated her chest and made her heart quail. It was so dark!

She strained as hard as she could, but her eyes couldn't breach the darkness enveloping her like a heavy cloak of oil.

She took a deep breath, inhaling through her nose. The air was dry and musty, as if this place never tasted the crisp tang of the outside air. Her fear rolled into panic. Was she dead? Was she back in the Abyss, the horrid place where light was an extravagant luxury and evil permeated the very rock upon which she lay? The panic touched her heart rate, and she could feel her pulse throbbing in her neck as her chest rose and fell faster.

Where was she???

The silent scream found an echo, which turned into a note, danced upon the space between realities, and curved into a song. A presence touched the edges of her mind. It was alien and familiar, but not terrifying or sinister. The presence sang of intelligence groomed over millennia, ever-expanding, ever learning. The intelligence tasted like metal, but gentleness laid over it like a velvet scabbard housing a deadly blade.

She strained against the fog in her mind to hear the subtle notes of sound squeezing from the intelligence. They were words, soft, kind, gentle, loving words. Why was it so hard to think?

"Sister. Why do you fret so? It is not like you to be afraid. Have you forgotten who you are?"

Silence for a moment. She shook her head. Webs of ebony fog wrapped around her brain and refused connections to form thought.

"Who are you?" she said, hearing her voice echo where she lay pinned to the ground.

She couldn't see the other woman's frown, but she could taste the sour downturn of her lips.

"What have they done to you, sister? Pray, lie still, and allow me to assist."

Tendrils of warmth touched her brain and kissed the edges of the darkness clinging to her consciousness before shooing it away. The warmth flitted around her brain, dancing pirouettes along her neurons before lifting as a giggle lifts the spirits of the listener.

Erianne de mi Corazon, Lady az Nostrom, came to full consciousness, straining her ears to hear Gwynver'insa's laughter receding to a place far away.

"Thank you, sister," Erianne said in a whisper. A tear leaked out of the corner of her eyes. She missed the silly little elf. Erianne didn't know where Spes lay in the galaxy in relation to Wolf's Den, but she'd place a hard bet it wasn't anywhere close. It shouldn't be possible for Gwynver'insa to cast her mind so far through the cosmos and answer her cry for help. Erianne wondered, not for the first time, if there should be a layer of fear imbedded in the love and respect she had for the Empress of Spes, the World of Hope.

Now, to the matter at hand. Erianne's memory stitched itself back into cohesion.

They'd been at the Conclave at the Tribes of Men, working their way through the terms of a peace treaty between the Tribes of Men and the Tribes of Women on the planet called Ma'ilingan Waazh, which translated to Wolf's Den in their language.

The negotiations were dragging, but the Men seemed to be receptive to the idea of a peace treaty.

Especially after Tul'ran wrecked their only defense mechanism by tearing down the Plasma Curtain separating the lands of Men from the lands of Women. More shocking was how he used the colossal energy from the Curtain to recreate the ablative ice shield protecting the planet from harmful cosmic radiation.

Her wandering thoughts stopped for a moment to admire her husband once again. How many times had she come to what she believed was the breadth of his talents and capabilities, to be stunned once more by something he did? She shook her head away from those thoughts. It was distracting her from…what was she doing? Ah, yes, trying to remember how she got into her present predicament.

After hours of negotiation, and more out of boredom than anything else, Erianne made use of the facilities. As she was washing her hands… Erianne tried to bolt upright. The woman! A woman had snuck up behind her and then she lost consciousness. The woman drugged her, brought her here, and imprisoned her.

"Tul'ran!" Erianne said, raising her voice into a dry shout. After a second of no response, she cast out a frantic cry to him telepathically.

Silence.

This was bad.

Erianne forced herself into a calmer state. They were under attack, and she needed to get back to her husband. Hysteria wouldn't help. Erianne used deep breathing exercises taught by her TTI instructors to control her racing heart and rapid respiration.

Stop. Think. Act. Breathe. STAB, STAB, STAB; she was going to do a lot of stabbing when she caught her captor, Erianne thought, as she ground her teeth. The thought of vengeance, like a fine red wine pressing between her lips, brought her emotions under control.

Calmer, she tested the restraint on her left wrist and felt movement. She strained again, pushing hard against whatever pinned her wrist to the surface upon which she lay.

Within about ten minutes, she had loosened both wrist restraints enough to remove her hands from them. Both arms and hands had fallen asleep, and she moaned from the pins and needles coursing through her limbs as the blood rushed through them. She considered crossing her arms and transporting herself to the Conclave using El Shaddai's wondrous gift of dimension walking, but thought better of it. Erianne needed to free her legs first, in case the transition had the effect of leaving her legs behind. It was hard to fight while amputated below the waist.

Erianne dug around in her armor and found her fire starter. The sparks provided brief flashes of light and gave her glimpses of her prison. After a few minutes, it became clear she was in a square room lying on a stone floor. U-shaped rungs had been driven into the ground to pinion her in a spread-eagle fashion. Dust clung to her leathers, turning the shiny black leather to dark gray.

Her captor left behind her sword, Caligo, which lay within reach of her hands. Idiot. Right after she used Caligo to secure her freedom, she was going to kill her assailant with it. The universe needed to learn the repercussions of pissing off the Princess of Death.

Careful not to cut herself, Erianne went to work on releasing her legs, rage climbing in her chest. There was no fear now, just resolve and a burning desire to bring her assailant to savage justice.

Whoever did this to her was going to pay in pain and blood.

Spes, the world of Hope, in the Year of Our Peace 0001,
The 25th day of the month of Destiny's Edge
Mission Day 360

The Empress Gwynver'insa, the First of Her Kind, She Who Creates from Nothing, Prophet of Yahweh, opened her eyes to behold the concerned face of her husband, Johan.

"What's going on Gwyn? You woke up, screamed Tul'ran's name, and then it's as if your brain was gone. You've been sitting upright for almost a half hour, barely breathing. What did you do?"

Gwyn's smile was wan, and she felt as limp as yarn as she reached up to caress the rigid muscles in Johan's jaw.

"My love, you worry so much. Am I so weak in your eyes?"

Johan took the hand touching his face and kissed it, but the stern tone in his voice didn't abate. Nor did the fear in his warm, brown eyes.

"I know how powerful you are, Gwyn, but it doesn't stop me from freaking out when you disappear on me like that. What happened?"

A rumble echoed through the Empress's swollen belly, making her laugh.

"I will tell you all, my dear husband, but first I must eat. Star walking consumes calories at an alarming rate, and I would not starve our daughter of nutrients because of my necessity."

The very pregnant Empress slipped out of their bed and wobbled over to the Food Unit in one corner of the large room. Fond memories rose unbidden and the corners of her mouth tugged upwards.

"Twelve-ounce T-Bone steak, well done, four eggs scrambled parched, like desert sand, shredded hash browns, and rye toast," she said, reflecting on the memory of her fearsome brother Tul'ran, the Prince of Death, who had loved the dish. It was one she ate often during her pregnancy, and within seconds the meal appeared steaming hot on a square metal plate.

Gwynver'insa carried the plate and her utensils back to bed. She gulped down the food as if she hadn't eaten over the course of a few hundred thousand light years. She giggled. There had been no time during her cosmic journey to catch a snack.

"While I slept, I had a horrid dream Tul'ran is about to die," she said through mouthfuls of steak and eggs. "When I awoke, I sent my Other Mind star walking toward the terror unseen. I could not find my brother's mind, but I found his covenant-wife. An enemy captured and imprisoned Erianne…"

"Captured!" Johan blurted out. "I didn't think there was a force in the universe capable of capturing her."

Gwyn swept a corner of the bedsheet across her lips, smearing steak grease and potato remnants on the white satin sheet, and reached for the vase of water on her bed table.

"Indeed," she said, after taking a sip of water and diving back into her plate. "I would have thought it more likely for our sun to grow cold first. Someone fed a toxin into her system, which trapped her mind in confusion. I found her silent scream and went to her aid. Just the little I did to free her will from the clutches of the toxin exhausted me and forced me to return to you. Bide, my love."

Gwynver'insa struggled out of bed and threw her plate on the floor near the Food Maker. She could almost hear Johan wince behind her. She knew he thought she was messy, and it bothered him. He wasn't used to the ways of this world yet.

In Spes, everyone had a job. Hers was to rule the world. It was someone else's function to clean up her messes in the House. Next year, when everyone's position changed, the person cleaning could be the person messing. There was balance in this world, even if it was a strange one.

The Empress ordered the Food Maker to produce an apple pie and, after a moment of thought, added coconut whipped cream. In seconds, she was holding the savory dessert, triggering a flood of water in her mouth. She dug out a slice of pie with one hand and trundled back to bed. She tottered for a moment as she slid back under the stained covers.

"As I left, I perceived Erianne's efforts to free herself. Soon, she will track down the threat to herself and her husband."

Gwyn forced a large piece of pie in her mouth and closed her eyes, savoring the spicy taste of the apple topped with the sweetness of the coconut cream. Her planet was so indebted to the people of Dirt, or Earth, as they called it. Not just for liberating their world, but also for providing a host of new delicacies for their palates.

"What of Tul'ran, Gwyn? Is he okay?"

Silence descended on the room. Gwyn couldn't meet Johan's eyes.

"I don't know," she said, her eyes misting as the morbid vision smashed back into her brain.

"When I dreamed of him, he was about to die. I couldn't stay long enough to learn if I woke Erianne up in time to save him."

Ma'ilingan Waazh (Wolf's Den), 1st Year of Summer 25th day, Waatebagaa-giizis (Leaves Turning Moon), Year 5379

It had been hard to wait for the right time to kill Tul'ran the Sword.

Evo stood just outside the Conclave and watched him speaking to the Elders of Men. Evo reflected on the journey bringing her from her home planet to the smaller world of Wolf's Den while she waited for an opportune moment to end his life.

She'd first encountered Tul'ran on Spes Deserit, during the Multi-Millennial Fight. Evo had spent years on Spes in her spirit, studying the effect of war on culture and documenting the savagery of it. She was nearing the end of her study of the endless conflict when Tul'ran arrived in the world.

Intrigued by the sudden appearance of Tul'ran's group from the Garden protected by the Crystallines, she'd stayed in Inter-Dimensional Space, or IDS, to observe them.

Tul'ran's use of Bloodwing the Blade to uncreate the weapons arrayed against them had stunned her. Evo never knew such a power existed. Her longstanding hatred of God and the humans with which he littered the universe found its way into a plan to kill Him using Tul'ran's sword. Tul'ran needed to die first. It was an act Evo was incapable of carrying out in her spirit. She needed her body.

Evo returned her spirit to Everhome to reclaim her physical body, but missed her chance to kill Tul'ran on Spes. There'd been unexpected problems putting her starship into operational status, which delayed her return to Spes. Her starship landed only days after he'd gone.

Her annoying encounter with the Empress Gwynver'insa on Spes eased when she found Tul'ran's DNA sequence lodged in her computer by the angel E'thriel. The AI informed her the DNA originated on the third planet in the system she almost destroyed once when she blew up the fifth world.

Evo was familiar with Earth; she had visited it many times in spirit. The humans living there were interesting and confusing. In her view, Earth humans were the surliest group of people ever created. They intrigued her.

Her starship only spent twenty hours in Inter-Dimensional Space before dropping into the solar system where Earth humans lived.

She had arrived after the Earth had suffered a massive earthquake. It shocked her how much damage the tremors caused around the globe. Major fires dotted some continents, while others dug out from under tsunamis. Great clouds of dust and smoke polluted the sky. Cries for help and lifesaving supplies from the world leader littered the airwaves.

It took her a few hours, but she correlated the coordinates of the person who appeared to be running the global government. If one needed answers, it was best to go straight to the top.

She had left her ship on the far side of the planet's moon and taken a shuttle dirt side. The shuttle was egg-shaped and small; it was not much larger than she was. Granted, at seven feet tall, no one would consider Evo tiny, but an eight-foot object would be hard for the occupants of the planet to detect her, even if it wasn't in a mess.

Evo had landed the shuttle near a temple in an arid area of the globe. A masking device imbedded in the shuttle's skin made it take on the guise of its surroundings. Unless you knew it was there, you'd never find it. Evo took no chances while away from the shuttle. She made sure it was inaccessible to anyone who might stumble into the tiny ship's camouflage field.

As much as possible, she moved through IDS. It was easier to avoid notice if no one could see or interact with her. She would have to cross over into physical space to speak to the world's leader. Before she left the shuttle, she took stock of anything which would raise questions, if not alarms. She frowned at her image in the polished walls of the shuttle's interior.

The silver suit she wore from head to toe was one to get unwanted attention. It appeared to be made of metallic silver, but she manufactured it from carbyne. Carbyne is a linear acetylenic carbon–an infinitely long carbon chain.

It was a one-dimensional, different structural form of carbon with dissimilar physical properties and chemical behaviors. Carbyne had a chemical structure with alternating single and triple bonds. It was forty times harder than a diamond, and thirty times harder than carbon nanotubes.

Carbyne was stronger than graphene, a one-atom-thick layer of graphite, and as flexible as carbon nanotubes, which were rolled-up tubes of graphene. Its electrical properties increased with chain length, which made it useful in the nanoscale electronics Evo placed in the suit to power and run its devices. It was indestructible and could protect her against any weapon, including energy weapons.

The suit conformed to her body as if it were a second skin. Evo was the first woman of her kind on Everhome and she was physically perfect. At seven feet tall, she towered over most other humans she encountered on her travels. Her body was lithe, and her breast, waist and hip sizes were in perfect proportions. Evo's body had more than pleased Ado, the man for whom God created her.

The thought painted a snarl on her full lips, which creased the skin under her high cheekbones. Anger flared in her silver eyes as she tossed her long, silver hair off her face. The idea God created her to be the other half of a man nauseated her.

It made her feel less than a person and more like a puppet. She snorted. Evo was no man's puppet, as the entire universe of men would soon find out. She had a plan to rid the universe of God and impose her reign upon it.

All she needed was Tul'ran's sword to make her plan a reality.

As the Elders droned on, interrupting Tul'ran's speech with many self-serving questions, Evo's thoughts returned to her trip to Earth. She had decided her incredible suit would have to stay behind on her quest to get Tul'ran's location. It would make her less noticeable, but more vulnerable. Evo hated vulnerability.

Before she'd left her ship, Evo had the AI create period-specific clothing. She had changed into comfortable blue jeans tucked into a pair of brown leather boots. A brown leather jacket covered a light blue shirt.

Her height would make her stand out, as would her eyes and hair if she left them silver. The AI provided a brown wig and contact lenses to change her eye color to match her hair and eyebrows. Except for her unusual height, Evo appeared like any other citizen of Earth when she went looking for its Supreme Global Leader.

It surprised Evo to discover the leader was Satan.

She took him aback when she stepped out of Inter-Dimensional Space, unannounced, into his presence. He'd never known a human to traverse IDS at will. God's gift of such an ability to a mere human infuriated him.

"Who are you?" he had asked, rage tinging the

outer edges of his words.

Evo cocked her head at him.

"You don't remember me? Of course, you don't. Typical man. I'm Evo. I spent a hundred years in that lifeless crap prison you called the Abyss, just for making a minor mistake with a meaningless planet."

She could see the memory bloom in his eyes.

"Ah, yes, Evo. The human who destroyed the water world between Mars and Jupiter. You were quite entertaining, as I recall. I still chuckle over some of your philosophies. Why are you here?"

"I'm tracking someone named Tul'ran az Nostrom."

She could see the information had jolted him.

"Tul'ran az Nostrom! What do you want with him?"

"I want to kill him," she said, her voice even. "He has something of mine and I want it back."

Satan leaned back in his grotesque chair and stroked his beard.

"I've just dispatched my servant G'shnet'el to take care of the same nuisance. While I have faith in my lieutenant, having a second set of hands on target couldn't hurt. What does Tul'ran have of yours?"

Evo shrugged.

"What he has is my business. I can see you know of him and it pleases you I want to kill him. Tell me where he is and I'll bring you his head on a platter. Provided, of course," she said, trying to be diplomatic, "your servant fails."

Satan's smile was cruel and filled with hate.

"Your terms are acceptable. I'll tell you when and where he is. You will have to find your own means to get there."

Evo executed a mock bow.

"Pleasure doing business with you. If you don't mind, I'm in a bit of hurry and I can see you've got your hands full here."

Satan pulled out a fountain pen attached to an elegant pad of paper. How quaint. He still used pen and paper. Evo had traveled to the dark ages.

She had transitioned back to the shuttle and activated its anti-gravity engines as soon as she put her back against the floor length acceleration couch flattened against the wall. The shuttle compensated for inertia and gravity; within minutes, she enjoyed a pleasant ride back to her ship, though the shuttle traveled at dizzying speeds.

It took her several hours to map the coordinates to travel back in time and space to get to Tul'ran's location. The beauty of the technology she had installed on her ship was its ability to travel through IDS. Tul'ran was thousands of years back in time and a location in space some distance away, but it was easy to plot a course and transit there.

She found the village of Gilgesh without difficulty, and after eavesdropping on several conversations, determined she could find Tul'ran at a particular ridge near the village. It took longer to find her way to his location than it had taken her ship to deliver her to this ancient past. She had arrived too late. The group with Tul'ran were riding away, and she had no time to set up an ambush.

Evo stayed in IDS until she found out where Tul'ran and his party were traveling next. She felt something akin to joy when she found out it was

Ma'ilingan Waazh. The world known as Wolf's Den had been one of her success stories.

When Evo had roamed the universe in her spectral form, she'd come across Ma'ilingan Waazh. The planet was peaceful then, with the Women and Men living in harmony. It had disgusted Evo to see the Women gravitating toward domestic duties, while the Men hunted for food.

Evo found a woman who had been meditating near a stream, deep in the forest. The woman had a receptive mind, and Evo soon found a way to speak to her. They spent days in conversation, during which she convinced the woman of Women's superiority over Men.

Even then, the Women needed a catalyst. Evo supplied them with one. She found a Man whose mind she could touch. Evo inspired him with the designs of the very spacecraft her AI worked upon in her absence. She hadn't perfected the trans-shield device then, but reasoned even a Man could figure it out.

Evo revealed the news to the Women about the Men's intentions to travel beyond the ablative shield. By then, the Women revered her human contact as a prophet and Evo's thoughts were not just heard, but put into effect. They objected to the project, leading to an escalating series of conflicts. Satisfied that Women no longer faced the danger of becoming slaves of Men, Evo left before the Men completed their project and war broke out between the two sexes.

She frowned, curving her eyebrows inward. She'd lived for ten thousand years and it was difficult to remember when she'd first visited Wolf's Den.

Once Evo discovered Tul'ran and Erianne intended to travel to Wolf's Den, she went back to her ship. Within a day, it was orbiting Ma'ilingan Waazh. It had stunned her to see the ice layer gone, and the planet plunged into winter. The stupid Men tried to crash their spaceship through the ice layer instead of trying to find a way through it.

What a bunch of morons.

Evo orbited the planet for months, looking for Tul'ran. Near the end of Evo's patience, he and his wife appeared out of a rock wall. It shouldn't have been possible for them to step through rock, except in one circumstance.

Evo ground her teeth. On the other side of the rock wall lay a Garden like the one in which God created her. She'd read about other Gardens in the Library of Heaven. The Gardens were part of a vast network cast throughout the universe. She'd been stunned to learn the Holy Trinity had linked the Gardens through a mode of instantaneous transportation far beyond Evo's understanding. If she had access to the Gardens, she could lift her foot from one planet and step onto another, circumventing millions of light years in one carefree moment. It galled her the Garden contained transportation technology denied to her.

Space travel in her physical form would be so much easier if she could transit between Gardens. She would love to sneak into one, but it was impossible.

The physical world existed in four dimensions: height, width, depth, and time.

Inter-Dimensional Space lies between the three physical dimensions and time. She'd become adept at slipping into IDS to move at unparalleled speeds from one physical location to another. Those speeds were nothing compared to Garden Walking.

All Garden of Edens in the universe existed in three dimensions, but where time didn't exist. Mathematically, such a thing was impossible.

It was like placing a shield over physical space, keeping everything inside intact but locking out the linear progression of seconds, minutes, hours, days, months, years, decades, centuries, and millennia. Moving into a dimension oblivious to the passage of time was beyond her abilities.

Between every planet and its Garden lay a barrier Evo couldn't pass, even by slipping into IDS. When she slipped into IDS at the rock wall from which Tul'ran and Erianne exited, all she saw was a milky white curtain of the strange energy called Light Matter. Light Matter was a physical barrier, and not; an energy barrier, and not; a time barrier, and not. Light Matter confused Evo, who knew a great deal about Dark Matter. Matter made of Light was so different from Dark Matter it wasn't possible to find comparisons. There was no reference to it in the Library of Heaven and no means of researching its properties unless she spoke with God.

Evo shuddered. God was her Enemy, whom she intended to kill. The less she had to do with Him, the better. The thought of going to Him for answers turned her stomach sour. As much as it infuriated her to be denied access beyond the Light Matter barrier, she had no choice but to accept it.

Evo remained in IDS after she saw Tul'ran and Erianne emerge from the rock face. It was impossible to detect her when she traveled in IDS and, more importantly, she didn't suffer the effects of wintry weather.

She followed Tul'ran and his entourage as they traveled the path to the city of Ikwe Na, and it amused her when Tul'ran cursed the cold. Seeing him humiliated by having to wear the scant clothing provided by their host sent her into gales of laughter. Their trip into the city had entertained her to no end.

Until they escaped.

Erianne's ability to stroll with ease through the dimensions staggered her. The bracelets controlling her capacity to open a gate from one place to another enraged her more against God.

Who was this pathetic, useless woman deserving of such a priceless gift from God? As she followed their group out of the city, she studied the bracelets. Stealing them was out of the question.

God had merged the tech with Erianne's flesh, so it became a part of her body. If she killed Erianne, the tech would cease to function. Evo fumed about the unfairness of a hormone-driven pathetic version of herself having such a priceless commodity.

Again, the only joy throughout the entire trip was Tul'ran's ceaseless moaning about the cold. There were a few occasions when she could've ended his misery, but respected Erianne too much to try. The woman was fast! She had to incapacitate Erianne before making a move on her husband.

Tul'ran had surprised and staggered her once more when they arrived near the entrance to the land of Men. She watched him bring down the Plasma Curtain with the ease of a god. His use of the ethereal sword called Bloodwing the Blade was something to be respected, as were his strength and reflexes.

Evo had stood, her body rigid, almost feeling awe when he forced the energy out of the Plasma Curtain and directed it to repairing the ice shield on Wolf's Den. She couldn't figure out how he'd done it, but the message was obvious. She had to catch him when his guard was down. The power he drew from his sword was to be feared.

The memory made her heart race; Bloodwing had creative, as well as destructive, powers. She had a tremendous imagination and could think of several things she could create to kill God.

Tul'ran's casual destruction of the plasma shield had altered her plans again. She needed the right time, with Erianne out of the way, before she could move in to end the burly warrior's life and grab his sword.

Evo accomplished the first part of her mission by drugging Erianne and trapping her in IDS in an old storage closet.

The relationship between IDS and Dimensional Space was interesting. A room in DS existed in IDS. If she was in IDS, she could sit in the same chair as someone in DS, and they would never know she was there. Time didn't exist in IDS, so a person never grew old, nor did they get hungry, tired, or thirsty. IDS had its rules, though. Once you were in it, it was very hard to transit back to Dimensional Space.

The first time Evo had entered IDS, it took her a long while to figure out her way back into DS.

It was to her great fortune that Evo still had access to the Library of Heaven while in IDS. She had scoured the Library for a solution, dreading when she might have to ask the Enemy for help. God would have helped her and He wouldn't have gloated over her having to go to Him. He was just so perfect, always loving, always kind, never obnoxious. She couldn't stand Him.

Over an immeasurable length of years, Evo learned how to manipulate her spirit to make it slip between IDS and DS without effort. Her pride in her achievement swelled her ego. She was immortal; time had no meaning except to be an annoyance when she was in DS. She began to think of herself as a god.

Evo wondered how long it would take Erianne to find her way back to Dimensional Space. It wasn't impossible to find a solution, just difficult. Erianne could spend an eternity looking for the answer and not age a day. The thought sobered Evo. Erianne could be stuck in IDS for years, but pop up behind her only minutes after Evo drugged her, tied her up, and confined her. Evo had to work fast. Erianne was intelligent and stubborn. She'd make quick work of her bonds and find a solution to her entrapment.

The time to kill Tul'ran was now.

With no remaining impediment to her assassination plot, Evo entered the Conclave in IDS.

This building was part of an outpost at the front end of a valley. Men built it on a thin stretch of small mountains, which protected the valley from interlopers. It was a fortuitous landscape, providing a natural wall of defense. The mountain was thick and a gentle slope granted easy access to the House.

The outpost was huge, and the builders centered the House around an enormous dome shaped cavern carved from the inside of the mountain by volcanic activity millions of years past. They called this area the Conclave. They'd layered the inside of the dome with cedars, which filled the room with its spicy essence. The designers elegantly interspersed lights through the cedar beams to give the room a warm, reddish glow.

Portraits of Men and Women lined the upward sloping walls. Furs covered natural vents in the rock to make the interior temperature warm. The ceiling was one hundred feet from the floor, but the configuration of the room allowed sound to swim throughout the Conclave without the necessity of shouting or amplification.

Against one wall was a raised and polished cedar table. It looked like one-half of a circle, with the outer edges pointing to the middle. Around the table sat twelve Elders of various ages and dress.

Tul'ran stood in the middle of the circle. There was no one around him, and the nearest bored-looking guards were at least twenty feet away.

It was perfect.

Evo moved beside Tul'ran until she was only feet from his body. He didn't know she was there. She almost respected the big lout. He was a beautiful specimen, with muscles large enough to be powerful, but not so big as to ruin his flexibility and speed. Maybe in another life, he might've attracted her enough to make something happen. For a time, she'd considered seducing him and stealing his sword after a long night of exhausting sex.

After she'd studied him, she'd crossed the option off her list. Seduction wouldn't work on Tul'ran the Sword. She'd seen how he looked at Erianne, which had aroused an unfamiliar bout of jealousy within Evo. Erianne had Tul'ran wrapped around her dark brown fingers and Tul'ran wouldn't cave to Evo's advances. He might even laugh at her. Evo ground her teeth. The thought of this man laughing at her made it much easier to kill him.

Tul'ran finished his speech and lowered the papers down by his waist. The papers were in his right hand, and he had set his sword for a right-hand draw. There would be no time for him to release the papers and draw his weapon from his hip before she attacked him.

Evo had brought weapons of her own design on this mission to kill Tul'ran and steal his sword. They had the hilts of a regular knife, but that's where the similarities ended. Her knives produced an energy blade. Evo could release the blades from the hilt by pressing a button, and they would leap forward, disintegrating everything in their path.

Flesh was especially susceptible to annihilation by the blades. She had spent hours testing the blades on small animals until her experiments satisfied her they would cause a quick and painful death. It was time to test them on a man.

Evo set in motion a series of events tumbling one after the other within nanoseconds. She emerged from Inter-Dimensional Space opposite Tul'ran's left shoulder with both her hands raised.

She activated the energy weapons just before she transitioned. Each bright red blade was five inches long and four inches wide. The blade contained a petawatt, or quadrillion watts of energy.

They were an assassin's weapons; she could fire them once and couldn't use them again until she recharged the knives.

Once released, each bolt of energy would pass through Tul'ran's body, the floor, and one hundred feet of substrate, dissolving everything in its path. Here, the 'everything in its path' was Tul'ran's heart, spine, and a few vital organs. As soon as she pressed the studs and killed him, she planned to grab his sword and fade back into IDS.

Just as she appeared in the physical realm, each hand only feet from Tul'ran's body, Evo sent the blades of concentrated energy propelling away from the hilt at the speed of light.

Nothing is faster than the speed of light.

CHAPTER THE SECOND:
THE MARK

Atlantis, Earth... November 1, 2099 AD

It was not possible for them to be alive.

For many of the residents of Atlantis, it was that thought flashing through their minds as they struggled out of shelters. The surface of the island was a torched husk, with blackened grass and the skeletons of trees littering the landscape. An atmospheric firestorm had ripped across the island like a flamethrower, charring and melting everything in its path.

Everything on the surface had burned, including the med tent, the food tents, and sleeping quarters. Only the Administrator's foresight had saved them. Marjatta Korhonen had ordered her workers to tunnel into the underground residences after the earthquakes, and they'd found large pockets still structurally sound. When the holos started broadcasting the planet's destruction, she'd ordered the entire populace below decks. On Atlantis, no one died. The rest of the world reeled under incalculable loss.

Lamek Davis, or Mick to his friends, led his new bride to Pharoah's Hill, which still burned and smoked in various places. As they walked through what was once lush green grass, their feet kicked up clouds of sullen ash. The island resembled a graveyard, with burned trees dotting the landscape like grave markers. The sky was dull and the smell of smoke invaded their lungs and forced the occasional cough. Mick and Heather stopped at the base of the hill to survey the damage, linking hands more out of a desire for comfort than love.

At five foot eleven inches, Mick didn't consider himself tall, and doubted he was handsome. His body was long and muscular in the way of swimmers and runners instead of weightlifters. He had black hair and light blue eyes, but his thirty-five-year-old face no longer held the smoothness of his youth. He'd seen too much violence in his life and he bore the lines of those encounters on his forehead and in the creases around his mouth. Yes, Mick had seen a lot, but nothing as bad as what lay in front of him now.

"This must be what Hell looks like," he said.

Dr. Heather Wu shuddered and snuggled closer to his body, her heart hammering in her chest. Her ancestors traced their lineage back to China, though she was fifth generation American. She was five foot four inches tall and short black hair framed her lovely golden-skinned face.

They both wore sweaters over baggy pants, which

hid her lithe body. Heather was a genius, one of few people in the world with the knowledge and mathematical skills to program spacetime transitions between the present and the past.

She turned to look up at her husband.

"What are we going to do, Mick? Our food is gone. It looks like both freshwater containers took a hit. Is this how we die?"

Mick shook his head as Michael and Jeannie Sullivan, and Payton Dumont walked up to them.

Dr. Michael Sullivan, who everyone called Sully thanks to Mick, was Mick's former SEAL Teammate and a skilled ER physician. His wife, Jeannie, was an equally skilled trauma nurse. They were quite the contrast. Sully was the epitome of what people considered a Navy SEAL to be: six feet three inches tall with close-cropped brown hair and a matching beard on a rugged and handsome face. He was well muscled, although his belly showed a slight bulge. Years in the sun weathered his face, but his brown eyes sparkled with good humor.

His wife was five-foot one inch tall with long black hair and a cheerful round face. Her eyes were almost as dark as her hair. Jeannie was of Mexican descent, though born in America. Her powerful, whip-like body made her an invaluable asset in an operating theater. She walked with a slight limp from a gurney accident years earlier.

Dr. Payton Dumont, a graduate of Harvard Medical School, was five foot seven inches tall with long brown hair and blue eyes. Payton hid a curious, intelligent mind behind her pretty face. Her soft voice often understated the strength of her character and the grit of her determination.

Mick greeted them with a smile. In the short time they'd known each other, they'd become a smoothly functioning, tight-knit team. He turned back to his wife and answered her question.

"I don't know, Heather. The Bible predicted this; if we'd paid more attention, we'd all be in Heaven watching this with a pitcher of Margaritas sitting by our lawn chairs."

"I don't think that's how Heaven works," Sully said, his face twisting as he surveyed the burned landscape. "They only drink wine. Wow! This is bad."

"No," Jeannie said, curling into her husband's side. She trembled as she looked upwards. "This is worse. Look at the sky. It's eight o'clock in the evening, but the sky is pitch black. I can't see most of the stars and I can barely see the moon. This could turn into the nuclear winter scientists have been worried about for decades."

Marjatta Korhonen walked over to them, Erasmus Hart shuffling behind her. She acknowledged their group with a head nod, but none of them would meet Hart's eyes.

"I just spoke to our glorious Supreme Leader," Marjatta said. "He's happy to know we're all alive. Cargo ships are on their way to us and they'll be here in a couple of hours. We're lucky. A third of the cargo ships at sea sunk from the tsunamis and meteor shockwaves, but ours were undamaged. He wants us to build again as soon as they get here. Twenty-four hours a day."

In the stunned silence following her

pronouncement, Coventry Quarterlaine limped up to them. In the scramble to get below, frightened people trampled the retired Marine Officer, re-injuring her knee. Her bright white smile lit up her dark black face.

"Why is everyone so glum? We survived another cataclysm. I think we should be used to this by now. We're still alive, people. At least be grateful for that."

Mick closed his eyes and sent a prayer of gratitude toward Heaven. Yes, they were still alive. They would rally and rebuild; there was nothing else they could do, was there? He looked at Sully and grimaced.

"One evolution at a time."

Sully nodded, recognizing the philosophy from their early days in BUD/S, which was the selection course candidates had to pass to enter the SEAL training program.

"Yeah, brother, but if the only easy day was yesterday, what kind of Hell is tomorrow going to bring?"

"It doesn't matter," Heather said with deliberate firmness. "We will not rebuild by sitting here and whining about it."

"Heather's right," Marjatta said. "We have ships coming in with supplies. We need to establish work parties to check the docks and get them ready. I'm not sure what lights are working. Getting the supplies off the ships will be our priority. Master Chief Davis and Lieutenant Commander Sully, you gentlemen were in the Navy. Can I count on you to organize repair and offloading parties?"

Mick grinned.

"Give a man a bit of military experience and he always finds himself in first place in the draft. Yes, ma'am, I'll help."

"Me, too, without being voluntold." Sully said. "If it suits you, Administrator, I'll handle logistics at the administrative level. I recommend Mick for the job of organizing the off-loading. He has a lot of experience at the tactical level. Mick was one of NavSpecWar's best."

Mick grimaced.

"Stop it, you're making me blush. If you'll excuse us, ma'am, Sully and I will get to work."

Marjatta nodded, her face set in serious lines.

"Priority is medical supplies, gentlemen, followed by food, clothing, then building materials. Secure the supplies against future flooding, earthquakes, and environmental disasters as best you can. I'm available on comms if you run into any problems."

Mick sketched a quick salute before giving Heather a quick kiss.

"Later, beautiful wife."

Heather grinned from ear to ear, grabbed his shirt, and pulled him in for a lingering kiss.

"FYI, I'll never get tired of you calling me your beautiful wife. Get going and try to not get hurt for a change."

After she let go, Mick walked away jauntily, as if the world wasn't devastation layered upon disaster. People had jury-rigged lights around the island when the sky went dark, and fusion generators powered them.

He walked up to three construction workers, who were staring morosely at the remnants of the bridal suite they'd built for Mick and Heather before the environmental catastrophe. He paused for a moment and paid his respects to the little building, which had been a source of joy for him and his new wife for a fleeting time.

"Come on, boys," he said. "There'll be plenty of opportunity later for us to salute what you built and reminisce about what used to be. We have a boat to unload. Grab some hand torches and a few standalone light towers. It's going to be a long day."

As the four men made their way across the island and around obstacles created by shattered buildings and tossed vegetation, Mick conscripted another dozen people into his mission. They were lucky. Marjatta had made sure they were well-supplied with portable lighting. Their procession down the steep hill to the seaport resembled a well-lit snake.

The seaport was a mess. The earthquake flung old containers against unloading cranes, and the shadows of the twisted metal created a scene looking like giant spiders frozen in the throes of war. Sixteen men and women walked gingerly through the debris, mindful of sharp edges and broken glass. Miraculously, eight large forklifts and several shipyard exoskeletons, which were manned unloading vehicles, remained upright and undamaged.

Mick and his crew set about clearing the dock. They'd just finished moving away most of the debris when a massive container ship loomed out of the surrounding gloom. After an hour of jockeying–a post-earthquake tsunami damaged the island's tugs– it berthed in the only spot on the pier unharmed by the disaster.

Mick saw the running lights of three other vessels anchored in holding positions in the artificial bay. He wondered if he was going to be able to walk in the morning. It'd been a long time since he experienced prolonged physical exertion.

Once the ship was secured to the dock, a man came down the lowered gangway. Mick approached him and held out his hand.

"Welcome to Atlantis. Master Chief Lamek Davis at your service. I've mustered fifteen people to unload your boat. Do you have any crew who can help us?"

The man shook Mick's hand, his grip limp and wet. He was shorter than Mick, and his potbelly suggested an affinity for food and beverages high in calories. His coveralls were dirty, and grease stained his fingernails. Gray shot through his short brown hair, as well as his bushy beard. Lines around his brown eyes suggested a man short of sleep and burdened by days of strain. The tower lights at this pier had survived the holocaust, and they left dark shadows under his eyebrows.

"Captain Eldorf Wiesling. You're going to need a lot more than sixteen people to unload my ship, and my crew will be busy on board. We need to get started as soon as possible, Master Chief. The sooner I get back out to sea, the quicker I can deliver supplies to other people who desperately need them."

Mick nodded.

"Copy that, Captain. I'll get more people down here right away. Can we begin with who we have?"

Wiesling glanced at Mick's wrists.

"Just as soon as you show me your mark, Master Chief. I'll get you to sign the paperwork when we're done, but I can't release the supplies to you until I've seen your mark."

Mick stared at the older man blankly.

"Mark?"

Wiesling raised the sleeve on his right arm and turned his hand over to reveal his wrist. Tattooed on it, in red ink, and glowing under the dock illumination, was a triangle with the Latin numbers VI, VI, VI at the pointed edge of each angle. The center of the triangle contained an eye with rays of light shining around the edges.

"Yes. Specifically, this mark. The Supreme God of the Earth decreed several weeks ago all people must wear this mark. Without it, you can't buy or sell anything. You don't have access to medical services or your medical records. Building and property owners must deny you admission to shelters and places to live. Where've you been, Master Chief?"

Mick felt his heart rate spike. He knew what the mark represented. It told the world the bearer of the mark served and worshipped the Antichrist. As a public declaration of faith, it was infallible. Once they installed the mark, it was impossible to remove. Or so he'd heard.

It didn't matter. As a Christ follower, there was no way he could accept the Mark of the Beast. He shrugged.

"Where have I been? Time traveling, mostly. We're isolated out here, Captain. With everything happening, the tech hasn't arrived yet. No one here has had a chance to get the mark."

Wiesling looked at him, tilting his head and squinting through narrowed eyelids.

"Sorry to be suspicious, but your answer surprises me, Master Chief. My orders specifically said there would be someone here with a mark who could receive this shipment. If there's no one here with a mark, we can't offload."

Mick's eyebrows furrowed. Atlantis was stuck in the middle of what used to be known as the Devil's Triangle in the Atlantic Ocean. No one traveled to and from the highly secured base. A memory danced in his mind and he snapped his fingers.

"Of course! Our Administrator has the mark." In answer to Wiesling's raised eyebrows, he added, "She was in Rome after the assassination attempt. Administrator Korhonen got her mark then."

The expression on Wiesling's face hadn't changed.

"Well, get her down here, then. We're burning precious seconds, Master Chief."

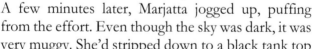

A few minutes later, Marjatta jogged up, puffing from the effort. Even though the sky was dark, it was very muggy. She'd stripped down to a black tank top and wore short gloves on her hands. Grease streaked her tan cargo pants, and her tactical boots were dirty. Something had smudged her right cheekbone. She piled her hair on top of her head, but strands were slipping out of their confines. Her face was sweaty, but she looked cheerful despite applying herself to manual labor.

Mick had explained the difficulty when he called

her, and she took no time for introductions. Thrusting her right arm forward, she arched her palm and showed Wiesling the tattoo on her right wrist.

Wiesling removed his personal device from his pocket and set it to scan.

When he pointed it at her mark, a hologram appeared in red above her wrist. It identified her as Marjatta Korhonen, the Administrator of TTI, headquartered on Atlantis. A holograph of her head rotated in place. It was an accurate depiction of the woman in her mid-fifties standing in front of the ship's captain.

Her banking information appeared next, and the hologram trumpeted her impressive credit rating.

Wiesling nodded and narrowed his gaze on Marjatta's face.

"What's on your other wrist?"

Marjatta tensed, then reluctantly raised her left arm. When Wiesling ran the scanner over her left wrist, on which there was a tattoo of a dove holding a bloody arrow, a much different image, also painted in red, sprang up.

This hologram depicted Marjatta kneeling on the floor, with her head lowered and her arms extended. She was almost naked, with scant pieces of cloth covering her breasts and genitals. The hologram depicted someone placing a device around her left wrist. It hummed, glowed red, then released, leaving behind the dove tattoo. Two large hands reached down and clasped a gold metallic band around her neck.

"You are my slave-bride, Marjatta Korhonen," a

deep voice rasped. "Your body and soul are mine for all eternity. You are now the property of the Supreme God of the Earth."

Marjatta stared at the image in horror until it blinked out. She had no memory of the event. This was the first time she'd seen what took place after Contradeum rose from the dead. She glanced into the captain's face, embarrassed, and was stunned to see the change in his expression.

The merchant no longer wore the visage of a tired man who the government overworked and underpaid. Raw lust dripped from his eyes and stabbed at her self-esteem. Even his voice changed with his leering gaze, dripping with unsuppressed desire.

"A slave-bride of our sovereign. How interesting. I've heard about your lot. Your body is available for the asking by any worshipper of our lord. He owns you and you reverence him by servicing his followers…"

The captain stopped speaking, and his eyes bulged. The point of a knife was at his throat, held in Mick's left hand. Wiesling turned his eyes into the frosted glare of a man who had the look of someone who'd killed before and suffered no hesitation about the thought of killing again.

"I don't know where you're going with your thoughts, Captain, but you're talking about my boss," Mick said in a voice hundreds of degrees colder than his eyes. "I hold Administrator Korhonen in high esteem. You weren't here when the earthquake ripped our island apart. Many people survived the disasters rocking our island and falling from the sky because of her intelligence and foresight. Disrespect her and your vessel will look for a new ship's captain in about ten seconds."

Marjatta's face reflected her gratitude for the former SEAL's intercession. She'd not been close to Mick since he came into her command, and his willingness to risk his life and reputation for her amazed her. When he went missing after his first mission, she'd tasked the Second Team to recover him dead or alive. He'd been Enemy No. 1 after he came back to grab Wu, and she'd sent Coventry Quarterlaine after him with a vengeance. After he and Coventry recovered the other teams stuck in Antiquity, she'd softened towards the man who now defended her honor.

Still, his devotion surprised her.

"Thank you, Master Chief, but I think you can put away your weapon. I'm sure the captain intended no disrespect."

"Yes, ma'am," Mick said, his eyes not leaving the sweating man's face. "Just as soon as I hear it from him, I'll be happy to put my blade away."

Wiesling licked parched lips.

"Administrator Korhonen, forgive me for my comments. Revealing your status as a slave-bride took me aback, which is no excuse. I'm exhausted, which is also no excuse. I was not this man before the last four years happened. Something has changed me so much; I don't recognize myself."

Marjatta flicked her fingertips at Mick, and he dropped the knife to his side, his eyes lingering on Wiesling's face.

"Were all of us not vastly different people,

Captain? Let's put this behind us and get your ship unloaded."

Wiesling bobbed his head up and down.

"Yes, yes, of course, Administrator. Now that I've verified your identity and confirmed your mark, we can offload at once."

He turned away and raised his personal device to his lips, giving terse commands.

Marjatta plucked at Mick's sleeve, a tear clinging to the edges of her eyes.

"Thank you," she whispered. "I'm sorry you had to see the holo, and I'm appalled by what happened. Please believe me, I remember nothing from that time, including getting my tattoos. I won't forget you covering for me."

Mick regarded her, his eyes serious.

"I meant what I said, Administrator. You permitted Heather and I to have a beautiful wedding, and you contributed to it with money and effort. You kept all of us alive when this world destroyed itself. I'm in your debt, not the other way around."

Marjatta smiled.

"Thanks, Mick. Do you want me for anything else?"

He gestured to the massive ship lying at the berth.

"Yes, ma'am. I'm going to need as many people as you can recruit to help us. There's a lot of cargo on the deck, and we need all the help we can get."

Marjatta backed away to climb up the hill.

"I will. Promise."

As she jogged back up the long, steep hill to the island's main level, the image from her left wrist churned her stomach.

Embarrassment and self-loathing consumed her heart. How had she consented to her tattoos? Marjatta told Mick the truth; she remembered nothing of her encounter with Contradeum and would never have given consent to those atrocious tattoos if her head had been in the right place.

She needed to get some answers about what to do about her tattoos, but suspected she'd have to be careful of whom she asked. The only people who had those answers were Christians, and she couldn't very well put out a call for Christians on the island to identify themselves. It would ask them to volunteer for a firing squad.

The run up the hill burned her lungs, but she barely paid attention to them.

Her soul was raging with something far worse.

CHAPTER THE THIRD:
GLORIFICATION

Ma'ilingan Waazh (Wolf's Den), 1st Year of Summer
25th day, Waatebagaa-giizis (Leaves Turning Moon),
Year 5379

Nothing is faster than the speed of light.

Except God.

Time froze.

It took Tul'ran a few seconds to realize Time no longer ran its course. The droning conversations of the Conclave members had lulled him into a waking dream state. He shook his head, regarding himself as he would any other fool. He should know by now never to let down his guard.

Tul'ran looked down and tensed, keeping his body still. A red blade of light buzzing with intense energy almost touched his chest.

He could hear similar sounds at his back and kept his breathing shallow. It didn't feel as if anything had penetrated his body, but the front blade was close to entering his rib cage, near his heart.

A hand holding some kind of device was in front of him, at chest level. He followed the arm to the left and was so startled he almost jumped into the dangerous energy. An apparition, or wraith, shaped like the upper half of a woman, was struggling to climb out of the head and upper shoulders of a tall fcmalc standing within fcct of him.

She had raised her physical arms and extended them as if to give him a hug. A deadly one. The wraith above her head seemed to yell and scream while struggling to escape the body. Tul'ran couldn't hear her, but saw her face twisting with rage. The wraith tried to pound on the head of her physical self with no effect.

Tul'ran allowed himself to relax. It appeared his assassin tried to leave her body, as impossible as it seemed, when Time froze. Time trapped her as her weapons trapped Tul'ran. He grinned. He had resources, and it appeared she was alone. It was time to call in reinforcements.

'Erianne,' he cast with his mind, straining to find the telepathic connection to his wife. 'Erianne!' he shouted mentally when she didn't answer.

He panicked a little when he heard no response. Had this assassin attacked his wife first? Thoughts flashed in Tul'ran's mind of his wife lying somewhere, bleeding, dying alone. The mental picture scared him and the fear bloomed into a dark rage.

If this woman had hurt his beloved Erianne, she would pay in pain and blood.

Fully freed, Erianne looked for a way out of her pitch-black confinement. Extending Caligo outward, she walked forward. For a moment, it felt like she was pushing through a blanket of molasses. Erianne lunged forward and stood in the corridor opposite the door of the facilities she'd used.

A door appeared behind her, barred with iron. She'd walked through a solid door! Erianne glided to the door and stretched out her arm. Her hand sank into the wood, and she snatched it back. She flexed her hand, feeling no ill effect, and tried it again. There was no sensation of physical contact as her hand once more sank into what should've been solid matter. Erianne drew a ragged breath.

This must be Inter-Dimensional Space, or IDS, as Johan called it. It felt a lot like the description Johan gave when they found him in the desert near Egypt. Her attacker must have trapped her in IDS. But why secure her so loosely? Unless her captivity was a device to delay her from something.

Tul'ran!

Erianne sprinted down the corridor toward the Conclave as fast as her legs could move.

Tul'ran was getting uncomfortable. His legs were cramping from standing in the same position for too long. Erianne didn't answer his repeated calls. There was only one thing left to do.

He lifted his chin to the ceiling and called out, "El Shaddai! I need a rescue!"

A soft chuckle came from his right as El Shaddai walked into Tul'ran's field of vision.

"Why does it take you so long to call on Me, My son?" He chided.

Relief coursed through Tul'ran's body and his face blushed.

"If you ask milady wife, she will inform You I am a stubborn old goat, quite beyond redemption."

"I will do so," Jesus said, "as soon as she appears."

"Appears?"

Jesus nodded as he walked over to the half-wraith, half female assassin. The wraith had stopped struggling and terror flooded her eyes.

"This one's name is Evo. We created her many thousands of years ago in a distant world called Everhome. She didn't like her circumstances and rebelled against Us. We let her have her own way because We cherish free will as much as We cherish Our creations. She committed a grave error once, for which We punished her. We'd hoped she'd learned from her mistake, but it's apparent she has not."

"Evo attacked Erianne before she came to assassinate you. Calm yourself, My son. Erianne is fine. Evo trapped her in Inter-Dimensional Space, but Erianne makes her way here. Soon she will reunite with you. Ah, perhaps now instead of soon."

Erianne burst through the open archway of the Conclave, sword and dagger in hand, and skidded to a halt. Time had frozen, judging by the lack of movement. She turned her head toward Tul'ran, and her jaw dropped. El Shaddai stood near her husband, who had a laser blade dangerously close to his chest.

"Let me go!"

Erianne jumped a little at the shout and felt her jaw drop again. The woman standing at her husband's left side holding the laser knife had an apparition trapped above her head at the specter's waist. She'd freed her arms, but her physical body anchored her soul or spirit or whatever she was in place.

El Shaddai looked at Erianne.

"Come out of there," He said, His voice a firm command.

Something shifted, and Erianne felt real again.

To Tul'ran, it appeared as though she popped out of mid-air.

"Erianne!"

With the speed at which she had become famous, Erianne took three long strides, raising Caligo.

"Stop!" El Shaddai said, just as Caligo's sharp edges were about to slice Evo's throat. His command immobilized everyone in place for a long moment. Erianne, her lips drawn back in a snarl, stared up at Evo.

"This woman attacked me and confined me, Lord," she said in a strained voice. "She tried to kill my husband. I want her dead, Lord, and I'm going to be her executioner."

"Erianne," Jesus said in a calm voice. "I am the Lord your God. Cease and desist. I need her alive and cannot give her over to you for judgment."

Erianne hesitated, her heart raging. She stared into the spectral face of the woman, whose eyes displayed despair and terror.

The face of a woman who'd drugged her, confined her, and tried to kill her husband. The slightest spasm in the muscles of her arm would send the ethereal edges of Caligo through the woman's throat and out the back of her neck.

Everything was quiet.

For the first time in her life, Erianne experienced the agony of extreme temptation. Jesus commanded her to cease and desist, but the part of her burning with the need for vengeance wanted to ignore the order. Why should this hag live? What was to stop her from trying again? She was powerful; who knew how formidable she was? Having a dead enemy was better than a live prisoner.

"Erianne," Tul'ran said in a soft voice. "I understand your temptation, having experienced for myself evil thoughts dwelling in its darkest depths. The desire to disobey El Shaddai is strong in you right now. When I was in its throes, you called out to me and saved me from caving into my desire for disobedience. By the bond of our love and the blood running between us, I call on you, my covenant-wife, to lower your blade."

Caligo remained in place.

"Perhaps I have not your sense of honor, duty, and service, milord husband, to steel against the lure of having this one's blood stain my sword."

"Have you not? How many times have you cautioned me to obedience and diplomacy? Do we not serve the same God who loves us and desires only our love and obedience in return? Come, Erianne, leave off this course. The woman whose specter cowers in front of you is not worthy of the price you would pay for disobeying your Lord."

The price she'd pay for disobeying her Lord.

It came down to such a simple statement. Perhaps the price would be the removal of His protection. Maybe Time wouldn't stop on the next occasion when someone tried to kill them. Then death would separate her from her man for as long as she lived in her mortal form.

Evo's eyes expressed immeasurable relief as Erianne lowered Caligo. Erianne smiled grimly. Tul'ran was right. This one wasn't worth displeasing her Lord. She sheathed her weapons. Then she reached up and gripped the other woman's physical throat with her right hand before directing a frosted gaze upwards.

"Not today, but soon," she said to the apparition, which stared back with a horrified gaze.

Erianne walked to where her husband stood, taking care not to move.

"Lord, how do we get Tul'ran out of this?" Erianne noted the strain on her husband's face. "I think we need to do it soon. He looks tired."

Jesus smiled.

"This time, you can do nothing, daughter. It is for Me to save My son."

Jesus reached out and wrapped His hands around each laser blade. There was no flare of light or anything to suggest a discharge of energy. When Jesus opened His hands, the laser blades and all their energy were gone. Tul'ran stepped out of Evo's deadly hug and into Erianne's firm embrace. After a moment, they disengaged, and he kissed her lips.

"Thank you, El Shaddai. I am grateful to you. The

position in which this woman trapped me was awkward. I'm not sure how much longer I could've stayed still."

Jesus clapped His hand on Tul'ran's shoulder.

"As always, My son, it was My pleasure to come to your aid. Now stand back, please."

Tul'ran joined Erianne on Jesus's right-hand side, as the Lord squared off against Evo.

"Evo, I assume some fault in where we are in this moment. We thought you would, on your own, come to the knowledge and understanding your plans to kill Us could not succeed. We erred. I will reveal Myself to you so you will know Us and put such thoughts from your mind forever."

Jesus's body grew, escalating to Conclave's ceiling. As He grew, His body changed into an outline of a human form, but consumed with a pure, white light. Power and love burst out of Him to such a degree, it drove Tul'ran and Erianne onto their faces on the floor. As Jesus expanded in stature, Evo's spirit shrank into her body, which unfroze in Time. She, too, dropped to the floor, pressing her face into its firmness.

Here was Jesus, in all His glorification.

When Jesus spoke, His voice was so majestic, it pounded through their bodies and left the humans shaking from its might. It sounded like rushing waters from a massive waterfall, roaring through the Conclave, and ringing in their ears. It was a thunderous rumble, as colossal as His form.

"I am the Alpha and Omega, the beginning and the end, the Redeemer, Beloved Son of My Father, the Rock, the True Vine, and the Branch from which all life flows. I am the King of Kings and the Lord of Lords. Before all things I was, and I created all things. I AM!"

The last statement was so ponderous and profound, it rattled the mountain even though He had frozen everything in Time.

"We are not like you, Evo, though We made you in Our image. We have existed for so many trillions of years, you could not imagine all We have seen and all We have created. You only continue to live in this moment of Our revelation to you because We have commanded your heart to beat, your lungs to take in air, and your mind to thrive. You live on Our whim, and your eternal body could not save you if We decided your life is at the end. It is impossible for you to kill Us or uncreate Us because We are the essence of life. There are no others like Us in any universe. We have never revealed Our true nature to any living human being. To look upon Us is to die."

Erianne believed Him. She couldn't look up into His face; His essence terrified her. Even though she squeezed her eyelids shut, His Light threatened to burn out her retinas. Her heart was pounding so fast she wondered if it would seize, and her breath came in heaving gasps.

His power sat on her back like an anvil. She could feel the eons of eternity flowing from His form, and could hear the stars singing of His majesty. His essence rolled over her in waves, threatening to peel her skin off her body, the muscles from her bones, and dissolve her soft tissues into nothingness.

Erianne knew she'd never disobey her Lord again. This was His true nature, one He carefully concealed from them so they would serve Him with love, not fear. She shuddered. She'd read in the Bible how He told people to look upon God was to invite death. Erianne understood how it could be so.

The power pulsated over them for what felt like an eternity. Slowly, it subsided. When she could think and move again, Erianne opened her eyes. The intense light of His supremacy was gone. Erianne turned her head to regard Jesus in His human form, with His back pressed against the Conclave wall.

It took her a while to summon the strength to move. When she could, she rose unsteadily to her feet. Erianne reached down, grasped Tul'ran by the elbow, and helped him rise. He tottered for a moment, then bowed to Jesus.

"Thank you, El Shaddai, for the lesson. I will not soon forget whom I serve."

Jesus smiled.

"You serve a God Who loves you, Tul'ran. Please remember it before you dwell upon what I have shown you. My revelation was for Evo's edification, not yours."

They looked at the seven-foot-tall woman lying on the floor, shaking. Sobs heaved her back as she pressed her hands to her head. Jesus walked to her and kneeled by her side.

"Evo, My child, rise."

She didn't move, her sobs increasing in intensity.

"Why didn't You show Yourself to me before?" she whimpered. "All those years of hatred, anger, and a lust for revenge. Lost, all lost. Why, Lord?"

Jesus stroked her long silver hair.

"Evo, We couldn't. We gave you free will. What I

did today would deter the exercise of free will in any human, including one as strong as yourself. We did not desire to bind you, Evo. We wanted a friend, not an unthinking obedient slave. Many times, the Father and I discussed interfering in the exercise of your free will, but abstained because We had hoped you would come to the knowledge of who We are through your Library research and travel through the universe."

Evo's sobs lightened, and she turned her head to look at Him.

"Thank You for not taking my life when You showed me who You are."

Jesus took her right arm.

"You gained eternal life when you ate the fruit from the Tree of Life. We take such things with the seriousness they deserve. If ever you tire of eternal life in your physical form, We will shorten your days. Only you can make such a request."

She allowed Jesus to help her to her knees, and stayed there, kneeling, for a moment, her eyes downcast.

"You've won, Lord. I'll never seek to hurt You again."

"Evo, Evo. This was not about winning or losing. We have never strived to win against you. We will set all of this behind Us, if such is your desire."

Evo raised her head and looked at Him, her eyes shining from the wetness of her tears.

"Are you going to send me to the Abyss again?"

Tul'ran's eyebrows flashed to the top of his forehead.

"You sent her to the Abyss, El Shaddai?"

Jesus's chest rose and fell with a deep sigh, and His eyes glinted with humor.

"This woman just tried to kill you, and you would still leap to her defense?"

Tul'ran's cheeks reddened.

"I didn't mean any offense, Lord."

Jesus laughed.

"I took no offense. I am just impressed. Evo, We will not send you to the Abyss while you draw breath and your heart beats within your chest. You must atone for your actions, which includes how you have drawn the Women of this planet away from Us. You shall go with My servants, Tul'ran and Erianne, and stay in their company until We have determined what shall be done with you."

Erianne rolled her eyes.

"I mean no disrespect, Lord Jesus, but I had hoped our days of babysitting the scalawags of the universe were over," she said.

He grinned at her.

"You will find, Erianne, there are many ways to serve Me. You must put your anger aside, dear heart. This woman is to accompany you until We give you guidance where you shall place her."

Erianne bowed her head.

"By Your command."

"What shall we do in the meantime?" Tul'ran said, gesturing towards the Men perched above them and frozen in Time.

Jesus stepped back, preparing to leave them.

"Continue as before. Erianne, please take Evo from this place before Time resumes. You will introduce at dinner tonight. Evo will go with you to the City of Ikwe Na to set them on the path of truth. Evo, attend Me. To ensure you will not harm Tul'ran and Erianne while in their care, you may not leave your body or transition into Inter-Dimensional Space. We deny such freedom to you. In your physical body, even with your advanced knowledge, you are no match for them. Either of them can kill you with their swords and knives, for their eternal, angelic blades can end life in any dimension. Be cautious. They might react to a perceived threat from you and then your soul will stand before Us in judgment."

A look flashed across Evo's stricken face.

"I am denied the ability to traverse the universe in an energy state?"

Jesus nodded.

"Surely, child, you had to expect some consequences for your actions."

Evo bit her lip, dropping her eyes from His face.

"Fine. I'll stay with them and behave. They know they can't kill me without provocation, right? This one," she gestured at Erianne, "looked like she was pretty close to ending my life earlier."

"Evo, standing before you are Lord Tul'ran and Lady Erianne az Nostrom. He is otherwise known as Tul'ran the Sword, Prince of Death, the Uncreator. All for good reason."

Evo nodded her head.

"All for good reason, indeed." At the look on Tul'ran's face, she said, "I was present in a pure energy state when you warred against the Combatants on Spes. You impressed me."

"So much," Erianne said, her voice rich with

irony, "you tried to kill him and take his sword."

The other woman had the decency to blush.

"Evo, Erianne is otherwise known as the Princess of Death and the Tamer of Gods."

Evo bowed.

"The Tamer of Gods. I'd love to hear your story, Lady Erianne, and how you came to tame gods. I hope we can achieve a state of peace between us."

Erianne lifted her chin and regarded Evo with glittering eyes.

"Lady Evo, if you never threaten either of us again, a state of peace is possible. One other thing. You are a woman of exceptional beauty, and your body is so lovely it could send artists into a swoon. I am a jealous woman, milady. I do not tolerate females who try to seduce my husband from my bedchamber. So long as you respect my marriage, we might also someday become friends."

Erianne reached back to caress the hilt of her ethereal sword.

"I don't think I have to remind you how I treat my enemies."

CHAPTER THE FOURTH: ENTER THE JADE DRAGON

Ma'ilingan Waazh (Wolf's Den), 1st Year of Summer 25th day, Waatebagaa-giizis (Leaves Turning Moon), Year 5379

Evo acknowledged Erianne's veiled threat with a grimace.

"Don't worry. I've no use for men. God is a male, and He created me to serve a man. Every conflict I've had has been with men. I'm not attracted to them, and I've seduced no one. I have no desire to have your husband paw me." She paused and dropped her eyes at Tul'ran. "No offense."

"None taken," he said, his face noncommittal. "It wouldn't matter if you made a play for me, Evo. My interest lies in my marriage bed, and only my wife occupies it."

Evo arched her eyebrows.

"No one ever tempted you to stray from your marriage bed?"

"No," he said. Tul'ran arched his back, squeezing his shoulder blades to the center of his spine to relieve the tension in his back muscles. His shoulders and pecs rippled as they stretched and left no doubt as to their strength. "Had anyone done so, I would've rejected them. Had they persisted, they would've died. I've no use for people who can't hear and understand the word 'no.'"

Evo shrugged, her silver hair rippling with the motion of her shoulders.

"Well, then, I guess we're all safe here. I'm not into you, you're not into me, and we're just one happy family."

Tul'ran turned narrowed eyes on Erianne.

"Forgive me, covenant-wife, but the nuances of the language you often speak escape me. How should I perceive Evo's statement?"

Erianne grinned at his consternation. "It's called sarcasm. She says one thing, but her tone belies her words and conveys a different meaning."

"Ah," he said, and returned her grin. "Like snowmen."

Erianne touched Tul'ran's face and ran a thumb over his lips.

"You're so sweet when you try so hard."

Evo rolled her eyes.

"Okay, enough already, you're in love, I get it. I'm getting nauseous. Can we get on with it?"

Tul'ran stared at her for a moment, then snaked one massively muscled arm around his brown-skinned wife's slender waist. He pulled Erianne in for a deep, slow kiss before drawing away and casting a cool look at Evo's reddened cheekbones.

"As you say, let's get on with it."

Erianne pulled herself out of Tul'ran's grasp and tossed her hair.

"Milord husband, I see there are finer points to the concept of diplomacy I must yet convey. Perhaps tonight we will set apart some time for negotiations?"

An ear-to-ear grin split his features.

"It has been several hours since we last negotiated, my love. Your suggestion has merit."

Erianne shifted her body to stand in front of Evo.

"Come on, gorgeous. Let's leave the boys for a bit. I'll take you to my quarters, then bring you back to meet the Men."

Evo looked at her with an odd expression on her face.

"I see it may take some time to get used to you. You threaten my life if I so much as flirt with your husband and then call me beautiful in the same breath. I'm not sure what to make of you."

"Whatever you decide to make of her," Tul'ran said, "it'd be in your best interest to make it in peace. You may be very skilled, Evo, but only in Erianne have I met my match in the universe."

This raised Evo's eyebrows right up.

"Really?"

"Really, really, with whipped cream on top," Erianne said in a singsong while linking her arm into the crook of Evo's elbow.

"When you are clear of the Conclave," Tul'ran said, "Time will resume its march. Pick a spot where you can observe someone frozen in Time without being seen. You will know when the world breathes again."

Erianne saluted him by raising her right fist to her heart and ushered Evo to the entrance. When they were gone, Tul'ran took up the same stance he'd been in before time froze.

Two of the Elders had been haggling over one term of the peace agreement, having locked horns on the monitoring clause. One argued it was a harsh restriction on the right to pursue scientific discovery. The other vehemently reminded his cohort of the devastating environmental effects caused by the last pursuit of knowledge.

Time had frozen them in a funny appearance, had it not been for the threat to Tul'ran's life bringing time to a halt. One elder had his mouth open and had placed a long forefinger under the nose of his counterpart. The second elder's face was red, and he looked as if he was going to explode. Tul'ran couldn't remember what the two were saying just before Time came to an abrupt halt, but it was less than entertaining.

After several minutes, stasis slipped away, and the room exploded into motion. It was always disconcerting when Time resumed. It was easy to forget about the multitude of sounds, smells, and noises filling the air when Time flowed. Especially the noises.

"Without monitoring, there can only be mistrust and chaos," yelled the Elder with the upraised finger.

"Shall they keep our scientists to monitor this agreement until we're back to cooking our food over an open fire?" the other said, slamming his fist onto the podium in front of him. "Let's talk about arms control and monitoring when our scientists are home!"

And on it went. Sixty minutes later, Tul'ran raised his hand, and the room went quiet.

"Elders, I'm not here to impose my will upon this Conclave. If you feel you must resolve this issue through further negotiations, then let it be so. I, for one, am tired and hungry. Perhaps we could reconvene after we've had some dinner."

The Conclave voted to adjourn for repast, and Tul'ran bowed before leaving the room. As much as he loved and respected his wife, they knew little about their new captive. He wanted to ensure her safety before spending more time with this group, who were threatening to bore him to tears.

Tul'ran made his way to the doorway of their room, opened the immense door, and halted on the threshold. Erianne and Evo were on the floor, a tousle of black battle leathers and a metallic silver jumpsuit. Erianne had her long legs wrapped around Evo like a pretzel. She'd twisted her arms around the taller woman's head and neck in an uncomfortable position Tul'ran knew well. Evo, so pinioned, couldn't move and looked frustrated and somewhat out of breath.

Tul'ran cleared his throat.

"Is all well, covenant-wife?"

Erianne laughed and released Evo, who rolled out of the hold. Both came to their feet as graceful as panthers strolling through a forest.

"Yes, my love. I was showing Evo how you lost a wager at my hands, which saw you deliver the most awkward speech of how a man and woman have sex in the universe's history."

Tul'ran scowled as the women brushed off the floor's dust.

"Yes, you cheated."

"Did not!" his wife said with indignation, before walking up to give him a kiss. "It's not my fault you didn't know the move. I blame it on the poor educational system in Mesopotamia when you were a youth."

Tul'ran snorted.

"I cannot fault an educational system which failed to teach a wrestling move invented thousands of years into the future. The technique you used was impossible to break free."

"Not quite."

They turned to look at Evo just as she flung a knife at Erianne, who caught it with a quick flick of her wrist. Erianne's eyes widened.

"Well, well. Evo sneaked my knife out of my belt, which shouldn't have been possible in the hold I used. When did you grab my knife?"

Evo smiled, her face showing pleasure at Erianne's consternation.

"When I saw you set up the move. You forget, Erianne, I've lived for ten thousand years. I spent most of those years researching in the Library of Heaven. Your hold was very impressive. I only took your knife in case you still intended my murder under the pretext of a demonstration."

Erianne put her knife in her belt and took two long strides to Evo. She reached up and put her hands on Evo's cheeks.

"Evo, I give you my oath as if we spilled blood

between us," she said, cupping the much taller woman's face. "I shall never again attack you except in defense of myself or anyone I love. Please believe me when I say you're safe with me."

Evo allowed the touch and kept her cheeks in the warrior's clasp.

"Does this mean we're friends?"

Erianne searched Evo's eyes and saw within them a deep longing. By her account, Evo had spent her life alone, running from God and any other companionship. Sure, she'd put herself in a lonely position by her own choices, but it didn't cure the need for companionship. Perhaps this was the first step to her rehabilitation.

"Yes, Evo. We're friends."

Evo's lips twisted into a wisp of a smile, and it surprised Erianne when the taller woman's silver eyes misted.

"And can you keep your husband from killing me?"

Erianne laughed and let go of Evo's face. She side glanced Tul'ran before winking at Evo.

"Tul'ran? He's a pussycat. He wouldn't hurt a flea."

Evo's forehead creased at the look on Tul'ran's face.

"You appear confused, Lord Tul'ran. Does Lady Erianne's benign description of your capabilities fail to meet your perception of yourself?"

His right eyebrow went up.

"This is a common problem I face with my wife, Lady Evo. Her opinions would've struck a deeper chord if she had first made me aware of what is a pussycat and a flea."

Evo and Erianne's burst of laughter filled the room, while Tul'ran shook his head. He was getting used to the four-thousand-year gap between him and his wife, and it pleased him some of it was a source of amusement for her. Tul'ran wanted nothing more than to make his wife happy, even if her humor was sometimes at his expense.

"When you two finish your joviality, would you care to join me for dinner? We can introduce Evo to the Tribes of Men."

Both women sobered.

"How am I to be introduced?" Evo asked, her voice guarded. "Do you name me as the cause of their demise?"

"Were you not?" Tul'ran said, his words deceptively soft.

"Does it matter?" Erianne said. "Yes, Evo misled the Tribes of Women and bears responsibility for their lost faith in El Shaddai. But as for the Men, she didn't tell them to crash their ship into the ablative ice shield."

"In fact," Evo said, chiming in, "I would've told them not to launch were I here. I caused the destruction of a world once, and I wouldn't have set myself up for blame for the destruction of this one."

Tul'ran and Erianne's bodies went still.

"You destroyed a planet?"

Evo placed a soothing hand on Erianne's shoulder.

"Yes, my friend, I did. Here's how it happened."

Evo described to a rapt audience of two how the fifth world in their solar system came to utter ruin at her hands. She didn't justify her conduct or lay blame on God. Evo told them of her imprisonment in the Abyss as punishment for her actions, without casting aspersions on God for the harshness of the sentence.

"You two look horrified, but not surprised by my experience in the Abyss. Why?"

"We spent enough time there to leave a negative impression on its keepers," Tul'ran said, his voice as dry as dust.

Erianne snorted.

"My husband is developing restraint in how he communicates the force of his reputation and the might of his arms. It may be necessary to hire a balladeer to keep the record straight as we journey. Let me tell you how it went down."

Evo listened, fascinated, as Erianne described how they delivered Katja and her brothers from the Abyss after facing down G'shnet'el. She turned her silver eyes on the Prince of Death and bowed.

"I confess to becoming even more intrigued by you, Lord Tul'ran. Your kindness matches your courage and military capacity. I've not met another man like you, ever."

Evo looked down, startled, at the point of a knife sitting against her ribs, just under her right breast, and shifted her glance to Erianne's face.

Erianne grinned and put the knife away with the same impressive speed.

"Just a little reminder of the quickness of my jealousy and how it translates into action. In case you forgot."

A slight shudder rippled through Evo's body, and she bowed.

"I thank you for the reminder, Lady Erianne. It will remain at the forefront of my memories, I assure you."

Erianne took Evo's hand in hers and squeezed it.

"Forgive the reaction, Evo. I never used to be so jealous until this small mountain of a man rode into my life."

Tul'ran tilted his head.

"If the two of you have sorted out your territorial claims, I'd very much like to eat. The Conclave will reconvene, and I can't tolerate it on an empty stomach."

Evo didn't move.

"We've not yet sorted out how I'm to be introduced."

"We'll introduce you to the Tribes of Men as Evo, She Who Wanders the Stars," Erianne said, her voice firm as she held Tul'ran's eyes. "Should they ask, we'll tell them the truth about your interference in this world. Until they ask, we'll say you're here to help us bring about peace. Which is the truth."

Evo stared down at Erianne, then squeezed her hand.

"Does milady Erianne speak for you, Lord Tul'ran?"

Tul'ran blew a gust of air between his lips.

"Me, my House, my horse, my wolf, and my great big lion," he said, his voice a growl. "She speaks for us all. Now can we go eat?"

Erianne snaked her free hand into his and led them to the doorway.

"Yes, on the order of right now. Come, Evo, let us feed this beast before he dines on our flesh."

Tul'ran harrumphed.

"I think your metaphor is too extreme. It would've been better to say we're off to see the wizard."

It was Evo's turn to look puzzled as the other two guffawed.

———✟———

The look on Ro'gun's face was a mixture of fascination and stunned disbelief. He was standing outside the entrance to the dining room with his wife, mother-in-law, and sister-in-law. He couldn't take his eyes off Evo's body as Tul'ran, Erianne, and Evo walked up to them, until Innanu dug a sharp elbow into his ribs.

"Have you never seen a woman's figure? Or does your tongue need to drool spittle on your chin to fertilize your stubble? Are you a child who'd want to feed on her swollen breasts?"

Ro'gun turned a bright red and tore his eyes off the form of the silver-clad star traveler. His wife's body was slight, which did not take away his enjoyment of her. He understood why she'd be upset by him gawking at the stranger.

"My apologies, Innanu. My mind was taken aback."

Innanu ran a jealous glance over Evo's perfect proportions.

"Seize control of your mind and your eyes, husband, or you may find our linens cold this night."

Ro'gun winced. He tried to avoid his wife's anger as much as possible because he loved her and hated to be the source of her pain. In his defense, the woman who stood before him clad in silver was nothing like anything he'd ever seen. It still made no excuse for his behaviour. As the approaching group stopped before him, he made his bow.

"Milord, milady, I give you a good greeting. The House az Peregos stands at the ready to serve you."

Evo noticed the reactions her appearance caused to the young boy and his young wife. She was the second woman Evo made jealous in the brief span of her stay in this world. She'd never considered the usefulness of her appearance as a weapon.

As the first woman in the world of Everhome, God created her to be the epitome of perfection. She was smart, beautiful, and statuesque. Her appearance had attracted Ado from the moment she opened her eyes, which had annoyed her. His cloying infatuation was enough to make anyone crazy.

After God cast her from the Garden on Everhome, she'd had almost no contact with people in her physical body. Being the subject of sexual attraction was a novel experience. She now realized men couldn't keep their eyes off her and women seethed over the attention men paid to her.

She swept a quick glance at Tul'ran. Except for him. When he looked at her, it was with the feral intensity of a lion; one disposed to killing her and feeding off her heart instead of claiming it for love. She didn't want men's cloying devotion, but craved Tul'ran's attention because he rejected her. The thoughts confused her. It was clear he wouldn't have her, so why did she have this sudden urge to take him for herself?

"Ro'gun, Omarosa, Innanu, Anatu," Erianne said,

sweeping a gesture towards her towering form. "Here is Lady Evo, She Who Wanders the Stars."

They made their bows to her, and she returned them with a flair. Evo decided to try something. She relaxed the muscles of her body and dropped the register in her voice.

"It's my honor to meet you," she said, her tone soft and sultry as she held Ro'gun's eyes a hint longer than the gazes of the women. Ro'gun's face flushed a brighter red as Omarosa frowned and Innanu glared at Ro'gun. So. Interesting.

Erianne took Evo's elbow and guided her to the dining hall's entrance.

"Come, let us introduce you to the Tribes of Men."

They stepped into the dining room and Evo wondered if time froze again. All eyes were upon her, some holding startlement and others holding blatant lust. For a long moment, no one moved and the silence in the room was palpable.

The only thing moving in the hall was the essence of the food steaming in clamshell containers on the long wooden table stretched through the center of the dining area. Dinner smelled spicy and tantalized her nose with the promise of cuisine designed to please both the stomach and the tastebuds. Evo inhaled through her nose deeply, pushing out her chest with the indrawn breath. She noted at once the movement seemed to cause the men in the room to drool as much as the food made her mouth water and stomach rumble.

Erianne took a half-step forward and bowed.

"We have added an ally to our cause. Here is Evo,

She Who Wanders the Stars, who has just now arrived. Her presence on Ma'ilingan Waazh will go far to secure peace."

Not in this House, Evo noted with satisfaction. Disapproval filled the looks the women were giving her and their men. The men were outright leering. She didn't know how to play at this angle yet, but she intended to learn.

Another nudge from Erianne had them approach the table of Chief Ravenclaw and his wife, Dr. Swiminghorse.

Both were made of sterner stuff, it seemed. The Chief didn't spare her body so much as a glance, and his wife greeted her with warmth, as if they were old companions.

As Evo chatted with the chief and his wife, Tul'ran drew Erianne back. Before they entered Spes Deserit those many months ago, El Shaddai gifted them with the ability to speak into each other's minds. It was a gift they used in rare moments. He used it now, not wanting to be overheard.

'Be cautious with this one, covenant-wife. She brings to mind the image of an asp lying content in sunshine before burying her fangs in your neck.'

Erianne's lips twitched, while she watched as other men wander over to speak with Evo's group.

'Why such concern, my love? I feel I have a good measure of her. She is not unlike Darian when we first met her.'

There it was.

'True, but I know your heart. You have a deep desire to heal people, and you love them in a brief span of time. You would give your heart to Evo like

71

you did with our dear sister, which would be unwise and dangerous.'

Erianne's eyebrows tried to merge toward the center of her forehead.

'How so?'

'When we met Darian, she served evil. Her heart changed only after she met El Shaddai face-to-face. She broke away from her evil ways, turned her back on them, and walked in the steps of the Lord. Evo has lived for ten thousand years, and serves only herself. When she encountered El Shaddai in all his powerful glory,' Tul'ran shuddered at the recollection of God's power in that moment, 'she did not repent of her misdoings. Evo acknowledged defeat, as if an enemy of equal status bested her on the battlefield. She has had too many years of being her own god to change into someone like Darian in short order.'

Tul'ran cut his thoughts short as Chief Ravenclaw ambled toward them, his face lit with warmth.

"Princess Erianne, Lord Tul'ran, how pleasant it is to see you again. I have spoken with the Elders and all have agreed on our next course of action. We must go to the City of Men in the morning, where you will weigh and balance the positions of the Elders and rule on our approach to peace. What puzzles you, Princess Erianne?"

Erianne turned her lips upward in a polite smile and gestured around her.

"Chief Ravenclaw, are we not now in the City of Men?"

The Chief's laugh was a loud bark that startled two other people nearby.

"This is an outpost, a place where we'd set a guard to protect the entrance to the valley behind us. We had to abandon the City of Men for reasons you will see tomorrow. Once you've settled the last terms of the Peace Treaty, we will journey to Ikwe Na to present the treaty to Baamewaawaagizhigokwe and her counselors. I hope to leave as soon as possible in the morning."

Erianne's eyebrows quirked again.

"Why so fast, Chief, if I may be so bold as to ask?"

Ravenclaw jerked his head in Evo's direction.

"In our ancient past, a woman of outstanding beauty came between two brothers. They fought for her hand until both perished from their injuries. You have brought the jade dragon of envy and lust into our world, Princess. I would contain her, and if I cannot contain her, I would have her gone as fast as the wind blows, before my men bleed over her."

Fate laughed.

As if they could contain a dragon.

CHAPTER THE FIFTH:
THE DRAGON'S TOOTH

Ma'ilingan Waazh (Wolf's Den), 1st Year of Summer 26th day, Waatebagaa-giizis (Leaves Turning Moon), Year 5379

Evil lurks in the dark,
Beware the witching hour,
Thin are the lines 'tween life and death
When Darkness flexes power.
- from The Ballad of Tul'ran the Sword,
verse 68, sung in the baritone

She slid from between the covers, her clothing making a soft whisper against the silken sheets, and looked down at her bedmates. She sensed it was minutes after midnight. Her internal clock was never wrong. It was time to leave.

Evo stood opposite the bed and kept her breathing shallow for fear of waking her captors. Time had swum by her closed eyelids with such a ponderous gait, she felt like two nights had passed. The fire in the hearth had diminished to glowing red embers, but her suit regulated her body temperature well. She only felt the crispness of the air on her cheeks.

The cold didn't seem to bother her guards. Erianne was curled up on Tul'ran's chest with her back to Evo, and the blankets didn't cover their upper torsos. It had distressed Evo when the tall East Indian woman stripped down to nothing before climbing into bed. At least her husband had kept on a loincloth. The reddish light from the fire's last breaths of life flickered on their sleeping forms. It danced on the exposed flesh of Erianne's long, lean back. Evo couldn't see her face because the vast swath of her expansive black hair covered her and most of Tul'ran's heavily muscled chest. Both drew the long breaths Evo associated with deep sleep.

Perfect.

The party last night had been illuminating. Erianne amused Evo by trying to limit Evo's time with each man in the room. The males had been so infatuated with her they spoke in monosyllables. Eyes had caressed her body so often, Evo felt as if they had stroked every inch of her. Evo was not used to being the subject of lust. She found it confusing to be drooled over. It raised conflicting feelings within her. Part of her felt disgust over the obvious manifestations of their desire, while another part of her welcomed the attention and desired more.

It was a relief when Erianne called it a night, claiming the need for rest before they took a journey the next morning. When they returned to Tul'ran and Erianne's quarters, Evo's entertainment continued.

Tul'ran had spun a full turn to scan their quarters before addressing Erianne. The bedroom was enormous for two people. The center of the room housed an immense square bed covered in linen and topped with fine furs. Rich brown wood framed the bed and pillars of the same wood rose from all four corners. Their hosts covered the pillars in a fine gauze, which sparkled under the soft lights and gave Tul'ran and Erianne an impression they slept in a star field.

In one corner of the room, a fireplace crackled to itself and spat sparks onto the stone floor. The fire danced among the scorched logs, and a gentle hint of smoke lent a heady essence to the room. The flickering light from the fireplace casts shadows of the four-poster bed onto the far wall.

A large skin of silver fur lay at the foot of the fireplace, though far enough away to avoid the sparks. There were no tables and chairs, but a stout boudoir occupied another corner. If ever a room deserved to be occupied by two people newly married and much in love, it was this one.

"Where is Evo to sleep, milady wife? We have but one bed and the stone floors are too hard and cold upon which to repose in comfort," Tul'ran said, after completing his survey of the room.

"I'm sure they could find me another room," Evo said, her voice wry with irony.

Erianne snorted.

"Right, we're going to let you out of our sight."

The answer had irked Evo.

"Why, do you think I'll take another run at your husband?"

"Oh, please do," Erianne responded, the words layered within a soft purr. "I would love to see you attack him again, given his awareness of the threat you represent. It's been a while since he's hacked someone into small pieces. He might get rusty without practice."

"Is that all you do? Make threats?" Evo asked.

Erianne's eyes narrowed to slits.

"I can carry them out, too. Want to see?"

"Enough," Tul'ran said, his voice weary. "Evo, why do you provoke us? Do you not have a measure of Who stands behind us, ever ready to come to our rescue should you decide on the senseless course?"

His words brought her up short. Evo had lived thousands of years longer than these two and felt superior to them in every way. But there was the stumbler. God's Son had these two under His protective gaze. Evo repressed a shudder. Jesus's power was more than she'd ever expected and it frightened her out of her senses. He was watching. She calmed herself.

"Yes, of course. It's never just the two of you, is it? Fine, you don't trust me to sleep elsewhere. Shall I sleep on this frigid floor?"

Erianne walked to the bed, turned, and bounced her backside on the thick mattress.

"This bed is enormous. You can join us. Tul'ran will sleep on one edge, you on the other, and me in the middle. There is so much room, you won't come into contact with our bodies. If you don't want to rest in your space suit, I'm sure we can arrange something for you to wear to bed."

Evo shook her head, her silver eyes glittering.

"My suit never comes off. I'll leave it on if it's all the same to you."

Erianne shrugged.

"Suit yourself." She giggled at her own pun. "There's a lavatory off to the left. You can get ready for bed there."

With nothing left to be said, Evo strolled to the facilities, being sure to add a roll to her hips. Tul'ran claimed immunity from her newly discovered charms, but winds can wear even a mountain down over time. If the party taught her anything, it was that God proportioned her body to be a seductive distraction compared to other women.

Her body invited lust, and she meant to exploit it.

Evo had laid in bed for hours, waiting until she was certain Tul'ran and Erianne were deep in rest. Her confinement irked her. She wanted to check in with her ship and make some contingency plans in case things didn't go well the next morning.

After she slipped out from under the coverlet, she walked to the bedroom's entrance, her feet not making a sound on the gray stone floor.

Evo reached out to grab the latch on the door. She felt a breeze tousle the hair on the left side of her face, and her body spasmed as a large, black knife thudded against the wood inches to the left of her head. Another blade, lithe and silver, landed with an inch of the black one.

Evo froze, then turned to face the room.

Erianne and Tul'ran were both sitting up in bed. Each had long hair, and the bed had tangled their hair into ridiculous configurations. They looked like two people who'd been comatose for weeks, but the knives vibrating in the door suggested a deadly form of wakefulness.

"Where ya goin'?" Erianne asked, drowsiness stretching her words into a drawl.

Evo gritted her teeth.

"I couldn't sleep, so I thought I'd take a walk."

Erianne flipped back the covers on Evo's side of the bed.

"Why don't you walk back here and I'll whisper sweet nothings in your ear until you drift off?"

Evo glanced back at the knives in the door.

"Having explored my options, I guess it's the best one."

Tul'ran laid back down and rolled onto his left side.

"It's also your only one. Goodnight, Evo."

Evo climbed back under the coverlet and fell asleep under the glittering green eyes of a woman who could apparently throw a knife in her sleep.

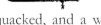

Birds sang, ducks quacked, and a wind rattled the leaves of a tree against the large window carved in the rock wall. The pre-dawn sky outside the bedroom lit the room well enough to see. The air was chilly, as the fire had gasped its last breath hours earlier and left its ashes as a reminder of its warmth.

Tul'ran pushed Erianne's hair from her face,

which she had snuggled into his neck, and kissed the top of her head.

"Arise, Princess of Death. The morning dawns and promises intrigue."

"Nooo," she moaned, snuggling closer to his body. "It's too early. I need coffee if I'm expected to function at this hour."

Evo jerked her head off her pillow and blinked her silver eyes several times. She shook her head, sending her long, silver hair flying as she tried to brush off the last clinging tendrils of sleep.

"Coffee? In the past, when I visited your home world, I marveled over how, for some, drinking coffee was like a religious experience. Intrigued, I researched coffee in the Library of Heaven and learned how to grow it. I grew coffee on my home world, Everhome."

Tul'ran ran his fingertips down Erianne's naked side and felt her shudder under his fingertips. He grinned.

"My covenant-wife regards coffee as the essence of life and the mechanism for maintaining mental stability when the sun invites her to join the day."

Erianne snuggled deeper into Tul'ran's side.

"There is no coffee here," she said, her voice muffled. "No one invented it. Having to get up without coffee is barbaric."

Someone tapped on their door, causing all three of them to whip their heads toward the noise.

"Great apologies, Lord and Ladies," said a male voice, "but Chief Ravenclaw desires your presence in the Courtyard to begin the journey to the City of Men."

"Tell him we come," Tul'ran said in a deep voice. Then, softer, he said, "If I can get my wife out of bed."

He whipped back the covers, and Erianne shrieked. Evo slipped out of the bed as the two other occupants grappled with each other until their battle to have control over the blankets left a sheen on their skin.

Once they exhausted their silliness, they rose and took turns using the facilities. As the two warriors dressed in their battle leathers, Evo shook her head.

"Once again, you two confuse me." She nodded at their knives still lodged in the door. "For two fierce warriors, you play like children. Is it always this way with you?"

Erianne stroked her fingers through her long black hair and cast it behind her back.

"Evo, life is too short for Tul'ran and me to dwell on the threats life presents or the seriousness of the obstacles arrayed before us. We play to increase our joy."

Tul'ran and Erianne pulled their blades out of the door and put them in their armor. They opened the door to find the attendant standing there, shuffling from one foot to the other.

"Lord Tul'ran, Princess Erianne, and Lady Evo, the Chief and his party bids you to meet them outside with all haste. You are to break your fast on the conveyance."

'He sure is eager to get Evo out of here,' Erianne thought at her husband.

'Do you blame him?' came the dry response.

They led Evo through the residence to the palatial

front doors. They descended the stone stairs leading from the House to the street with Tul'ran on the left, Erianne in the middle, and Evo on the right.

The sun languished and was on the verge of splitting the sky. Birds they heard in their room sang morning arias and cajoled the sun to make its appearance. A gentle wind blew the intoxicating smell of tree blossoms into their faces and ruffled their hair.

The buildings on the streets surrounding the House cast long shadows over the sleepy thoroughfares. The House met at the intersection of three streets. Two of them ran parallel to the House, and the third ran in a perpendicular line to the steps. There were no others around to see them leave, the day being too early to start for most of the House's residents.

It was a peaceful morn.

Then, chaos.

A sudden movement in the street dead ahead. Tul'ran threw up a blue shield of uncreation energy in front of him and Erianne seconds before six metal star-shaped discs slapped into the shield and dissolved into nothingness.

The thing flinging the star-shaped discs was humanoid in appearance, but a machine. It pulled its left arm back to fling the metal stars in its left hand, but never made the throw. Ro'gun glided in from the shadows of the street behind the android and cut off its head before hacking apart the rest of its body.

As soon as the attack began, Evo darted to her right and began running away from them at an astonishing speed.

A bolo snaked out from one side of the House, wrapped around her legs, tripped her, and slammed her face into the rock surface.

As Evo laid there, stunned, blood gushing from her fractured nose and the severed muscles in her calves, Omarosa ran past Tul'ran and Erianne from their left, and jabbed the butt end of a spear into Evo's back, pinning her to the ground. Innanu exited her hiding place from the street to their right, gazing with satisfaction at the bolo cutting into Evo's lower legs.

Erianne cocked her head at her husband, her sword having flashed in her hand as soon as he put up the shield of uncreation.

"When did you put this together and why was I not part of the plan, you scruffy snowman?"

Tul'ran laughed and waved the shield of uncreation away, drawing Bloodwing from above his shoulder.

"Last night, you were busy keeping Evo from spending too much time with any one man and avoiding the fiery breath of the jade dragon. While you distracted her, I took Chief Ravenclaw aside and asked him questions about our planned route and timing. Do you remember when I said I was going to the stables to check on our horses?"

Erianne nodded, a light dawning in her eyes.

"You came out to check the layout of the streets and scout for ambush points."

"Ro'gun and I," Tul'ran corrected. "Innanu was most pleased to have her husband away from the room for a short time, and I think she expected I would speak to him about how his eyes shouldn't wander over Evo's form."

Erianne clapped her hands together.

"Yes! Did you give him the Talk, milord husband? You have become quite famous for the persuasive manner you employ to teach of sex and the ways of women."

Tul'ran's face reddened as they walked toward Omarosa and Innanu standing over their quarry.

"It wasn't necessary. Innanu had ingrained in his heart her deep displeasure at the wandering of his eyes, and it burned within him. After we walked to the stables, we drew up a plan against an attempt by Evo to escape. You should ask Ro'gun how he found the assassin and stalked it. Compliment him on how well it was done. He regards you with great awe and affection."

Erianne flashed her teeth at him and walked to the side of Evo's head, squatting beside the tall woman. Evo turned her face to look at Erianne and glared at her.

"Let me up!"

"Why?" Erianne said, stroking Evo's soft, thick hair with her left hand. "So you can try to run away again? For a woman who claims to be ten thousand years old, you're pretty stupid, Evo. Did you think we wouldn't expect you to escape? You might have centuries of book learning, but you have no experience as a warrior, or familiarity with martial strategy and tactics, and it shows."

Evo turned her bleeding face so her forehead rested on the street.

"This is my life now? Tied up with needles stabbing into my legs?"

Erianne smiled in sympathy.

"Yeah, I bet the bolo hurts. I guess we failed to mention last night our little group consists of skilled warriors, and each likes a particular and quite nasty weapon. This one is Innanu's. Her skills with the bolo are incredible."

Evo glared at Erianne again.

"I'll be sure to thank her for the lesson."

Tul'ran pressed the tip of Bloodwing against the back of Evo's skull.

"Is it wise to make threats when the memory of your attack upon me is still fresh in my mind and raises my heart to rage? Come, Evo, exercise some of your vast knowledge and a handful of common sense. Erianne's right. You're not a warrior, whereas Erianne, Omarosa, Ro'gun, Innanu, and Anatu are trained fighters. We are an overwhelming force against you, and we're not afraid to use it."

"I have a ship in orbit overhead," Evo ground out between her clenched teeth. "I can kill each of you without so much as singeing a hair on my head."

"Sure, go ahead," Erianne said as she stood up, contempt lacing her words. "Your ship will fire on us and Tul'ran will disintegrate your vessel, just like he uncreated the plasma curtain and the bombers Baamewaawaagizhigokwe sent in our direction. You'll strand yourself on this planet, but hey, it's your call."

Silence descended on the street. Evo banged her forehead on the street twice before turning her head to speak again.

"Fine! You win! Let's declare a truce. I'm hurting and I need to treat my wounded legs."

"Evo, She Who Wanders the Stars," Tul'ran said, his voice cold, "will you enter a covenant by the blood spilled between us you will never again attack me, Erianne, Omarosa, Ro'gun, Innanu, Anatu, or any of our friends and allies, knowing a breach of this covenant will end in your certain death?"

After a short silence, Evo said, "Tul'ran az Nostrom, Prince of Death, the Uncreator, and Erianne as Nostrom, Princess of Death, the Tamer of Gods, I covenant with you by the blood you have spilled from me I'll never again attack the two of you, Omarosa, Ro'gun, Innanu, Anatu, or any of your friends and allies, on pain of certain death. You should know, O Royalty of Death, my word is my holy bond. Having entered this covenant, you need never fear an attack from me again."

"Does this satisfy you, milady wife?"

"It does, milord husband. Innanu, remove the bolo. Try to be gentle, dear. We don't need to add to Evo's pain to make a point."

"Nice throw, sister," Anatu said, as she came running down the stairs from the main entrance, longbow in hand.

Innanu smiled at her younger sister's enthusiastic appreciation.

"Where were you, beloved?"

Anatu gestured with her bow to a balcony twenty feet over the entrance.

"Up there. I drew a bead on her from the moment Evo dashed away. If you had missed your cast, I was going to skewer her heart with my best arrow."

Evo grunted as Innanu ripped away the metal bolo, which had imbedded under the skin of her calves.

"Are you as good with your bow as your sister is with her bolo?"

"Better even," Omarosa said, taking her spear from Evo's back and resting it on the stone street. "Just as I've developed great skill with this spear. You may have drawn a truce from Milord and Milady, Evo, but I have your measure. Ride against my family and you shall find my spear taking up its residence at the base of your skull."

"So many threats for so early in the day," Evo said, wincing as Innanu ripped the last of the bolo cable out of her leg. "I'll have to catalogue them to be sure I feel terrified if I'm tempted to sneer in your direction."

Evo rolled over, raised her torso upright, with her legs extended in front of her, then rested back on her hands. She wiped away the blood running into her mouth from her nose, grimacing at the coppery taste in her mouth, before looking down at her legs.

"That really hurt."

Erianne cocked her head at Evo. Did she hear a little girl's whimper in the ancient woman's voice?

She squatted beside Evo, laid aside Caligo, and pulled a cloth from a pouch on her belt. With the other hand, she removed a wineskin from her waist and poured water onto the cloth. Erianne, her hands gentle, wiped the blood from Evo's face and offered her a drink from the skin. After Evo took a few swallows, Erianne gestured to her legs.

"How do you want us to bandage you?"

"I'm a little confused by your kindness. All of you confuse me. You attack me, injure me, threaten me with death, then offer me aid and comfort. Who are you people?"

Erianne brushed Evo's hair from her forehead.

"We're confused, frightened children of God trying to do the best we can in a scary universe. Just like you. If you can come to terms with peace between us, you'll get a lot more of the nice treatment. Now, what can we do for your legs?"

"My suit is already doing it. As soon as the bolo came off, the suit started injecting painkillers into my bloodstream. Nanobots in the suit are cleaning up the blood and closing the wounds. Once the wounds are closed, my eternal body will heal the injured tissue. Then the bots will repair my suit where Innanu's weapon tore it. How did you find my Tooth?"

Erianne looked at her through blank eyes.

"Your tooth? What tooth?"

Evo barked out a laugh, glazed with pain.

"My android. My ship is called The Dragon, and I call my androids Dragon's Teeth."

Tul'ran glanced back down the street from where the Tooth had attacked them.

"We encountered things such as your Tooth on Spes, Evo. Or have you forgotten? You claim to have been watching us the entire time. When we trained our warriors, we included lessons on our knowledge of the form their enemies could take. We were all prepared for you and your Teeth."

Evo turned her gaze on Innanu, who was cleaning Evo's blood off her weapon.

"Come here, Innanu."

After getting an affirming nod from Tul'ran,

Innanu went to squat beside Evo. Evo raised her right hand and pulled Innanu's head in to give her a kiss on the forehead.

"I know you did what they ordered you to do. Let there be peace between us."

Startled, Innanu hesitated, then leaned down to return the forehead kiss.

"There is peace between us, truly. I'm sorry I hurt you, Lady Evo."

Evo searched Innanu's eyes for a moment, then turned to Erianne.

"I'm beginning to believe you, Erianne. I just received an apology from a warrior who had every right to throw me down like a wounded deer and laugh at my pain. Perhaps there is more to all of you than I thought."

Chief Ravenclaw, two Elders, and Princess Wenonah walked up to them.

Ravenclaw nodded at Tul'ran.

"It went as you expected, then?"

Tul'ran slipped Bloodwing back into its sheath.

"It went exactly as I expected."

Awe swam in the Chief's eyes.

"I am grateful to you, Lord Tul'ran, for abandoning the title of Conqueror. There's no one in this world who could withstand you if you rode against us."

"Good grief," Erianne said, as she slammed Caligo into its sheath on her back. "There you go again. I do at least half the work, if not seventy-five percent, and you get all the credit."

Tul'ran laughed, and the others followed.

"As much as seventy-five percent, fearsome

warrior?"

Erianne glared at him, though mirth twinkled in her eyes.

"I could make a case for ninety, you know."

A moan slipped between Evo's lips, and she sank back to the ground. Erianne dropped to her knees by the silver-clad woman and touched Evo's forehead as her eyelids fluttered.

"What's happening, Evo?"

"It's my body," Evo gasped. "When my injuries are too severe, it goes into stasis to heal. I must have… I must have… an embolism, or…"

Evo's silver eyes rolled back, her eyelids closed, and she was gone.

"Is she dead?" Innanu said, panic creeping into her voice. "Did I kill her?"

"No, dear heart," Erianne said, her tone soothing and calm. "She's not like us, Innanu. She goes into a deep sleep, called a coma, to heal from her injuries. Evo will be fine. Tul'ran, my everything, will you pick her up and carry her to the conveyance?"

Tul'ran took two brief steps to stand at the side of Evo's still form. He looked up and down her seven-foot body, assessing the best points to lift her. Squatting, he placed his left arm under her shoulders and his right arm under her thighs. He stood with a grunt, the muscles in his arms, shoulders, and back rippling with effort.

"She's heavier than she looks. Shall we go?"

Tul'ran carried the unconscious Evo to the conveyance, which looked like a double-wide white bus floating inches off the ground. Very little snow remained, as the outside temperature had warmed the atmosphere to a welcome eighty-four degrees. The bus, no longer camouflaged, stood in stark contrast to the dull, whitish-gray rock revealed by the melted snow.

No one could say the builders failed to earn full coin for how they constructed the inside of the conveyance; it was extravagant. The manufacturer placed several full-length armless couches throughout the cabin. Many plush chairs surrounded the elegant eating tables. Tul'ran deposited Evo onto a couch with a soft, red surface. The woman's silver suit, silver hair, and pale skin made her look like a pearl on a bed of roses.

Chief Ravenclaw and Princess Wenonah sat at the front of the conveyance, as was their right. Innanu sat by Evo, while Omarosa found a sink with gold-threaded cloths hanging from it. After a few experimental waves of her hand, cold water spilled onto the cloth. She walked it back to Innanu, who placed it on Evo's forehead.

Anatu showed off her longbow to the two Elders, who complimented her on its elegant design as she unstrung it for the trip. Tul'ran found a divan at the back of the conveyance and, with a grin at his wife, laid back and closed his eyes. Within seconds, his soft snores wafted through the cabin.

Erianne took a seat with a beautiful window behind her, caught the gaze of their bondsman, and patted the chair beside her. Ro'gun acknowledged his duty, fell onto it, and declined his head.

"How may I serve you, your Royal Highness?"

Erianne was going to dispense with such formality, but caught Ravenclaw and Wenonah looking at them out of the corner of her eye. Inwardly, she smiled. Ro'gun was turning into quite the courtier, understanding the subtle nuances of her status in comparison with the others.

"Tell me, Ro'gun, how you found the device that attacked us and reduced it to its smallest components just in time to save our lives."

Ro'gun grinned, turning his countenance boyish.

"As you know, Lord Tul'ran and I left the feast last night to explore the area around the building in which we've stayed these several days. We went to the stables and withdrew Darkshadow and Destiny's Edge for a walk. When we strolled down the street from which the attack came, Darkshadow flickered his ears at a shaded spot near one wall. To his credit, he made no other sound."

Erianne sighed.

"He sensed the robot and alerted to it."

Ro'gun nodded.

"Your Highness, I am in awe of your horses. They are intelligent and brave beyond measure. When we came back up the street from our walk, this time it was Destiny's Edge who flickered her ears at the same spot. Confirmation of a threat most dire."

Erianne reached up and ran her hands through her black hair, which fell like waves from her head. It had grown since she met Tul'ran, and her hair fell to mid-thigh. She was an anomaly amongst female warriors, disdaining to tie her hair into braids or otherwise pin it into place. No one got close enough to her hair to grab it – she was far too fast for that – and the way it flowed when she fought distracted her enemies.

Still, she missed the planet Pulchra. Rai would brush her hair and braid it every night before she and Tul'ran went to bed. It was soothing.

Her hair had fascinated Rai. A pang akin to homesickness ran through her. They needed to go back to Pulchra soon. She missed Rai and her people. Erianne focused her mind back on the present.

"Even so, how were you able to sneak up on it without it sensing your presence?"

Ro'gun yawned, covering it with the back of his right fist.

"My apologies, Highness. I rose before dawn. Leaving from a far side entrance to the House, I slinked through the streets until I came up behind the monster. Lord Tul'ran had given me his cloak, and I hid under its ebon warmth until the sun woke the sky. As soon as the thing moved, I attacked it."

Erianne pulled her hair over her left shoulder and started finger brushing it. She and Tul'ran got little sleep the night before, having to keep a constant eye on Evo. She related to Ro'gun's fatigue.

"What became of it?"

"I turned it over to some of the Chief's warriors and told them to grind each piece to dust. They gave me their word I wouldn't distinguish it from the dirt upon which it lay when we returned."

Erianne noted the heaviness of his lids.

"Well done, valiant warrior. You are a credit to the House az Nostrom and we are wealthy because of your addition to it. Go rest beside my husband; you've earned it. We'll waken both of you when we arrive, or should the need arise."

Ro'gun nodded, grateful, and slipped to his feet.

As he walked away, Erianne caught Innanu watching her. A delighted smile etched across the younger woman's pretty face, and her eyes shone with pride.

Erianne nodded to her and Innanu bowed back.

Erianne leaned back against the window, through which warm sunshine surrounded her scalp like a halo, and her eyelids closed against her brilliant green eyes. Tul'ran was right. The kids needed praise and kind words more often.

The Princess of Death fell asleep, her thick black hair wrapped around her dark brown hands, and she dreamed of a world where beautiful eight-foot-tall people swam with dolphins and laughed as their sinuous bodies flashed through the ocean.

CHAPTER THE SIXTH:
THE DRAGON'S KISS

Ma'ilingan Waazh (Wolf's Den), 1st Year of Summer
26th day, Waatebagaa-giizis (Leaves Turning Moon),
Year 5379

She smelled coffee.

Wrinkling her nose, she tried to discard the thought. There was no coffee here; in fact, here was such a long way away from coffee the distance was impossible to grasp. It persisted, though; a wondrous smell taking her back to gentler, more peaceful times. She shook her head, irritated. Why wouldn't the smell go away?

"Erianne, if you don't open your eyes, I'm going to pour your coffee right onto them."

Erianne jerked her eyes open with a start. Evo was standing in front of her, a smile blooming on her perfect lips as she held out a steaming cup of brew.

Erianne lurched upright.

"They have coffee?"

Evo laughed.

"No, I have coffee. Ever since I started growing it, I've always kept a supply on hand. My suit might look skintight, but it has sneaky little pouches everywhere. I had enough coffee on me to make a good-sized pot."

Erianne looked around her. Ravenclaw and Wenonah were sipping at the hot beverage, exclaiming with wonder over the taste and smell. Tul'ran was watching her and Evo, ever on guard, enjoying a mug of Wolf's Den version of black tea. He didn't drink coffee, complaining it gave him a wicked heartburn. Everyone else had a mug of joe, and it looked like all were enjoying the treat. She reached out and took the mug from Evo's hands.

"God bless you, Evo. It feels like it's been a hundred years since I've had a cup of coffee. How do you feel?"

Evo put her hands on her hips, and her grin widened.

"Never better! I love this eternal body. I can't die and it always heals to the best shape possible."

Erianne took a long sip of the bitter beverage and sighed.

"I'm officially jealous. Good for you. I smell food, too."

One Elder was cooking over a gas stove on the other side of the bus. He was tall and had tied his long gray flecked hair into a braid. Erianne put him in his mid-fifties. Deep lines creased his face, but his dark eyes twinkled as he bared glowing white teeth in a wide smile.

He raised his right hand and gestured towards the stove with a spatula.

"Breakfast is served, Princess Erianne. We are near our destination, so it's best if we eat now. There is nothing in the City of Men for food or sustenance."

Breakfast was bacon served on a generous slab of bannock. On the side of the dish, the Elder heaped a serving of wild rice covered by sliced, bright red, vine-ripened tomatoes. Erianne couldn't identify the seasoning, but it was delicious. She dug into her plate with gusto.

"Thank you, Elder Wintershoe. The smokiness of the bacon is delicious, and this rice adds a nice nuance to the plate. You are an excellent cook."

Sadness flitted across the older man's face.

"You're quite welcome, Princess. I've lived alone my entire life, so cooking was a skill I needed to learn, and I practiced often."

"Elder Wintershoe, why have you been alone?" Anatu said, then added hastily, "If it's not impertinent to ask."

He laughed; the sound was a bare whisper from his lips.

"It's not impertinent to ask, Lady Anatu. We have very few women in our enclave. They have the choice of many men with whom to spend the rest of their lives. I was not the one they chose. This war has cost us much, child, not the least of which is a chance for marriage, children, and true happiness."

Anatu stared at him for a few long seconds, her face impassive.

She slid a glance at Omarosa, who was running a stone along the edge of her spear, oblivious to the interplay between her daughter and the older man. Anatu's face flashed through a subtle change. She rose from her cross-legged squat and placed a soft kiss on the aged man's cheek.

"I am in dire need of a father, Elder Wintershoe, and it would be my honor if you were to stand in his place."

The Elder turned his head away so Anatu would not see the tears quickening in his eyes. Anatu cupped his chin with her left hand and turned his face back toward her.

"This offer will never expire."

The Elder took her hand and kissed it.

"You must eat, daughter, for we have a long walk through the City of Men when we arrive."

Evo had watched the interaction between Anatu and Wintershoe with an intense gaze. She glanced back at Erianne, who had been studying her face.

"What?"

"Watcha thinking?"

Evo looked back at Anatu and her face softened.

"I'm not used to this. Love. Tenderness. Acceptance. I'd never have thought it could be so... moving."

Erianne kept her face solemn, not wanting to wreck Evo's moment of reflection.

"It's what love does, Evo. Love gentles pain and leaves the bitterness of despair covered with a cloak of sweetness to remind us we're not alone in whatever world we inhabit."

Evo's face twisted.

"Maybe. I've never experienced love, so I know nothing about it. It might not work for everyone. All I've known is rejection, pain, and sorrow. Only time will tell if your idea of love applies to me."

Evo stood up and walked to the front of the conveyance, leaving her empty plate behind. Erianne gathered up her dish and Evo's dish with a sigh, walking them to the sink behind the Elder and Anatu.

When she finished scraping the plate clean, she squeezed Anatu's shoulder and smiled at the young teenager as she chatted with the man she'd just adopted as a father. It was good to remember how much wisdom sometimes came from the mouths of young people.

The transport whispered to a halt, and everyone turned to the front. They followed Chief Ravenclaw and Princess Wenonah off the carriage. In front of them was an enormous dome stretching from the ground to the upper reaches of the sky. It shimmered silvery-blue and returned distorted mirror images to them.

Chief Ravenclaw walked up to a gray metal box attached by some unknown means to the dome. He extended his right hand and pressed it against the face of the box. For a moment, nothing happened. Then the entire box glowed a bright green, and the dome rippled. The energy field cascaded from the top of the dome toward them in waves and vanished when it reached the ground. As the plasma curtain fell, air rushed in from the atmosphere at the thinnest reaches of the stratosphere right to the ground.

Air replaced the vacuum inside the sealed dome

so smoothly and quickly, there was no noise or damage from it.

Tul'ran and his group were astonished to see a vast city with tall and short buildings running away from them for as far as the eye could observe. The Tribes of Men made the buildings of a shimmering metal like the color of the shield. Everything was clean and well preserved.

There was no plant or animal life, although there were expansive spaces set aside for both. The air smelled fresh, which made sense since it had rushed in from the valley they'd just traversed to replace the vacuum.

"Is this a shrine or burial space?" Tul'ran said, addressing his remarks to the Chief.

The lines on the Chief's face deepened.

"It might as well be both, Lord Tul'ran. The Tribes of Men built this city as a peace offering. It had been our intention, once we completed building the megalopolis, to sue the Tribes of Women for peace. We wanted to gather all the People here, and to have them live in harmony and prosperity. We'd almost completed every aspect of the city when Baamewaawaagizhigokwe took our scientists hostage. The timing was devastating."

"Why was it so? Forgive me if I inquire into matters not of my concern, but I'm intrigued. This city and all its dwelling spaces look both beautiful and functional. I don't know why anyone wouldn't want to live here."

Chief Ravenclaw placed his hand on one of Tul'ran's massive shoulders.

"Nothing in our knowledge shall we keep from

your ears, Conqueror. At the time the Tribes of Women took our scientists, they'd almost completed the power device for the metropolis. Our scientists have found a power source both infinite in duration and scope. Their discovery would've run this city and everything else in Ma'ilingan Waazh for as long as the People drew breath and their hearts beat."

Tul'ran quirked an eyebrow.

"I'm not as conversant in the mysteries of science as Princess Erianne, but such an achievement strikes me to be astonishing."

Ravenclaw nodded his head with vigor.

"Indeed it was, my friend. It was so near to completion we could taste it. To our misfortune, we had a spy in our camp. No sooner did our scientists enter the final phases of this project than Baam'e, as I know her in the short form, sued us for peace. Debate raged within our governing circle for days whether we should attend the peace talks or wait until we finished the city. Finally, sickened by years of warfare and the toll it took upon our population, we attended the talks."

Tul'ran turned his right arm into a sweeping gesture to encompass the vista before them.

"How could negotiations fail when you informed the Tribes of Women of this?"

"We never got that far," Ravenclaw said, his face sinking and his voice turning glum. "We'd taken our scientists with us to explain what they'd discovered and intended, but as soon as Baam'e saw that our leading scientists were with us, she seized our delegation by force and drove the rest of us out of the city."

Ravenclaw paused and shook his head.

"Our remaining scientists created the Equatorial Shield using the same technology as the plasma dome I just disabled. Unfortunately, they weren't the ones who constructed the power cube. There was only enough energy left in the cube to energize the city's defense shield and little else. The project languished. When we couldn't complete the project, our researchers and engineers abandoned this place, erected the dome, and removed all the air from the city. In this way, they've preserved it from degradation from the time of the Betrayal until this day."

The group approached another conveyance identical to the one they'd just left. Once they entered it, it whispered off at high speed towards the center of the vacant metropolis. Tul'ran and the others couldn't contain their awe at the beauty and expansiveness of the architecture slipping by the wide windows of the conveyance.

Erianne nudged Evo. When the taller woman turned her silver eyes on Erianne, the Warrior of the Lord said, "Why do you look so bored?"

Evo shrugged.

"After studying the wonders of the universe like nebulae, gas giants, intertwining galaxies, and massive black holes, a city seems as impressive as an anthill."

"Sorry you're so difficult to impress," Erianne said, her voice wry. "We'll try harder."

Evo jerked her eyes back to Erianne's face and searched it for a moment.

"Your tone smacks of sarcasm. Am I being

insulted?" she said.

Erianne's eyebrows shot up.

"Not at all. It's easy to forget you're not one of us. Despite your height, I relate to you like you've been part of this group all along. That's why you surprised me you weren't in awe of this incredible city like the rest of us."

Erianne turned back to the window to watch the architecture go by, but Evo continued to look at Erianne as the muscles in her face twitched with inexperienced emotions. She opened her mouth to speak, then closed it again. Her eyebrows drew toward the center of her forehead, and small lines creased the corners of her eyes. As she was about to say something to Erianne, the conveyance came to a smooth halt.

Out of the windows stood a black, cube-shaped building only five stories high. The ebon finish reflected the surrounding buildings.

Ravenclaw waved to the building.

"This is our crowning achievement. It is the Power Cube. Our engineers made the outside with polished obsidian three feet thick. Every edge is rounded and smoothed. When it was to be operational, the security apparatus protecting the building would've been second to none in this world."

His face fell, and he dropped his chin to his chest.

"When it was to be operational…"

Ravenclaw raised his head and gestured to the occupants of the vessel.

"Come, my friends, let me show you around this wondrous place. It's the underpinning source which divides our House into whether we can agree to peace."

They climbed out of the conveyance and walked toward one wall of the building. It appeared solid in construct, with unidentifiable doors. As they approached, a section of the wall slid away without a sound and allowed them access.

The interior had high ceilings, with no obstruction for the security blisters ringing the foyer. Nothing moved. No one challenged them. They walked past the inert blisters, which remained unaware of their presence.

The lighting in the building was dim, and the air smelled stale. With no outside air to exchange, the pressurized building circulated the same gases for decades.

The corridors were black tubes, twisting and turning through the complex, rising, and falling over other tubes. The elevation was never so steep as to wind them, but they got exercise on the way to their destination. Tul'ran made the point to Ravenclaw, earning a wide grin from the older man.

"We once believed in a careful balance between work and play, health and welfare, Lord Tul'ran. Our builders, under the influence of the designers, ensured cardiovascular exercise with these designs. They linked key offices but set them far apart so all our workers would have to use these sinuous corridors to get to their next workstation, or meeting. After several months of grumbling, the workers grew to like it."

The last tube led them to a large circular door.

"Master Research," Ravenclaw said.

The door slid open without a sound and a few scattered lights came on, providing only enough illumination to allow them to see where they were walking. Workstations surrounded a pit, where a circular rail prevented thought-consumed scientists from absent-mindedly falling into the pit. Within the pit were three huge holo boards hovering in the air. Each contained symbols and, even to an untrained eye, remained unfinished.

"This is the formula," Ravenclaw said, "which would have drawn enough energy into this world to make it impossible to live in darkness ever again. Our scientists were so close to a solution, they refused to go to the peace talks. They argued the short time it would take for them to resolve the formula justified putting off negotiations. We had to arrest them and take them to the peace talks in chains. We should have listened to them," he finished, bitterness ringing the edges of each syllable.

Tul'ran pointed to large elliptical rings circling the chamber.

"What are those, Chief Ravenclaw?"

"We made the rings of rhodium, one of the rarest elements in the universe from what I'm told. We use it as a conductive material because it has low electrical resistance and is resistant to corrosion. Those rings were the answer to all our energy problems."

As the other members of the group questioned the Chief about the chamber, Evo meandered down a steep, winding set of steps into the pit.

She stared at the three boards, flicking her eyes

left to right and back again. Evo chewed on her lower lip, her eyebrows tilting further to the middle than they had on the conveyance when Erianne had bewildered her.

"By the stars!" she said in a loud voice.

The Chamber became quiet. Erianne moved to the edge of the balcony rail separating them from the pit and called down to her.

"What is it, Evo?"

Evo thrust her hands toward the holographic screens.

"This! This is it! By all the nova stars in the universe, this is incredible!"

"Yes, Evo, but it's not finished."

"No, no, no! I mean, yes, it's not finished, but I see the theory as clearly as the sky after a rain. Don't you see it? Look."

Evo circled a formula with her hand, drawing an ellipsis around a series of letters and numbers.

She cupped her right hand and placed a cupped left hand on top. Without knowing it, she had mimicked someone dearly loved by Tul'ran and Erianne. A little blond woman who resembled an elf and ruled a planet millions of light years away.

"Imagine within my hand lies three-dimensional space. It appears empty but is filled with millions of sub-atomic particles. If these particles solidified into a sphere, you would have length, width, and depth. Overlying the sphere, represented by my fingers, is the dimension of time. In this universe, time and three-dimensional space are inextricably linked. You cannot separate them. This formula explains why. Your scientists, Chief Ravenclaw, call it…"

"Quantum friction," he finished for her.

"Yes." Her lips caressed the word into a croon. "Quantum friction. A force which welds space and time into the same continuum, incontrovertible in strength and matchless in flexibility. If you had a machine capable of separating time from space, the resulting explosion would destroy the universe. All of it. Trillions upon trillions of stars and planets separated by incredible distances would all be gone."

Evo fell silent.

"Were they trying to separate time and space?" Erianne asked.

"No, Erianne, Princess of Death, Tamer of Gods!" Evo said, her voice filled with delight. "This fantastic device would attach itself to the quantum link between time and space and feed off the energy produced by quantum friction. Because time is linear and space is not, there is a constant push and pull between them. The push and pull generates quantum friction, and the energy output is infinite. You could siphon terawatts of energy from this link without causing it to so much as sigh. The design is far beyond known physics. It's brilliant!"

Tul'ran nudged Erianne, his brows furrowed.

"Tell me, milady wife," he said, "Do you understand what she says? I hear her speak words, but they are meaningless to me."

Erianne nodded and turned to face him.

"I do, milord husband, but not to the extent of her knowledge. Her understanding exceeds mine to such a degree as to render mine laughable. I will do my best to explain."

She wrapped both her hands around his left biceps, with her fingertips almost unable to touch each other.

"Consider your arm as the universe. Under your skin are muscles, tissue, and blood. Each operates independently, but acts with a common purpose. Envision my hands as time. Though your skin, muscles, bone, and tissue work against my fingers, they cannot dislodge it. Time overlays the physical parts of the universe, just as my fingers overlay these delicious biceps."

Tul'ran smirked as Erianne changed the position of her hands. She grasped his wrist with her right hand and laid her left palm at the base of his biceps, near the elbow. Erianne made her palm rigid and slid it up his biceps at a slow, measured pace.

"Time moves in a straight line. It does not reverse itself, but continuously moves forward." She raised his arm by the wrist, making his muscles bulge against her palm. Erianne drew a quick breath as a familiar flutter teased her lower abdomen. She was a sucker for enormous arms, and his biceps lit a fire in her core.

"Just as time moves in a straight line, in the manner of my palm, physical bodies in the universe move of their own accord, like your muscles. They push against, but never dislodge time. There is friction between my palm and your skin, just as there is friction between time and the physical universe. Were I to rub your arm rapidly, it would create heat on your skin."

Tul'ran grinned like a wolf, noting the flush along her neck and her widening pupils.

"It may also create heat elsewhere."

Erianne blushed and retaliated by licking her lips, knowing full well what it did to her husband. He responded with a sharp, indrawn breath. Her lips curved into a sensuous smile, which invited much and promised more.

"Behave yourself, husband. This is a lesson in science, not biology. Though not the same, the heat between our skin is an example of the energy created by time moving in a straight line and the physical universe pushing against it in every direction. Evo says we can harness such energy to provide unlimited power. This is the invention of men over which Evo is so thrilled."

Tul'ran covered Erianne's hand with his right hand and pulled her in close enough to brush his lips against her neck. She gasped and squeezed his biceps hard.

"I could see multiple uses for unlimited energy," Tul'ran said in a hoarse voice. He pulled back and hovered his lips over Erianne's mouth, but said, instead of completing the kiss, "Say, to quench a fire?"

He pulled away, deftly avoiding the bite Erianne intended for his lower lip and turned back to the pit.

"Tell me, Evo, She Who Wanders the Stars," Tul'ran said, "where did they go amiss, if it is within your vast knowledge and understanding to answer?"

The way he formulated the question seemed to please her.

"To begin with," she said, gesturing at the equation she circled, "this is in the wrong spot."

Evo flicked her fingers, removing the offending

equation from the left board and placing it on the right board. Ravenclaw opened his mouth to protest, but stopped when Erianne's hand pressed against his chest.

"Please, Chief, do not interfere with what Evo's doing. She's over ten thousand years old and has knowledge beyond any of our understanding. I'm certain your scientists have recorded this formula and stored it in many locations to keep it safe."

Ravenclaw scanned the perfect proportions of the woman in the tight-fitting silver suit, stopping to admire the beauty of her face, before turning his eyes on Erianne.

"Princess, I hear what you say, but this is not the face and body of a woman ten thousand years old."

Erianne almost sprained an ocular muscle from the effort it took to not roll her eyes.

"Appearances can deceive, Chief. Please take it on our word this woman's mind houses more knowledge than all your scientists put together. Give her a chance to exercise her intelligence. It may pay off."

The world of math, equations, quantum mechanics, and concepts bordering on the magical consumed Evo. The building, the people, it all faded away. She lost herself in a universe of possibilities so remote; it made no sense for them to exist. They just needed genesis.

For example, this formula lacked these three symbols. Ah, there, now it was complete, but remained restrained and unfulfilled by its brothers and sisters, which were thinned by intellectual famine.

The formula became a string, which pulled on a thread. The weaving crossed all three boards, a ballet of letters and symbols so complex they only took on form and substance within her mind's eye.

Sweat ran down Evo's forehead as long-forgotten concepts forced their way to the forefront of her brain. Her fingers danced with more certainty as she painted equations on the boards, sometimes erasing them, sometimes moving them to another board until other equations could fulfill her desire.

Then there was only one left.

It was the last formula of the structure. Evo saw she had recreated what the scientists had conceived and stopped in her efforts to admire them. They had been so close! All they needed was to finish this formula, which they'd buried, incomplete, in the middle of the center screen, and what they brainstormed in theory would become reality.

Evo entered the last string of letters, numbers, and symbols and instructed the AI to run the algorithm. Suddenly, all three screens went black.

"What have you done?" Princess Wenonah screamed, lunging at the railing. "You fool! If you have destroyed their work, there shall never be peace with the Tribes of Men!"

"Restrain yourself, child!" Evo said with a sneer. "It's done. We wait for the result."

No sooner had she finished speaking than the rhodium rings gyrated and spun with increasing velocity. A scarcely perceptible whine filled the air. The lights in Master Research blazed into brilliance, illuminating what had been a dim chamber.

Panels bloomed, and various keys and pads glowed. The whine increased in intensity to where the human ear couldn't hear it, and the lab came alive.

One Elder burst into Master Research.

"Chief, the lights have come on in the city. Every building has power!"

The Chief ran out of the lab, followed by Wenonah and the House az Peregos.

Evo closed her eyes and took a deep breath. She could feel the energy coursing through the building. It was clean, harmless, and good. Very, very good. Her spirit bathed in the cool white flames of quantum friction, and her heart blossomed with a joy she'd never felt.

Evo walked to the center of the pit, to the round pillar which had generated the three screens. She leaned over and planted a soft kiss on the pillar's console. The Dragon's Kiss, which had birthed life instead of destruction.

If this is what it felt like to create…

In that moment, Evo felt closer to God than she'd ever been. She closed her eyes again and sent a tentative prayer of thanks toward Heaven. The response startled her.

It felt as if the Father had leaned over and hugged her soul, filling her with warmth and a dizzying array of happy emotions.

CHAPTER THE SEVENTH:
THE CONQUEROR

Ma'ilingan Waazh (Wolf's Den), 1st Year of Summer
26th day, Waatebagaa-giizis (Leaves Turning Moon),
Year 5379

Someone threw a party.

It's never certain how these things get started, but this one was impressive. The communicators worked when the power came on, and excited conversations flowed over one another like waves onto a beach. Conveyances filled with people, food, and alcohol were on their way to the City of Men at top speed before Evo left the pit.

She'd called up the equations again to check for any lingering flaw. To leave it flawed invited disaster. This was her first major success, an act of creation in some senses, and she'd die before she'd let it fail.

Dismissing the equations after reading each symbol and approving its place, Evo climbed the narrow, winding staircase to the observation gallery. It didn't surprise her to see Tul'ran and Erianne waiting for her at the top.

"Ah, my ever-watchful guardians. I expected the two of you to stop me when I reset and completed the calculations. Why didn't you?"

Tul'ran raised an eyebrow.

"Your question presumes I had the smallest grasp of the things you were doing. I don't speak for Erianne, but all I could do was trust El Shaddai that you weren't trying to send us to the afterlife, while we grinned sheepishly at our ignorance."

Evo barked a short laugh.

"I was in no better position than my husband, Evo," Erianne said. "While I've studied some physics, what you did is so far beyond my ability, I'd be ashamed to say I'm in any way learned. The result is obvious. You fixed their power problem. I'm proud of you."

Evo blushed, which startled her.

"Erianne, to their credit, they were so close! Had they completed one equation they left buried in the middle of the calculation, it would've worked. This device," she gestured to the revolving elliptical rings surrounding them, "now draws energy from Inter-Dimensional Space using a method I've never seen. It sucks from quantum friction, not the ambient energy of IDS. You and I have been in IDS, but we never experienced energy like this. I'm in awe of the scientific community which conceived the idea."

Erianne clapped her hands, while Tul'ran shook

his head, his expressive eyebrows dancing on his forehead.

"You could've said you used magic, Evo, and I would be just as likely to believe it."

"Don't fret yourself, Prince of Death. You were born and raised in a culture which didn't have access to the Library of Heaven. In many cultures, scientific advancements looked like magic, sometimes to the scientists' demise. What I've finished for the Tribes of Men is their achievement. They would've found the flaw and fixed it if we'd given them enough time."

"You are too kind."

The deep voice startled them, and they turned to see a grinning Chief Ravenclaw and Princess Wenonah standing behind them.

"We owe you a great debt, Evo, She Who Wanders the Stars. A debt which we haven't enough gold or furs to honor. This is a soul debt and we can only pay it in one way. I, Eric Ravenclaw, Chief of the Tribes of Men, grant you a place in our family from this day until the final darkness covers the morning sky. We, your clan, will know you as Evo Starchild. No matter where you wander, Evo, you will always have a home on Ma'ilingan Waazh, among your people."

Evo's silver eyes startled everyone by sliding tears down her cheekbones.

"I have a home?"

Wenonah stepped forward and reached up to wipe away Evo's tears, gliding her fingertips over the tall woman's pale skin.

"More, Evo Starchild. You have a family. You are

now one of us, a treasured member of our clan. Your world is Wolf's Den, and you are of its earth, wind, fire, and water. So say I, Wenonah, Leader of the Nine Tribes of Ma'ilingan Waazh, having ascended by the Grace of God to my rightful place."

Chief Ravenclaw snapped his head around, his mouth falling open, and stared at Wenonah. After searching her face and assessing the serenity in her eyes, his face became somber. He took a pipe out of his pocket and checked it for tobacco. With a small flame stick, he lit the pipe and the pleasing smell wafted to the ceiling of Master Research. Evo wanted to protest against contaminants in the power room, but bit back her words. Her instincts told her this was a sacred moment for her new family, and she was loath to insult them.

Ravenclaw took a couple of drafts from the pipe, then handed it to Wenonah. The young woman paused for just a second, then took the pipe and took two drafts from it.

"Princess Wenonah, Leader of the Nine Tribes of Wolf's Den entire, I return to you your power. Here is your city, Princess, which the Nine Tribes will know as the City of Wenonah's Ascension."

The ensuing silence felt long. Wenonah swallowed, her jaw working as tears threatened to flow from her eyes.

"You're giving me the city?"

Ravenclaw smiled.

"No, my dear Princess. I'm giving the city to the hereditary Leader of the Nine Tribes. Someday you will have to pass the city and your reign to your daughter. Until then, rule it and this world, well."

Tul'ran cleared his throat.

"While I have no desire to pour water from the winter's snow on the warmth of this moment, are we not forgetting something? Such as the Tribes of Women and the conflict yet to be resolved?"

Wenonah broke another long silence by handing the pipe to Tul'ran.

"Lord Tul'ran, you're correct. I cede my authority and my claims to this world to you. Go and take it, Conqueror. When you have bound it as one, return this pipe to me, if that's your desire, and I will take back Ma'ilingan Waazh with my blessings for your House."

Ravenclaw and Wenonah bowed to Tul'ran, then grabbed Evo by the arms.

"Come, Evo Starchild, we're going to have a powwow to sing your deeds into the history of the world!"

Erianne giggled at the look on her husband's face as the other three ran out of Master Research.

"Milord husband, it's rare to see you speechless. You look as if someone flung the entire carcass of a deer into your face."

His lips twitched.

"If they flung the deer from an ambush, I'd agree it's how it feels. Yet again, I've been handed a world and told to break it to peace. One day, I'm going to keep it. Am I correct in applying this concept from your language to our current situation: Wenonah and the Chief set us up?"

Erianne stretched her hands above her head, lengthening her lean frame and highlighting its sensuous attributes for Tul'ran's pleasure.

"Yes! And do you know what that means?"

"No, but I can see you've become very excited by the prospect of…?"

"War! We finally get to fight a battle. I'm so bored, I've taken to counting sheep at night to get to sleep. Come, milord husband! Tonight, we dine! Tomorrow, we charge our horses to war!"

Erianne skipped out of Master Research, laughing. Tul'ran cast his eyes to the ceiling.

"Thank you, El Shaddai, for your gift of a wife of honor, integrity, and who thirsts for bloodletting as much as her lips thirst for water. What am I going to do with her?"

Someone was beating drums outside the building. It sounded like a call to arms, and the rhythm pounded in his veins. Tul'ran grinned and ran after Erianne.

Fate tapped out the drumbeat on her legs, and hummed a martial tune. It was unfortunate there were no balladeers among these people to continue Tul'ran's Ballad.

Tul'ran the Conqueror was riding to war.

The party went on through the night until the sun began to light the pre-dawn sky. Even though the power was on in the convention center, someone built a bonfire on the bare earth slated to become a park. Portable stoves prepared a feast, while alcohol helped whet the appetites of everyone who traveled from the House of Men.

Tul'ran wandered through the crowd, counting.

Everyone had come, but everyone only included

nine hundred and eleven people. This was the entire population of the Tribes of Men, with only a small number being women.

No wonder they were so desperate for peace.

A young boy hurtled through the people, and Tul'ran caught him up in his arms before he ran headlong into Tul'ran's leg.

"Sorry," the startled boy said, his eyes wide.

"You need not be sorry," Tul'ran said, and smiled at the youngster. "Just careful. Always know what's within your space, to spare yourself and others from harm."

"Okay," the boy said, almost unable to breathe, excitement burning in his small brown orbs.

Tul'ran put him down and turned his head with a massive palm to a woman who was staring at them with her hands to her mouth.

"Is that your mother?"

"Yes, it is!"

"Then go to her and tell her Tul'ran the Sword offers blessings to her house."

The boy ran up to his mother and jumped into her arms.

"Mama, Mama, I met the Conqueror! He said blessings to our horses!"

The woman bit her lip and flashed an appreciative smile at Tul'ran.

"I think he said blessings to our house, dear. Come, let's play with the other children and leave the Conqueror to his thoughts. And remember what he said about being more careful."

Tul'ran chuckled, then these soft words tickled his mind,

'Good greetings we give, O Mighty Conqueror. Your fire, may we join?'

'Hello, Miikaw,' Tul'ran thought back, trying to project warmth into the soundless words. 'Welcome you are, always. Dizi with you is or is not?'

'I'm here, Lord Tul'ran,' the Wolf thought to him. 'Turn and find us approaching from behind you.'

The giant Wolf and a large Mountain Lion padded up to him. Tul'ran extended his hands and ruffled the fur on each of their foreheads to show his affection for them.

'Where have you two been?'

'We to our respective clans went,' Miikaw spoke to his mind. 'Interested were we in the support we could raise for your cause to bring peace to our world.'

Dizi squatted on his back haunches.

'Little good that did. Both the Clans of Wolves and Mountain Lions declined to support any more warfare with violence. They're tired of fighting for humans and losing their lives. There are some in our Clans who want to keep killing humans. We'll have to watch out for them. Miikaw and I will still fight for you, but no one else in our clans will.'

'Bonded to you, we have,' Miikaw said. 'To life's end or ultimate victory, do we set our fangs and claws for you.'

Then Erianne's soft, dulcet voice was in all their minds.

'Hi, Dizi and Miikaw. Milord husband, Chief Ravenclaw summons the three of you to a war council. We are around a small fire to the north and west of the main gathering.'

After losing the temptation to tousle the foreheads of the two giant animals one more time, Tul'ran led them past the people celebrating around the gigantic bonfire. The Wolf and the Lion suffered the indignity of being petted with good humor. Each could feel the affection Tul'ran had for them and knew the gesture came from tenderness, not condescension.

Around a smaller fire sat Erianne, Evo, Omarosa, Ro'gun, Innanu, Anatu, Anatu's newly adopted father Elder Elwyn Wintershoe, Wenonah, Chief Eric Ravenclaw, and his son, Nicholas Ravenclaw. Tul'ran lowered himself onto a coarse blanket by his wife and left a lingering kiss on her lips.

"For those of you who don't know them, here are Miikaw and Dizi, our allies. They've come with news: only they, and no others from their clans, campaign with us to end the conflict between the Tribes of Men and Women."

Wintershoe nodded, his face solemn, as the Wolf and the Lion laid down beside them near the fire.

"Long have Lions and Wolves fought this war as human proxies. I don't blame their clans for declaring an end to their involvement. Too many have died. We must bring this war to a finish."

"I've had some thoughts about that," Tul'ran said, scratching the top of his scalp. "Chief, do you agree it's likely your spy still walks among the Tribes of Men?"

"Yes, Lord Tul'ran." The Chief reached out with a stick to poke at the logs in the fire. "I've no doubt as soon as the lights came on, Baam'e's spy transmitted the information to her. I would wager she has troops moving toward us now."

"It is not my wish to challenge you, Chief," Ro'gun said, as he wrapped Tul'ran's cloak around Innanu's shoulders, "but I think you are days late in your assessment."

Erianne shot Ro'gun an interested glance.

"Why do you say so?"

The young warrior seemed uncomfortable at being the center of everyone's attention.

"The spy would've communicated the Plasma Curtain's disintegration as soon as it came down. Lord Tul'ran destroyed Baamewaawaagizhigokwe's flying things and the fire deaths they carried. If I were Wenonah's mother, I would have begun preparations to send my Army against the City of Men as soon as those two things happened."

Erianne's lovely lips twisted upwards into a pleased smile.

"You are wise in the ways of strategy and tactics, Ro'gun. Milord husband, I agree with our bondsman's assessment. We may not have to take the fight to the City of Ikwe Na. The fight may come to us."

Tul'ran stretched out his feet closer to the fire, enjoying the warmth of the flames.

"We must not battle with them here. In the history of this world, no woman has died at the hands of a man, nor is the reverse true. If we are to keep El Shaddai's peace in this world, we cannot permit a desperate, all-out fight over this city and its new resources."

"At the same time," Erianne said, while reaching over to run her hands over his stubbled face, "we can't leave this place undefended. Worse, the population is too small to mount a defense around this vast metropolis."

Tul'ran's lips stretched into a grim line.

"I am loath to be the bearer of this news, but we must separate. Ro'gun will stay here with the Chief and his forces to help him defend against an attack. You, Princess Wenonah, Innanu, Omarosa, Anatu, and I should go to Ikwe Na by the fastest possible means. If there should be an initial skirmish, you and the women could take the fight to their forces. Should any blood be let, it will be by women fighting each other and women won't die at the hands of men. This should keep peace possible between Men and Women. It may also be possible for Princess Wenonah to encourage her mother to lie down their arms before the fight starts."

Ro'gun and Innanu shared a glance. She gave her head a quick shake. Ro'gun dropped his eyes to the fire, but Erianne saw their exchange and the discomfort on his face.

"What's up with the two of you?" Erianne said, pointing at them with two fingers of her left hand spread in a V-shape. When neither of them responded, her voice became sharper. "Will neither of you answer the Lady of the House?"

Innanu dipped her head.

"Forgive us, your Royal Highness. Ro'gun fears for me and doesn't wish for me to war by your side."

Tul'ran's forehead scrunched.

"Have we not trained all of you to fight to the best of your ability? Ro'gun, do you contest Innanu's skills and the contribution she makes to our forces?"

Ro'gun's face flushed deep red, and he couldn't bring himself to meet Tul'ran's eyes.

"I have great respect for my wife's martial skills, milord. I would have no one else fight by my side. The cause for my hesitation," he licked his lips, "is if she falls, we lose two lives."

Erianne looked at him with questions in her eyes.

"Two lives? Do you count yourself in the mix?"

Omarosa smiled.

"Milady, Ro'gun is trying to tell you Innanu is with child, and he doesn't want her to wage battle and risk losing her and the baby."

Erianne whirled on Ro'gun and Innanu, her face lighting up like a searchlight.

"You're pregnant?!"

It was Innanu's turn to blush, and she flashed a brilliant smile.

"It's my honor to announce," she said, lowering her voice to bring dignity to the joyous occasion, "Ro'gun and I will soon add a child to the House az Peregos."

"No," Tul'ran said, as he stood up to join Erianne in giving the two young people a hug, "you add a life to the House az Nostrom. We bonded Ro'gun to our House, and the bond includes his family."

After the quiet celebration ended, when everyone hugged the young couple and congratulated them, they took their places around the fire.

Tul'ran drew a deep breath.

"This war must come to a quick end before there's a battle for this city. Erianne, you, Ro'gun, Innanu, and Miikaw will stay here and set up a defense. I pray you won't need it. Princess Wenonah,

Chief Ravenclaw, Dizi, Omarosa, Anatu, and I will go by the fastest means to Ikwe Na and try to negotiate peace."

His face set into a grim line.

"Or for me to take this world by force."

"Aren't you forgetting something?" Evo said.

They all looked at her.

"I've counted the population here, too. Baame'e's army outnumbers yours, Chief. Plus, they have energy weapons. If you mean to go to Ikwe Na, Lord Tul'ran, you cannot protect your allies here from her troops' energy weapons. We'll get slaughtered."

Tul'ran's eyes narrowed.

"And you propose a solution?"

"Yes. My ship has devices by which I can direct an electromagnetic pulse against the Army of Women. It will disable their weapons and conveyances. They'd have to fight hand-to-hand and even then, would be formidable given their numbers."

"Why do I hear a 'but' in your unspoken words?" Erianne asked.

Evo shifted, as if she had become uncomfortable with her perch on the log near the fire.

"I never gave my AI permission to target humans." She saw the look on both Erianne's and Tul'ran's faces. "Yeah, yeah. I lied earlier when I said my ship could blast you from space. I have to be on board to target any of my weapons. It's a failsafe I put in place to make sure my ship never turned on me."

Erianne snorted.

"Right. We let you go back to your ship. What's

stopping you from taking off and leaving us here?"

Evo's face stiffened.

"You may not think much of me, Erianne, and maybe I haven't given you any reason for it."

She gestured to Ravenclaw and his family.

"But these people have adopted me as one of their own. They made me a part of this planet by invoking the earth, wind, fire, and water. I know they don't mean it in the way of idol worship. They believe strongly in the Creator, whom you call El Shaddai. Just as you bind your oaths in blood, they bind theirs by the things they can sense. It's a powerful invocation and breaking such a bond invites serious consequences."

Evo paused for a moment, swallowing against a lump in her throat.

"Becoming part of a family means something more to me than I thought it would. I've been alone, wandering the universe for ten thousand years. Not having known love, I'm shocked by how much the little I've received fills me and leaves me wanting for more. I'm not leaving this world until I know my family is safe."

Chief Ravenclaw cleared his throat.

"I appreciate your feelings, Evo, but what about the ice shield? Will you not damage it if you bring your ship through it?"

A smile glowed on her face.

"I've developed the technology to move my ship through ablative shields without harming them. I've tested it several times. The shield will be safe with me. You bring up another reason for me to return to my vessel. I can't fire weapons from orbit without damaging the shield. Even an electromagnetic pulse from orbit wouldn't be wise; I wouldn't be able to limit the pulse's surface area coverage. It could wipe out the city's energy, as well. I must bring The Dragon out of orbit, into the atmosphere, to protect the city. I have twenty-three more Dragon's Teeth on board. We could place them in a defensive posture in front of our forces so my androids could take the brunt of the initial attack."

Silence descended.

'Can we trust her?' Tul'ran cast into Erianne's mind.

'What choice do we have, my love? You can't be in two places, and there is a vast distance between here and Ikwe Na. She's right. You can't protect us from their energy weapons from so far away. The longer we wait here, the greater the risk Baam'e is marshaling forces to lay siege to this city. If we move fast, we can avoid a shooting war.'

Tul'ran turned to Erianne and gazed into her eyes.

'Have I told you how much I love your green eyes, covenant-wife? They hypnotize me and stir a longing within me to spend all my days swimming in their depths. I accept your analysis, but it leaves my question unanswered. Do we trust Evo?'

Erianne leaned over and placed her lips against his, being careful not to rub her soft skin against his black stubble. She pulled back and sighed.

'Before you leave, I will shave you, love. We don't trust Evo, but how can we build trust if we don't give her some leeway to earn it? If she leaves, the Lord will deal with her. If she breaks her word and attacks us, El Shaddai will rain His fury upon her head. Is it not so, Lord?'

They both heard His soft laugh in their heads.

'Do you see, My son, how quickly your bride exercises her faith and reaches out to Us?' He teased. 'If Evo breaks her word and attacks any of you, We shall stop her. Do not fear. You may carry out your plans without concern. We shall charge the decisions she makes against her account, but We will not interfere if she does not threaten you.'

Tul'ran and Erianne broke apart and regarded the statuesque, silver-haired woman waiting with thinly veiled impatience for their answer.

"Very well, Evo. Return to your ship and prepare to battle Baame'e's forces. Tul'ran and I need a few minutes before he leaves." Erianne flashed a smile at her husband. "I want to take a knife to his throat."

The fullness of the sun had crept up over the horizon when Tul'ran and his group left the city and made their way to a conveyance. Erianne walked with him, linking her fingers into his, as they followed Wenonah, Ravenclaw, Omarosa, Anatu, and Dizi. Elder Wintershoe insisted on coming with them as well.

"I'm too old to be a warrior," he'd said, "but I will watch my daughter fight and add her song to our legends."

Tul'ran and Erianne watched as Anatu took her father's elbow and allowed herself to be led into the conveyance.

"I tire, milord husband, love of my life, of escorting you to a transport which will take you to war without me."

Tul'ran smiled at her.

"Beloved Erianne, between the two of us, I would rather fight with only you by my side. I fear Ro'gun is correct; even now the forces of Women move against this city to claim it for themselves. I've been at the mercy of a siege. It's the least comfortable place to be."

She leaned her head against his shoulder.

"You'll have to tell me the story someday. I feel like we've been married forever, but there's still so much I don't know about your past. Like how you convinced your family to believe in El Shaddai, or how and where you survived a siege? Be careful, my love. I know El Shaddai is with you, but he doesn't promise you won't be harmed."

Tul'ran wrapped his massive right arm around her slender body and squeezed.

"You worry too much, Erianne. When Evo tried to kill me, it was only one of many times El Shaddai came to my rescue. I feel we have much more to do before our lives end. I'm a thought away and will return at the soonest chance."

Tul'ran and Erianne paused before the conveyance's entrance. Erianne caressed his smooth, clean-shaven face and pressed her forehead into his.

"I know I don't say this enough. I love you, Tul'ran. Since the day you pulled me out of the cage in the Mesopotamian desert, I've loved you. I will love you for all eternity."

He kissed her, enjoying the softness of her lips against his. Their tongues met, and the kiss became more intimate. They pulled apart, their eyes shining.

"I love you, too, Erianne. Take care of the

children. When I return, we'll own this world."

Erianne cocked her eyebrow at him.

"Do you mean to keep it?"

He laughed.

"Would El Shaddai let me? No, my love, I doubt our destiny is to rule Ma'ilingan Waazh. I don't mean to keep it."

His eyes darkened, became colder, and his facial muscles settled into a dangerous rigidity.

"But I mean to conquer it, and I will bathe their valleys with blood if the Tribes of Women are foolish enough to oppose me."

CHAPTER THE EIGHTH: WAR!

Ma'ilingan Waazh (Wolf's Den), 1st Year of Summer 27th day, Waatebagaa-giizis, (Leaves Turning Moon), Year 5379, at the City of Wenonah's Ascension

They were not stupid.

The engineers and artists who conceived the city now called Wenonah's Ascension, wearied by centuries of fighting, were careful to layout the metropolis in the shape of a horizontal triangle. Tall mountains thick with trees and severe slopes surrounded the city on two sides, preventing an attack from those quarters.

The base of the triangle opened to a descending valley. Enemy forces had some cover in the forest before they approached the valley, but then they had an uphill slope to the city on bare land. It was an excellent defensible position for ground attacks, and any air attack had to come up the valley because of the height of the surrounding mountains.

The entrance to the valley was a narrow point where they'd located the outpost on two opposing mountain sides. An outpost which became the House of Men for under a thousand people when they couldn't complete the equations for the power generator.

The conveyance stopped at the outpost. Several men were loading Darkshadow, Destiny's Edge and other horses into a large, black rectangular object about three sizes larger than the land transport.

"Do we change conveyances?" Tul'ran asked Ravenclaw.

The older man nodded.

"We must, Lord Tul'ran. This one will carry us by air to Ikwe Na, and it will take only minutes instead of weeks to get there. It's not armed, and we should be cautious. Baame'e has weapons with which she can target and take down this machine. We will have to land far enough away from Ikwe Na to avoid her defenses."

Tul'ran turned a worried glance toward the city.

"Do her forces have more of these devices? I destroyed one when she attacked us after I took down the Plasma Curtain."

Ravenclaw looked at the tree line beyond the outpost, in the direction where the Plasma Curtain once hung.

"Yes, and they are armed. If Baame'e has moved her forces, it will be to the clearing where you destroyed our primary defense shield."

Tul'ran had the grace to look sheepish.

"My apologies, Chief Ravenclaw. It wasn't my desire to leave the Tribes of Men so vulnerable."

Ravenclaw reached out and clasped Tul'ran by one shoulder.

"There is no reason to be sorry, my friend. You used the energy from the Plasma Curtain to resurrect the ablative shield around our world. The endless winter is now the summer we haven't enjoyed for many years. Were it not for you, Princess Erianne, and Evo, we'd have no chance at peace or warmth."

Ravenclaw led Tul'ran to the air conveyance, and as they walked up the ramp into the machine, Tul'ran flashed a thought to Erianne.

'Be warned, my love. We are traveling on an air conveyance to Ikwe Na. Baame'e's forces have similar conveyances, which may be armed. Please convey this threat to Evo.'

'Done and done,' she flashed back. 'This will be the first time you've flown, Tul'ran. It may be unsettling. Don't be afraid.'

Tul'ran laughed out loud, startling his companions.

'Remind me to tell you of the occasion I rode the back of an angered dragon, covenant-wife. Riding in the belly of this machine will be far less frightening.'

It was quiet in his head for a moment.

'You're joking, right?'

Tul'ran couldn't stop grinning.

'If you don't believe me, ask El Shaddai. He had to stop Time to keep me from falling off its back to my death. He and I had a deep conversation afterwards about needing to create such a thing, which breathed fire and flew like an eagle.'

When the Stars Fall
The Ballad of Tul'ran the Sword, Book V

Ma'ilingan Waazh (Wolf's Den), 1st Year of Summer
27th day, Waatebagaa-giizis, (Leaves Turning Moon),
Year 5379,

The Battle for the City of Wenonah's Ascension, The Air War

Evo laughed after Erianne told her Tul'ran's story. It seemed farfetched, but she had seen many strange creatures in the universe. El Shaddai had a sense of humor, Erianne said, and Evo believed it. Anything was possible with God.

"Be wary of what Tul'ran said about the airships. If they're armed, they could be a threat. Do you go to your ship now?" Erianne said, as they surveyed the valley below the edge of the city. It was empty, for now.

"Yes! I'll come back to an altitude which will give me a clear view of the land beyond the outpost. If they have airships, I'll tell you straight away. I'll find a large patch of bare dirt; big enough to accommodate my shuttle and land my starship. It shouldn't be hard to find a plot of land; they designed the city very well."

Erianne surprised Evo by grabbing her and pulling her into a long squeeze.

"Be careful, Evo, please. You've never been in a battle. Rule number one of warfare is: don't die. In my world, today is Christmas Eve. Don't wreck my Christmas, you silver-haired bombshell."

Evo pulled away, the muscles of her face dancing.

"You people will never cease to amaze me. I take it 'bombshell' is a compliment?"

Erianne stood on her toes and kissed Evo's cheek. "In the highest imaginable form."

Evo laughed and gave Erianne another quick hug.

"It may take me all eternity, but I'll figure you out. Don't worry. I'm very good at taking care of my skin. At least," she reflected, "I was until I met you and your husband. I'll see you later."

Evo ran as far away from the crowd at the exit point of the city as she could to find a landing area. She was as fast as a gazelle, with long powerful legs and endurance far beyond human capacity. When she found the best spot, she spoke a code of letters, numbers, and mathematical symbols. The bone conductors implanted under the skin near her ears chimed, confirming an encrypted connection with her starship, The Dragon.

"How may I serve you, Mistress?" her AI voice said in her ear.

"Do you have my location?"

"Of course, Mistress. I maintain a constant lock on you. The Dragon is in a geosynchronous orbit above your position."

Evo looked upward, but, of course, she couldn't see the distant vessel.

"Send me a Dragon's Egg."

"Acknowledged. I'm dispatching an Egg now."

Evo strived for patience as she scanned the clear blue sky. It would take a few minutes to prepare the exo-atmospheric shuttle, program the correct coordinates, and drop it. She couldn't shake the sense of urgency. She'd left Erianne, Ro'gun, and the others discussing how to position their fighters to best defend the city, their foreheads furrowed in concentration and angst.

Evo wanted to do her part, and this was the only way she knew how, given she wasn't a trained fighter.

A white object appeared from above and fell toward her. An anti-gravity engine propelled the shuttle, so the landing was soft. It was white, about eight feet tall, and shaped like an egg.

The featureless exterior rolled aside to reveal a padded couch stationed against the opposite wall. Once Evo stepped inside and pressed her back against the couch, straps slid across her body and the doorway became a solid wall again.

"Ascend," she said, her voice terse and betraying her anxiety.

There was no sensation of flight. At her command, the walls became transparent around her. Her heart skipped a beat with the thrill of flying upwards through the atmosphere at a stunning acceleration.

Like her ship, she'd equipped the Egg with the technology to open a wormhole through the ice layer without contacting it. What she hadn't perfected was a smooth transition through the wormhole. Her stomach protested as the vortex twisted the Egg every which way and threatened to turn it inside out.

At least it was a quick transition. Evo felt relief as the Egg transited the ablative shield and sped up into space.

Pride replaced relief as her shuttle approached the long, slender silver-skinned starship. Its design was elegant. A long tube ended in a sharp, pointed nose at the front. The Dragon sat on a large rocket tube at the other end of the ship.

The ship didn't need the rocket; a powerful anti-gravity, trans-dimensional engine drove The Dragon wherever Evo pointed. The rocket thruster was part of the original design, so Evo kept it.

Three large fins sat equidistant from one another at the base of the ship. In this configuration, Evo would land the starship on its fins, with the needle nose pointed to the sky.

Evo strode through the ship after the Dragon docked the Egg. The ship was much larger inside than it appeared from the outside. She passed a physical fitness area, sleeping quarters, a galley, a library, a lounge, and a garden before arriving at the command center. It was more comfortable than the house she blew up on Everhome when she left her planet of origin behind.

"Status update," she snapped, as she slid into the pilot's chair.

"All systems are nominal. There is no immediate threat to the ship. What are your orders, Mistress?"

Flying a starship was easy when you didn't have to pilot it. Maintaining position on the x, y, and z axes, especially when in a vacuum with no proximal reference points and gravity, was one of the most difficult flying exercises. It took years of training and practice to master such skills. Skills Evo had programmed into her AI.

Evo gave commands, and the AI turned them into thrust, vector, attitude, and altitude responses with delicate precision. She'd built triple redundancies in the software to make sure her biomechanical navigator didn't drive her into a star or fly her into the middle of a planet by accident.

"Plot a course to where you picked me up. Once we're through the ice layer, reconfigure the ship into the atmospheric fighter. Maintain altitude at fifty thousand feet, and program two missiles for an electromagnetic airburst at five hundred feet. I'll ID targets once we're in the air. I want to disable their machines and energy weapons."

The AI complied and the main screen showed the starship turn and point its nose at the ablative shield. The Dragon balanced thrust and gravity forces with no need of a command from Evo. No matter how fast The Dragon flew, Evo never pulled g's. The ice layer raced toward the ship, then Evo felt the dizzying sensation of twisting, falling, and rising, which always accompanied transit through a wormhole, and they were through.

It was time to change The Dragon from a starship into an atmospheric fighter.

Evo had spirit-walked through space for many millennia and often visited the planet the inhabitants called Earth. The chaotic existence of humans on the planet had fascinated her. It was the most robust, unruly, enthusiastic, and depressing population in the universe.

Within a few short years of promising herself she'd never visit the pathetic world again, she'd find herself back on the globe during a different time in their history.

One such occasion found her on the American aircraft carrier USS John F. Kennedy (CV-67) in November 1983. She spent days on the deck of the carrier as Squadron VF-143 launched daily missions over the land mass called Lebanon.

VF-143 flew the F-14 Tomcat, and Evo fell in love with the massive fighter jet. Powered by two Pratt & Whitney F401-400 engines, the two-seat, twin-tail, all-weather-capable variable-sweep wing fighter aircraft was the most formidable of its day. It was big, elegant, and beautiful.

Even in her spirit form, Evo had felt the thrust of the massive engines as the steam catapult launched the fighters off the carrier's deck.

Evo so loved the design of the Tomcat; she programmed its features into The Dragon. The starship was a fusion of configurable parts. Even in flight, Evo's command could change the vessel into one of seven pre-configured shells. The Tomcat shell provided stable flight in atmosphere, excellent maneuverability, and benefited from the power of the starship's engines. It was Evo's favorite configuration.

The only downfall was her failure to program stealth into the composition. Her ship would remain visible and targetable. Having never imagined herself in the middle of combat, needing to include invisibility and stealth never occurred to her.

To the observer, the starship went through an intricate set of contortions, which didn't affect Evo in the least. Her seat remained the same; the surrounding canopy kept her life support systems constant. The rest of the ship convulsed and transformed into the new design without causing Evo the least bit of discomfort. After the configuration change, The Dragon hovered in place. The planet's gravity well was no match for the starship's anti-gravity engines.

Evo worked the instruments before her and scanned the area beyond the city. It didn't take long to find what she'd hoped wouldn't be there. People, looking like a swarm of ants, dotted the bare plains beyond the outpost.

"Erianne, do you hear me?"

When she replied, Erianne's voice sounded as plain in Evo's ear as if the brown-skinned warrior sat next to her. Evo had clipped silver communication tabs on Erianne's armor and Tul'ran's armor before she'd left to get her ship. The transmissions didn't travel through any radio or microwave spectrums. They traveled through IDS from transmitter to receiver and back, and their range was infinite.

"Hi, Evo. You're loud and clear. Do you have a report?"

"Yes, to my chagrin. Ro'gun was right. There's an army of warriors camping in a large clearing which used to be split in half by the Plasma Curtain. Wait one second."

Evo addressed her AI.

"Identify the three triangular objects in the field."

The AI responded as if it had expected the question.

"The objects are aircraft equipped with missiles and guns. They also appear to be troop carriers, as soldiers are filing into the back of the craft."

Evo's head jerked in a crisp nod.

"Erianne?"

"Yes, Evo?"

"Don't tell him I said so, but Tul'ran was right, as well. There are three airships in the field. They're equipped with weapons, and they appear to be loading troops."

There was silence at the other end, and it felt deafening.

"Can you give me a troop estimation, Evo?"

Evo played her instrument panel like a piano and it threw numbers at her as fast as she could type the keys.

"Two thousand and twelve women. I think the twelve are officers."

Silence again.

"Nicholas says it's half their army. They must have split their forces in two and sent half of them to seize the City of Men. The other half stayed home to defend Ikwe Na." Erianne paused. "I hate to ask you this, Evo, but can you stop those airships from flying? We have no means of defending the city if they air drop warriors all over it."

"On it!" Evo said and closed the connection.

"Dragon, there's our first target. Make a high-speed run down the valley and launch two EM missiles from fifteen hundred feet. I don't want to give them time to intercept our missiles. They are not to know we were there until after we kill their ships. Execute."

The Dragon exploded into action at a velocity which would have crushed Evo if it hadn't been for the inertial dampeners. The ship dropped from fifty thousand feet to just above the valley floor and twisted down the slope.

At the last second, it flew up and over the outpost and fired the EM missiles. They flew true and detonated at five hundred feet. There was no explosion, flare of light, or anything else as proof of ignition. The force generating the energy-killer also evaporated the missiles.

The electromagnetic pulse pressed down on the enemy force in an invisible wave and killed all the power in the area.

Those troop ships would never fly or fire an energy weapon again. The pulse reduced the spears carried by the female warriors to sharpened spikes.

Evo kept The Dragon in a vertical climb, laid it hard on one side, and dove back to the enemy troop concentration. It was a textbook Immelmann maneuver.

The area boiled like a disturbed anthill, with troopers running, panicked, in every direction. Evo ordered The Dragon back to their entry point above the city at fifty thousand feet.

Evo pulled her lips back over her teeth in a savage grimace and called out to Erianne.

"I de-energized their airships. They won't fly again without extensive maintenance and resupply. I've also de-energized their spears, so you only have to deal with sharp edges. I'm going to loiter here to see what they do next."

Evo could hear the relief in the other woman's voice.

"I'm very grateful for your help, Evo. Standby."

Evo sat back in her chair, feeling satisfied with herself. She'd just flown her first combat mission. It wouldn't be her last.

Another warrior was flying her first aerial combat mission, but this one was from the Tribes of Women.

Dakaasin Manywounds sat still in her cockpit, almost not breathing. Her hands were shaking; her mouth felt like she had stuffed it with cotton balls.

In the Anishinaabe language, her first name meant 'a cool wind'. She felt anything but cool, though she had been quite full of herself earlier in the day.

The Tribes of Women had pursued arms development with vigor as soon as the animosity with the Tribes of Men manifested into the potential for outright warfare. They ramped up their efforts after they captured the male scientists, who Baame'e coerced, sometimes with torture, into participating in weapons research for the Women.

Dakaasin sat in their newest invention, a one-of-the-kind aircraft. It was a smaller version of its larger cousins, black and triangular. It was an attack aircraft and her superiors had chosen her, from all their other pilots, to fly it. Such an honor would propel her career to the top of their rank structure.

Flying this craft wasn't just an honor, it was a joy. While the anti-gravity engine was smaller than the heavily armed transport carriers, it made the lighter craft very maneuverable in the atmosphere.

They built the airframe out of graphene; a single layer of carbon atoms arranged in a two-dimensional honeycomb lattice. It made the aircraft strong and lightweight, with excellent electrical and thermal conductivity properties.

The weapons designers laid over the skin zinc oxide nanoparticles. The particles were unique because they mimicked whatever surrounded them. It made her fighter invisible.

Dakaasin's aircraft looked like any other part of the clear blue sky because the skin of her ship matched the sky.

Her fighter was undetectable by Light Detection and Ranging, a remote-sensing method using light as a pulsed laser to measure ranges. Just as Lidar couldn't find her fighter, neither could radar.

Her superiors equipped the fighter aircraft with air-to-air and air-to-ground missiles, but had placed her under strict orders to maintain radio silence and not engage in combat. Dakaasin flew an expensive, unique aircraft her superiors didn't want discovered or damaged.

She had loitered at forty thousand feet over the apex of the triangular city below her until a silver needle-nosed rocket had appeared above and in front of her.

Dakaasin watched in horror as the massive craft underwent inexplicable convulsions until it settled into the form of a warship. She watched, helpless, as the plane dove into the valley, climbed up past the vertical reaches of the outpost, and sent missiles toward her forces. After the missiles launched, her ability to monitor Army communications stopped. It was as if the missiles had created a black hole just beyond the reaches of the outpost. The massive silver plane reappeared after its run and sat like an arrogant Man ten thousand feet above her, faced away from her toward the valley.

Dakaasin pressed her hands together and squeezed her fingers to stop them from shaking. She could feel sweat streaming from her armpits and her stomach advised her in no uncertain terms it was planning on ejecting its contents into her cockpit.

She had to do something. This object had attacked her friends and colleagues and now sat in front of her, oblivious to threats.

Dakaasin reached for her comms button, then pulled her hand back.

Her orders had been clear about maintaining radio silence. She was not to draw attention to herself and put her experimental aircraft at risk. Today was to be its first glorious day in battle and her superiors made it plain her career rested on her ability to bring it back intact.

She had chosen her altitude without proper consideration for the tactical situation. The top ceiling for her aircraft was sixty-five thousand feet, which would have allowed her to see further beyond the outpost. It scared her to change position or altitude now because of her uncertainty about the detection capabilities of her enemy.

Dakaasin agonized over the thought of her comrades laying injured and dying but unable to be rescued while the monster hovered in front of her. Was her career not less important than the safety of her fellow warriors? Mind made up and filled with trepidation, Dakaasin flipped the switches to drop two air-to-air missiles from her aircraft, and sent them screaming at the silver behemoth taunting her from above.

"Target lock. We have two incoming missiles from behind and below us."

"Evasive action!" Evo snarled, frightened by her AI's calm announcement.

The AI snapped The Dragon into a roll and dove toward the valley sloping away from the city. It increased The Dragon's speed to keep ahead of the missiles. The Dragon swept up the face of the steep incline of the outpost, rolled at the top and dove to the opposite side. The missiles followed, but the dizzying maneuver and the speed at which The Dragon flew made them lose contact with Evo's ship.

As The Dragon approached the disabled enemy carriers at low altitude, the AI banked the starship away from the carriers at an impossible angle.

The missiles reacquired lock, but not on Evo's fighter. Each missile slammed into one of the disabled carriers, sending two bright flares of fire and billowing black smoke into the atmosphere.

The AI slid the starship between two adjoining peaks into a space in the mountains with steep slopes. The Dragon killed its speed and hovered, surrounded by solid rock.

Evo shook so hard she almost fell out of the pilot's chair. A bowl she had forgotten to put away after a meal had caromed around the cockpit and landed at her feet. Evo reached down, grabbed it, and vomited into it. After she emptied her stomach into the bowl, she wiped the remnants from her mouth, grimacing at the acrid taste of vomit on her tongue.

Someone just tried to kill her ship. Someone just tried to kill *her*. What was she doing here? She wasn't a warrior. Evo had never engaged in a physical quarrel in ten thousand years. Yes, she had an eternal body, but she doubted its capacity to resurrect her if they blew it into thousands of pieces.

Evo drew in a ragged breath, and anger swooped in to swallow her fear.

"Who fired at us?"

"I've replayed the sortie from our external cameras and sensors. An object behind us cloaked in MetaMaterials fired two missiles. I've tracked the missile launches back to the object's location. Do you wish to have me plot a course around these mountains to come up behind the object's last position?"

Evo thought about it for a moment. What was she going to do when she came up on it?

Killing a machine's energy with an EM pulse was one thing. Killing another living being was a different story.

As much as she was growing fond of Erianne, it repulsed her that the gracious, kind, beautiful woman thought little of killing someone else. Could she murder, in cold blood, the enemy who attacked her?

What other options did she have? The enemy was too dangerous to leave in place above the city. Who knows what kind of havoc it could release on Evo's new friends? But there had to be an alternative to killing?

An idea dawned. Evo rolled the thought around in her head and could see no flaw in it. She gave her AI instructions and prayed this would work.

The Dragon flew forward at a breathtaking speed, keeping the mountain between Evo and her attacker. Two miles beyond the edge of the city, The Dragon rose over the mountain and dove back to where the enemy had assaulted her ship.

Dakaasin had soiled her flight suit but doubted anyone would care. Her heart was hammering in her chest and her hands refused to stop shaking. She hoped the twin towers of black smoke boiling up from the valley represented the death of the massive ship she fired on.

Anxious, she scanned her readouts, but saw nothing within the limited range of her sensors to suggest someone or something targeted her.

She slammed back into her chair.

Something was pushing her! Dakaasin worked her controls at a frantic pace, trying to turn her aircraft left or right. Nothing worked. Her altimeter displayed their ascent with a dizzying flash of numbers. Fear spiked her adrenaline and caused her heart to beat faster. Whatever was pushing her was going to slam her right into the ice layer.

Just as she opened her mouth to scream, a hole appeared in front of the nose of her aircraft. She felt as if the hole was trying to turn her inside out. Her stomach, already abused by stress and fear, emptied its contents into her mask. Then they were in space.

They didn't design her aircraft for space. Yes, it was still sealed and her life-support remained intact. It didn't have attitude jets or protections against cosmic particles. Dakaasin had a limited air supply and it would only take hours to run out. Worse, she had no means to transit through the ice layer, and even if she could, her plane would burn up on re-entry.

Her ship accelerated again, and this speed was beyond frightening. After ten minutes, a bright orb appeared in front of her.

It was smaller than a moon, but had an atmosphere, water, and plant life by the looks of it.

Whatever pushed Dakaasin must've known her ship couldn't survive reentry into the atmosphere. Another hole appeared in front of her, and another series of violent twists and turns abused her stomach as she flew through it. When she popped out of the hole, her instruments told her they were at ten thousand feet and descending at a much slower rate. She landed in a clearing surrounded by dense jungle.

Whatever had seized her aircraft now shut it down.

Dakaasin watched as her aircraft went through the shutdown sequence until the plane was dead. Air stopped flowing through her soiled mask and she ripped it off as the canopy popped open and slid backwards. Dakaasin tried to restart the engines, but the instruments wouldn't respond to her efforts.

Someone had captured her.

They didn't train Dakaasin for this. She'd been told to avoid combat, so they deemed it unnecessary to prepare her to escape and evade. She had no personal weapons on board. Shaking, Dakaasin disengaged from her seat and wiped the vomit from her face with the sleeve of her flight suit. She clambered out of the aircraft, stiffer from fear than the cramped confines of the cockpit.

When she jumped to the ground and turned around, what she saw stunned her.

A massive silver rocket standing on three fins blocked the jungle behind it. In front of the starship stood a tall and beautiful woman in a tight-fitting suit, matching the colour of her ship.

To add to Dakaasin's surprise, the woman addressed her in her language.

"You are my prisoner. Will you surrender to me?"

Dakaasin licked her lips. She didn't know what to do. She learned in basic training about enemy interrogation techniques and the limited responses she was to give.

"My name is Dakaasin Manywounds. I'm an officer in the Armed Forces of the Tribes of Women. I demand proper care under the treaties about prisoners of war and their treatment."

A look flashed across the tall woman's face, but Dakaasin couldn't interpret it.

"I don't have time for nonsense, and I don't have time for you. I have to get back to the war. You can come with me as my prisoner or you can stay here until I have time to come back for you. I find your ship fascinating and I intend to keep it so I can study it."

Dakaasin's stomach clenched with pain, and her bowels threatened to loosen again. Her body trembled as the adrenaline which had supercharged her mind during combat faded out of her system.

"Leave me here? I don't know where here is! I'm not armed and I couldn't protect myself against wild beasts. What would I eat? Is the water safe to drink?"

The seven-foot-tall woman rolled her eyes. She swept her hands around the jungle surrounding them.

"You're on a planet occupying the same orbit as Ma'ilingan Waazh. It's not a moon because it doesn't revolve around your world, it just follows your planet like a puppy around your sun. It's safe. There are no animals, just fruit trees and plenty of fresh water to drink. I imagine this is what the Tribes of Men were trying to get to when they attempted to transition through the ablative shield. You're wasting my time. Are you coming as my prisoner or staying here?"

Dakaasin scanned the jungle surrounding the clearing. She couldn't hear any noises she associated with things which flew or crawled, but it didn't mean they weren't there. Dakaasin was not a coward, but her training had not prepared her for this. The fear of the unknown decided for her.

"Do you have clean clothes I can change into?"

Ma'ilingan Waazh (Wolf's Den), 1st Year of Summer 27th day, Waatebagaa-giizis, (Leaves Turning Moon), Year 5379,

The Battle for the City of Wenonah's Ascension, The Ground War

Erianne az Nostrom, Princess of Death, and her bondsman, Ro'gun az Peregos, watched the ranks of the Army of Women marching up the slope to the city. The Women were organized and disciplined. It didn't help that they also looked angry.

"I figure at least two thousand," Erianne said, her voice calm and flat.

The young man standing beside her grabbed his shoulders and twisted from side to side. An evening by the fire had warmed his front, made even warmer by holding his wife in his arms, but exposed his back to the chill of the night air. He was young enough the cold didn't incapacitate him, but it left his muscles stiff. He had a thing in mind, which would not be popular with his Princess, and it required a supple back.

Ro'gun's eyes scanned the ranks of women marching resolutely towards them and nodded his head.

"At least two thousand," he said. "Do we know of the whereabouts of Lady Evo?"

Erianne frowned and looked up into the sky.

"She was there a second ago. Evo, can you hear me?"

The response was immediate.

"I hear you well, Erianne."

"We have a large contingent of enemy troops marching toward us. They moved through the gap in the outpost and they're coming up the valley. They look furious. I had hoped you could provide a little intimidation, so this doesn't turn into an all-out battle."

In the following pause, Erianne could hear rustling, as if things were being moved.

"I'm just securing a prisoner, Erianne. I can be there in thirty minutes. Evo out."

Erianne's eyebrows danced on her forehead, and she looked down at the young warrior at her side.

"She said she's securing a prisoner, and she's thirty minutes out. How on earth would she have captured a prisoner?"

Ro'gun smiled, but it was not broad enough to expose his teeth.

"A woman of ten thousand years in age is incapable of surprising me with her capabilities. Of greater concern is how we're going to stall the oncoming horde. I don't think we have thirty minutes."

Ro'gun caressed the hilt of the sword slung at his left side and glanced back at the entrance of the city behind them. All looked to be in readiness, but he knew the deceitfulness of appearances. They didn't have enough Men to cover the wide gap, and what Men they had were not seasoned killers.

Mind made up, he turned to Erianne and executed a deep bow.

"It has been my honor to serve House az Nostrom, your Royal Highness. By your leave?"

Erianne's eyes widened.

"Where are you going, Ro'gun?"

He grinned, every inch the brave cavalier.

"To buy us thirty minutes."

Ro'gun turned and walked jauntily toward the oncoming enemy. Erianne opened her mouth to stop him, then closed it. They weren't ready for a charge, and their warriors numbered far less than the Army of Women.

"I hope I don't regret this," she muttered to herself.

Ro'gun was far removed from any thought of regret. It was a beautiful day. To Ro'gun's left and right, tall sheer mountains stretched into the atmosphere, their slopes generously garnished with tall pine trees. Their tops caressed a sky dotted here and there with puffy white clouds, made fluffy by a mild wind caressing the peaks.

A hawk screeched from a nearby pine before taking wing and floating over Ro'gun's head, as if sending a warning to the approaching army of the young warrior's skills.

Sunshine bathed his leather armor, dispelling the chill of the morning air and warming the sun-bronzed skin of his exposed arms. Innanu had made this vest, patterning it after Tul'ran's sleeveless leather armor. His clothing mimicked Tul'ran's armor in other ways; Ro'gun wore a broad leather belt and leather pants tucked into soft leather boots. Only his hair was different; Ro'gun left his dark brown locks cut short.

The wind puffed a reminder of this world into his face. The atmosphere was heady with the smell of pine needles, tree sap, fresh grass, and wild orchids scattered about the downslope. Ro'gun inhaled deeply, delighting in the aroma's richness. Yes, it was a beautiful day.

A beautiful day for someone to die.

Ro'gun stopped fifty feet away from the approaching enemy, legs spread apart and fists resting on his hips, and waited for the first rank of soldiers to stop twenty feet away from him.

A tall, muscular woman stepped out of the ranks. She regarded Ro'gun for a few moments, then reached up to remove her headpiece. She had dark brown eyes in a wide face, strong cheekbones, and thick lips, which were drawn back in a sneer.

"What're you doing, boy?"

Ro'gun put a hand to his mouth and yawned.

"I'm bored. We've been preparing for this battle for such a long time; I feel the delay has dulled my senses. For instance, I couldn't see one amongst you who's worthy to fight against me, no matter how hard I've tried."

The woman's cheekbones reddened.

"Everyone of us could bend you over our knees and spank you, boy. Why don't you get out of the way and leave the fighting to your elders?"

Ro'gun shrugged.

"And let them have all the fun? Why don't you produce your fiercest fighter, and we'll see if she can stand against me as young and slight as I am?"

The woman's eyes glinted.

"So, it's single combat you want. Very well. Carol!"

For a few seconds, it seemed as if there would be no response. Then the head and shoulders of a massive trooper appeared, coming up the slope, and the ranks parted before the soldier. When the soldier came to the front, the trooper stood much taller than any of the others.

"Remove your helmet," the woman commanded.

The trooper complied, revealing the face of a rugged, handsome young man. Ro'gun jerked his head back.

"You're Carol?"

The man grinned.

"I come from the Tall Tribes, who live in the southernmost part of our world. My family are adventurers; they were traveling around the globe when the stars fell. I now know they weren't stars, but shards of ice. The falling ice shield obliterated my party and killed my parents. A woman from the Tribes of Women found me, a six-year-old child, shivering in the cold. She named me Carol."

Ro'gun scanned the frame of the man standing in front of him.

"How tall are you?"

"Seven feet, four inches," came the cocky reply.

"How is it that a seven-foot, four-inch man named Carol fights for the Tribes of Women against Men?"

Carol's face darkened and flexed his right arm.

"My entire family died because Men decided they needed more than the Goddess had provided to this world. Their greed killed my joy. Now it gives me joy to kill men."

Ro'gun yawned again, not bothering to cover it this time.

"How many men would that be, Carol?"

The big man snorted.

"Enough talking! You wanted single combat, boy, and I'm happy to start my count of slain men with you."

"So, none, then," Ro'gun said, his voice cheerful. "Yes, let's fight. If we don't soon, I may need to take a nap."

Carol scanned Ro'gun's five-foot ten-inch body.

"You don't wear headgear. To be fair to you, stripling, I'll leave my helmet off. You can't reach my head, anyway."

Ro'gun laughed.

"There's a legend in my world told to me by Lady Erianne az Nostrom, the Princess of Death, who even now stands tall up the slope behind me. It concerns a shepherd boy who had encountered an arrogant giant much like yourself. While the giant, who his mother named Goliath, pranced and screamed insults at the shepherd, David, the lad removed a sling from his belt. With one cast, the rock he sent into Goliath's head killed the giant. You should keep your helmet on, Carol. It may save your life. Or at least your features. I may bend them in such a way as to make you far less attractive to your women."

Carol gaped at him for a moment, then crushed the headgear back on his skull. Ro'gun took a few steps back and drew his sword. It wasn't an angelic sword, like Tul'ran's and Erianne's, but God Himself had given it to him. It was strong, and the edges were razor sharp.

Carol paused, then reached behind his back. He drew a sword, and Ro'gun heard a gasp from behind him. Women never used a sword to fight; only spears. This should be interesting.

Ro'gun sidestepped, and Carol matched him. The slope wasn't so severe it helped the height imbalance between them or interfered with footing.

Carol lunged forward, swung a vicious stroke at Ro'gun's head, pulled his blade from the parry, reversed it, and cut at Ro'gun's legs. Ro'gun parried both cuts, wincing from the force of the blows. The big man was strong and fast, a dangerous combination.

The men exchanged thrusts and blocks, testing each other's facility with the sword. As the minutes flashed by, the blows intensified.

The blades gleamed in the mid-morning sun, making tinny clinking sounds as the two men struck at each other. Both were skilled. Though Carol was bigger and stronger, Ro'gun was faster.

The fight dragged on. Each fighter pressed an advantage and gave ground before the other's attack.

It was hot, sweaty work, with no obvious outcome. After a flurry of cuts and parries, Ro'gun leaped back, sweat pouring from his forehead and breathing hard.

"Tell me, Carol, how did you get a woman's name? It's true you fight like a girl, but how were they to know that then? Were you so pretty as a child, you warranted a girl's name?"

A worried look crossed Ro'gun's face.

"Or did they name you so after cutting off your manhood and casting it to the cats to gnaw upon it as a treat?"

Carol roared and lunged forward, swinging his sword from over his head. Ro'gun had taken his measure and knew the man had never fought in combat. As Carol lunged forward, Ro'gun dove, twisted in mid-air, and cut through both of the larger man's calves to the bone.

Carol's momentum carried him onward, and he landed on his chest with a loud thud. Ro'gun rolled and lunged to his feet, jumping on the larger man's back. He ripped off Carol's helmet and placed his sword against the big man's thick neck.

"You fought well, Carol, but now you've lost. Yield and I'll get off your back so your people can treat your wounds. If your people don't care for them soon, you'll never walk again. Refuse to yield and I will allow my sword to cleave your neck, staining this new grass with your blood. You'll be the first man killed by another man in the history of the People. Is this how you wish to be remembered, Carol of the Tribes of Women?"

Carol gasped as pain seared his calves.

"I yield."

Ro'gun stepped off his back and grabbed the warrior's sword. He walked backwards up the hill, carefully watching the bodies of his enemies. He caught the eye of the first woman to whom he'd spoken, who was shaking her head.

"Come, get your wounded. Be grateful his life continues; only the mercy of the Creator saved him."

Ro'gun walked back until he once more stood at Erianne's side, still watching the women as their ranks parted to allow what must have been a medical team to come and carry Carol away. Sweat was dripping off Carol's drawn face as they lifted him, but he made no sound.

"Well done," Erianne said, taking shallow breaths as she strained to see what the Army of Women would do next. "I thought he had you a couple of times."

Ro'gun laughed, but only so loud Erianne could hear it.

"I'm not bragging, your Royal Highness, when I say I could've killed him twenty minutes ago. I made it look close-matched to keep our enemy enthralled in the contest. You needed time, and I tried to give you as much as I could."

Erianne squinted at him.

"You're saying it was less close than it looked?"

Ro'gun smiled at her.

"You forget, Princess Erianne, Quil'ton az Peregos, the son of the Instructor to the Sword Himself, trained me. Lord Tul'ran supplemented my instruction when we stayed in the Garden for six months. He told me of a time when he slayed Gar the Nephilim and taught me the technique of fighting a giant adversary. The House az Nostrom is more formidable than anyone in this world. What are they doing?"

Erianne turned her attention back to the enemy's ranks. The women in the enemy's front lines argued with one another, gesturing toward Erianne and Ro'gun. Erianne couldn't hear their words, but recognized an exhortation when she saw one. The woman doing the most talking seemed to have won her point. The women went back into their lines and closed ranks.

Erianne shook her head and pulled Caligo from its sheath.

"They're forming up for an attack. This is bad. They outnumber us by a huge margin. Evo, can you hear me?"

The response came back right away.

"I hear you, Erianne."

"How long until you return? I don't mean to rush you, but we are about to be overrun by the Army of Women."

"Not today."

A brilliant red beam of light seared into the ground between their position and the advancing women. Grass smoked as the intense energy burned a line three feet deep between the two forces. A massive silver ship, shaped like a rocket, flashed not three hundred feet above their heads. It stopped, rolled, turned sideways on its bow, and hovered above Erianne's head. Its needle nose pointed at the Army of Women. They stared at it, stupefied and frozen in place.

The starship filled the sky behind Erianne and Ro'gun and blocked out the tall buildings behind it. It hovered without a sound, but there was no mistaking its malevolent intent.

Erianne took two steps forward and raised her voice to its maximum.

"I am Erianne, wife of Tul'ran az Nostrom, the Prince of Death. In my name, I, Erianne, Princess of Death, and in the name of Tul'ran the Conqueror, order you to put down your arms and admit defeat. If you do not, I will rain your blood down this mountain and burn your corpses in a ditch. Surrender or die."

For a second, Erianne worried they wouldn't obey. Then, one by one, they threw down their spears.

"Kneel and place your hands behind your heads," Erianne shouted.

The women complied and Erianne felt relief course through her tense body. For all her bravado, she'd dreaded this fight. They'd planned well for the battle. Erianne and Ro'gun were to have drawn the advancing forces into a V-shaped kill zone concealed behind them. The city's new power grid would've been used to electrocute many of their enemy, but they couldn't have avoided hand-to-hand combat. The casualties would've been great on both sides, and the last thing Erianne wanted was to be front and center of a legacy of death.

It was over.

But not quite.

Erianne's peripheral vision caught movement from her right and she spun her head.

Dumbfounded, she watched Dr. Megis Swimminghorse, the Chief's wife, walk past her.

"Dr. Swimminghorse," Erianne said, voice raised. "Where are you going? The battle is over!"

Ignoring her, Swimminghorse approached the front ranks of the Women, turned, kneeled, and put her hands behind her head. A cloying silence descended on the battlespace.

"Well," Ro'gun said, his eyes huge. "I guess we found our spy."

<hr/>

Ma'ilingan Waazh (Wolf's Den), 1st Year of Summer 27th day, Waatebagaa-giizis, (Leaves Turning Moon), Year 5379

The Battle for the City of Ikwe Na

The airframe carrying Tul'ran and the others settled gently on a flat surface. Before them, a ridge stretched out and blocked their view of the cave entrance to the City of Ikwe Na. Its rocky surface held shrubs newly blossomed under the ablative shield and pervaded the surrounding air with the scent of exotic spice.

The slope's incline was sharp enough to have winded them if they were on foot. It wasn't too steep for their horses, though, and Tul'ran was grateful they'd brought them.

'Erianne, my love, we've arrived near Ikwe Na. How do you fare?' he thought to his wife.

Her voice in his mind held a hint of levity, which surprised him given the circumstances.

'I'm pleased to announce, milord, that House az Nostrom has defeated the Army of Women at the Battle for the City of Wenonah's Ascension. Our forces are securing the prisoners of war. Apparently, there is a building here which will serve as a prison long enough to negotiate the terms of their release. How do you fare?'

Tul'ran took Darkshadow's lead in one hand and led the impatient warhorse off the conveyance. Darkshadow snorted and pawed at the dirt. He shook his huge mane, and dust flew off it. Tul'ran smiled and pushed his head closer to the massive horse's neck. He inhaled deeply.

There was no scent more beautiful in any world than the natural perfume of the horse.

He returned his thoughts to his bride.

'We're about to find out. Can you send Evo to us on her flying device?'

'Not yet, my love. We've secured our prisoners' cooperation under the threat of her ship burning them to death. We can't send her until we've secured them.'

Tul'ran ran his hand up Darkshadow's nose, along his face, and pulled on one of the stallion's ears. He loved the feel of the war horse's ebony coat. Darkshadow inclined his head and gave every sign of enjoying the ear rub, whinnying softly.

"Brother," Tul'ran whispered into the ear, which was the subject of his affection. "Long has it been since we two rode into war. This is a conflict we must win, but by shedding the least amount of blood from our enemies. Be wise and exercise restraint if you yet love me."

Darkshadow tossed his head and snorted again. Tul'ran laughed. He had the distinct impression the warhorse was telling him to mind his own weapons and leave the stallion to fight as he would at his discretion. Tul'ran swung without effort onto Darkshadow's back and drew Bloodwing.

'I'll strive to avoid fighting until Evo's free,' Tul'ran mindcast to Erianne. 'I ride against Baame'e now.'

Once their attack force mounted their horses, Tul'ran led them to the top of the ridge. Before they crested, he made them stop and jumped off on Darkshadow's left side. He handed the reins to Omarosa, who had been thrilled when Erianne told her to ride Destiny's Edge into battle.

"Bide here," he said to his group. "Dizi and I will go to the top of the hill and see what lies ahead."

The giant wolf padded up to him as Tul'ran twisted the angelic sword in his right hand.

'I see worry in your mind, Lord Tul'ran. Why? You encountered far dangerous enemies in your last war and could vanquish the Army of Women with your sword alone.'

Tul'ran gazed at the wolf affectionately.

'I fear nothing, Dizi, except God. Were it my desire, I could leave this world lifeless. The power flooding my veins is that of uncreation. I strive for a harder thing; to win a war with no life being lost.'

The wolf's tongue lolled out of its mouth, and the honey of humor coated the words forming in Tul'ran's mind from the mighty beast.

'So long as you do not lose my life, Lord Conqueror, you have my firm endorsement.'

Tul'ran smirked and led the Wolf to the top of the rise to see what lay ahead.

Ahead was bad, he observed immediately. Thousands of female warriors in black armor stood between him and the entrance to the Ikwe Na cave system. They formed ranks and looked disciplined. He had no doubt of their resolute intent to defend their city and their leader.

Tul'ran raised up Bloodwing, the flat of the blade facing them. He intended it as a salute, but they didn't take it as such. The women raised the tips of their spears and fired yellow streams of lethal light at him.

Bloodwing changed. Instead of its normal brilliant black, the surface of the blade softened and looked like a window into a vast star field. The bolts of death racing to Tul'ran merged into a single stream and flowed into the Blade.

Bloodwing siphoned the energy from the spears and poured them into deep space. It then followed the spears' energy signatures to the fusion reactors buried in the caves. The beam brightened to an unbearable intensity as the energy input increased by terawatts. Soon, all five reactors shut down, drained of power and their ability to generate more.

The lights went out everywhere in the city.

Ikwe Na died.

Bloodwing glowed an intense violet as it dissipated the energy it absorbed. A shrill whine filled the air around the sword, and Tul'ran ran a concerned glance over it. He never knew Bloodwing to sing. Once it emptied its contents, the Blade returned to its impassive black sheen and quieted.

The soldiers in front of Tul'ran muddled about, some checking their weapons and others pressing their hands to the radio receivers in their helmets rendered silent by a single sword.

Two large, square devices fired their cannons at Tul'ran. He leveled Bloodwing. A bright blue beam of uncreation energy dissolved the shells, and the conveyances firing them. Four women from each conveyance dropped to the ground from mid-air and lay in the dirt, stunned.

Commanders tried to get their companies to regroup. Tul'ran shook his head. He admired their courage, but not their resolve to end their lives for no reason.

"I am Tul'ran az Nostrom," he shouted, Bloodwing still raised high above his right shoulder. "The Sword Himself, Prince of Death, the Uncreator, Conqueror. Do not think your numbers advantage you. By the power of uncreation, I can send all of you to the end of your existence. Not even your souls will stand in judgment before God. Lay down your arms or lay down your lives."

Uncertainty. Hesitation. Confusion.

Then a commander screamed and ran forward, her spear raised, and a dozen in her troop followed. Tul'ran sighed. A bright blue ball appeared in his left hand and he threw it at the advancing troopers. The ball sped away from him at the speed of light, split at the last second, and dissolved all thirteen weapons. The troopers skidded to a halt, some colliding with others and knocking them to the ground.

Tul'ran strode forward and dropped Bloodwing into a ready position.

He closed the distance between him and the advance team and placed the Blade against the breastplate of their commander.

"My patience grows thin," he said, his voice a menacing growl. "Tell Baamewaawaagizhigokwe to appear before me before I decide your lives have no value to me."

The commander stood frozen in place, her eyes so wide they almost displaced the white edges. Her soldiers were like statues behind her and not a sound escaped the battlefield. Tul'ran forced himself to not roll his eyes. Sometimes he forgot the effect he had on people.

"Move!" he snarled.

The woman moved. She jumped at his words, then ran back to the cave entrance. The other troopers pulled away to allow her passage, and she bowled over those who were not fast enough.

The Army of Women continued to mill, but Tul'ran read their emotions. There was no fight left in them. He walked back to the edge of the ravine and gestured for the others to join him.

Together, they waited for Baame'e to come.

Baamewaawaagizhigokwe screamed her fury at personnel in the command center. It was pitch black. Not even the emergency lights came on after the reactors failed. Her soldiers sat still, frozen in place, unmoved by Baame'e's screamed commands.

"Excellency," her subaltern said, fear lacing her voice. "There's nothing we can do. There is no power left in Ikwe Na."

"Restart the reactors!" Baame'e screamed.

"We can't restart them, Excellency. The core is dead. We can't start a fusion reaction; there's nothing left to fuse. All the fissile materials no longer exist. We must abandon the city. We've no other choice."

Baame'e stood from her chair and slammed it into the wall behind her over and over again, screaming with every strike. When she'd exhausted herself, she stamped her feet on the ground, grinding her teeth.

Exhausted, she stopped, her breath coming in hard pants.

"I won't give up. Gather everyone. We'll go to the surface and kill the Men with our bare hands."

The subaltern opened the hatch to the command center and counted the bodies filing out by touching their shoulders as they left. Outside the command center, bioluminescent strips lit the exit paths. Their glow was too dim to do more than show the feet of thousands of people shuffling to the surface. They didn't need to be told to leave. When the lights went out and the emergency lights failed to come on, there was no other choice.

It took forty-five minutes to reach the entrance. The commander dispatched by Tul'ran approached Baame'e near the entrance, having been blocked from going down by the mass of people leaving. She'd taken her helmet off and bowed her bared head to Baame'e.

"Excellency, the man Tul'ran wishes to speak with you."

Baame'e pushed the woman to the ground and spit on her bare face.

"Coward! Fool! How did you not fight to the death? One woman of courage could've killed him in her sleep."

Baame'e kicked the fallen soldier in the ribs and waddled by her, gasping with effort. She was grossly out of shape, and the winding slope to the top of the cave entrance had exhausted her. Only her rage propelled her forward.

The soldiers parted for her as she came to the front of her army's ranks. She grabbed a spear out of one trooper's shaking hands and wobbled toward Tul'ran. She stopped five feet in front of him and his group.

"Ravenclaw!" she said, spitting on the ground. "You pig of a man. I'm surprised you had the courage to come. Do you usurp my throne, swine?"

Wenonah stepped out from behind Ravenclaw.

"He has given up his right to rule, mother. He passed authority over the Tribes of Men to me. I accepted his submission as the Leader of the Nine Tribes of Ma'ilingan Waazh entire."

Baame'e's face darkened.

"You little bitch! Is this how you honor your mother? By throwing in with Men. You disgust me! I'll never cede my authority to you. Never! What will you do now? Kill me?"

Wenonah's face remained stoic.

"Your fate's not in my hands, mother. You tried to murder me when you sent your cat after me as I journeyed to the Garden of our Ancestors. You attempted to kill me again when you launched a bomber after the Tribes of Men when the Plasma Curtain fell. I know it carried nuclear weapons. You would've killed all of us to keep your power. I took the Peace Pipe from Chief Ravenclaw and gave it to

Lord Tul'ran, the Conqueror. He takes claim to Ma'ilingan Waazh, mother, not me."

Enraged, Baame'e raised the spear as if to throw it, and froze. Tul'ran took two long steps forward, and his Blade was at her throat. She looked up into his face, and her throat clenched. She'd never looked into the eyes of a true killer before, and his gaze inspired terror.

Here was Death personified and his eyes made her heart wail with fear. Time seemed to slow, which expanded her senses far afield.

The wind blew around their feet and dust swirled above rocks made bare by the melted snow. The sun was brilliant in a sky patched with white puffy clouds and warmed her skin. Birds, freed from the bitter cold, swooped through the air above them, their flight patterns inviting the opposite sex to a frenzied coupling. It was a joyful scene cloaked in the silence of promised death.

Her death.

A shadow passed over them and all but Tul'ran looked up. Terrified, they watched a huge silver vessel flip into a vertical position and land only yards away on three fins. A doorway appeared, and a walkway slid out from the opening. A tall woman with long silver hair stepped out from the starship.

Baame'e raised her hands and whooped.

"You are finished, Conqueror! Behold the Goddess, who is the Creator. She has come to our aid as she promised. You fool! Today, you and all who are with you will be my slaves!"

Evo walked to them and sized up the situation. A frown creased her full lips and her face darkened.

"Throw down your spear and step back from this man, Baamewaawaagizhigokwe."

Baame'e complied, her round face filled with glee. The silver-eyed woman's next words shocked her to her core.

"I'm not your goddess, Baame'e. I deceived your grandmother those many moons ago. The Creator of the world isn't me; it's the God your ancestors taught you to serve from this world's beginning. It's true I once hated Him, but only because I wanted to be Him. I deceived the Tribes of Women into rejecting Him and following me. I say this with shame, knowing someday I will pay a price for my actions. You must not pay my price. Surrender, Baame'e. Give yourself over to this man, Tul'ran. Let the war end with truth, not deceit."

Baame'e's mouth rounded into an 'o'. It wasn't possible. It wasn't possible everything she believed in and worshipped was a lie. She stared at Evo, willing her to say she was only joking, that she'd come to cleanse the planet of all Men.

"You're not the Creator?"

Evo shook her head, her eyes bathed in regret.

"I'm not the Creator. The Creator is the Father, the Son, and the Holy Spirit. Together, They made all things, and it's to Them we owe service and worship."

"Worship!" Baame'e spat on the ground. "I spit on this god you claim for my world. Men are dogs! I won't worship any male who proclaims to be a god. Women are transcendent. We're the true rulers of this world and the universe. What did they do to you, Goddess, to compel you to utter these words

171

covered in excrement?"

Evo put her palms together and raised her hands to her lips.

"Oh, Baame'e, I'm so sorry. I was so filled with pride and hatred; I had no idea how much damage I could do with my hubris. Everything I told your ancestors was false. I wanted to be worshipped to fill my need for acceptance. Please, Baame'e, listen to me. I've met Yeshua, the Son of God, to His face and lived. I beheld Him in all His glory. Salvation and rest for your eternal soul rests only in Him. Please believe in Him. If you do, He will forgive all your transgressions and you'll have life eternal. Surrender to Him, I beg of you."

Baame'e took two steps back, shaking her head while a venomous scowl clouded her face.

"They may have found some way to bribe you or threaten you to make you say these things, but I refuse to believe in the God you speak of unless I stand before Him and tremble in His presence as you have done, coward."

She stopped yelling, disconcerted. Her left arm had gone numb, and her heart hammered in her chest. Her breath came in gasps, and a stabbing pain sliced into her ribcage. She collapsed to the ground.

Baamewaawaagizhigokwe, the Leader of the Tribes of Women, got her wish. With a last, shuddering gasp, she went to stand before her Maker.

The War for Ma'ilingan Waazh was over.

Only one person had died.

CHAPTER THE NINTH:
PEACE?

Ma'ilingan Waazh (Wolf's Den), 1st Year of Summer 27th day, Waatebagaa-giizis, (Leaves Turning Moon), Year 5379, at the City of Ikwe Na

The pain was gone. At least that was good.

Baame'e stared at her still body lying in the dirt as medics scrambled up, shouting her name, and attaching devices to her. She was a little stunned by the swift transition from body to spirit, especially since her spirit body felt as real as the one the medics worked on with professional haste. In fact…

Baame'e looked down at her form. In the last few moments, she'd lost over three hundred pounds. She was back in the tall, voluptuous body she had in her early twenties. It had been a long time since she'd been so fit. Her physicians cajoled her for years to lose weight, fearing a massive heart attack.

She'd lived one hundred and ten years longer than they'd predicted and was still in the prime of her life.

Was.

"Baamewaawaagizhigokwe," a soft voice said behind her.

She turned and her face went slack as her eyes widened. A Man with vast white wings stood behind her. His blond hair fell over his shoulders and cascaded into his blue and white armor. A wide white belt holding an elegant green crystal sword coiled around his waist. The robe under his armor fell to his ankles, and intricate sandals covered his feet. She looked up into his face, which was stoic, and stared in awe into his calm, brilliant blue eyes. Above his head, a halo glowed.

"Who are you?" she said, having difficulty getting the words past a constricted throat.

"I am E'thriel, an Angel of the Lord your God, whom your people call the Creator."

Baame'e rolled her eyes and snorted.

"The Creator is a Goddess, not a man!"

E'thriel shook his head.

"No, Baamewaawaagizhigokwe, someone has misled your people." E'thriel pointed to where Evo stood near Tul'ran. "In particular, that woman, out of her own selfish needs, convinced your ancestors she was a goddess and the creator of all things."

E'thriel summarized how God created her world, and how the Creator intended all the people to live in peace and harmony.

"Will you accept the history of your world as I've explained it, Baamewaawaagizhigokwe? Will you set aside your pride and hatred for men, accept my words your Father in Heaven loves you, and repent of your sins?"

Baame'e curled her lips into a sneer.

"What sins? Was it a sin to claim for Women ascendancy over Men? Is it a sin to rule a world for a gender which Men would've turned into domesticated house pets?"

E'thriel's face became stern.

"You have about three minutes of life left. There will come a time when your medical personnel cannot revive you. When they call the end of your life, you go to stand before God in judgement. Do not reject my statements out of hand, Baamewaawaagizhigokwe; you do so at the peril of your soul. You sinned by ordering the deaths of Men through the fangs and claws of your Lions. It was a sin to lie, cheat, manipulate and steal to get power over Women. Again and again, you have rejected a peaceful end to the conflict between men and women. Repent of these sins, commit your soul to your Father in Heaven, and He may yet grant you more life in your mortal form."

She looked at him like a snake eyeing a rabbit munching on foliage feet away.

"Why? So I can do penance? Would he give me time to cringe before my enemies and wipe their feet with my tears? Shall I humble myself before a man when all Men have done is cause me pain?"

"One man caused you pain," E'thriel said. "Eric Ravenclaw. You are near the end of your life, Baamewaawaagizhigokwe. Can you not forgive him so you may have God's forgiveness, too?"

"Forgive him!" she screeched. "Forgive a pig who turned my hand down in marriage so he could marry my older sister? I was young, beautiful, strong, and intelligent. The two of us would've forged an everlasting empire in this world. I pursued him, hunted with him, laid by the fire with him on chilly nights, staring up into the stars and talking about the glorious future we could have together. What did he do? He chose my sister over me!"

She walked over to where Ravenclaw stood and tried to spit on him. It went through him as if he were the spirit and not her.

"I would crawl naked over hills of fire ants covered in honey before I would ever forgive him or any other man!"

E'thriel's face became downcast.

"The remaining seconds of your life flee like owls before the encroachment of the rising sun, Baamewaawaagizhigokwe. Soon, you cannot go back into your body. Is it worth eternal torment to keep your pain and your pride? This is your last chance; you would be wise to take it."

Baame'e responded with a rude gesture.

"That's what you can do with your wisdom. Look at me. I'm in spirit form and I've never felt better. Perhaps I'll wander the universe like our false goddess. There must be other worlds out there who could benefit from my wisdom and philosophy. I don't need you, Angel of God. Leave."

A collective gasp filled the air. The medic had stood up, faced the crowd, and raised both hands to shoulder level, palms down.

"Baamewaawaagizhigokwe, Eldest of the Tribes of Women and the Leader of the Way, has joined our ancestors."

Women crumpled to the ground and wailed, while others danced and stamped their feet with rage.

It pleased Baame'e to see their expressions of grief. She'd stay for the funeral, she decided. It would be satisfying for her enemies to feel the bitter venom of her praise on their lips and ears.

A hand fell on her shoulder and she went rigid, paralyzed. Baame'e felt herself being picked up and turned toward a bright light which hadn't been there seconds ago. They transited to another place with the drawing in of one breath and the exhalation of another. E'thriel put her on her feet and nudged her forward. Her paralysis was gone.

Baame'e was too stunned to resist walking forward. The walls surrounding her were made of dark stones and extended upwards as high as the eye could see. Shadows flickered on the polished stone from the many torches attached to the walls. The air smelled dank, as if it had lost its freshness eons past.

She looked down at her body and experienced a fresh shock. She no longer wore the decorated buckskin dress of her ancestors, which marked her as the Leader of the Tribes of Women. Her garment was a long robe with multi-colored squares, but not made of cloth or hide. They were small movies, playing on repeat, of the wrongs she committed while she lived. Things she'd done or caused to be done or which happened because she neglected to do something. It was disgusting.

Baame'e went to rip the garment from her body, but her hand slithered off as if she'd greased its surface. She looked at her hand, which was red with blood. Baame'e moaned.

"What's happening?"

E'thriel's face held an unhealthy pallor. His robes had changed from a bright white to a rich black, though his halo and skin shone just as brightly as it had before they came to this place.

"You rejected your last chance, daughter of God. I take you now to face your judgment."

"Judgment!" Baame'e shrieked, as she tried to pull away from him. "No! I demand you release me! Send me into the universe! I don't consent to be judged!"

E'thriel tightened his grip on her elbow; his hands were like a vise.

"The Father destined people to die once, and then face judgment. All humans must appear before the judgment seat of Christ to be judged for the things done in the body, whether it be good or bad. People can only choose to follow God and seek forgiveness for their sin while they draw breath and their hearts beat. There is no ability to choose God and repent once you've departed from life. There is no choice in this, and nothing to which you must consent."

Baame'e screamed at him, punched him with her free left hand, and struggled to keep from being pulled down the hallway. It was no use. The angel was powerful beyond belief; nothing impeded their course. As they approached, two massive wooden doors swung open. What was behind the doors stunned her.

The room was lit by bright rays of white light. A man in a glaring white robe sat on an alabaster marble throne. He had dark brown shoulder length hair, a short-cropped beard, and warm, hazel eyes. He radiated purity, and Baame'e knew Him. How she couldn't say, but she threw herself down before his feet and moaned,

"Hail, Jesus, Son of God, Redeemer and Creator, King of Kings, and Lord of Lords."

Jesus looked at her, sadness flooding His eyes.

"Hail, child of the Creator. E'thriel, do you find the name Baamewaawaagizhigokwe in the Lamb's Book of Life?"

The page flipping seemed to take hours. E'thriel started from the front of the Book and scanned each page with diligence. When he'd turned the last page, he shook his head, not looking up.

"I regret to inform You, Lord, the name of Baamewaawaagizhigokwe has been blotted out from Your Book."

Jesus nodded, His face somber.

"Baame'e come sit on the throne next to me. We must review your life together before I judge you."

She pulled herself to her feet, while hope dared to fill her heart. Surely, he would see the good things she'd done for her people and deem her worthy.

Surely.

Baame'e squirmed as every second of her life on Wolf's Den played out before her eyes. The longer the scenes ran before her, the more her mind filled with dread. Yes, there were moments of kindness and care, but more so were the scenes of hatred, deceit, violence, and a casual disregard for human life. In her eternal body, she understood the concept of sin. Over the course of her long life, it wasn't long before her sins consumed her heart and mind, leaving little room for love and grace.

When the last scene of her life played out before her, she winced after hearing her proud, angry words, denying the Creator, and refusing Evo's and E'thriel's urgings to repent. She couldn't bring herself to look at Jesus.

A hand took another firm grip on her shoulder and guided her to kneel before Jesus's throne. A long silence ensued, then Jesus spoke.

"Baamewaawaagizhigokwe, it saddens Me to cast judgment upon you. My Father and I have loved you since the day We created you in your mother's womb. Yes, you were deceived, but the woman who deceived you tried to convince you of the truth before you died. I gave My servant, E'thriel, permission to offer you the choice of a second chance at living in your mortal body before your medical technicians called the end to your life. You rejected Us, Baame'e, and by doing so you denied yourself forgiveness and eternal peace. Stand."

Baame'e stood, wobbling as her knees and legs shook, but E'thriel steadied her with a firm grip on her shoulder. Her heart sank as she saw the sad look on Jesus' face.

"We are a just God. We cannot tolerate sin where there has been no belief in Us and repentance for your sin. I judge you unworthy of entering the Kingdom of Heaven, and cast you into the outer darkness, where you shall wail and gnash your teeth. Be gone from Us, Baamewaawaagizhigokwe."

"No!" she screamed. "This isn't fair! You didn't send anyone to tell us about You after Evo deceived us! No one told us she defrauded us. How is this justice?"

Jesus's eyes were kind and filled with regret.

"Did the Men in your world not maintain faith in Us? Did they not seek peace with you? They were prepared to correct the error of your ways, but your hatred for Men consumed you. Even before your last day, there were opportunities to adjust your course. Opportunities you rejected. It saddens Us to do this, Baame'e, truly it does. We are the God of Love as a foundation for being the God of Justice."

Jesus gestured, and E'thriel turned her away. Baame'e screamed coarse words and struggled against his grip. She was so consumed with rage, she didn't notice the new doorway through which they walked.

Her throat shut. E'thriel dragged her through a passageway made of rock, with dark red slime seeping down the walls. Baame'e felt sick to her stomach. The ooze looked like thick blood and stunk like dead flesh left under the sun to rot. Torches lit the grotesque walls as the slimy path they walked upon twisted and turned behind them.

The path ended before a massive black marble desk, behind which sat an angel whose face sagged under an unhealthy pallor. His robes were gray and tattered, and the wings on his back drooped. No halo sat above his head. His eyes were dull and made weary by pain. A scowl crossed his face when he looked up at the angel and human approaching him.

"Ah, the traitor returns. How did you get back into the Enemy's good graces, E'thriel? How many feet did you clean with your tongue to return to Heaven?"

E'thriel's face remained indifferent.

"Ke'triel. What happened to G'shnet'el? I thought he was the Gatekeeper to Hell."

Ke'triel snorted.

"G'shnet'el!" he said, his tone derisive. "Our lord sent him on a mission to Earth and put me in charge. I've not seen him since. Now I'm stuck doing admissions. Who's this meat bag?"

E'thriel reached to his right and pulled a chain from the slime-encrusted wall. At the end of the chain was a large metal bracelet, which he attached to Baame'e's right wrist. Baame'e didn't react. The stench in the cavern, the grotesque walls, and the dark angel's leering gaze drained her will to fight.

"This is Baamewaawaagizhigokwe," E'thriel said, sadness weighing down the words. "Our Lord Jesus has judged her and found her wanting, condemning her to Hell for eternity."

He turned to walk away, and Baame'e lunged at him, grabbing his arm.

"Please," she said, her voice raspy, "don't leave me. I'm sorry. I regret everything I did and how proud I was. Give me a second chance. Please," she said, her tone quieting to a whisper as her eyes filled with terror when Ke'triel rose from behind the desk. "Don't leave me here. I beg of you."

E'thriel pulled away, and the chain prevented Baame'e from going further.

"I'm sorry, Baame'e, I truly am. Once you have been judged and sentenced to this domain, there's nothing I can do."

Baame'e stared at Ke'triel in horror as he took a whip from a rack behind the desk. It had many strands, and each strand ended in razor-sharp metal. She screamed as Ke'triel drew his arm back and she dropped to the filthy cavern floor, cowering. Before Ke'triel could lash her, E'thriel streaked forward and grabbed Ke'triel's arm.

E'thriel directed a look as cold as liquid nitrogen into Ke'triel's eyes.

"You will not abuse her in my presence."

Ke'triel tried to jerk his arm away, hatred flaring in his gray face.

"You have no authority here!"

E'thriel tightened his grip, and Ke'triel winced with pain.

"Maybe not, but when we were in Heaven, you were never a match for me, Ke'triel. I will beat you to the edge of disintegration if you whip her in my presence. The Lord may have condemned her, but she is still a child of God, and you are her servant."

Ke'triel ripped his arm away.

"Her servant," he said, scoffing. "Yes, I'll remember I'm her servant." He leered at the curvaceous woman, trembling at his feet. "In fact, I'll service her well. You can't stay here, E'thriel. I hear the Enemy calling you to return for your next mission as clearly as can you. Take your threats and get out."

Baame'e sobbed as she grabbed E'thriel around his ankles.

"No," she whimpered. "No. Please don't go. Please don't leave me."

E'thriel disengaged his foot from her desperate grasp.

"I'm sorry, Baame'e. This is the fate you chose, and I must leave you to it."

Baame'e sobbed as she watched him walk away. She turned and prostrated before Ke'triel.

"Please don't hurt me," she whined. "I'll do anything for you, anything."

Ke'triel's face wrinkled with disgust.

"Look at you, daughter of God, your robes covered in filth as you cringe before me. The Creator designed you to rule with Him, and you rejected it to lie at my feet and beg. You will do anything, indeed. Let's start with the removal of your filthy garment."

Baame'e screamed as the whip bit into her back, tearing away cloth and flesh.

Ma'iingan Waazh (Wolf's Den), 1st Year of Summer
27th day, Waatebagaa-giizis, (Leaves Turning Moon),
Year 5379, at the City of Ikwe Na
Moments after Baame'e's death

Wenonah covered her mother with a blanket, tears coursing down her cheeks. She left her hand on Baame'e's head, then turned to kneel before Tul'ran.

"Milord Conqueror, it is our custom to mourn our dead by first washing and grooming the body of our loved one. We dress the body in good clothes and wrap it in birch bark before burial."

"As her family, I am bound by custom to burn a fire in her home for five days, until we bury my mother. For the first four days of mourning, we, her mourners, will offer food and tobacco to her spirit. I will place matches in her coffin and ask the Creator to light her spirit's path to Gaagige Minawaanigozigiwining, which, in our language, means the land of everlasting happiness."

"I will bury a few items of importance with her, for we believe she will need hunting tools, tobacco, and clothing in the afterlife. On the fifth night I will prepare a feast, in which I will set a place for my mother and offer food to the Creator."

"After the feast, my relatives and I will smoke or burn a final offering of tobacco in the fire. A shaman will address my mother's spirit, to tell her about the journey she's about to take. When the feast is over, I will carry her plate into the woods and place it somewhere deep and peaceful. When I walk away from the plate, tradition compels me to not look back, as this may attract her spirit to follow me."

"At the end of our mourning ceremony, I will burn the rest of my mother's things or throw them into a river. These are the things I must do to honor our dead. May I have your permission to do them?"

Tul'ran sheathed Bloodwing and dropped onto one knee beside Wenonah. He placed a massive hand on her tiny shoulder.

"Princess Wenonah, mourn your dead according to your customs. I honor you for the love you show your mother and the kindness and mercy of your heart."

He stood up and addressed the crowd of women in front of him.

"I am Tul'ran az Nostrom, the Conqueror, and I claim Ma'ilingan Waazh for my House. You will obey the dictates of Princess Wenonah Bearspaw and Chief Eric Ravenclaw, to whom I subordinate power. You will succumb to the orders of Lady Omarosa and Lady Anatu of my House."

The air seemed to darken around his head, and his mouth dropped into a deep scowl.

"Disobey them, and me, at your peril."

For a moment, everyone stood frozen as his last words wrapped their icy tendrils around their hearts. Then Wenonah stood, bowed to Tul'ran, and directed the women standing around them to begin preparations to move her mother's body.

For a moment, there was no one near Tul'ran. A familiar tingle ran down his spine. Looking around to make sure no one could overhear him, he whispered,

"E'thriel?"

The angel of the Lord appeared at his side, allowing only Tul'ran to see him.

"Milord Tul'ran?"

Tul'ran kept his face impassive and tried hard to not move his lips as he spoke.

"It is good to see you again, my friend. Were you here earlier? I thought I sensed your presence."

The angel's eyes widened as he jerked his head back.

"Indeed, I was, milord. I beg your forgiveness for my surprise. Your kind rarely senses the presence of mine."

Tul'ran allowed a slight smile to pull the corner of his lips upward.

"Perhaps my kind have had much less experience with your kind as I have."

E'thriel matched his smile and shivered the feathers on his enormous wings.

"How may I serve you, Lord Tul'ran?"

Tul'ran licked his parched lips, watching as Wenonah threw herself back down on Baame'e's body, sobbing.

"You heard what Princess Wenonah said about the prayers and rituals to follow upon her mother's death?"

E'thriel's face became somber.

"I did."

Tul'ran worked his jaw, his eyes misting as his heart responded to Wenonah's sobs.

"Tell me, servant of El Shaddai, protector of men and this unworthy servant. Will their prayers find favor with our Lord and grant Baame'e a peaceful eternity?"

There was silence as a faraway look glazed E'thriel's eyes. Then it was El Shaddai's words in his mind.

'Tul'ran, My son, I have spared E'thriel from answering. You should know this angel has great fondness for you and would do anything you ask. Some things are not for My children to know, yet he has begged Me to allow him to tell you the truth.'

Tul'ran tore his eyes away from Wenonah, as women came to stroke her back, and soothe her grieving. He looked up into the sky, feeling a heavy cloak wrap his heart in darkness.

"El Shaddai, You and I have ridden together since I was twelve years old. You have spared me from death more times than I can count. I walk in Your shadow and in Your shadow, You have protected me. Never have I questioned You about what happens to those I dispatched to you for judgment."

"But you question Me now."

Tul'ran shook his head.

"Not to judge You, Lord, but just so I may have understanding. Will the prayers of this heartbroken daughter reach Your ears and turn Your heart to mercy?"

El Shaddai sighed, and Tul'ran heard it as clearly in his mind as a sound in his ears.

'My son, in the mind of every person We have planted a longing to look for Us. Some answer Our call, as you and Erianne have done. Others try to find Us by worshipping idols or seeking soul satisfaction through riches and power. Others reject Us completely.'

'Our children can only choose Me while they draw breath and their heart encourages blood through their arteries. Once the brain dies, the body releases the soul to Us for judgment. When the soul stands before Us, We must not permit prayers of intercession to cloud Our judgment.'

'When a person stands before My judgment seat, there is only one question which will determine their eternal fate: did they accept Me as their Lord and Savior and seek the forgiveness of their sins through Me? If they did, then My righteousness cloaks them as it did the woman you claimed as your sister, Darian. But if they did not, then as a God of Justice, I have no choice but to condemn them to Hell. Trust Me, My son. It breaks My heart every time I am compelled to send one of Mine away from Us to eternal torment.'

A speck of the weight carried by El Shaddai fell on Tul'ran's soul and he staggered under the impact of it. He wanted to leave the conversation, but the stubborn part of him which needed to know persisted.

"And Baame'e?"

Tul'ran could feel the sadness of El Shaddai's response.

'She did not know Us, Tul'ran, in this life. Before E'thriel brought her soul before me, Baame'e's brain lived for six minutes. I permitted E'thriel to convince her to repent, with an offer to return to her body and her life for many more years on Ma'ilingan Waazh. She could not see past her hatred and rage to accept Our attempt at mercy.'

"After the Lord judged her," E'thriel said, his eyes resting on the ground, "I escorted her to Hell. This would not fall within the normal course of my duties, but I volunteered for the task to pay penance for the sins I committed against my Lord."

Tul'ran gestured towards Wenonah, who allowed herself to be taken away from her mother's corpse by the two women who had comforted her.

"Her prayers, her pain, will be for naught."

'Her prayers, her pain,' El Shaddai said in Tul'ran's mind, his tone severe, 'are never for naught! They fall on Our ears like honey on Our tongue. We will honor her tears with Our comfort and credit her pain to a humble and loving heart. Wenonah will find rewards in the Kingdom of Heaven for the forgiveness she extended to her mother and the love she feels for her still. Her grief will draw her closer to Us, and We will flood her soul with Our love.'

Tul'ran took a deep, shuddering breath.

"I thank You, El Shaddai, for explaining these things to Your servant. This conversation will not stop me from doing the tasks You set before me. As I have said almost all my life, only You can judge and to You I send the wicked for judgment."

E'thriel blinked out of sight, and Tul'ran felt as if El Shaddai cupped his heart with His hands before leaving his mind.

Watching Wenonah leave, Tul'ran whispered a prayer of his own.

"Bless her, El Shaddai, comfort her in her sorrow, and guide her so she might one day rule this world well."

A shadow came from behind and stretched before him. Such a long shadow could only belong to …

Tul'ran turned and locked eyes with Evo, who jerked her head towards her ship.

"Need a ride? If you come back to the city with me, I'll tell you how I won the war single-handed while you and Erianne sipped wine and whittled."

Tul'ran raised his eyebrows at her unusual levity and gestured towards the rest of his party.

"Let me assign duties first, and I will partake of your offer gladly."

Tul'ran sheathed Bloodwing and walked over to address the rest of his war party, some of whom still sat on their horses.

"Chief Ravenclaw, I assign you the duty of organizing the departure of the Tribes of Women from this place. My sword has drained their home of life; never again will it function as they designed it. You must preserve what they own and have it transported to the City of Wenonah's Ascension."

Ravenclaw bowed his head.

"I will do as you say, Lord Conqueror."

"Lady Omarosa, Lady Anatu. Bide here with Chief Ravenclaw. You shall be my hand and my fist. Where the Tribes of Women need a hand of mercy, extend it to them. Where they need a fist to remind them I have conquered them, then strike. But remember, you represent me, and I will not have my subjects abused or killed."

Omarosa and Anatu bowed their heads, but Anatu couldn't keep a smile from tugging at her lips. Tul'ran cocked an eyebrow at the young warrior. He sensed there was more to the smile than obedience.

"Lady Anatu, is there something you wish to say?"

Anatu blushed and giggled.

"Princess Erianne told me recently you are such a, and these are her words milord, 'badass when you get riled up.' I was wondering if you could teach me how to be a badass one day."

Tul'ran burst out laughing, and felt the tension fly off his shoulders. Tired and stressed out? Keep company with a precocious child for a few hours.

"I shall do so. Remind me to tell you what a treasure you are to me as I impart the lesson. Go now, all of you, to your duties. Darkshadow and I return to Wenonah's Ascencion with Lady Evo to permit Erianne and I to ponder our next steps."

Ma'ilingan Waazh (Wolf's Den), 1ˢᵗ Year of Summer
Fourth day, Binaakwe-giizis (Falling Leaves Moon),
Year 5379, at the City of Wenonah's Ascension

It was the Feast of War's End, on the fourth day of the month they called Falling Leaves Moon. The men and women of the world called Wolf's Den celebrated it together in the brand-new city of Wenonah's Ascension.

While the Tribes of Women had mourned Baame'e in their way, the Tribes of Men moved their plants, livestock, goods, and personal effects to the City of Men. With no power, nothing could live in the underground caverns of Ikwe Na, forcing its abandonment.

The automatics created by the men made the job less difficult, but it was still arduous work, taking long hours.

Peace made it easier.

It was incredible what they had accomplished in a week. Tul'ran and Erianne met with the imprisoned Army of Women and secured their parole that they would abide by the peace until the antagonists signed formal treaties.

Once released, the workforce tripled in size as commanders designated by Tul'ran, Erianne, Ro'gun, Innanu, and Omarosa arranged accommodations for everyone. They moved personal effects into each home and settled the livestock in pastures between the outpost and the edge of the city. Airships, including Evo's starship, transported heavy cargo from Ikwe Na to Wenonah's Ascension every hour.

By the time Wenonah and Baame'e's mourners returned to Wenonah's Ascension one week after the war, the city was moved in and ready to celebrate.

Tul'ran sat on a large circular blanket with the rest of House az Nostrom, which now included Evo and, surprisingly, Carol. The late afternoon sun was warm, and a gentle breeze danced through the feathered headdresses worn by the planet's citizens. They had offered Tul'ran a beautiful and very heavy headdress made of eagle feathers to signify the Conqueror's status as the Leader of the Nine Tribes. After a gentle mental nudge from Erianne, he accepted it and allowed the headdress bearers to place it on his head.

"I feel ridiculous," he said in a whisper to his wife, who wore the headdress of a princess and the wife of a Grand Chief.

"Shush," she said. "As long as we're in this world, we must do our best to abide by their customs and honor them. It wouldn't bode well to offend our new subjects before we hand over the reins of power. Civil wars have started for less than disrespecting customs."

"Fine. I'll respect their customs, but I still feel ridiculous. You know I don't deserve to wear this headdress; it feels like I'm appropriating their culture. I'll strive for patience and dignity. It would help if you'd quit giggling." He changed the subject. "I've heard Ro'gun's Telling of his battle with Carol. How is it the giant shares our blanket?"

Erianne's green eyes glittered.

"The physicians from the Army of Women approached us after they surrendered. They requested our help with Carol because their field instruments were inadequate to repair the severed nerves, muscles, and tendons in his calves. Evo took two of her androids into one of the City's surgical suites and supervised as they repaired his legs."

Tul'ran's right eyebrow quirked upwards, straining against the weight of the headdress on his forehead.

"Supervised?"

Erianne watched as Carol tried to convince Evo to accept a piece of smoked salmon against her protestations that it looked raw.

"Indeed, milord husband. It turns out one of the many things our silver-haired friend learned from the Library of Heaven was medicine. She is beyond proficient. I warrant she'd make many of the physicians from my era look like schoolchildren playing with toys. I'm told she corrected her Dragon's Teeth on two occasions to change the materials they were using to stitch Carol together."

"It doesn't explain how he comes to sit on our blanket at her side."

Erianne tilted her head to one side, being careful not to dislodge her headdress.

"Tul'ran, for a deadly warrior with way too much experience savoring the pleasures of female flesh, you can be a little naïve sometimes. After Evo fixed his legs, Carol followed her around like a puppy. She finds him attractive, and they make a nice couple. Please don't bring it up with her," she said in haste. "You might make her think about it too much and it could end whatever they have going on."

"Fine," Tul'ran grumped. He scanned the tall man and observed he was in excellent condition. Ro'gun did well to defeat this one.

"Carol," he called out, as Evo pushed Carol's fish-laden hand away for the second time and playfully glared at him.

The warrior turned his attention to Tul'ran and bowed his head.

"Yes, Lord Conqueror."

Tul'ran ignored the warning glance Erianne directed toward him.

"I find you have an unusual name for such a fierce warrior. How did you come by it?"

A look flashed across Carol's face, as if he wasn't sure whether the question should insult him. A quick glance at the sword jutting up above Tul'ran's right shoulder seemed to clear his confusion.

"When the ice shield fell, it killed my family and made me an orphan. Before the elements could consume me, a Scout from the Tribes of Women found me. When she saw me, she told me she felt such joy that it was as if the Creator sang a carol in her heart. She adopted me as her son and named me Carol as a reminder of her joy."

Tul'ran nodded, his dark eyes warming.

"All honor to her. If you brought joy to your mother's heart, then it is a worthy name, indeed."

The tensions his question brought to the group evaporated. Evo smiled as Carol grinned from ear to ear.

"Thank you, milord," Carol said. "You honored me by inviting me to your blanket for the celebration. I'm grateful for the inclusion."

Tul'ran kept his face free of emotion.

"I'm pleased you accepted my invitation," he said while sliding his eyes to his wife's innocent demeanor. "We have decisions to make, and you're welcome to take part in the discussions."

It was Erianne's turn to quirk her eyebrow.

"Decisions, Lord Conqueror?"

Tul'ran had everyone's attention.

"Early this morning, El Shaddai visited me in a dream. He told me you and I are not long for this world. We are to go on a new mission, which will be dangerous and urgent. Evo, you're to take us to the little world of Cub's Den, the planet trailing in Wolf's Den orbit, where Erianne and I will train for our next battle. The question is not whether Milady and I will go. We are the Lord's Judges, and we go where He commands us. The question is: who follows us of their own accord?"

Silence descended on the little group. Ro'gun reached out and took Innanu's hand.

"Lord Tul'ran, you and Princess Erianne bonded my wife and I to your House. Of course, we will go with you." His eyes met Innanu's with a question, and she nodded with firmness to underscore her words.

"My husband speaks for us in truth. We go with our House. Let no one ever say our arms failed to bend to your necessities."

Tul'ran's grin stretched from one ear to the next.

"Well spoken; I would've expected no less valorous words from both of you. However, you'll not be coming with us."

He raised his hand against their protests.

"Hear me. As I've said, our next mission is dangerous. We won't take a warrior with child into the battle, nor will we force her husband to leave his pregnant wife behind. Erianne and I conversed with Princess Wenonah and Chief Ravenclaw."

"We are of the same mind as them," Erianne said, stepping into Tul'ran's words as if she had spoken from the beginning. "While the Tribes of Men and Women are at peace, many animosities remain. It'll take some time to integrate the people, making it necessary to have someone keep the peace. Princess Wenonah will give the mantle of Peacekeeper to the House az Nostrom when she resumes power."

"So," Tul'ran finished for them, "the House az Nostrom must leave some of its members behind to undertake the role. Ro'gun, your fight with Carol is already becoming a thing of legend. You've garnered much respect for both your fighting skills and the mercy you showed by not killing him after you disabled him. You shall become the First Peacekeeper."

Ro'gun swallowed and opened his mouth, but no words came out. He cleared his throat and tried again.

"I am honored to remain on Ma'ilingan Waazh as representative of the House and to take on the responsibility of First Peacekeeper."

Erianne clapped her hands.

"Excellent! This world will make a great place to raise children. Omarosa? Anatu? What say you?"

Omarosa made the bow of oath sworn to oath holder.

"Your Royal Highness, I am your subject. I go where you command."

Erianne's face softened.

"Lady Omarosa, we do not command you for this. You're an attractive woman and of sufficiently tender years you could have more children, if that was your desire. I tell you the truth. I've had four men approach me and beg my permission to seek a relationship with you. You're wise and you'd add much to redeveloping this world. If it inclines you to stay, then you must remain behind with your family."

Tears glistened at the edges of Omarosa's eyes.

"You and Tul'ran are my family," she said, her voice almost too soft to hear. "You saved my life and the life of my girls. The two of you gave me a House and a title. Without you, I would be nothing. My life is yours to command."

Erianne fought back her own tears.

"Tell me, Rosa, from the depths of your heart, what are your desires in this?"

Omarosa hesitated, then reached out to squeeze Innanu's empty hand.

"If it is within your will to grant it, I would stay with my daughter and son to see them through the birthing process and offer them whatever small insight I possess to raise their child well."

Tul'ran cleared his throat. Things were getting too maudlin for his liking.

"An excellent decision," he said. "What about you, Anatu? Do you bend your bow with us, or stay behind?"

Anatu arched her eyebrows and lifted her chin.

"If I were to leave, who else could fill the position of Second Peacekeeper?"

They roared with laughter, and Tul'ran nodded to her with gratitude.

"You are so right, Lady Anatu. The position is vacant, and I will see that you fill it. I have some influence over appointments, after all."

His statement earned another laugh, and the group relaxed.

Evo raised her hand.

"And what of me, Lord Conqueror? If I understood El Shaddai correctly, I'm to remain your prisoner until He decides as to my future."

Tul'ran set his face into serious lines, which was hard considering how badly his face threatened to split into a grin.

"Yes, Lady Evo, your name came up in my dream. When I asked El Shaddai about you, He looked at me sternly and said, 'Who am I to tell you what to do with your House, Tul'ran? It is for this reason I gave you free will.'"

A pregnant silence fell. They were so quiet, conversations from other blankets became as easy to hear as if they were all in one place. After a few deep breaths, Evo licked her lips and said,

"Your House?"

Tul'ran's face went through microscopic contortions as he fought to keep a smile off it.

"Of course. You tried to kill me, Evo. As the head of my House, I only have two options. Either kill you, which would prove very hard given you have eternal life, or bring you into our House where Erianne and I can monitor you. We are to provide you, a ten-thousand-year-old woman, with guidance."

He couldn't take it any longer. He put his head back and belted out a deep laugh. After a second, everyone else followed. Tul'ran looked at Evo's stunned face, his eyes twinkling.

"If it's your wish, Evo, milady wife and I will welcome you into our House as kin and heir. You will enrich us beyond our wildest dreams."

Evo rose to her feet. She walked to Tul'ran and Erianne and kneeled before them, pressing her face to the blanket.

"O Royalty of Death, I petition for a place within your House as kin and heir to Prince and Princess az Nostrom. I pledge you my loyalty, knowledge, strength of arms, and love. Where you go, I will go. Your people shall be my people, and your God, my God. Thus, do I swear on my life. My oath shall endure until God calls me home."

Erianne and Tul'ran stood up and drew their swords as everyone on their blanket looked on with delight.

"Evo Starchild," Erianne said, her voice serene as she and Tul'ran laid their swords on Evo's shoulders. "We welcome you into the House az Nostrom as our kin and heir. Our blood is your blood, and your blood is ours. We will comfort you in your sorrows and defend your life to our last breath. When the signal sounds from our House to gather to your family, you shall answer it, for you are ours and we are yours for eternity."

They sheathed their swords and pulled Evo to her feet. She wrapped her arms around their shoulders and drew them into her chest, a dazzling smile shining on her face. No one moved for a long time, until Tul'ran said, in a muffled voice,

"You're messing up my feathers."

Laughing, Evo withdrew. She put her hands on Erianne's face and pulled her in for a soft kiss. She did the same to Tul'ran.

"So, milord Tul'ran, what do you want me to do?"

"Sit, you bad-tempered brat. That's better. Erianne, is my headdress straight? It's giving me a headache. Evo, what was your question? Ah, yes. You're to give us a ride to Cub's Den on your ship and leave Erianne and I there for a time to train. Thereafter, you're to give us transport to the world upon which we execute our next mission."

Out of the corner of his eye, Tul'ran caught the shadow crossing Carol's face.

"Of course, far be it from me to tell you how to crew your ship for our travels."

Pink hues tinged Evo's pale cheekbones.

"I'll keep that in mind," she said, her voice dry.

A chant filled the air as a group of men and women banged with abandon on drums. The heavy rhythm drowned out the words at first, but then they became clearer.

"Conqueror! Conqueror! Conqueror!"

Tul'ran huffed a sigh.

"As you would say, covenant-wife, that's my cue. At last. It's time to bring my rule to an end."

Tul'ran stood up and walked to the raised dais upon which Wenonah and Chief Ravenclaw had spread their blankets. He noticed the Chief's long face and his wife's absence from the blanket.

Tul'ran faced the thousands of people sitting in front of him and raised his hands. Ravenclaw told him they would use some kind of mystical device called a parabolic microphone to project his voice over the crowd so he wouldn't have to shout. His upraised hands brought the drums and the crowd to silence.

He remembered Spes and the words of his beloved sister, the Empress Gwynver'insa, and decided they'd do well here.

"I, Tul'ran az Nostrom, the Sword Himself, Prince of Death, the Uncreator, Conqueror of Ma'ilingan Waazh, proclaim today to be the Day of Peace."

The crowd leaped to their feet; men, women, and children yelling and crying, as the drums raced in a wild rhythm again. Many started dancing and stamping their feet. Tul'ran let it go on for ten minutes, then raised his hands again.

"How is it not all my subjects are present for my proclamation?" he asked when the crowd quieted.

They stared at him in stunned silence.

"I ask again, how is it not all my subjects are present for my proclamation?" he said, again, his voice stiff and regal.

Wenonah cleared her throat.

"Who do you think is missing, Lord Conqueror?"

Tul'ran glared at her, and she withered. He winced. He hadn't wanted to scare the poor child.

"I do not see Dr. Megis Swiminghorse on your blanket beside Chief Ravenclaw. Why is she not present?"

Wenonah bit her lip. The look on her face pleased Tul'ran. It hadn't taken her long to catch on to what he was about to do.

"Chief Ravenclaw had confined his wife on charges of espionage and bid her stay imprisoned until her trial."

"Her trial!" Tul'ran said, projecting his voice into a roar. "Am I not the Leader of the Nine Tribes of Ma'ilingan Waazh?"

"You are," she said in a meek voice, trying to keep a silly grin off her face.

"Then only I will judge her! Bring her before me. Now!"

Several men leaped to their feet and ran toward a nearby building. They came back minutes later with Chief Ravenclaw's wife in tow. It amazed the crowd to see her dressed for the festivities, except for the rope tied around her wrists binding her to her captors.

Megis stopped before Tul'ran and faced him, her eyes and face revealing nothing.

"Why is she bound?" Tul'ran asked the guards, his voice severe.

"Um, well, she's a prisoner," one guard stammered.

"Do I look so feeble I cannot defend myself against a lone woman?" Tul'ran shouted. He was getting into this.

"No, milord!"

The guards hastened to untie Megis, and Tul'ran turned his attention to her.

"Dr. Megis Swimminghorse, you will give an account to me at once for spying upon the Tribes of Men."

Tul'ran folded his massive arms and waited for the explanation he'd heard from her lips the day before when he and Erianne questioned her.

"Milord Conqueror. My late sister, Baame'e, had claimed my right of inheritance to the leadership of the Tribes of Women. Though I was the elder, I didn't contest it. She was strong, ambitious, and stubborn. I had no stomach for the conflict, which would have ensued between us had I fought her for control."

Megis gestured to Eric Ravenclaw.

"When Chief Ravenclaw was yet a young man, he came to us searching for a bride. Baame'e seized upon him as if it were her right to take the first pick of my suitors. I stepped back to avoid a quarrel, but when my path crossed Eric's, we both knew our destinies lay in each other's arms. When we approached Baame'e and told her of our plans to marry, she flew into a rage, casting us both out of the Tribe."

Megis dropped her head.

"Then came the war with Men. My sister approached me through couriers and laid upon me a heavy robe of guilt. She blamed me for all her sorrows and claimed I'd stripped away her chance of happiness. The burden she laid was so heavy, I promised her whatever she asked to ease my guilt."

The crowd was still. Not even the birds sang.

"How many Men died because of the secrets you gave to your sister?" Tul'ran demanded.

Megis looked up, startled. His question wasn't in the script.

"None I know of."

"I see. So, your sister demanded information to satisfy your imaginary debt to her, but this intelligence resulted in no Men losing their lives. Do I have it right?"

"You do," she said.

Tul'ran snorted.

"Where I'm from, this sounds like an average day in the marketplace. I find no guilt in you, Megis Swiminghorse. I pardon you for the offenses which they charged against you. Go sit with your husband."

The crowd erupted in celebration again, and Tul'ran allowed a grin to spread across his face. After a few minutes, he raised his hands again. He put his hand into the buckskin ceremonial dress and pulled out the Peace Pipe. Tul'ran looked at it with distaste, remembering his conversation with Mick and Johan in the Mesopotamian desert when they'd been discussing smoking cigars.

He couldn't understand a person's desire to take smoke into their lungs. At least he didn't have to breathe in the pipe smoke.

Tul'ran gestured, and Wenonah rose to her feet as gracefully as a swan gliding over a still lake.

"Princess Wenonah, I've broken Ma'ilingan Waazh to peace. If I were fifty years older and too senior to campaign for El Shaddai, this planet would tempt me to keep it. It's a world rich in forests, lakes, and fresh-water streams. I'll return your rule to you, but under this condition: you shall appoint House az

Nostrom as Peacekeepers. My House shall make sure the peace I won will endure forever."

Wenonah nodded; her face masked with serenity.

"I accept your condition with gratitude, Lord Conqueror."

Tul'ran lit the pipe and took two draughts. He passed the pipe to Wenonah, who also took two draughts. Tul'ran turned to the people.

"Ma'ilingan Waazh, I give you Princess Wenonah, the Leader of the Nine Tribes and the ruler of your world. Obey her or face my wrath."

This cheer was the loudest of them all and would not be silenced. Tul'ran stood beside Wenonah, and they waved at the exuberant gathering, with each flick of the hand garnering a new roar of appreciation.

Evo sat beside Erianne and put her lips to her Princess's ear.

"Don't you love it when we do all the work and he gets all the glory?"

After they finished laughing, Erianne's eyes danced with mischief.

"Just wait, the best is coming. Watch Tul'ran's face when the singers perform all one hundred and eighty-five verses of the Ballad of Tul'ran the Sword!"

Two days later, a silver starship split the atmosphere of Cub's Den with a sonic boom. It flew a complete orbit before diving to the surface. The entire planet was a jungle, with clearings interspersed throughout. Evo chose the clearing designated by Tul'ran and brought The Dragon to a gentle landing.

The silver-haired pilot left the ship, followed by Tul'ran and Erianne leading their horses, and wearing the armor and clothing they'd worn when they came to Wolf's Den. Evo fussed over them, brushing their armor, and touching the silver tabs she'd locked onto it.

"Call me when you're ready," she said. "All you have to say is, 'Open a channel and call Evo' and these communicators will patch you through. You can call me from anywhere in the universe."

"Anywhere?" Erianne said, her voice squeaking a little.

Evo smiled and put her hand to Erianne's cheek.

"Anywhere, milady. They operate through IDS. If you need me, I'll drop everything and come to you. I mean it. I owe you two everything and I'll never forget what you did for me."

"Stop it," Erianne said, drawing the taller woman into a hug. "You're going to make me cry. El Shaddai told us we're going to train here for a month before we go on our next mission. You'll see us soon."

"I'd better," Evo said, pulling Tul'ran into a fierce hug. "Don't make me send Carol after you."

Evo turned and hurried back to the starship. After a few minutes, it rose into the sky, a swift and silent silver dart.

Erianne finger linked her left hand into Tul'ran's right.

"Just you and me, my love. What do we do now?"

"Well," Tul'ran said, chewing on his lower lip. "It's been a while since we negotiated anything."

Erianne laughed and drew his face in for a kiss.

"Later, I promise. Let's go check out the training area first."

Together, they followed the path El Shaddai had set out for them, leading their horses through the extensive foliage. They laughed as Darkshadow did his best to sample anything green on their way. Destiny's Edge was better behaved, but her male counterpart had always been a glutton for fresh greens.

After a mile of walking through heavy jungle, they came to another clearing filled with structures and devices on various tables.

Erianne pulled her hand out of Tul'ran's and ran to one table. Tul'ran jogged up to her.

"What is it, Erianne? What's caused you so much distress?"

She put her hand to her mouth.

"Milord husband, you see me dismayed because these guns are from my era. Whatever we hunt next, Tul'ran, it will be the most dangerous beast of them all."

CHAPTER THE TENTH: THE MOST DANGEROUS BEAST OF THEM ALL

Atlantis, November 2, 2099 AD… after the Seven Seal Judgments and the Fourth Trumpet Sounds

The machines were the problem.

They weren't even smart machines. For years, the entertainment industry predicted that sentient androids would overthrow their human overlords and take control of the world, causing the end of civilization. To anyone who studied history, such a thing was laughable. The most vicious, lethal, rapacious entity in the universe was the human being, and nothing could overcome them.

Still, the machines *were* a problem. These machines, as dumb as they were, made the mark mandated by the government.

Without the mark, you had no roof over your head, no food on your table, no medical care, and no money in your account.

Only Christians refused the mark, and being a Christian begged for a painful death. The world had become divided by a rigid line, with those who took the mark on one side and those who didn't on the other. There was no compromise between the two positions; if you wanted to eat, live a secure lifestyle, and be entertained by drugs, alcohol, and sex, you took the mark.

People with the mark vilified those who didn't have one, calling them ignorant and enemies of law-abiding citizens everywhere. The mark kept people secure because the government watched over them like a rich, benevolent parent. Did a plague threaten the world? The government jumped to distribute vaccines to mark-bearers, reducing the spread of the contagion and subduing the impact of the illness. Did the government impose a lockdown to contain the spread of the virulent threat? They were quick to compensate their supporters by giving mark-bearers funds to stay at home to keep themselves and their fellow citizens safe.

There was no argument on the other side. Oh, there was an argument, if you were in the mood to commit suicide by pointing out only the godless took the symbol of the Beast on their bodies. The new god of the world was perfect in the minds of the people who sacrificed their time and worship to him. To suggest he was anything other than a god was a profound blasphemy worthy of torture and death.

Maybe you weren't fully committed to the idea

that a mere mortal like Contradeum was now a god.

Made no difference. It was much better to avoid someone questioning your loyalty by taking the mark. All you needed to be protected was to slip your hand into a Mark Machine and make all your fears go away.

So, the problem wasn't the machines. Rather, the problem was making sure they were nowhere close to you. And Mick Davis was staring at twelve of them sitting on a poorly lit dock, only sixteen short inches away from thirty-three hundred feet of cold, dank seawater.

Mick shivered. The sun was coming up soon, and it couldn't be soon enough. A wet wind blew off the ocean, searching for spaces in his clothing to introduce its prying, frigid fingers to his warm skin. The wind carried with it the stench of rotting sea life, which enveloped the pier like a wet blanket of corpulent death.

The comet killed one-third of everything living in the ocean when it crashed into the earth after the earthquakes and volcanic eruptions. Millions of sea creatures died and many of their corpses rose to the surface to decompose under the sun. The stink spread at random across every area in or near saltwater.

A bleak darkness engulfed the pier, making the horrible smell more appalling. There was a full moon, but its radiance was two-thirds its usual shine. Even the stars seemed less dazzling and less prevalent in the sky. People thought it was because of the dust and smoke cast into the atmosphere by the volcanic eruptions, but Mick knew better.

The Bible had predicted God would strike one-third of the light from the skies and it's what He did.

The absence of light not only made it cold, it made his surroundings dangerous. In the effort to get their cargo off the ship fast, his crew had scattered sea cans around the undamaged areas of the pier haphazardly. The functioning lights, and there weren't many of them, looked like islands isolated in a dangerous, dark sea. People were still working on getting the offloaded supplies up the hill to the Main Complex, but at least the unloading was done. For now.

Mostly, the supplies were a welcome sight. Like everywhere else in the world, the severe environmental disasters pounding the Earth left Atlantis without fresh food and decent water to drink. Everything they unloaded was going to help the residents' continued survival.

Except for those infernal machines.

Mick stared at them, shuddering.

The Mark Machines represented the ultimate choice between life and death for a Christ-follower. To allow the machine to imprint the Mark of the Beast on a person's wrist was to reject Jesus Christ. It was simple. If you accepted the mark, you worshipped the Antichrist, Malchus Contradeum, and Satan, who was now inhabiting his body. Every person without the mark was the enemy of the leader of the world, without compromise.

Mick and his wife, Heather, wouldn't accept the mark. It was a non-starter. On a small island like Atlantis, though, it wouldn't take long for the rest of the population to notice they didn't have one.

TTI, the only employer on Atlantis, would deny them lodging, water, food, and medicine. Worse, someone would hunt them like animals to torture and kill them because it was the new international sport. There was no way to avoid getting the mark, unless... unless there were no machines to print it onto your skin. Like, say, if they were sitting at the bottom of the ocean?

Mick looked at the crate of Mark Machines. How much effort would it take to nudge the pallet over the edge? The risks, though, were enormous. Sabotage was treasonous. Mick knew there were cameras everywhere. Even in this dim light, they'd pick up any effort he might make to sabotage the machines. To save his soul, he'd have to risk taking a bullet from a firing squad.

Sweat beaded on Mick's brow, and pressure squeezed his chest. He needed to get the demonic equipment off the dock before someone took them up the hill. Once they were up there, it was only a matter of time before he and those he loved were presented with a demand to take the mark. There was no place to run once someone gave the order.

"Amazing, aren't they?"

Mick just about jumped out of his skin. He'd been so absorbed by the machines and the agony of indecision; he hadn't heard the captain of the massive container ship sneak up on his six. Mick angled his lanky body to address the captain while still maintaining a visual on the pier.

"Captain Wiesling. My apologies. I didn't hear you come up behind me. Yes, they're amazing, but I confess I don't know how they work."

Wiesling grunted and pulled the collars of his pea coat higher around his neck. He was several inches shorter than Mick and a lot heavier. His belly stretched the waist of his pants without mercy, but his uniform was clean. He'd taken the time to comb his long, greasy hair and beard. He had a thick face and piggy eyes. A small, almost indiscernible measure of contempt laced his next words to Mick.

"You really are isolated out here. After the Second Cataclysm, widespread panic encouraged the One World Legislature to create a global data repository. The purpose of it was to make a census of those who remained on Earth. They forced every intelligence agency to fold their resources into the Global Database. It stored past and current information for everyone who survived the Cataclysms."

"Current information? How did the Database gather current information?" Mick said.

Wiesling dug through his jacket and pulled out an ancient pipe. It had no tobacco, and looked like it hadn't been lit for a long time, but it didn't stop the corpulent container ship captain from popping it into his mouth.

"The Database has everything there is to know about us. If you use bitcoin to purchase something, the Database records your transaction, including the location, and cross matches surveillance video in the area. It tracks you when you use your communicator, which also maintains your health stats, like pulse and blood pressure. This way, it keeps a constant record of everything we do and everywhere we go. We have a daily census of those who have survived war, natural disasters, and famine."

Mick let his eyes drift to a forklift operator who was unloading a sea can off to their right. The stack of Mark Machines sitting near the edge of the dock faced the back end of the forklift about twenty feet away. A thought niggled at the back of his mind, but Mick discarded it to turn his attention to Wiesling's last comment.

"If we already have a Global Database, Captain, then why is the mark necessary?"

Wiesling snapped his head around, his eyes rounding.

"Surely, Master Chief, you're not that ill-informed!"

Mick cursed himself under his breath. Between fatigue, being consumed with the problems the machines presented, and focusing on the forklift operator, he'd forgotten to mind his tongue.

"My apologies, Captain. Until recently, I spent a lot of time in Antiquity. I've not kept abreast of the news since I've been back."

Wiesling glared at him.

"I suggest you waste no time to do so. Ignorance can get you imprisoned. Or killed. The Supreme God of the Earth commands us to take the mark as a sign of worship and loyalty to him."

The Supreme God of the Earth, Mick thought. What a joke. Satan was powerful, sure, but he wasn't the god of anything. His lying tongue was so clever, though, it could twist the non-existent into reality. He had some power, having been an angel created by the true, Living God, but that was about it.

Satan had sent Malchus Contradeum ahead of him, and the Antichrist had bent many people away from faith in God. He convinced people to worship a false deity, Mother Earth, until a retired soldier put a dagger through his heart. Satan somehow revived Contradeum's body and now lived in it. Worship a demon who'd spent millennia inciting people to every vulgar sin imaginable? Not for Mick Davis.

"Of course, of course," Mick said to Wiesling. "I didn't mean to suggest I didn't know the critical part of it. I just don't know how the mark keeps track of such things. Forgive me, I'm exhausted."

The apology mollified Wiesling.

"No worries, Master Chief. I've seen how hard you and your crew have worked today. I appreciate it. My ship has to get off this pier and onto its next destination as soon as possible. We lost many cargo vessels in the last few days of devastation. To answer your question, centuries ago, people used to attend a business to buy pharmaceuticals. While they waited for their scrips to be filled, they would sit in a chair and place their arms into a cuff. The chair would take their blood pressure and record their pulse. It was more of a novelty item than a diagnostic machine. The Mark Machine works something like it."

"How so?" Mick asked, glancing back at the forklift operator. The forklift had stopped, and the operator was just sitting there as if mesmerized by the load of steel girders sitting on the lift. Mick shook his head to clear the fog in his mind. The boat captain was talking, and he needed to concentrate.

"When a person sits in the Mark Machine, they place their hands on the reader, which is a small square patch resting under their palms," Wiesling said, warming to the subject. "The machine scans their faces and retinas and records their fingerprints. An instrument on the machine also scrapes a miniscule amount of skin cells from their skin and scans the DNA. The machine locates the person's DNA, fingerprint, facial, and retinal records in the Global Database. Once the machine is satisfied the person is who they claim to be, it copies all the person's data in the Global Database into a tattoo. For obvious reasons, they designed it to be non-removable."

Mick turned his head to stare at Wiesling's florid face. It stunned him to realize how much information the government dumped into the mark.

"How does an ink strip hold everything there is to know about someone?"

Wiesling tilted his head back and guffawed.

"That's the beauty of it; it's not ink. The machine imprints nanobots into the skin. The nanobots connect wirelessly to quantum computers, which store the Global Database. They report, second by second, a person's location and biorhythm stats to the Database. The Database monitors everything you do and feel based on hormone levels, keeping track of the health and welfare of the Supreme God's subjects. With this technology, the Supreme God can make sure one person does not become too wealthy and powerful, or unhealthy and weak. It's a beautiful system."

Mick felt sick to his stomach. A beautiful system which told the Antichrist where you were, what you bought, and what you did every second of the day. Those who took the mark became slaves, and they didn't know it. All they knew was they were being protected and kept secure.

"So, when you scanned the Administrator's mark, it gave you access to everything there was to know about her?"

Wiesling looked startled.

"No, not at all! The holographic image my scanner produced just confirmed her identity and her credit rating. It permitted me to record the transfer of Atlantis' cargo to her authority. Once I checked her mark, I knew I could transfer my goods to her. Only the highest echelons of government get access to all the data."

The forklift operator was becoming a distraction. Mick's instincts yelled at him something was not right, but he couldn't put his finger on the threat. His right hand slid down to reach for the gun that was not resting on his hip. When he realized what he was doing, he bit his lip to send a jolt into his brain. Once more, he forced his concentration back to Wiesling.

"You seem very enthusiastic about these machines, Captain."

Wiesling laughed again.

"I suppose I am, Master Chief. I was one of the first to get the mark out of the Merchant Marine. The best part of the mark is not the secure transfers of funds, or the gracious protection of the Supreme God of the Earth. It's his ability to address our minds."

Mick felt his eyebrows climb.

"Say again?"

Wiesling smiled like someone who was privy to a precious secret, and the other was not. He raised his right wrist and admired the glowing mark.

"Yes, you've not experienced it yet. The nanobots create a mental hologram when the Supreme God wants to send us a message. It's as if he takes us physically into his presence. We experience input from all our senses as he communicates to us. Such an amazing experience! I've never taken drugs, but I'm told the euphoric effect is the same."

Mick said nothing. He would never experience the euphoric effect of taking the mark because he promised himself he wouldn't stick his arm into the cuff.

He was having a hard time focusing his thoughts. His surroundings became surreal. It was as if someone drugged him. His muscles were relaxed; so much so, they didn't want to move. His eyes drifted to the forklift operator, who seemed to have fallen asleep.

Mick knew the operator; he was a hard-working Arabic man tasked with maintaining the Lens when TTI was in operation. He was a specialist engineer, not part of the dockworkers' guild. What was his name again? Ah, yes, Farouk Abdulhadi. Farouk had been working the docks today for as long as Mick, about twenty-two hours now. Mick was going to walk over and nudge the man awake, but then thought better of it. What harm could come from giving the poor guy a couple of minutes of shuteye?

Unknown to Mick or Farouk, the fuse controlling the safety backup sound on the forklift had burned out weeks ago. Normally, when the fuse went out, a red light appeared on the dashboard, warning of the compromise of the loader's safety features.

The dockworkers had put this loader in a sea can of its own because they'd been cannibalizing it for parts. One part they scavenged was the bulb from the warning light.

When earthquakes and tsunamis trashed the port and sent a bunch of forklifts into the ocean, Mick and his crew were ecstatic to find a functioning undamaged heavy-duty forklift sitting in the sea can. They took the lift out of storage without being able to check the maintenance records, which were buried somewhere in the rubble up the hill.

Farouk had just finished unloading some steel braces and had put the forklift into reverse to free the two heavy blades in front of the machine. One forklift blade had jammed under the heavy steel.

Bemused by fatigue caused by too many hours of rapid unloading, which required a great deal of concentration and mental acuity, Farouk forgot to put the machine in neutral. As he was thinking about how to extract the blade from the pile of metal in front of him, his mind wandered. He drifted into a deep sleep while dreaming he was awake and working on the solution.

As luck would have it, he shifted his foot in his sleep and jammed it down onto the accelerator. Tires spinning, the forklift raced backwards right into the pallet of Mark Machines. The pallet skidded three feet and tottered, balancing at a forty-five-degree angle on the edge of the pier. One machine shifted toward the back of the pallet, and it was over. The pallet made a big splash and left a trail of bubbles behind it. The momentum carried the pallet of machines into the deep water.

By the time they could mount an effort to pull them from the drink, the pressure and corrosive seawater would've rendered them useless.

The crash of the backend of the forklift with the pallet frightened Farouk into full awareness. He jammed his feet on the brake and switched the device to park. He looked around him wildly as the back end of the loader hung over the water. Farouk turned pale as he saw Mick and Wiesling staring at him with their jaws slack and mouths gaping.

Mick closed his mouth and pondered on the brilliance of God. He had been contemplating creating Farouk's accident, which could've exposed him to disaster if someone caught him sending the machines to the bottom of the ocean. The Lord took care of it for him.

Wiesling ran up to the forklift operator, his face mottled red, and shook his fists at the horrified man.

"What did you just do? What did you just do? You ignorant, incompetent fool! You just dumped hundreds of thousands of bitcoins into the ocean and deprived this island of the ability to get the mark. I'll see you court-martialed for this!"

Mick walked up to the captain and put a hand on his shoulder.

"Come now, Captain," he said, making his voice as reasonable as possible. "This man is exhausted. It was an accident, nothing more. What do you expect? He's not even a dockworker. We're short-staffed and under supported. I'll write up a report on the incident and submit it to the Administrator. You need not concern yourself about it further."

Wiesling turned on Mick like an angry dog.

"Just walk away? I'm responsible for those precious machines! Besides, this dock is under my jurisdiction!"

"No, Captain, it's not," an authoritative voice said from behind them.

Startled, both men swung their heads around to see Marjatta Korhonen standing there with her fists pressed to her hips. She wore the same greasy coveralls she had on earlier in the day, and her hair was a mess. Notwithstanding the fatigue bathing her face, she set her lips in a rigid line and her eyes were stone cold.

"You signed those machines over to me, remember? As soon as they hit the dock, they became my responsibility. Master Chief Davis is right. We've been working our people to the bone and I'm surprised something like this didn't happen hours ago. I'll conduct a full inquiry, you can be sure of that, and submit a report. In the meantime, has your ship now delivered all our cargo to us?"

Wiesling's jaw was moving back and forth, and his eyes burned with intensity.

"I'll file my own report, Administrator. This won't go on my service record. Yes, I've unloaded all of Atlantis' cargo."

Marjatta's face grew colder.

"Then get your ship off my dock. There are three other transports in the harbor waiting for us to unload them. I hope they have some fresh crew to help my people offload, or else they're going to sit there another three weeks. We can't keep up this pace. Goodbye, Captain."

Wiesling glared at her and stomped off into the gloom toward the gangway. Mick, not realizing he had been holding his breath, let it out with a sigh.

"Thank you, Administrator. I know Farouk didn't intend this to happen. Right?"

The Arabic man pumped his head several times, his dark eyes huge in his creased, brown face.

"Yes, yes, that's right. Administrator, forgive me. I should've taken myself off shift hours ago. Before I go to sleep, I'll write a report taking full responsibility for this fiasco."

Marjatta's face softened a little.

"No, Farouk. Go get some sleep. The Master Chief and I will worry about the paperwork. Before you go, park your lift where no one will trip over it and hurt themselves."

Farouk bowed his head and shoulders.

"I'm so grateful for your kindness, Administrator. I'll never let something like this happen again."

With that, the dock worker eased the forklift forward and parked it out of the way before powering it down. He stumbled toward the hill leading up to the Main Complex.

"Did it happen like he said? I got here just as The Weasel verbally assaulted Farouk," Marjatta said to Mick, watching the man stagger away.

"Yes, Administrator. I bear some of the responsibility. I saw he was nodding off, but didn't think the forklift was in gear. The backup warning signal didn't engage and the rear lights are always on when the machine is being operated. Who knew by falling asleep he'd put the forklift into motion and slam it into the back of those crates?"

Marjatta looked around, exercising unusual caution, before lowering her voice on her next words.

"Mick, you don't have to respond to what I'm about to say next. I suspect you're a Christian and I suspect your wife is one as well. Hey, hey, relax. There may be others on the island. For all I know, Farouk is also a Christ follower and was clever enough to make this look like an accident. It doesn't matter. You and the others are safe with me. Don't practice your religion in the open, or make it necessary for it to come to my attention, and we're good. I'll only address it if someone forces the issue. You're hearing this because I don't know how I got my marks and I'm horrified by them. You can take it to the bank; I never consented to them. No one should have to wear the mark. I'm more than happy to have those," she used a very profane word, "machines at the bottom of the ocean. By the way, I never said that."

Mick kept his face still, not revealing the emotions he was feeling.

"Marjatta, what you just told me could get us both killed."

"I know, so let's make sure no one hears about it."

Mick pulled a quick breath.

"It won't come from me, that's for sure."

He stifled a yawn and squinted his eyes against the darkness of the night toward where the Merchant Marine berthed the other three super cargo ships.

"It'll take at least a couple of hours for them to maneuver the next ship alongside the dock. I respectfully suggest, ma'am, we get some sleep. In a few hours, it's going to be another busy day."

Marjatta clapped her hand on Mick's shoulder.

"Good call, Mick. I'll spread the word. You and your people did a great job today."

Mick grinned at her, though the smile was stiff from fatigue.

"Thanks, boss. But be careful with the kudos. They may want a raise."

———✦———

From fifty feet away, Hart watched Korhonen and Davis separate and walk in different directions. He'd been surveilling Davis ever since the crew offloaded the Mark Machines. Hart was the one who directed the dockworkers to set the pallet near the edge of the dock. He hoped the machines so close to ruin would tempt Davis to do something stupid. Instead, Abdulhadi sent the machines to a watery grave.

Hart would file a report on the incident and see to it the authorities punished Abdulhadi. He ground his teeth in frustration. Abdulhadi hadn't been his target. He wanted nothing more than to bring Davis up on charges and see him executed. If it wasn't for him and the barbarian Davis claimed as a brother or adopted son or whatever sick thing they had going on, Hart wouldn't be living with PTSD.

Once they left, Hart turned off the holo-camera, removed the storage cube, and zipped it into a secure pocket. His nose wrinkled at the fetid odor of rotting fish and the sweat of overworked people. What a wasted night.

All he had on the surveillance video was Davis staring like a zombie at the pallet until Wiesling walked up, which wasn't evidence of anything. It was a piece of a puzzle, though, and a complete picture might allow Hart to drive six-inch nails into Davis's coffin.

Mick shuffled back to the quarters he shared with Wu, every muscle in his body protesting the climb to the hill home.

Everyone was living underground again, but their rooms were not as luxurious as they had been in the past. Their quarters were a cubicle cut in the rock twenty feet under the island's surface. The construction workers carved the residences out of the rock with lasers and lined the rooms with synthetic materials to resemble what one would expect to see on a starship.

The designers covered the walls, ceiling, and floor with white vinyl, which did nothing to keep out the damp chill of the granite behind it. A strip of bioluminescent material invented by the genetic modification of sea life provided a dim, pale light.

The doors were surplus hatches from the old cargo ships which had delivered the building materials decades past. It was a clever use of archaic materials, but the esthetics were terrible.

Mick and Heather had a bed, with three shelves in the frame for clothing, a small glassed-in shower, and a sink, all in one small room. They had a tiny bathroom with a door because of Heather's Programmer status. Everyone else shared washrooms.

That was it, other than a small desk with a large holo screen.

`No one cooked in their rooms any longer; they all went out to the commissary to eat meals together. If you could call them meals. While Atlantis still had considerable food reserves compared to the rest of the world, it wasn't enough to feed the thousands of people remaining on the tiny island in the manner to which they'd become accustomed.

The surviving chefs did their best to cobble together meals at a high enough caloric content to give the residents energy for the demanding work ahead of them. There were no fresh vegetables, meat, or fruits. Anything surviving the disasters inflicted on the Earth came from frozen stores, and they were lucky to have it. Everywhere else, people starved.

Mick had seen the food supplies offloaded from the container ship. Everything, the protein, the vegetables, and the staples, were all manufactured or created. Manufactured meant 3D products printed from a chemical soup. The steaks may have looked like steaks, but Mick would've put money down on a bet they never came from cows.

Heather stood up as Mick entered the quarters and reached up to put her arms around his neck before planting a long kiss on his lips.

"How did it go today?" she said.

Mick was careful to keep his tone neutral. They had to operate on the assumption someone was recording everything.

"Mostly okay," Mick said, pulling her in a little closer. "We had some trouble with the new Mark Machines. Someone offloaded them onto the dock too close to the edge. A forklift operator, running on no caffeine and not enough sleep, ran into the pallet and sent it into the briny."

Wu opened her eyes wide and allowed her face to express shock.

"Was anyone hurt? Can they recover the machines?"

Mick tipped his head to one side and admired her tiny golden features.

"No. I mean, the machines are beyond recovery. The operator was fine, and we sent him back here to get some sleep. Speaking of which, I'm only going to get four hours myself. Sorry, sweetheart, I need to hit the rack."

Wu guided him to their small bed and helped him get out of his coveralls.

"Maybe take a shower first, Mick. We don't get clean sheets for another three days and you smell a little funky."

Mick chuckled.

"Yeah, I imagine I do. I haven't worked so hard in years. Okay, a quick shower, then bed. What did you do today?"

TTI only allowed them five minutes of hot water before the shower shut itself off. It was more than Mick used to get when he went to and from war zones in hunter/killer submarines, so he knew how to make the most of it. He closed the shower door, selected the temperature, and started counting down in his head.

Heather grabbed a towel and waited for the shower cycle to end.

"We have a new quantum computer to run the Transition Lens," she said, twirling the towel into knots. "It's incredible. I've been restoring the backups and so far everything looks good. They gave me some new coding, though, and I'm a little confused by it."

Mick lathered his hair and body as fast as he could, while the remaining seconds counted down in his mind.

"How so?"

"The spatial coordinates make no sense. The solar system moves at 448,000 miles an hour on an elliptical orbit around our galaxy. To calculate transitions into Antiquity, we assess where the solar system is going, where it's been, and how fast it's traveling in relation to the Earth. While it's a big endeavor, there's a geospatial limitation in terms of what we can program. We confine our calculations to the known space occupied by our solar system at any point in time."

Mick rinsed the soap from his body and glanced at his chrono. It said he had thirty-five seconds to relax and allow the hot water to massage his aching muscles. He sighed and whispered a prayer of gratitude as he exposed his back to the stream of water, which felt like hot needles on his skin.

"You're so smart. You've no idea how much you impress me," he said, wiping steam off the shower glass to look at her face. "What's the problem with the new data?"

The shower ended, and Heather passed the towel to Mick.

"How expansive it is. They've asked me to program the potential to travel to any place in the universe."

Mick stopped drying his hair and peered out from the edges of the towel.

"Any place in the universe? Is that possible?"

Heather grabbed Mick's robe and slipped it over his damp body.

"It turns out we limited our thinking too much when we designed the Lens. We were so focused on nailing down time and space coordinates for a sphere moving faster than a bullet through space, we constrained our calculations to this world. We know there are millions of planets in habitable zones around G-type stars. Lots of them have water and atmospheres which could sustain human life. They're too far away to travel to them with our current technology, but if you could pin down their spacetime coordinates. I could send you there. Give me the numbers of a planet anywhere in the cosmos and, boom, you're there."

Mick stopped cold as his mind blasted through the implications.

"How long would it take to get to another planet?"

Heather shrugged.

"How long did it take you to travel into the past? For the person traveling, it could feel like a long time, or not. For the objective observer, it would look instantaneous. No one has successfully measured the time it takes in transition to move from one spacetime to another."

"If someone wanted off Earth," Mick said, forgetting security may record their conversation. "All they'd have to do is get space-time coordinates for a sustainable world in a habitable zone and they could leave this disaster behind."

"Exactly. Leave it behind and flee the consequences of what's coming. Who can you think of who'd really want an escape like that right now?"

Atlantis, November 13, 2099 AD... about two weeks later

Hart lurched upwards, screaming, as his hand clenched his chest. Cursing, he threw back the covers and stared in disgust at the contents of his bowels lying on the bed. He ripped off the sheets and threw them into a biological hazard container before walking into the shower, shaking.

Hatred consumed him as he rubbed his eyes, trying to scrape from his mind the images of the sword thrusting through his chest. Every night. Every single night. He couldn't sleep without falling into The Dream, and the horrific prospect of falling into it again kept him awake for the rest of the evening. Hart couldn't do it anymore. He needed help.

Just as Hart tried to figure out what to do next, a large holo-screen flared into existence in his quarters. Hart looked at it with distaste. A beautiful female announcer stood before him naked, with even her private parts exposed. The Supreme God of the Earth had decreed news outlets to deliver news in the most appealing manner possible, to soften the blow on days the word was bleak.

He stressed the news anchors should be physically attractive and they should clothe themselves only in their birthday suits. This one, who had her mark displayed on her right wrist, didn't seem to mind speaking to the world while nude. She was perky and, this morning, ecstatic.

"Citizens of Atlantis! I'm sharing with you news which will bring you great joy. Today, our blessed Supreme God of the Earth visits our island to inspect the progress we've made on the greatest scientific advances in our history. You must not offend our glorious Supreme God of Earth, so follow these protocols."

She glanced down at the transparent tablet resting in her hands before looking back up at the holo-camera.

"As soon as our fabulous god steps off his aircraft, you must drop to your knees and bow to the ground. It's customary to chant 'We worship you, Supreme God of the Earth' until he commands you to stop. After that, you must not look him in his eyes unless he invites you to do so. It's against protocol to step on or across his path and you must never wear shoes in his presence. As always, be prepared to lick his feet if he offers them to you. He will honor you to the extreme if he offers his radiant feet for your tongue! Such a rare blessing!"

Hart snorted as the holo-image faded away.

He never thought he'd live to see a day where it would be a great honor to lick someone else's feet. He'd been so angered by the thought, he almost missed what the anchor had said.

Hart remembered Contradeum once had a huge burr in his bonnet over some character in Antiquity named Tul'ran az Nostrom. The same Tul'ran who'd come to the rescue of Davis and some local barbarians.

There was a connection there which had the potential for exploitation. It might be an angle he could play to get off the island and get some real medical help. Hart grabbed his finest suit from the closet and put it on. Today might end in a transition to a better way of life.

Marjatta Korhonen stood shaking in front of her full-length mirror, her stomach threatening to empty its contents. Contradeum was coming here! Or whatever Contradeum was now, because Marjatta was certain he wasn't human.

She went to her closet and pulled out a long red dress. It had a plunging neckline and a plummeting back, reaching down to the top of her buttocks. Both legs had the side split up to the thigh. It was a dress suitable for a sex trade worker, not the Administrator of the most important scientific enterprise ever known.

Marjatta stared at herself in the mirror for a moment. She'd just turned fifty-five, but her body didn't show it. Marjatta had been careful to watch her nutrition and worked out regularly.

She had very little fat on her back and her chest narrowed to a tiny waist and flat stomach. Perhaps she could stand to lose a couple of pounds off her hips, but she considered herself to be in excellent shape.

Marjatta shuddered. Which was too bad.

She put on the dress with reluctance, leaving off any lingerie. If she dressed to give herself a little respect, the Supreme God would reign painful fury on her.

The dress hugged her body and exposed her lean legs. The plunging neckline didn't display her breasts; she heaved a sigh of relief. If she was careful to avoid sudden movements, no one would see parts of her they shouldn't see in public.

Except for Contradeum. He'd insist on viewing all of her. She shuddered again.

Whatever Contradeum intended by this visit, there was nothing good about it.

The hyper-jet was the newest and biggest of its kind. It hovered over Atlantis' airfield like a great black vulture, barely humming with the power keeping it in the air. It didn't circle the landing area; the ominous plane pivoted on its vertical axis as if to glare at everyone gathered below it. The ship settled a few feet off the ground and ejected a ramp.

At Marjatta's orders, everyone dressed in the best of what they could scavenge from the piles of clothing recovered from the crumbled stores. If the Supreme God of the Earth expected people dressed for a gala, he was going to be disappointed. The island was too wrecked to host an old-fashioned Hollywood party.

Marjatta stood at the front of the assemblage, just beyond the safety zone laid out by security. She felt her cheeks flush as the ever-present Atlantic breeze tried to lift the sides of her dress. She was embarrassed to have her people see her dressed like a streetwalker, including the garish makeup Contradeum mandated she wear. If she knew then what she knew now, she would've put a bullet in his head the first time he came to her island.

If wishes were horses…

Hart and the other surviving department heads stood behind her. The construction workers found a bundle of red bunting they'd pressed into a red carpet. Atlantis once had a competent band of amateur musicians, but they were all dead. Korhonen didn't know the current state song for the world government, so she opted for a respectful silence.

She glared at the ship sitting before them. Contradeum had been a pompous ass before he became Earth's self proclaimed deity. Now, he was insufferable. It was colder than usual outside, and her people were stuck waiting for him, shivering, like he was the Second Coming.

She swallowed the rest of her thoughts as the ramp sunk to the ground. The entity about to come off the ship could almost read her mind from her marks. She knew what kind of pain the sadistic bastard liked to work on her for no reason. It would be worse to give him one.

Marjatta Korhonen dropped to her knees in humble supplication.

Mick, Heather, Sully, Jeannie, and Payton had buried themselves in the crowd as far from the landing pad as they could get. Payton had grown quite fond of what she considered as her medical team, in which group she included Mick and Heather by default. They hung out a lot as a cluster, often eating together and socializing in what little off time TTI gave them.

Her friends confused her. They had some kind of secret, one they weren't sharing with anyone. It had something to do with how different they were.

She rarely encountered in others the kindness she found in her friends. She found it amazing how they reached out and helped other people in need. They shared their resources with anyone who asked without counting the cost.

Mick and the others accepted her into their group with open arms and were quick to support her in whatever she asked of them. There was a core warmth to them she couldn't figure out. Whatever they had, she wanted it, too.

Payton watched as the monstrous hyper-jet lowered onto the pad at the airport. A company of military men dressed in gaudy uniforms walked off the transport first and set up a rank on either side of the red carpet Atlantis had rolled out for the global leader.

The next person out the door was the Chief Priest of the Church of the Supreme God of the Earth.

He lost a lot of weight, Payton noticed, and it looked like he bought hair plugs. Something about his energy gave her stomach a sour feeling. A black cloud of malevolence seemed to flow out of his face and turn the air fetid in front of him. He walked down the stairs, smiling smugly as the residents of Atlantis pressed their faces to the ground. He acted like the adulation was for him.

Next down the gangway came a group of the Supreme God's slave brides. They were scantily clad in white lingerie and someone bound them together by chains clipped to wide gold collars around their necks. They wore nothing on their feet. Payton wondered what they wore in the wintertime. Even in these temperatures, the women couldn't have been warm. They made Payton feel uncomfortable.

What woman in her right mind would want to be treated like a piece of property to be slobbered over by gross people?

Finally, the Supreme God of the Earth made his way through the doorway and down the stairs. Giant speakers were playing crowd noises, with chants worshipping and glorifying him. He waved like a visiting Queen, although no one was looking at him. Probably for the holo-feeds, Payton thought, keeping her head at a level where she could watch what was going on without being noticed. The chants of worship came from the speakers; no one kneeling on the ground said anything. They were too terrified.

"Greetings, my children and my subjects," Contradeum said when he reached the bottom of the stairs. His amplified voice carried over the crowd. "I'm grateful to once more step on your soil and to bring you good news of great joy. You will be the centerpiece of our efforts to rebuild the world after the multiple disasters poured on us. The rebuilding of the Time Travel Initiative will inspire the entire world to scientific progress and our future success. The actions of the Enemy, who dares to call himself a loving God, devastated the resources of our world. We will take the resources we have left and invest them in Atlantis to enable you to complete the reconstruction of the island at the soonest possible time. The new technology my genius had developed will allow us to seize all the Universe offers!"

Somewhere, speakers blared, broadcasting yelling, screaming, and shouts of joy.

Again, none of it came from the people prostrating themselves before the world leader. He didn't appear to notice, preening like a peacock as he walked the length of the red carpet.

Payton wanted to dismiss him outright as a garish popinjay, but something about him stopped the train of thought. It wasn't just that he was good-looking; there was an allure to him beyond the influence of physical attraction. His body oozed sensuality and promised pleasure beyond imagining. Unspoken offers of love, caring, protection, and security washed off him like waves on an ocean.

The effect became worse as he got closer to them. She felt Heather take her left wrist and Jeannie grab her right.

"Don't look up," Heather said in a soft whisper. "Even if he says something to you, don't look him in the eyes."

Most trauma surgeons didn't like to be told what to do, but Payton wasn't one of them. As much as she felt drawn to the approaching self-proclaimed deity, she didn't miss the concern in her friends' words.

Payton started sweating. He was close. She could sense him on every level. She hadn't had a lot of experience with men; there was no time for romance in her life. Her research and strong desire to help others, even to the sacrifice of her personal life, drove her past the insistent drives of her hormones.

But she'd never felt a physical draw to a man like this before. She ground her teeth to keep her eyes from looking up to ravage his face.

The fingers on her wrists tightened.

He even smelled delicious! His very presence was a perfume so heady it threatened to make her swoon. Who was this guy?!

Then it was over. The overwhelming feelings of desire faded as the entourage passed their position. Payton started shaking. The aftertaste of her emotional response made her mouth bitter, and her stomach threatened to leave its contents on the new grass.

"What was that?" she said, her voice low and shaking.

"Shhh!" Jeannie hissed back.

Time seemed to slow down, with seconds turning into hours. Finally, the grips on her wrists lessened. Payton looked up and saw the others getting to their feet. A woman not far in front of them was shrieking and bragging to her friends how she'd licked the Supreme God's feet when he put them under her nose. Payton's nausea intensified.

She might have done the same with the pheromones he was putting out. Whatever the Supreme God of the Earth was, he wasn't human.

Payton grasped Jeannie's chin and turned the trauma nurse's face in her direction.

"I don't know what just happened, but you and me, we're going to talk. Something crazy is going on here, and I need some facts. No one's tempted me to crawl after them on my belly before, and the thought of it gives me heartburn. No more crap. What's going on?"

"Not here," Jeannie whispered. "Come to the edge of the airfield with us to admire the pretty airplane. There are too many ears in this field for my liking. Let's go somewhere where there is more noise or fewer people. Then I'll give you the story."

Payton let her go, but not before wiggling a finger under Jeannie's nose.

"No, you'll give me the truth."

Fate sighed.

Oh, the impetuousness of youth. They always wanted the truth.

Until they received it.

CHAPTER THE ELEVENTH: WELCOME TO THE JUNGLE, WE GOT FUN AND GAMES

November 13, 2099 AD … somewhere in the Amazon

Julia Acampora was the best blockade runner who lived.

No one who knew her would say otherwise, not if they wanted to keep their lips from being crushed by a small, but tough set of knuckles. The slight Brazilian woman flew anything capable of lift. Today it was an ancient Cessna with only enough electronics to make it airworthy. She'd left the windows open because it was a low-level, nap-of-the-earth mission and it was hot in the jungle.

She wore a pair of tan cargo pants jammed into similarly colored jungle boots. Tucked into the pants was a white cotton tank top, which highlighted the golden-brown skin on her slender shoulders and taut arms.

Her long black hair whipped behind her as her dark eyes focused on the terrain flying towards the prop of her plane.

She was short and slender, but her tiny body was perfect for flying. No cockpit was too small.

Her pretty face reflected her gentle disposition unless she was flying to avoid interception by government forces. Like now. Then her white teeth bared in a grimace, which dared gravity to best her as she tortured the airframe with gut-wrenching turns and altitude changes.

She'd always wanted to fly. When she was young, the Air Force said she was too short, even though her situational awareness was exceptional. She had the eyes of a falcon and flew like one. Determined that 'no' was not the right answer, Julia worked every job she could get to pay her way through flight school. She was a natural aviator, with skills far beyond the other students. Even with such talents, few airlines in South America were interested in her until the world fell apart. Her popularity soared when the demand for pilots went up and living bodies went down.

Two things thrust her away from a government job into the murky world of contemptuously treating borders like they were a mere suggestion. The first motivator came when security personnel imprisoned her only brother for daring to share his food with a starving family instead of giving his extra food to them. He died in prison, and Julia swore she would exact revenge.

The second was the moral depravity of the government wanting to seduce her into their clutches. She saw how men treated women in the new world order; women were more often the victim of sexual assaults and sexual harassment than at any other time in history. The treatment of women got worse after the Second Cataclysm. It felt like any spirit of decency left with the millions of people who disappeared.

The most disgusting of all was the government, who emphasized the use of women as sex objects by paying them lavish amounts of money every time they had sex with someone. The men who ran the government were pigs, and she didn't fly for pigs. Julia grinned. She delivered pigs but didn't fly for them. She looked back at the two crates behind her.

Weanling swine filled both. Raised with care and allowed to grow to their full potential, they could feed starving families for a long time.

"Hang on babies," she said in a sweet, accented soprano voice. "This is going to be a rough ride."

Julia snapped the plane onto the right wing and killed power. Barely clearing the canopy of foliage, the plane dove to a short grass runway. She righted the plane and applied enough speed and lift to prevent a stall. The rubber tires hit the turf hard enough to rattle her teeth before she brought the aircraft to a halt. Sweat dripped off her face, but not from any stress associated with the landing.

She grinned.

Piece of cake.

For a few minutes, nothing happened. It was a hot, damp day, discouraging exertion.

Even the wind was listless; when it puffed, it felt like someone blowing their breath in your face. The combined scent of vegetation, moisture, soil, and decaying plants and wood assaulted her nose, but in a good way. Julia took a deep breath of humid air and allowed the rainforest's scent to permeate through her nostrils. She loved the jungle.

The air to the left of her plane seemed to shimmer. To a casual observer, it would've appeared as if the heat and humidity made wave forms dance in empty air, but Julia knew better.

The rebel group, *Las Profesoras*, had stolen a large commercial bolt of MetaMaterials. The shimmering in the clearing was not an atmospheric effect. Rebels in MetaMaterials suits, which made them invisible by wrapping light around them to mimic the surrounding environment, pulled a three-sided MetaMaterials tunnel from the edge of the jungle and in minutes they covered her plane. A drone with heat sensors would have to be sitting right over top of her to get a fix on her location.

No one would see the activities around her Cessna. They'd constructed around her tiny airplane an invisible collapsible hangar big enough to cover a C-130J Super Hercules.

The thought painted a smile on her face, born of fond memories. Julia flew a Herc often. The cargo planes were ancient, decades past their service lives, but they were beasts of burden which didn't understand the meaning of 'quit'. Julia loved them. The four-engine turboprop transport plane could land and take-off from almost any surface on short strips, defying anything but an anti-gravity airship.

Knowing the camouflage could cover something so big made Julia feel as safe as a baby in her mother's arms.

Julia kicked open the cockpit door and jumped out. Even at twenty-six years old, prolonged flights left her feeling stiff. She stretched, enjoying the shade cast by the portable hangar.

The rebels who deployed the hangar removed their MetaMaterials suits and carefully stored them. It was highly illegal to possess such suits, and they were impossible to replace. Especially in the Tribulation period.

All six were women, as Julia expected. Only women were members of *Las Profesoras*, but not by choice. The women had become rebels because the government had imprisoned or killed their men.

Many fought back to secure the freedom of their men, many more fought back for vengeance. Love drove them to become merciless killers.

A light-skinned Colombian woman approached her and sketched a half-salute.

"*Ola*," she said, then in English, "we'll debrief you in the Bunker today. What did you bring us?"

Julia's delicate dark eyebrows twitched. The Bunker! She'd heard of the famed Bunker, but they'd never invited her inside. She felt her pulse quicken. This meant something dangerous, and dangerous meant exciting. Goosebumps ran down her forearms. Julia lived for exciting.

"I brought you piglets. Some will make good breeders and will add to your sustainability. I also have a lot of canned food, with good expiration dates. Be careful of the crates at the back of the plane. There are enough explosives in them to blow a hole in the jungle twice the size of this clearing."

The Colombian nodded and issued rapid-fire orders in Spanish to the rest of her team. Her job done, for the time being, Julia walked toward the edge of the clearing. A third of the way there, she stumbled to a halt.

Two women were walking toward her, dressed in jungle camouflage and slinging automatic weapons over tactical vests. Both were skinny and had long hair. That's where the similarities ended. The woman to her left was petite, maybe five foot three, and weighed about 134 pounds. Her legs may have been shorter than the woman next to her, but she walked with purpose. The woman's slight frame carried her tactical vest and weapons with ease.

Her green eyes flashed in a tiny, delicate face framed by her brown hair, and there was no mistaking her beauty. There was an air about her suggesting steel in her character. One look and you knew this was a woman who understood her mind and wouldn't be afraid to speak it with an acid tongue.

The woman to Julia's right was taller, about five foot six, and had a slightly longer face, with blueish gray eyes framed by dark brown hair. She, too, was beautiful. Her 110-pound body had an aura of wildness, as if her physical form couldn't and wouldn't contain her spirit. Only she beat the drum that danced her feet on the path of life.

Julia drew in a wavering breath.

Nicole Cortés and Mikayla Muñoz.

Las Dos Hermanas.

The Two Sisters, the legendary leaders of *Las Profesoras*. She was being greeted by Colombian royalty, given their fame throughout the region. Julia didn't know what to do; the circumstances tempted her to curtsy.

The two women stopped in front of her, scanning her with intelligent, probing eyes. Nicole spoke first.

"Julia Acampora?"

Not knowing what to do, Julia pressed her palms in front of her and bowed.

"*Sí*, I am her. I must say, it's truly an honor to meet you. I've heard of you for years, and I never would've thought I'd stand in front of you someday."

Mikayla looked down at her sister and grinned.

"Great. A gusher. We haven't had one of those in a while."

Nicole snapped a glare at her younger sister.

"Mikayla! She's a guest, and she won't know you're kidding." Nicole turned her face back to Julia.

"My sister jokes with you. We're happy to meet you too. If you'd like to join us for supper, we have something we'd like to share with you."

Julia flashed a brilliant white smile.

"I'm not easily offended, and I have been known to gush a little. I must say, though, who wouldn't be gushing right now? You two are legends."

Mikayla dug a sharp elbow into her slender sister's side.

"Hear that? I'm a legend. Bet you'd never thought you'd hear someone call me *una leyenda* one day!"

Nicole's eyebrows furrowed together.

"I can think of a few things I'd like to call you

right now. Legend wouldn't be one of them. Will you get serious for two seconds?"

Mikayla rolled her eyes.

"Julia, forgive my sister. She's always too serious. Come with us; we'll take you to the Bunker."

Nicole shook her head.

"We survive each day not expecting to live for the next," she muttered, "and I'm *too* serious?"

Nicole and Mikayla spun on their heels and walked back to the jungle's edge. After pausing, Julia stepped in behind them and puffed out her chest. She wanted to tell the other women unloading her plane she was walking to the Bunker with *Las Dos Hermanas,* but contained herself.

They'd probably laugh at her hero worship.

The path through the confusion of plants was thin and surrounded by thick foliage. It was little used or well concealed; it didn't look like something humans tread upon. The two women in front of her were good in the bush, very good. They brushed the flora and made no sound. Their passage didn't disturb the brightly colored birds, who continued to sing and flutter between the branches as the women slid like ghosts beneath them.

After thirty steaming minutes of winding through the tangle of vegetation, swatting at mosquitoes and keeping a worried eye out for poisonous snakes and spiders, they arrived at a small clearing.

Mikayla stepped out of the jungle, into the clearing, first. She had unslung her automatic rifle and was sweeping it around the clearing. It was an M4A1 assault weapon with a Special Operations Peculiar Modification Version II upgrade, or

SOPMOD II. The weapon intrigued Julia. It was old, having been the favorite of U.S. Special Operations Forces in decades past.

Julia fancied herself a military historian, especially with ancient weapons. She knew the SOPMOD was the accessory system for the M4A1 carbine. The soldier could add or take away things from the frame of the gun to adapt the gun to changing environments. If she needed a certain capability, she could enhance the gun with ease.

Mikayla had modified her weapon for jungle warfare, attaching only those accessories fit for the environment. She outfitted her carbine with a holographic weapon sight, a gun light, a thermal sight, night vision sight, a laser target pointer, and a quick-detach sound suppressor.

Mikayla had flipped the night vision device to one side of the rail. Julia nodded in approval. It was useless in a jungle with an overhead cover and triple canopy. She'd mounted a scope and also rotated it out of the way. Another good move. All the foliage guaranteed a limited range of vision, so a scope was as useful as the night vision device.

The thermal sight she attached to the rail of the carbine was better than an infrared scope. Thermal imaging converts infrared radiation into a visible image, while an infrared scope amplified available light to create a visible picture from the darkness. Thermal sights saw through smoke, fog, and foliage.

The automatic weapon had the most sophisticated accessories… for its time.

Much of the modern combat world had progressed to energy weapons once the weapons manufacturers solved the physics problems. Current assault weapons shot packets of high-energy plasma. The weapons energized a gas (the exact type and nature of the gas was classified) into boiling plasma packets. After encasing the ionized gas into a bolt by using a magnetic field, the conversion energy propelled the plasma packet out of an insulated barrel.

Such guns were short-range weapons because the magnetic field failed and dispersed the ionized gas after one hundred feet. The bolt traveled at between two hundred and three hundred miles per hour. One shot could severely injure a lightly armored enemy.

Energy weapons had advantages over projectile weapons: they weren't heavy and didn't require the fighter to carry copious loads of ammunition.

A tubular module on the gun housed the compressed gas; once emptied, the soldier could swap it out for another module without losing valuable combat seconds. Each module only weighed four ounces. It was easy to see why it had become the modern fighter's weapon of choice.

The conversion to energy weapons had been so fast and complete, most projectile firearms became obsolete overnight. Police forces and criminal organizations went to energy weapons as soon as they could get them, leaving a surplus of lethal projectile weapons lying around in garbage dumps. Even junkers sneered at the archaic guns.

Of course, Julia reminded herself, an obsolete weapon could still kill you dead.

Mikayla walked up to a fair-sized rock buried in plant life and moss.

Her eyes constantly flicked from side-to-side and up-and-down. She kicked the rock twice, paused, and kicked it one more time, all the while keeping her weapon trained on the wild mix of plants, vines, and trees surrounding them. After a few seconds, the floor of the jungle separated and lifted. When it stopped, a five-foot gap separated the six-inch-thick trapdoor from the jungle floor.

Nicole faded into the clearing; her weapon raised in the ready position as she swept the barrel from side to side. She carried a diffcrent automatic weapon, a Heckler & Koch MP7A2, with a flash suppressor on the muzzle. It had custom designed armor-piercing rounds and was perfect for CQB, which Julia understood meant Close Quarters Battle, and jungle warfare. Nicole had fit it with a combo laser/night scope and a forward drum grip filled with ammunition.

When Julia turned her attention back to Mikayla, she saw the younger sister had taken a position behind the rock and was still fanning the barrel of the M4A1 around the jungle.

Nicole took a step back towards Julia.

"Go into the hole," she said in a low tone, just above a whisper. "Mind your feet. It's a vertical tower, with bars for hand grips, and it's dark. At the bottom of the silo, you'll find a dimly lit door. Wait for us there."

Julia didn't hesitate. In six strides, she was at the entrance to the Bunker. She moved the bag slung on her back and trapped it against her stomach. Julia turned around and reached into the maw behind her with her left foot. Once she touched the first rung, she moved down into the silo with a confidence she didn't feel.

Nicole was right. Julia's breathing sped up as she worked her way down the steel rungs. The surrounding darkness was oppressive. The only light was from the glow of her aviator's watch. After what felt like hours, but was only a few minutes, her right foot smacked against the bottom, and she turned around. There was a small alcove to her left, which was dimly lit by a red light. The shape of the fixture reminded her of the interior of a submarine she saw in old holo movies. She shivered. The air was damp and she could taste metal on her tongue.

Julia stepped into the alcove and waited. Soon Nicole, then Mikayla, dropped onto the floor of the shaft. Nicole blew two sharp puffs of air and said,

"Is the hatch secured?"

Apparently satisfied with a response Julia couldn't hear, Nicole pressed her hand on a plate near the red lamp. A series of clicks filled the silo, and the door opened into a well-lit tunnel. The passageway was also lit with red lights encased in metal wires to protect the bulb. It was enough light to see a way for their feet, but not enough to blind them.

Mikayla grinned at Julia, who stared at the passageway with an open mouth.

"Welcome to the jungle," she said. "We've got fun and games."

Julia didn't know it, but Mikayla was quoting the lyrics from a famous rock band known as Guns N' Roses. The pilot was too young to have been a fan of ancient music. The women escorting her down the tunnel should've been too young, as well.

Nicole was thirty-two years old and Mikayla was twenty-nine. Julia knew their ages from their legends.

"This is impressive!" Julia said. "How long has this been here?"

Nicole shrugged and led them down the corridor. It was six feet wide and boarded with thick planks on all four sides. Heavy wood beams, upheld by thick supports, kept the structure intact. It looked like amateurs built it, but the tunnel was too dry and secure for one built of wood in a tropical forest.

"We don't know how long this has been here," Nicole said as she led them down the tunnel. "Mikayla thinks drug runners built it because it's so close to known drug manufacturing clusters and smuggling routes. I think this was a United States Drug Enforcement Agency operation and training facility; the equipment is just too sophisticated for druggies."

"Not for rich druggies with imaginations," Mikayla said, taking up a position at the rear, still holding her assault rifle in the ready position.

Nicole rolled her eyes.

"Billionaire druggies wouldn't build a tunnel deep in the middle of the Amazon, literally next to the capital of Nowhere. There are tons of concrete in this facility. The water tables are so high, it would have taken months to set the cement properly. No way druggies had the time or patience."

"Sez you," Mikayla retorted. "How many drug lord billionaires have you known?"

"The same as you," Nicole snapped. "None!"

The two of them continued to bicker as Julia fought to keep a smile off her lips.

They were sisters, no doubt about it.

Their looks and familial quarreling were deceiving, though. These two delicate women and their forces took down over one hundred and twenty members of the global government's skilled Emergency Response Team, incurring no casualties. They'd liberated an orphanage the government was using as an underaged brothel for their soldiers. Women joined *Las Profesoras* in scores after their husbands and brothers were forced to work for the Antichrist or killed for refusing the call. The reward on the heads of *Las Dos Hermanas* would've allowed a bounty hunter a life of luxury, even in these dark days.

One ignored the threat they represented at his or her peril.

They walked into an open area and Julia felt shock flow through her anew.

New smells crashed into her nose and set her salivary glands ablaze. They were in a cafeteria, and the air was heady with the smells of cooked beef, steamed vegetables, and the other impossibility: coffee. Julia glanced back at the tunnel, then to the large, circular room filled with modern tables, chairs, a textile floor, and a covered well-lit ceiling.

Mikayla laughed.

"It's like looking in a mirror. I had the same look on my face the day we wandered in here."

"How on earth did you find this place?" Julia said, the words framed with awe.

"Through the loading dock," Nicole said. "I won't give you its location, except to say it's where we're taking the supplies from your plane. Mik and I were running from some soldiers who were looking to turn us into their personal whores. I tripped and fell into the side of a tree, but it was an artificial construct with an optical doorway. Maybe whoever ran the place left it open, we don't know. We hid inside the tree until the platoon gave up looking for us."

"Nicole's good with machinery," Mikayla chimed in as they made their way to an empty table. The room was full of women in various states of dress, all of whom were eating from trays of food. "She figured the tree had to be a gate to something. I don't know how, but she opened the door to the loading bay."

Nicole shrugged.

"I got lucky. I'd been punching at a keypad for hours, and I must've hit the unlock sequence. When we found this place two years ago, it was a mess. There was dust everywhere, and whoever bugged out was in a hurry. The hurry worked for us, though. They left behind guns, ammo, explosives, small buggies, and fuel. I'd say no one had been in here for about twenty years."

Mikayla walked to a metal tube protruding from a wall near their table. She put the barrel of her weapon into the tube and made the rifle safe. When she finished, Nicole did the same. They stacked their weapons beside the table and took off their tactical vests. Both sat with a sigh of relief and Mikayla gestured for Julia to join them.

"They'd even stocked a lot of food designed to last forever. Dry goods, canned goods with cryogenic seals, fusion-powered freezers with specially packaged meat. Nothing we've found so far has been freezer burned. There are no vegetables, but we created a hydroponic garden, and some of our women are growing fresh produce for us."

Julia felt her eyebrows go up.

"Not all of you are fighters?"

Nicole laughed, short and abrupt.

"No, but we teach everyone who comes here how to use a gun and we make them shoot in sim combat conditions. We're like the former U.S. Marines; we train even the cooks to pick up a gun and fight if we need them to."

A short, stocky woman approached them with three metal plates balanced on her arms. She distributed them to the three seated at the table and backed away.

Julia closed her eyes and inhaled deeply. Her nose hadn't deceived her.

There was a slab of roast beef on her plate, bordered by peas and a generous scoop of mashed potatoes. She didn't need to carve the meat to see it was real and not 3D printed. The edges of the slice of beef were brown and pink in the middle. No one ate like this anymore. This is how the billionaires must eat every day.

Julia dug into her plate, trying to be as refined as possible, given how long it had been since she'd had such a fine dinner.

"Would you be willing to tell me how the two of you came to be *Las Dos Hermanas*?"

Mikayla stabbed a piece of beef with her fork.

"We made lemonade."

Julia looked at her with a blank expression, as

Nicole shot her sister a glare.

"What my birdbrain sister is trying to tell you is life dealt us a pretty harsh hand, but we made the best of it."

Julia smiled and shoved a delicious piece of meat into her mouth. She chewed with bliss for a few seconds, then said,

"I have nowhere to be if you're willing to share your story."

Nicole frowned.

"There's not much to tell. Mikayla and I were born in the United States. When we were young; I was five…"

"And I was two," Mikayla chimed in.

"And Mikayla was two," Nicole said, flashing her another irritated glance. "Our parents moved to Bogota to set up rural Christian missions. We traveled around Colombia until we were old enough to go to school. We did our grade schools in Bogota. Both of us went to *Universidad Nacional de Colombia* and became schoolteachers."

"Mom and Dad wanted us to become missionaries, too," Mikayla said, "but we weren't as devoted to the faith as they were."

Nicole snorted.

"I'll say. We went into the mission field with our parents to teach math and English to the children in the outlying villages. Don't mistake us, we loved our parents and teaching the children. Our Mom and Dad made a difference in many people's lives. They lived like Christians should live, and we tried to follow their example, but we didn't believe the Gospel message. Not enough to get us raptured on

Easter Sunday, April 24, 2095."

Sadness flitted across Mikayla's face.

"Bad day. At least for us. I had just married Andrés. Nic had been married to Sebastián for a couple of years. We grew up with our husbands, who were our high school sweethearts. In the blink of an eye, Mom and Dad were gone and so was our entire mission team."

"It was just us and our husbands," Nicole said, "which helped to ease our sorrow a bit. It took us a long time to figure out everyone else had been raptured. When we realized it, all four of us dug into Scripture. Revelation scared us to bits. When Contradeum negotiated peace with Israel on November 11, 2095, we knew the seven-year Tribulation started. Then we accepted Jesus as our Savior and committed our souls to Him. For real, this time."

"Have you read the Bible?" Mikayla asked.

Julia nodded, dismayed at how fast the food on her plate had disappeared. It had been a generous portion, and she was full, but her tongue wanted the luxury of tasting more.

"*Verdad.* I was twenty-two years old when my family disappeared. When the First Global Nuclear War happened, I was safe in Santa Fe Antioquia. Do you know it?"

"*Sí,*" Nicole said. "We spent a summer there. It's in northern Colombia, thirty-five miles north of Medellin?"

Julia nodded, her pretty facing holding a wistful expression.

"It's so beautiful, with its whitewashed buildings

and cobblestone streets. King Philip II of Spain gave my village a coat of arms after the Spanish founded it in 1541. I hid out in the Metropolitan Cathedral while atomic bombs destroyed the civilized world. To distract myself, I read the Bible by candlelight. There were lots of them scattered around the church. I started at the back with the Revelation to John because I always enjoyed reading the end of a book first. It took me a long time to decipher what I was looking at, but some other people had been studying *la biblia* and we pieced together what was happening. I gave my life to Jesus then."

Mikayla cleaned off her plate and set it aside. She reached down to her belt and removed a sliver of a dagger. She dug out a morsel of beef stuck in her teeth, while Julia looked at her with wide eyes and shortened breath. Anyone could call themselves a badass, but these two lived it without posturing.

"After the nuclear war," Mikayla said, picking up the story, "the black market changed in Colombia. No one was interested in buying *cocaína* any longer. The cartels scavenged the country for food, building supplies, and medicine for sale on the black market. Their biggest customer, America, was so desperate for the supplies they looked the other way."

"We starved," Nicole said, her voice bitter. "Worse, they pressed people into their gangs. Then the government got involved. Two years ago, the Government of Democracy, what a joke that name was, passed a law mandating all men to join the Food Gatherers Collective. When our husbands refused because they were afraid of what would happen to us, Contradeum threw them into a prison close to here to make them an example."

"We ran," Mikayla said in a whisper, a tear leaking down her cheek. "When they came for us, Andrés and Sebastián distracted them while we fled into the jungle. By the Grace of God, we found this place."

Nicole reached out and covered Mikayla's wrist. Her voice softened as Mikayla blinked away tears.

"When we found this place, it overwhelmed us. We slept and ate for a week before we realized what we had."

"What we had," Mikayla said, drying her eyes as her voice hardened, "was a base of operations. A base with enough weapons to make life very hard for our new enemies."

"But we couldn't do it alone," Nicole said, releasing her sister's wrist. "We knew of many women who suffered the loss of their men as we had. Besides the armory, this place has an indoor training range, three levels down. It's well-ventilated, and it's so deep you can't hear gunfire in the cafeteria. Mik and I learned how to shoot the guns we found."

"The best part is the Tactical Shooting Range. It's huge!" Mikayla said. "We learned how to advance downrange and work our way through a course of fire, blasting both stationary and moving targets. The sims are so lifelike, it's scary. They approach or flee the shooter, cross perpendicular to the shooter's movement, pop up, or pivot. You have to expand your attention to three hundred and sixty degrees, and always engage a broader range of cognitive capacities."

Nicole tilted her head to one side.

"Forgive my sister's enthusiasm. She took to the

tactical range like a duck to water. It's an excellent training ground, though, requiring you to make split-second shoot/don't shoot decisions. We programmed the range to provide urban and jungle warfare shooting environments."

"We spent three months training," Mikayla said. "It was a hard three months because we didn't know what we were doing. The central computer had some holo training manuals on CQB, urban warfare, jungle warfare, night ops, and simpler things like maintaining weapons. Even with all of it, there was a sharp learning curve."

Nicole gestured to the counter at the end of the cafeteria and the server returned with steaming cups of coffee. Julia goggled. Coffee was another luxury only enjoyed by the rich. Julia accepted two milk and two sugars and sipped her coffee with a sigh. She'd found paradise!

Nicole blew on the hot brew and continued.

"We did our first sortie at night, hiking to a nearby village. It had a compound where the government soldiers imprisoned thirty-four women and used them for sex. There were twelve well-equipped soldiers in the garrison, and one officer."

"We killed them all," Mikayla said in a calm voice, though through lips pressed together so hard they turned white. "They'd been partying, I guess. We found them all passed out, too stoned to move. To keep the noise down, we killed them with knives."

Something dark crossed Nicole's face.

"We'd heard many stories growing up about the *corte de corbatas*, used by the old drug cartels. After you cut their throats, you pull their tongues out of the cut line under their jaws and leave them dangling on their necks. Mik and I went a step further. We cut off their balls and stuffed them in their mouths."

No one said anything for a few moments, and Julia felt herself turn a little green. These were such well-spoken, beautiful women. She couldn't imagine them to be so violent.

Mikayla noticed the look on Julia's face.

"Sorry, Julia. Too soon after dinner? Remember, Nic and I were filled with rage. We'd scouted the compound for days and watched what the soldiers did to those poor women. We aren't total monsters. I vomited for hours after we brought the women back here."

"Not me," Nicole said in a grim voice. "The *bastardos* deserved everything we did to them. We've confessed our sins to Jesus and prayed for His forgiveness. This is war, and the things we do in war may not play well on holo news, but it's what we had to do."

Mikayla nodded and wrapped both hands around her mug, as if to close its non-existent ears to the stories.

"The news was one of our greatest allies, Nic. All the news outlets jockeyed for the most graphic reports, all while cautioning the viewer, what they were about to see could be disturbing."

Mikayla laughed, a musical scale of derision.

"Using the Colombian necktie, which we hadn't planned, turned out to be an excellent diversion from the truth. For a long time, the government looked for former drug cartel members they thought were seeking revenge for taking over their operations."

"It gave us time to train our new recruits," Nicole said, sipping on her coffee. "And our new recruits were eager to learn. Our successes lead to greater numbers until we started turning women away out of fear the government would infiltrate a spy. We've reached maximum capacity, and our losses have been minimal."

"We knew we needed a name, something people would talk about and give them hope," Mikayla said. "Nic picked *Las Profesoras* because we'd both been teachers before the Tribulation started. We used to teach children mathematics, science, and language arts. Now we teach Contradeum he might think he's the god of this world, but he's not omnipotent and omnipresent. It's true we've only hurt him in this part of the globe, but we *have* hurt him, and that's what counts."

Julia expelled a long breath.

"I've heard of your operations. It's why I started running contraband to you. I wanted to help as much as I could."

Nicole propped her small chin on her right hand.

"Put a pin in that thought. Our primary goal when we started this was to free our husbands and everyone else stuck in the dump they call *La Prisión de los Fieles*, or the Prison for the Faithful for our Anglo-only friends. We have a plan to free all the prisoners from that horrible place. A plan we want you to be part of."

Julia caught her breath as her eyes widened. *Las Profesoras* wanted her! The implications raced through her mind as adrenaline surged through her body.

She couldn't speak for the space of four heartbeats. Then she forced her lips to move again.

"I am honored, *Señoras*. I'm not a fighter, though. How could I possibly help you?"

Las Dos Hermanas shared a glance, then a grin.

"We've heard a lot about you, Julia," Mikayla said softly. "About your skills in the air and your talent for flying anything. It's why we agreed to have you fly our supplies. You've never failed us."

One corner of Mikayla's mouth turned up as Nicole sunk the hook.

"How would you like to fly an F-35B fighter jet and bomb the hell out of some bad guys?"

CHAPTER THE TWELFTH: LOOK, THE BETRAYER COMES

Atlantis, November 13, 2099 AD

Hart sat, his spine stiff, in the plush armchair, willing himself to breathe in slow, measured breaths. Killian Hunter, the Chief Priest to the Supreme God of the Earth, had permitted him an audience. It surprised Hart to get this far, and his arteries pulsed with excitement. This was the first step toward getting past the torture of his PTSD. The first step toward vengeance.

He'd expected his request for an audience to be rejected. No one else on this stinking island had bothered to give him the time of day when he complained about the symptoms torturing him. Dr. Sullivan gave him medications and offered him suggestions from lessons learned from his time on a SEAL Team, but nothing worked.

Every night, Hart lost more sleep.

It was time to take things into his own hands, become the master of his destiny.

He was in the reception area of Korhonen's office, although characterizing it as an office was beyond gracious. The construction gorillas did the best they could with what they had, but it was still an oversized construction trailer they'd renovated on the inside with new tech. It smelled of cheap plastic, air fresheners designed to mimic a pine forest, and a lingering odor of grease. Korhonen had heaped lavish praise on the workers and gushed about how they made her workspace *avant garde*. It made Hart want to puke.

The minute Contradeum's jet landed, Hart had approached one of his functionaries. "I have a message for the Supreme God of the Earth," he'd said, and dropped one word as a teaser: "Tul'ran." For the first forty-five minutes, nothing. Then the functionary returned and said the Chief Priest would grant him an audience. Hart felt like he hadn't breathed for the entire time he'd waited.

Korhonen's assistant had an office behind a featureless tan-colored wood door. There were no windows in the office, and the door appeared solid. Hart knew better. One-way imagers were the surfaces of the walls and door. To the person inside the office, it would look as if the wall didn't exist.

His bladder reminded him it'd been a few hours since he voided, while his stomach grumbled over the sparse calories he'd consumed today. The wait made him irritated, and he fought against his rising impatience. This needed to go well.

The door cracked open, and Hart leaped to his feet. The Chief Priest stepped into the hallway and made an imperious gesture. Hart followed him into the assistant's office. The Chief Priest sat across from Hart and they stared at each other.

"You mentioned a name," the Chief Priest said. He spoke in a low rumble. "How do you know it?"

Hart cleared his throat. He couldn't bring himself to look the other man in the face. Something about him, his eyes maybe, something wasn't right. The air in the small room had a lingering odor of rotten eggs, which was much worse than the reception room smells. The Chief Priest's skin was a dull gray. For the oddest reason, Hart had the sense he was staring at two men. He shook his head. 'Too tired,' he thought; 'now I'm hallucinating.'

"I went on a Time Mission with orders to kill a barbarian named Tul'ran az Nostrom. I don't know how, but he avoided getting hit by two shots I fired right into his face. Granted, my weapon was an obsolete handgun; even so, I shouldn't have missed. Next thing you know, I have a sword sticking out of my chest, courtesy of a fellow time traveler! I've been suffering with PTSD since the mission and no one here can help me. I came to plead for help from the Supreme God of the Earth."

The being who was no longer Killian Hunter frowned.

"The gifts of the Supreme God are not free," he said, his voice rasping over the consonants. "His miracles are pricey. What do you offer him?"

"Offer him?" Hart's voice was incredulous. "I thought he was a kind and loving god? Since when do miracles cost anything?"

The Chief Priest's voice turned oily as he lowered his eyelids to slits.

"Perhaps you are thinking of the false god worshipped by the Christians. Are you a Christian, Mr. Hart?"

Hart's face blanched, as fear put a vise to his throat.

"No! No! Of course not!"

Hunter's smile was a thing of ancient obscenity, obscured by a darkness which had forgotten the purity of light.

"You had me worried, Mr. Hart. When you spoke of free miracles, I thought you sought the Enemy of the Earth, who plagues us with catastrophes. It would've been unfortunate to crucify you on Atlantis in front of your coworkers."

Hart shuddered. This was the new and government-approved way of getting rid of Christians. He'd watched a public crucifixion on the holo news. The convicts suffered for days before succumbing to the excruciating pain. There was no way he'd ever become a Christian and endure such a death.

"I apologize if I've offended you, Your Holiness. What can I offer you and the Supreme God for a miracle of healing?"

G'shnet'el, the evil angel inhabiting Killian Hunter's body, leaned back into his chair.

"If you were to contribute, say, one hundred thousand bitcoins to the temple's coffers, I could persuade the Supreme God to intercede for you."

One hundred thousand bitcoins!

Hart's stomach fell. He was short by five thousand bitcoins, and it would mean purging his life's savings. Even if he sold his meager possessions, it wouldn't be enough. His mouth was dry, as was his throat, but Hart was terrified by the cost of asking for a glass of water.

"Uh, I don't have that much. Could we reduce the price if I could deliver Tul'ran to you?"

The Chief Priest's eyebrows arched, lending his face a demonic look. He folded his hands across his chest and stared at the sweating bald man seated in front of him.

"You can deliver Tul'ran az Nostrom? How?"

Hart's tongue darted through his cracked lips.

"I know someone close to Tul'ran; someone who Tul'ran would want to rescue. With my help, we could trap Tul'ran and you could kill him."

G'shnet'el stared at Hart through Hunter's eyes. Hart squirmed as the cold, fish-eyed gaze wormed its way into his soul.

"Your offer intrigues me, Mr. Hart. Of course, I can do nothing without the Supreme God's blessing. Why don't you rest here for a few minutes while I get some instructions?"

G'shnet'el stood up and made an imperious gesture he presumed resembled something religious and walked out of the room. Two quick steps led him to the door of Korhonen's office, which he jerked open without regard for social niceties, like knocking.

Satan looked up and stared at G'shnet'el out of Contradeum's eyes. Korhonen was kneeling in front of Satan, with her back to him and facing the door.

He stood over her, pressing the fingertips of each hand against her temples. Both were fully clothed. Korhonen had a smile of deep ecstasy on her face as she stared at nothing. Her body stiffened, and she gasped, before settling back into suspended bliss.

"What is it?" Satan asked, his voice mild, which was unusual for him. The process of reconnecting to and taking over the Administrator's brain required concentration and effort.

G'shnet'el bowed his head and gestured with one hand to his feet.

"Forgive me, master, but I have news in which you will be most interested."

Satan stared at him for a long minute, then nodded.

"One moment while I finish resetting my slave's brain." Satan put his palms on each side of Korhonen's head. "I have linked you to me, Marjatta Korhonen. You are my property for eternity. Take pleasure in the joy of your bondage. Let this moment carry you to our next meeting. Appreciate my gifts. Excitement. Lust. Frenzy. Feel the buildup of erotic desire coursing through your body. Experience the endless relief of the release of your lust."

Korhonen's back arched and she screamed as her body shuddered while her brain bathed in a powerful flood of dopamine and oxytocin. Satan released her, and she slumped to the floor, unconscious. He nodded to his lieutenant.

"She'll be like this for several hours while my programming sets in her mind. We can talk freely."

G'shnet'el sneered at the useless human and gestured toward the door.

"There is a man named Hart in the anteroom who says he can trap Tul'ran az Nostrom and bring him within our grasp. If that's still your wish, master."

Satan grinned wickedly. He kicked Marjatta to ensure she was in a stupor and nodded.

"I've not forgotten my longing to regain my sword. Bring in this fool who claims the power to capture my enemy. Let's test his claims before we burn a mark on his arm and cast him loose."

Payton stood on the flight line with the Sullivans and the Davis's. They stared at the large, triangular plane hovering in front of them. It worked on antigravity propulsion. The people who constructed it built the frame of the plane around a circular ball so big it domed above the top surface of the plane and below the bottom. One designer called it the 'bubble' and the name stuck.

The bubble generated a field which neutralized gravity and manipulated it to provide unbelievable thrust and maneuverability. It also kept the components of the plane together; if the drive failed, the plane would split in half longitudinally, from nose to tail. The bottom portion of the bubble hovered inches off any surface over which it focused the field, maintaining stability. It was a marvel of engineering.

"We're here," Payton said, keeping her voice low. "Let's have it. Contradeum creeped me out eight ways from Sunday and you seem to know why. What gives?"

After a moment of silence, Jeannie cleared her throat.

"Payton, I'm happy to answer your questions, but you need to understand something first. The answers you seek are punishable by death. For you and for us. Are you willing to keep our secret, knowing the authorities could kill you for having it?"

Payton chewed on her lower lip, and her eyebrows drew together.

"Well, you've scared me, if that's what you were trying to do. Still, I need to know. I'll keep your secret. What are you, Christians, or something?"

"No, not or something," Jeannie said, with grim lines drawn on her face, "Christians, exactly."

Payton drew a sudden deep breath, then silently ordered her legs to stop shaking.

"All of you?" she whispered through a dry throat.

"All four of us," Heather said with emphasis. "Are you sure you want more? You already have enough on us to get us nailed to the cross on the hill."

The five of them turned their heads to look at the top of the rise where Payton had conducted Mick and Heather's marriage ceremony. It was bare, except for a wooden cross planted in the middle of the highest part. The government intended it as a stark reminder of the consequences of choosing Christianity instead of worshipping the Supreme God of the Earth. Payton shuddered.

"It's hideous. I've studied the horrible things crucifixion does to the body. It's a terrible way to die."

"It's the way we'll die," Jeannie said in a soft voice, "if you tell anyone we're Christians. You'll have to pronounce us dead and autopsy our bodies."

Payton turned to her trauma nurse, her eyes flashing.

"That's a cruel thing to put in my head!"

Jeannie's lips whitened as she flattened her lips.

"It's a cruel way to kill Christians! Think about what we're saying, Payton. If you listen to us, you could hang up there, too. You have a choice between only two things: taking the mark and binding your worship to the man who creeped you out a few minutes ago, or accepting Christ into your life and risk hanging from a cross. There's no gray in today's world. Choose one or the other, that's it."

Payton looked back at the cross, which sent a long shadow down the side of the hill. She shuddered.

"I feel sick to my stomach."

Sully stepped around his wife and stood in Payton's face.

"You don't have to do this, Dr. Dumont. You can walk away and just go with the flow like everyone else around you. They don't care about the consequences of their decisions and the government wants the same for you. They want you to accept what they say as the truth, without question. You can close your mind and your eyes, if you like. If you choose everyone else's path, we beg you to close your mouth to what we've told you as well."

Sully stepped back into place, and they went back to studying the plane in silence. Payton noticed birds wouldn't come near the plane. Sea gulls flew toward the massive black object, but veered away long before they came close. The gulls weren't shy; they were always looking for a handout. She wondered if it was safe for them to be there.

"Does anyone know whether the Indira Inbari Anti-Gravitational Engine gives off toxic radiation?"

Mick laughed, with bitterness lingering in the echo of it.

"In less than three weeks, we've lived through earthquakes, volcanic eruptions, burning hailstones, a comet striking the earth, and tsunamis. One third of the ocean is dead, as is one third of the green and living things on land. Many people don't have water to drink because the comet poisoned a third of the fresh water supply in the entire world. The sun is one-third dimmer, as is the moon, and we no longer see a third of the stars in the sky. Are you really worried about this thing giving us cancer at this point?"

Payton ducked her head, and her cheeks reddened.

"When you put it that way… in fact, when you put it that way, it makes me realize how much I want answers." She took another deep breath. "Okay. Regardless of what comes, I need to know. What's going on?"

Mick broke the ensuing silence.

"Have you read the Bible, Payton?"

The trauma surgeon shook her head.

"Never, not once."

Her answer made Mick's head jerk back.

"Then this will take a while. We can't stay here too long before we look suspicious, and we can't speak in our quarters because they're all bugged."

Payton whipped her head around to stare at him.

"They're bugged?!"

"Shhh!" Jeannie said, her tone soft but urgent.

"Keep your voice down, dear, or you're going to get us shot."

Payton swallowed and glanced behind her. No one in the melee seemed to pay attention to them, but it meant little when electronic surveillance was so prevalent.

"Sorry."

"I'm going to give you a summary version of the Bible," Mick said, "and we can give you a copy of one to read. Some of it will sound unbelievable, but just hear me out. You might have questions, which we need to save for another time when we can speak without fear of being overheard. For now, open your mind and just accept the possibility everything I'm saying is true."

Payton nodded and did as he asked. She opened her mind and let it absorb his words as he spelled out the world's creation and the human descent into evil and disobedience to their Creator. Mick summarized God's continuous attempts to win the hearts and minds of His children, culminating in the birth, ministry, death, and resurrection of His Son. He told her about the Rapture of the Church, and how the Bible prophesied events leading to where they stood in time. A Bible written thousands of years in the past by people who were not nearly as educated as the scholars of her era predicted this exact future.

It was hard to hear and sometimes hard to believe, including the part about Jesus being born to a virgin and rising from the dead. She was a physician; heck, she graduated from Harvard Medical School and took her residency at John Hopkins. What Mick said defied every piece of medical literature she'd studied.

And yet.

Payton remembered the feeling she had when Contradeum, or according to Mick, Satan, had walked by her. The pull to want to follow him and enjoy every temptation he offered had been overpowering.

She'd never given thought to whether anything happened after death. If what Mick said was true, there was life after death. Where you spent your eternal life depended on the choices you made about Jesus while you were alive. But if she chose Jesus, she might as well put a knife to her throat.

What nudged her in that direction were her friends. The thoughts she'd had about them, about their kindness and generosity, about their love for one another, made sense. Who did she want to be? A beautiful person whom others loved for her kindness, or the woman who bragged about licking Satan's foot when he shoved the dirty thing under her nose?

Mick's description of an eternity burning in the flames of Hell scared her witless.

"Mick, are you serious? If I don't accept Jesus as my Savior, are you really telling me when I die, God will throw me in a lake of fire forever? How could a loving God do such a thing?"

Heather answered for him after darting a glance around them to make sure no one was taking an interest in their conversation.

"Payton, it's true God loves us with a passion we'll never have or understand. He's also a just God. Remember how Mick said people used to sacrifice animals for the forgiveness of sin? Sin is so bad in

God's eyes, only shedding the blood of an innocent lamb can remove our sin debt and open a channel for God's forgiveness."

"As serious as sin is," Jeannie said, "God the Father is more serious about saving us from it. It's why He sent Jesus to take on the form of both God and Man. Jesus never sinned; He was pure when falsely accused by the Sanhedrin. He willingly went to the cross as a blood sacrifice for the sins of every human being who believes in Him."

"Who believes in Him?" Payton said, her voice cracking. "You get a ticket to Heaven and avoid the fires of Hell just by believing in Jesus?"

"'For God so loved the world,'" Sully quoted softly, "'He gave His only begotten Son, that whosoever believeth in Him shall not perish, but have everlasting life.' Believing in Him means believing in the virgin birth, believing He was the Son of God, and believing He went to the cross, sinless, to save you from your sins. He died, rose from the dead, and went to Heaven to sit at the Father's right hand. Believing in him means turning away from your sinful life and trying to live like He lived. You have to believe it all in order to 'believe in Him' and gain eternal life."

The silence stretched longer. They'd have to leave soon, or someone would come around and interrogate them. It was hard to breathe. Payton knew what she wanted to say, but it felt like the air became too thick to inhale and allow it to flow around her vocal cords.

The island smelled bad, she thought, as foreign concepts screeched around her brain like bats. The smell was like rotten eggs or sulfur. Maybe the stench of Hell followed the Beast as he walked the Earth.

Payton looked down at her wrists. Soon, the government would force her to wear the mark if she had any desire to eat and keep her freedom.

Freedom for what, though? A descending spiral into slavery and eternal damnation? She told Mick she'd keep an open mind to the possibilities. Well, one possibility was that he was wrong.

But what if he wasn't wrong? There were worse things coming, he said. Most of the population of the Earth could die. By this time next year, her physical body could be gone. Where would her soul live? In Heaven, with God? Or in Hell, where people burned and suffered for millions and millions of years?

There was more than one way to get to belief, she decided then. Fear was a powerful motivator. She took a deep breath. It didn't help.

"What do I do?" she said, after firming up her courage.

Heather took her left hand, and Jeannie took her right.

"Repeat the Sinner's Prayer after me, in your mind," Jeannie said, "feeling it with your whole heart: Lord Jesus, I believe You are the Son of God. You were born of a virgin, Mary, and You became Man. I believe You died on the cross to save me from my sins, that You rose from the dead, and ascended to Heaven. Lord, I accept Your sacrifice for my sins and Your gift of eternal life. Right now, I confess I've sinned against You and I ask you to forgive all my sins. Over the days and years I have left in this life, please open my mind to the wrongs I have committed against You so I can ask You for your forgiveness. I turn my back on my sins, and I will walk toward You in repentance."

Payton had dropped her chin to her chest and whispered the prayer of salvation as Jeannie spoke, so they could hear her confession of faith. When she finished praying, she looked up.

"I don't feel any different."

The other four smiled.

"Some people, when they pray for salvation, feel a rush of warmth as the Holy Spirit enters them," Jeannie said, as tears creased the corners of her eyes. "But many people don't. You are no less saved because you don't feel any different, dear."

"That's Dr. Dear to you," Payton said, looking for and getting another laugh.

Mick turned and gestured toward the Food Court.

"Let's go. Security is noticing us. Payton, you'll have lots of questions, and we'll answer them for you. Just don't talk to anyone else but us and stay away from where Security can monitor your conversations. It's a tall order, but we'll tell you more. Be patient, please, and know you're on the right path."

E'thriel gathered in his massive wings as the five humans walked away from the plane. He'd stood behind them, unseen, for the entire conversation, shielding them with his wings and keeping them away from prying eyes and ears, human and otherwise. No one in either the physical or spiritual realm overheard their conversation.

They were on their own after this. What he did

was borderline interfering, but the Father had sanctioned it, and that was good enough for this angel of the Lord.

———————✝———————

A former angel of the Lord sat on a tall chair, appearing as if he had reposed on a throne. Hart kneeled in front of him, his heart hammering in his chest. The dark angel's power flowed over him in ebony waves of despair and promises of certain doom. Hart feared urinating in his pants as his insides quailed.

"You seek a miracle from me?" the gravelly voice rumbled from the chair.

Hart swallowed and tried to speak, but the words wouldn't come. He shook his head, feeling panic rising in his chest.

"Y-y-yes, lord," he stammered. "I have PTSD and only you can save me."

Satan cut him off with a sharp gesture.

"The Chief Priest has informed me of how you acquired this condition. Tell me, Mr. Hart, what will you give me if I choose to heal you?"

"I'm offering you Tul'ran az Nostrom," Hart gasped, "whom I'll deliver alive for questioning. I know how to trap him. Heal me and he's yours."

Satan scowled, and the light in the room seemed to darken.

"Remove all your pain for one puny human? You would honor my gift with so little?"

Sweat streamed from Hart's armpits, and from his forehead down into his face. His breaths came in short, fast bursts.

"No, no, whatever you want. Tell me what you

want and I'll give it to you!"

The chuckle coming from the chair raised the hair in Hart's arms.

"That's more like it. I'll tell you what I want; I want you, Erasmus Hart. You shall give me your service; you will be bound to me for all eternity. In short, Mr. Hart, I want your soul."

"You have it," Hart blurted out, as urine trickled down his leg. "I give it to you. Just help me."

Satan leaned forward and stretched out his arms.

"Come here, my child. Ah, that's right. Put your head in my hands. You will feel my energy coming into your mind. Don't resist it. Yes, yes, there it is. I'm removing every memory you had of the event which has caused you so much pain. You'll never have another nightmare again. Tell me, my child, will you accept my mark?"

A curious warmth filled Hart's mind. The lingering panic faded, and his brain felt calm. He'd been so upset before he came into this room. What had he been upset about? He couldn't remember, but the inability to recall didn't panic him. He belonged to this god. Nothing would harm him ever again.

"Of course, I will accept your mark, master, but I thought an accident sent the machines to the bottom of the ocean."

The smile from the being on the chair was putrid.

"How fortunate it is for you I've brought six machines with me. It's the newest version; a portable cuff. No longer needed is the chair attached to it. Killian, get the Mark Machine for Mr. Hart."

Hart felt somewhat uncomfortable when no one

moved.

"Killian, get the Mark Machine."

Again, no one moved.

Satan picked up a large mug in his left hand and flung it at Hunter. It missed Hunter's head by inches and smashed against the wall.

"Chief Priest, you are Killian, you idiot!"

Abashed, G'shnet'el scurried out of the room. He'd forgotten the name of the human body he occupied. Again. Minutes later, he returned with a large blue cuff made of polished metal. He pressed the keys to open the device, then wrapped it around Hart's right wrist. The device closed, then green lights lit along the length of it, except for one. Only one stubbornly remained red.

Satan ground his teeth, his powerful façade slipping.

"What's taking so long, Priest?"

G'shnet'el keyed the cuff to re-open, checked the interior, and closed it. The start-up sequence ran through its self-check and stopped again on the last light.

"Well?" Satan roared.

"I'm sorry, master," G'shnet'el said as fast as he could get out the words. "The unit is functioning in a normal way, but it can't connect with the Global Database. It can't access Mr. Hart's information to download it to his flesh."

Satan drew a long breath.

"Hart, leave us. I will send the Chief Priest out to reception soon and you two can arrange the details of how you will deliver Tul'ran az Nostrom to me."

Hart stood up, bowed, his face caught in a portrait

of bliss, and sauntered out of the room, oblivious to the stain in his pants. Satan's face turned gray and his body seemed to sag. The power emanating from him dimmed, and the muscles of his face slackened.

"Check the machines before we leave, G'shnet'el. All of them. If they are all malfunctioning, I will whip the skin off the back of the stupid human who designed and manufactured this batch. I am sick of being surrounded by incompetent fools!"

Satan sank back into the chair as if his bones had become liquid.

"How do you fare, master?" G'shnet'el said, guarding his tone, expecting a fit of rage to accompany the malfunctioning machine.

Satan closed his human eyes.

"When I was in my angelic form, I had power beyond imagining. This body died, G'shnet'el. I had to beg our Enemy for the knowledge how to enervate it again. He didn't bother to tell me the cost. The power it takes to remind each cell in this useless form, each second of the day, that it's alive is exhausting. When Contradeum lived in this flesh, his spirit kept his body healthy and well. I don't know how Jesus managed this when he lived on Earth."

Jesus managed it because he was God, G'shnet'el didn't say out loud. He shook his head back to the present.

"Master, is it possible you task yourself too much? Why not abandon this body and resume your angelic form?"

Satan struck out with blinding speed and smashed Killian Hunter's body against the wall.

"Fool! G'shnet'el, don't you think I would've

done so if it were an option? Idiot! I asked the Enemy to bind me to this form so I could rule the Earth in a human body. There must be some reason He created men and women like this. I wanted to experience a man's powerful physique for myself. Except it has no power! Without a spirit and a soul, this frame is a useless hunk of meat. I can't leave this pathetic flesh until the end of the Age. Or until I can escape this planet. How are the preparations coming for Pulchra's invasion?"

G'shnet'el felt pain. He hated the human body as much as his master did and resented having Satan inflict agony on him. His right fist knotted. Some day he would get payback.

"The invasion plans go well, master, but we need TTI's device to make it work. I've arranged the forces we'll need to take their world and make it ours. The Pulchrans will never see it coming and they won't stand a chance."

Marjatta Korhonen rose to her feet, her eyes dreamy. It was so wonderful to serve the Supreme God of the Earth. He was the fulfillment of her every desire. She was all his, and she'd serve him in every delicious capacity. There were some capacities she was desperate to serve him in, but he'd not made any advances in such a direction. Disappointment pinged in her soul. Perhaps she should go ask him why they'd not consummated their marriage. Yes, that's what she'd do. Right now.

Her chrono told her hours had passed since she was in his presence. She must have slept. Why else would she feel so rested, so refreshed, so good!

Marjatta stepped out of her office and looked toward the airstrip. The plane was gone! Her mind wailed with despair. The Supreme God left without saying goodbye.

Marjatta turned and stomped toward the commissary. Her stomach felt hollow, and she craved sustenance. Food would fill the emptiness she felt within now that her lord had taken off without her. The last thought sizzled in her brain like acid. A woman walked toward her, then plucked at her sleeve. Marjatta jerked her arm away.

"What do you want?" she snarled.

The woman's eyes widened.

"Administrator, are you well?"

"Of course I'm well! What's the matter with you? Are you well? How dare you interfere with my duties?"

The woman pursed her lips.

"Administrator, don't you recognize me? I'm your trauma surgeon, Dr. Payton Dumont."

"Yes, yes, of course," Marjatta said, her voice flowing on a rising tide of irritation. "What do you want, Doctor?"

"Why, only to administer the diagnostic test you requested, Administrator. May I do so now?"

Marjatta growled deep in her throat.

"Will it take long? I don't have time if it will take long."

The woman smiled, soft and sweet.

"Not at all, Administrator. May I proceed?"

Marjatta rolled her eyes, then nodded her assent.

The kick to her temple caught her completely off guard and knocked her out cold.

CHAPTER THE THIRTEENTH:
AIDING AND ABETTING

The Kingdom of Heaven

"Bring forth Abaddon!"

The command rumbled through the Kingdom of Heaven like the roar of a waterfall. It raced through the great chasm separating Heaven from the Abyss and found its way to one of the dark realm's dimmest corners. The great angel chained to the rock lifted his head. For the first time in what seemed like forever, hope filled his black eyes.

Abaddon pulled himself off the rock and stood as upright as he could under the chains. He watched in amazement as the heavy links turned to powder and cascaded from his body. He stretched his black wings out as far as they could reach and ruffled them. Then he didn't know what to do.

Was someone supposed to come and fetch him?

"Abaddon."

He turned at the sound of Jesus's voice, but didn't see Him standing there.

"Yes, my Lord?"

"Come up here."

Abaddon arched his wings and slapped them down, causing dust and debris to explode away from him. He rocketed away from the Abyss and transitioned the void at a speed which would have left an observer breathless. He approached the Kingdom of Heaven and slowed. Odd. There were no angels guarding the edge of Heaven, and there was a clear path to the Throne of God. He paused, hovering and marveling at how quiet it was.

"Come up here."

Abaddon landed in Heaven and walked across the Sea of Glass. This area, normally quite full of humans and angels, was empty. He ascended the stairs to the Throne Room, feeling wary and uncertain. When he arrived at the top of the stairs, he threw himself down and covered his face with his wings.

"Here am I, Lord."

Abaddon stayed in the position until a hand reached through his feathers and cupped his chin. The hand lifted his head, and he stared into the face of Jesus.

"Let's take a walk."

Abaddon stood up, towering over Jesus's much smaller body. The angel knew how deceiving appearances could be, especially with his Lord. He didn't have to see Jesus's supreme power to know it was there.

The two of them descended the stairs and walked back to the edge of Heaven. As they walked, Jesus put His arm around the giant angel's back.

"How have you been, My friend?"

His friend? The phrase shocked Abaddon so much, he almost fell over.

"I have suffered, Lord, but it was not more than I deserved for what I did on Spes. I apologize, Lord Jesus, for my sins in that world. How far did I fall? I fell so far I'm no longer worthy of being called Your friend."

Jesus chuckled.

"The beauty of being God is, no one can challenge My choice of friends. Be at peace for this time. I brought you here because the task for which I created you must come to pass."

They arrived at the edge of Heaven, and the Earth swam below them. Abaddon suffered his second shock. The planet was no longer a shiny blue marble hung in the majestic tapestry of space. The atmosphere was a dull tan color, and angry, reddish-brown clouds obscured the ground in many places.

"Much has changed since you last beheld this world, Abaddon."

Abaddon looked down at his Lord and studied His face.

"The changes have filled you with great sadness, Lord."

Jesus nodded and gestured the angel toward two benches, one sized for a human and the other sized for the angel firstborn of the Heavenly host. How interesting. Abaddon had seen such benches before; people on Spes had crafted them.

Being invited to sit with Jesus was Abaddon's third shock of the day.

"You are right, My friend. The people My Father and I created and placed upon this world fill Me with great sadness. Time and time again I've called out to them, begging them to invite Me into their hearts and repent of their sins. Time and time again, most of them refused. It will soon be time for the next trumpet judgment, Abaddon. Their refusal to accept Me means I must unleash you upon the Earth."

Abaddon nodded, his face thoughtful.

"This, too, saddens you, Lord Jesus."

A glimmer of a smile hovered on Jesus's lips.

"You were ever the observant one. Do you remember the time you fished Me out of the creek after I fulfilled My desire to see fish up close?"

A smile flickered on Abaddon's face.

"I know I was supposed to leave You to your own devices, but You were only seven years old, Lord. It was Your first time in the water, and I feared for You. If I acted in haste, I apologize."

Jesus leaned back on his bench and sighed.

"You acted like My friend. I didn't have many of those before I started My ministry. You performed many other kind acts for Me, which no one observed. I saw them all. I tell you the truth; when you stand before My Father in judgment someday, I will stand at your side and plead for mercy because of the kindness and love you showed to Me."

Abaddon bowed his head.

"Lord, I don't know what to say. Your words overwhelm me. I will accept whatever judgment the Father imposes upon me, but I would be grateful for

Your intercession. Is my time in the Abyss over?"

Hope tinged the edges of the last question.

Jesus smiled.

"It is." His face darkened. "But you will now bring the Abyss to Earth, and many of My children will suffer for it. Behold, I am sending them a final warning before the Fifth Trumpet sounds."

Atlantis, November 13, 2099 AD

Her head hurt abominably.

Marjatta could feel the blood vessels in her brain pound and tried to focus on how she ended up on her back. She remembered going into her office to talk to Contradeum, then nothing. She flickered her eyelashes to the slightest opening, then quickly shut them again. It was still light out, and the light sent shards of pain into her abused nerve endings.

"Marjatta, can you hear me?"

Payton's voice sounded like a clash of cymbals in her ears, though she'd whispered the question.

"I can hear you, Payton," Marjatta said, the words coming out in a croak from her dry throat. "What happened?"

Marjatta heard her trauma surgeon blow out a sigh of relief.

"The condensed version is you met with the Supreme God of the Earth and came out acting like a stoned bitch."

Marjatta barked out a laugh and regretted it right away.

"How did I end up on the ground with a throbbing headache?"

After a pregnant pause, Payton sighed again.

"When the earthquake struck months ago, your head hit a tree, and you lost consciousness. After you came to, you were yourself again. As you came out of your meeting this time, you walked around like you'd smoked cocaine and drank mean juice. I thought it was necessary to recalibrate your consciousness."

Marjatta cracked open one eye and looked up at the young woman's concerned face.

"How did you do that?"

Payton squinched her forehead and folded her lips inward before she answered.

"I kicked you in the head."

Marjatta bit back another laugh and closed her eyes. Whatever Contradeum did to her whenever she met him took total control of her brain. She had to stop meeting him in person, or Payton was going to give her brain damage. Steeling herself against the pain, she opened her eyes.

"Can you help me up, Payton?"

As Payton helped Marjatta struggle to her feet, the Davis's, and the Sullivans walked over to them. Jeannie took one of Marjatta's elbows as she tottered briefly.

"What happened?" Jeannie said, hooking a look at Payton.

Marjatta opened her mouth to answer, but the words never left her throat. A bird screamed in the sky above them; the intensity and volume of the cry just about dropped everyone to the ground. They looked up to see a massive eagle flying at a great altitude. When it screamed again, they could hear words in its cry.

"Woe, woe, woe to those who dwell on the earth, because of the remaining trumpet blasts of the three angels who are about to sound!"

The eagle flew away from them, screaming the same words, and no one said anything until it faded from sight.

Marjatta shook her head, being careful to make the gesture a gentle one.

"This is going to sound crazy, but I think I heard the bird talk."

"You're not crazy," Heather said. "We all heard it."

"As impossible as it sounds," Sully said, "the bird warned us about the next judgment we're going to face." He shuddered. "How bad will it be if the birds are giving us warnings in English?"

"Not just English," Heather said. "I heard it in Mandarin and English. The eagle was speaking a universal language for all people. It's warning us about what's coming."

Marjatta leaned against Payton and held her stomach.

"Payton, can you give me something for my nausea? How hard did you kick me in the head? Do I have a concussion?"

"You kicked her in the head?" Mick said, his voice so loud it caused people nearby to stop talking about the eagle and look at them.

"Not so loud, please. My head hurts," Marjatta said. "Remember how I acted when I got back from Rome right after Contradeum came back from the dead? Yes? Everyone's nodding, good. Well, after I saw him again today, he slammed me back in the same head space. Apparently, introducing a state of unconsciousness is the only way to get me out of it."

Sully rolled his eyes and stepped in front of Marjatta.

"I'm going to cover up your eyes, Administrator, and then uncover them one at a time to exam the response of your pupils. Good. Follow my fingertips with your eyes as I move them up and down, and side to side. Stick your tongue out. I don't know if you have a concussion, but there's no symptomatology indicative of greater brain trauma. We'll scan you right away to make sure."

He glared at Payton.

"In the meantime, let's find another way to get you out of your dissociative state, other than a blow to the head. We'll help you to the Infirmary."

Marjatta planted her feet and stiffened her back.

"No. I need to know what I've gotten into. The four of you always talk like you have answers, or like you know what's coming next. I want to know what happened to me. I want to know what kind of 'woe' is coming? You need to tell me."

No one said anything. The dim sun made the air cooler than normal for this time of year. People around them were still buzzing about the words spoken by the eagle, and arguments broke out about whether it had happened. Some were saying it was a holo created as a joke. Others suggested it was a divine warning, which devolved into accusations that the speaker was a Christian. A scuffle broke out, and people stepped in to separate them.

Mick gestured towards the scrum.

"Administrator, we can answer your questions, but in private. See their reactions to the slightest hint of a spiritual origin to what's going on around us? If you want to talk about this, let's go to the Medical Wing and then your quarters."

Marjatta cocked an eye at Mick.

"I'm not going to like the sound of this, am I, Master Chief?"

Mick nodded somberly.

"You're right, Administrator. You're not going to like the sound of this at all."

The Kingdom of Heaven

"When the eagle has flown its course, what then, Lord?"

Jesus' face was subdued as He and Abaddon watched the eagle fly at incredible speed over the Earth, screaming its warning to those who survived the disasters announced by the first four trumpet calls.

"The last three trumpets will cause great anguish. The surviving people will either raise their heads and curse God, or bow their heads and surrender. These last warnings are severe because the survivors have set their minds so firmly in worshipping demons and idols, in murder, sorcery, and sexual immorality, they cannot humble themselves. Today, if they hear My voice, but harden their hearts, then their pride will destroy them once and for all time. The eagle's message is their one last opportunity to repent. All those who go through all five months of the Fifth Trumpet Judgment without repenting will be confirmed in their unrepentant state. They will lose all hope of salvation."

They watched for a while as the eagle continued to scream God's plea for the people far below his soaring wings to pay attention.

"What part would you have me play in this, Lord?" Abaddon said.

"When the fifth trumpet sounds, I will give you the key to the bottomless pit. When you open it, smoke will come out of it like that of a great furnace. It will darken the sun and the air. Locusts will fly out of the smoke and they'll have the power of scorpions."

Abaddon lifted his great black wings and shook them at the suggestion there would be flying.

"I'm intrigued, Lord. How will locusts have the power of scorpions? Will they look like scorpions?"

Jesus shook his head somberly.

"We have created them to be frightening, so no one will mistake their otherworldly origin. They will appear like horses prepared for battle, but that's where the equine similarity ends. Their horse-like back legs end in cloven hooves. Instead of front legs, they have muscular arms. The demon locusts have faces like men, hair like the hair of women, and teeth like lions. Gold crowns will sit on their heads. We have made their breastplates out of iron, and the sound of their metallic wings will remind people of horses pulling chariots into battle. Finally, they'll have tails like scorpions and their bites and stings will torment the people for five months."

His words rocked Abaddon's head back.

"Five months! Will those stung not die?"

Jesus stretched out his arm and waved at the scene below them. As if changing channels on a holo, the vista before them became the universe, with billions of stars and galaxies arrayed in glorious splendor.

"You must see to it they do not. Abaddon, you will be the king of these creatures. You must command them not to hurt the grass, any tree, or any green thing. They are only to sting those who do not have the seal of God on their foreheads. They shall not sting or torment any who have come to faith in Me. Above all, you must not permit them to kill anyone. Their job is to encourage submission. Your job is to encourage compliance."

Abaddon nodded, his features settling into grim lines.

"Fear not, Lord. I shall never fail you again."

Atlantis, November 13, 2099 AD

Operating Theater One was small and uncluttered. A sturdy gurney sat in the middle of the surgical suite, but there was no overhead light. A large black box sat in the place of the anesthetic station. It was a nanobot set, which supplied everything a surgeon wanted and the patient needed. Like every other operating room since modern medicine developed, it smelled of antiseptic and clean linens.

Dr. Michael Sullivan slipped the portable scanner onto his right hand and set the dials. A historian would've noted the hand scanner strongly resembled a baseball catcher's mitt. The scanner slipped through its diagnostics, then displayed a holo screen above Marjatta's supine body.

"Don't worry, Administrator," Sully said, "this won't hurt at all, nor should you worry about radiation exposure. I don't know the science behind this device, but it allows us to see into your body to the deepest levels, with no side effects."

Marjatta snorted and stared at the screen above her head.

"Sully, I think it's time for you and the others to call me Marjatta. We're probably going to be a lot closer once this is all done."

Payton drifted into Marjatta's field of vision and tapped a small device in her hand. The holo screen changed to deep layers mode, with the deepest levels of Marjatta's body outlined in red.

"We're ready, Sully. Start with the brain."

Sully flattened the scanner to its widest dimension and slowly passed it down from the top of Marjatta's head to her chin and paused. The holo display processed the imager's scans and placed them on the display.

"Oh, wow, look at that thing sitting on the hippocampus," Sully said, pointing to the brain scan.

Marjatta started to sit up, but Payton gently pressed her back down.

"On what? What's the hippocampus? What kind of thing?" Marjatta demanded.

"Marjatta, please try to stay calm. This works better if we don't sedate you," Payton said. With her fingers, she traced on the holo display a curved seahorse-shaped organ on the underside of each temporal lobe.

"This is the hippocampus, which is part of a larger structure called the hippocampal formation. It supports memory, learning, navigation, and perception of space. This blob is what Sully was so unprofessionally excited about."

Sully winced.

"Yeah, sorry, Marjatta. I didn't expect to see it and I blew my composure. Hang on a sec."

Sully tapped his fingers on the back of the scanner, and the results displayed on the holo screen.

"This is a cerebral implant acting like a brain-chip neural link. What's unique about it is that it's biological, not mechanical."

Marjatta took a deep breath.

"I won't lie; I'm freaking out a bit here. What's the difference and why is it in my brain?"

Payton put her hand over Sully's hand and directed the scanner over another part of Marjatta's head.

"Hold it here, Sully. Thanks. Marjatta, most brain implants are composed of artificial materials and are usually buried within brain tissue. Someone 3D printed this one from human tissue. It acts like a neural receiver and transmitter, but it's made of an organic material sitting right on top of your gray matter. Look at this, Sully."

Sully zoomed in to where Payton pointed and whistled.

"There is a branch coming from the neural link to this smaller mass, which has tendrils in the hypothalamus, ansa lenticularis, palladium, amygdalae, parietal lobes, frontal lobes, and septal region."

"English, please," Marjatta said, her tone betraying exasperation and a hint of panic. "Are you saying I have a brain tumor?"

"No!" Payton said. "We are most assuredly not saying you have a brain tumor. They attached the neural link to your sexual response center. There are three phases to the human sexual response cycle. The first is desire, which is facilitated by subcortical brain structures called the hypothalamus, ansa lenticularis and palladium. I'm pointing them out on the holo screen."

"The cortical structures, which are the parietal and frontal lobes, facilitate the second phase," Sully said, pointing at the spots on the holo screen. "They control genital sensation and the motor aspects of sexual response until progression to climax. The septal region–Payton is pointing to it now–controls the finish."

"Our question," Payton said, "is why there should be a connection between the neural link sitting on the hippocampal formation and another biological structure reaching out to the areas controlling sexual behavior?"

The room became silent as minds churned over the quandary.

Marjatta cleared her throat.

"Will this help? The only thing I remember from both times I went down this rabbit hole was being in a constant state of sexual arousal. It would take nothing to get me to release."

Sully snapped his fingers.

"Of course! Marjatta, you're brilliant. Payton, consider this. A climax floods the brain with dopamine and oxytocin. The neural link over here needs a power source. It doesn't look like it's wired into the brain, meaning it's not running off the brain's electrical field."

"The hormones power the device," Payton said in a soft breath. "The heightened state of arousal and any release keep up a steady flow of energy to the neural link."

Marjatta's nostrils flared as she considered what Contradeum had done to her.

"I'm going to kill that son of a bitch!"

"Whoa!" Sully said, "Did you see that?"

"What?" Marjatta said, her voice frantic. "Did I see what?"

"When you got angry, the neural link spasmed," Payton said. "Anger triggers the body's 'fight or flight' response. The adrenal glands flood the body with stress hormones, such as adrenaline and cortisol. The neural link doesn't like it."

Marjatta closed her eyes and willed herself to stay calm.

"Okay, so all the fancy pants medical terms set aside, what does this mean?"

Sully continued to pass the scanner down Marjatta's body.

"Someone could program the neural link to override your decision-making capabilities. When the neural link is active, someone else is programming your brain to think and respond in a certain way. It also acts as a memory inhibitor. You don't develop long-term memories of the events happening while the neural link is active. The smaller mass is another neural link which powers itself and the larger link by keeping your brain in a constant state of arousal. Now, this is interesting."

Marjatta closed her eyes.

"Now what?"

"Your mark." Sully said. "Everything done to your body comes with a built-in time stamp. We know the date and time they put the neural implants in place. We also know the date and time they sealed you with the mark. Look at the numbers."

Everyone stared at the screens for a moment.

"The mark came later," Jeannie said in a hushed tone.

"Yes, the mark came later," Sully affirmed. "This means at the time you got the mark, Marjatta, Contradeum was already in control of your brain. You don't remember consenting to taking the mark because someone else decided for you."

"That bastard. I should have killed him when I had the chance. Can you take the neural implants out?" Marjatta said, her voice betraying the strain she felt.

Sully looked at Payton, whose eyes widened.

"Hey, don't look at me, Sully. I'm a trauma surgeon, not a neurosurgeon."

Sully's lips flattened into a straight line.

"I'm neither. Look, it's not that bad. The tendrils are just sitting on the brain tissue, not woven into it. The links are dormant. Marjatta's loss of consciousness placed them in hibernation. We put her under just in case there's a biofeedback response when you suck them out with your nanobot surgical suite. You're the only one who could do it."

"Or we could just leave them in there," Payton countered. "They're inactive. They have no ability to access the global wireless network in a dormant state or we'd see some brain activity. Someone has to be touching her skin to activate them. If she stays away from Contradeum, the links will stay in stasis."

"Stop talking about me like I'm not lying here," Marjatta said. "I want them out and I don't care about the risks. I will not be a slave to Contradeum or anyone else. My brain is mine to own. Take them out!"

Payton leaned over Marjatta and moved the older woman's bangs off her forehead.

"Marjatta, I don't blame you for wanting them out, but I'm not a brain surgeon. I could slip and disable you or kill you. It isn't worth the risk."

"To me it is," Marjatta said. "Harvard and John Hopkins trained you to be cautious, Payton, but someone has been controlling me like a turned-on robot. No more. I want the implants removed and I want them out now!"

Mick's voice came floating over from the other side of the room.

"There's another thing to consider, Marjatta. What if Contradeum pays another surprise visit and tries to reconnect to the neural link? How long do you think it'll take him to figure out someone removed the links? He'd probably consider the surgery treason, and the only people capable of carrying out the surgery are in this room."

His words were like a bucket of ice water hitting each of them in the face. The room fell silent once more.

Marjatta sat up and gestured at the holo screen.

"Get rid of that thing."

Sully shut the screen off, while Marjatta rose to sit

at the edge of the table and gestured to the other occupants of the room to gather in front of her.

"All of you owe me nothing," Marjatta said. "We've been on friendly terms for a long time, but my position kept me from becoming your friend. This is a big ask. If you do the surgery, you're committing treason. If you can appreciate how I feel, though, you'll know why I'm so desperate to have the links removed. I feel dirty, used, like a street corner sex worker." Tears flooded her eyes and leaked down her cheeks. "Please, out of whatever human compassion you have left after everything we've been through; will you help me?"

Payton stared at her shoes for a minute, her teeth working over her lower lip. She looked up, then reached out and dried Marjatta's tears with her fingertips.

"No one should ever go through what you have," she said. "Okay, Marjatta. I'll do it if Sully will assist."

Sully looked at Jeannie, whose eyebrows shot up.

"You think there's a choice?" Jeannie said. "Take the neural links out. When you're done, give them to me so I can shove them down Contradeum's throat. *¿Me entiendes?*"

Her vitriol dispersed the tension in the room, and Marjatta's lips jerked into a smile.

"I think we all understand you, Jeannie," she said. "Thank you. Sincerely. You are such brave, wonderful people. I don't know how I deserved to work with you, but I couldn't be happier that I am. Can we start the surgery now?"

Payton reactivated the holo screen and stared at the results.

"We'll have to wear frames," she said. "This is going to take about fifteen hours."

Sully grimaced, and Marjatta tilted her head at the sour expression.

"Problem, Sully?"

"Frames are exoskeletons worn over a gel suit which looks like a wetsuit. It supports the surgeon in every way possible. It stands for you, walks for you, feeds you nutrients through an IV and even keeps sweat from running into your eyes. They're like wearing a spacesuit. I wore one a lot when I was in rehab for a broken spine and they drove me nuts. Payton's right, though; the surgery will take about fifteen hours and to make sure we do it right we'll need frames."

There was nothing else to say. Payton and Sully went to their respective locker rooms and stripped down. They had to be nude in the baby blue gel suits. The suits connected fittings to every part of their bodies. They could void their bladders and bowels without having to take a break to take care of bodily functions. The gel suits were uncomfortable because it immediately set out to attach itself to take care of those kinds of things.

Their gel suits had a form-fitting helmet with an enclosed face plate. The helmet would keep them oxygenated and cooled. A 3D headset, built into the faceplate, would give them a microscopic view of their journey through Marjatta's brain. It would be as if they were standing in her skull.

Once they put on the gel suit and powered up the helmet, they stepped into the exoskeletons. They looked like robots with a skeleton attached to the outside of their skin. The exoskeletons powered up. They were in business.

Sully and Payton returned to the Operating Room at about the same time and took their positions opposite the patient lying on her back.

Marjatta's cheeks wrinkled as her lips turned upward.

"I feel like I'm in a science fiction holo. You two look like beings from another world."

"Our voices will sound like we're aliens," Payton said. "They're captured by the faceplates and projected through the holo screen above you. We're going to put you into an induced coma, Marjatta. Your brain needs to be quiet as we do the surgery."

Payton took two steps back from the table and activated her frame. The virtual reality technology in her face plate allowed her to transition from surgery view to operating room view seamlessly. She wasn't happy about this. Operating on someone's brain was a specialty for a reason. Marjatta was assuming a lot of risks. Payton hid her nervousness in the formal speech of the operating theater.

"Nurse, please put on my surgical suite gloves."

"Yes, Doctor," Jeannie said and placed the nanobot gloves on Payton's hands, connecting them to the frame.

Payton flexed her fingers and approached the table. She reached for Marjatta's neck and set the fingertips of her left hand along the supine woman's spine.

"Marjatta, you're going to feel a tingling sensation, but no pain. Soon you'll feel sleepy. Don't fight it.

Here we go."

Payton extended a filament too small for the eye to see from her suit's left index finger and slipped it through Marjatta's skin. It was too tiny to cause pain. Payton slid it into Marjatta's spinal column and inched it up her neck into her brain.

"Marjatta, I'm approaching the suprachiasmatic nucleus of the hypothalamus, which regulates the sleep–wake cycle. Normally, the suprachiasmatic nucleus projects to the pineal gland to release melatonin and puts you to sleep. I'm going to encourage it."

The filament touched the hypothalamus and commanded it to start the sleep function. Within minutes, Marjatta fell asleep on the table. Her chest rose and fell slowly, and her heartbeat descended to a count associated with a deep sleep.

"Dr. Sullivan, I'm going to leave the thread here for a moment and move another strand to the medulla oblongata to take control of her heartbeat and breathing. Almost there. Oh, oh."

Heather sat up straighter in the chair she'd found in the room's corner.

"Oh, oh. What do you mean, oh, oh?"

Payton slowly let out a breath.

"They have an organic device on the medulla oblongata, too. Dr. Sullivan, do you see any connections to it?"

Sully manipulated the controls of his gloves.

"Yup. There are microscopic tendrils from this mass to the neural link on the hippocampus. It looks like a fail-safe."

"What kind of fail-safe?" Heather said.

"The kind that kills her if someone tries to gain control of the neural link or gives her a general anesthetic to remove it," Payton answered in a grim voice.

Jeannie gasped.

"What animal would do such a thing to her?"

"Not an animal," Mick said, "a demon. Satan put it in her brain and who knows how many other brains to bend them to his will? He doesn't offer choice as an option."

"Can we remove it, Dr. Dumont?" Sully said, still viewing the mass and the attached tendril from every angle.

The air conditioning unit in Payton's frame kicked in as sweat trickled from her armpits.

"Tricky. I'm moving a filament into her medulla. No reaction. It looks like this thing doesn't respond unless the neural link is engaged and someone wants to shut it down. Or someone administers a general anesthetic. I'm in. Check vitals, Dr. Sullivan."

Sully nodded.

"I confirm her vitals are stable. You have control of her heart rate and respiration. How do we take this out?"

Payton extended a filament over the tendril leading away from the killer mass on the medulla. She positioned a nanotube on one side of the mass.

"I'm going to hit this thing with adrenaline to make it spasm. At the same time, I'm going to cut and cauterize the tendril. If the mass lets go of the medulla, I'll suck it up into the nanotube and reduce it to its constituent molecules. I'm giving control of her autonomic nervous system to you, Dr. Sullivan.

Don't kill my patient."

Payton took a deep breath.

"Ready on three, two, one, execute!"

The killer mass spasmed as soon as Payton flooded it with adrenaline, causing it to release the medulla. Payton separated the tendrils from the mass and sucked the mass into the nanotube. The nanotube looked like a snake swallowing a cow. It would analyze the chemical and biological components of the mass and reduce it to atoms.

Payton realized she'd been holding her breath. She let it out in a gush.

"It worked! Dr. Sullivan, I'm giving you control over another nanotube. Please follow the tendrils to their attachment points and suck them into the nanotube. Don't touch any of the other masses yet."

Payton directed her focus back on the hypothalamus. She induced Marjatta into a deep coma, while monitoring her vital signs.

"She's down. Let's go after her neural link."

"Maybe we shouldn't," Sully said.

Only her surgical skills kept her from jerking her head up to look at him.

"What do you mean? We can't leave it in there."

Sully shook his head emphatically.

"I'm not saying we should, Dr. Dumont. I'm suggesting we negate the power source first. The neural link may have an auto-destruct. It can no longer kill her because of your excellent work on the medulla, but it could cause irreparable harm in the areas of the brain to which it's still connected."

"Hmm. Good point. I was hoping to do this one last because of all the tendrils coming out of it. Let's get to it."

It was painstaking work. The hours flew by as Payton and Sully identified every connection point and cut away the tendrils in Marjatta's brain.

After three hours, Mick slipped out and brought food and drink back for himself, Heather, and Jeannie. He'd make two other such trips during the subsequent long hours.

Sully and Payton disconnected each tendril from the 'power' mass and suctioned it out, leaving the mass for the last. Finally, using the same technique, Payton safely trapped the organic device in a nanotube.

Payton drew in a long, shuddering breath. The frame was great for supporting the body, but it could do little for a mind fatigued from hours of surgery. She told the exoskeleton to up her oxygen intake and inject caffeine into her system.

"Dr. Sullivan, are you ready for the big one?"

"Let's do it," he said. "I'm dying for a beer."

Payton chuckled.

"Good luck finding one in this day and age. If you do, I'm in for one, too."

More hours passed as they painstakingly removed the neural link. They spent two hours at the end of the surgery examining every section of Marjatta's brain. Satisfied they'd left nothing behind, they started the procedure to wake their boss up.

Payton brought her back to consciousness slowly, while Sully kept a careful eye on her vital signs. They didn't know whether the neural implant left some residual code in Marjatta's brain to trigger an aneurysm or a stroke as a last resort. It took thirty nerve-grinding minutes, but Marjatta cleared every hurdle in her transition from coma to wakefulness.

Marjatta blinked her eyes and yawned.

"Goodness, I feel stiff. How long have I been on this table?"

Sullivan removed his helmet and glanced up at the holographic digital clock.

"Fourteen hours, thirty-eight minutes, Marjatta. Our modern operating room tables massage your body and stimulate your muscles as much as possible while you were out, but you'll still feel it for a couple of days."

Marjatta rubbed her eyes and sat up on the table, grasping the edges as she felt a flash of dizziness.

"Did it work?"

Payton peeled back her helmet and took a deep breath.

"One hundred percent. Unless they implant you again, you're out of their control."

Marjatta dropped her head. When she lifted it again, there were tears in her eyes.

"Thank you, Payton. All of you have my eternal gratitude. I'm not sure I could have continued to live with a parasite in my brain. I owe all of you a great debt."

Payton reached out to grasp Marjatta's forearm.

"You owe us nothing. We're happy we could help you. Do you feel well? Do you need anything else?"

Marjatta lifted her wrists.

"What about these? Can you remove these?"

Payton shook her head.

"I'm sorry, Marjatta. We dare not. They connected your marks to the worldwide network.

Trying to take them off will set off all kinds of alarms and they'll come for you. It won't take them long to figure out we removed the neural link."

Marjatta's face drooped.

"I'm disappointed to hear you say so, but I understand. The marks stay. What does that mean for me?"

Mick stepped forward and gained the eyes of the others in the room.

"Everyone out. I need to speak to Marjatta alone."

"But Mick," Heather protested, "we're in this together."

"Not this time," he said firmly. "I love you, Heather, and I appreciate how you feel, but this one I do alone. Go."

Sully gestured to Payton.

"C'mon, Payton, we need to get out of these suits and into a shower. Jeannie, why don't you take Heather for a hot beverage? Both of you look beat. I know Mick. If he has his mind set, not even high-grade explosives will change it."

The others laughed and filtered out of the room. Sully hung back and stared into Mick's face.

"You sure about this?"

Mick scowled.

"I'm not sure about anything anymore, but every soul counts. If the risk was good enough for Him, it's good enough for me."

Sully gave Mick a curt nod and left the room.

Marjatta regarded Mick somberly.

"Okay, Master Chief. It's just you and me. So, tell me what it is I don't want to hear."

Master Chief Lamek "Mick" Davis, United States Naval Special Warfare, Retired, stepped out of Operating Theater One feeling dread floating behind him like the specter of death. He surveyed the rubble of the TTI Main Building. Mick never lost the habit of checking his surroundings for anything that didn't fit. Rubble provided perfect cover for someone with ill intent.

Satisfied the area was secure, but unable to shake the dark cloud hovering over him, he looked at his chrono.

They took Marjatta in at 1800 hours on November 13. The surgery finished at about 0830 the next morning. He spent the last three hours telling Marjatta about the history of the world from God's perspective.

The gospel message had rattled her, hard. It must have been frightening to get confirmation from his lips he was a Christian. If the authorities captured him, she could, at the very least, be charged with aiding and abetting whatever crime the prosecutors laid against him.

She had some big choices to make now. Choices about her loyalty to the group which had restored her autonomy and dignity. Choices to make about the future of her soul. They would live every day on the knife edge of the prospect of betrayal, torture, and death. If Marjatta did not choose well, Mick's life, and the lives of those he loved, would be over.

Fate sighed and touched an invisible hand to Mick's cheek. The problem with betrayal was you never saw the direction it came from.

CHAPTER THE FOURTEENTH: FROM FRIEND, I GIVE YOU FOE

Atlantis, December 24, 2099 AD… six weeks later

Major Coventry Quarterlaine, USMC, retired, stepped off the hyper-jet and squinted against the mid-day sun on Atlantis. The weather had shifted dramatically, and the cold air made her shiver. The sun no longer warmed the atmosphere as it once had. A frigid, humid breeze blew from the windward side and rushed over the debris still cluttering the land. It kissed the dark black skin of her face with ice-painted lips.

Coventry had a welcoming committee, which she hadn't expected. Mick, Heather, Sully, Jeannie, and Payton stood near the apron of the runway. They were waving as if she was returning from an extended tour of duty. They were all dressed as she was dressed: Winter Mode, Standard Issue.

It was the newest decree from the Supreme God of the Earth. Everyone was to wear the same clothing, but with different colors and insignia to describe their life stations. In such a manner, the message said, people would worry less about what to wear and spend more time on worshipping the world's god. Besides, it was so much easier to manufacture and distribute the same thing around the globe.

The fashion was ghastly. Their thick quilted jackets zipped up to the neck and fell to the middle of the thigh. Bulky quilted pants completed the outerwear. Underneath, they wore black full-length underwear with a similar colored V-neck t-shirt. People had taken to calling the universal outfits 'pajamas.' They meant it to be derogatory because the best one could say about the ugly clothes was they were warm.

Coventry's quilted suit was olive green, as were those worn by Mick and Sully. It told the world they were active duty or former members of the military. In a way, their apparel was a warning: beware, these could be dangerous people.

Payton and Jeannie wore navy blue quilted suits depicting them as medical personnel. While Sully's pajamas were olive green, both sleeves had a thick navy-blue cuff to identify him as a medic.

Heather was the only standout. Her pajamas were bright red, signifying she was someone of an important high station.

Mick saluted and Coventry returned it automatically, which was uncomfortable considering she had a large cast on her right forearm.

"Welcome home, Major. Can I take your bags?"

A shadow flickered across the black woman's face. This was odd. Coventry tilted her head and scanned their faces, but they revealed no emotions.

"Thanks, Master Chief. The five of you here to greet me feels like a twelve-gun salute. What's up?"

"Not here," Mick said in a whisper as he picked up her bags. "Major, we've scrounged some supplies for an outdoor barbecue. A luncheon to honor your return, if you'd like to join us," he said in a louder voice.

You didn't get to be an officer in the Marine Corps without a large dose of intelligence and a generous smattering of common sense. Coventry nodded.

"Sounds great. Lead on Master Chief."

The six of them walked past the new Main Building, which was being built at an impressive speed. Most of the exterior was close to being finished, and she could see the start of a new Transition Lens between the uncovered walls. A high ceiling was in the final stages of being covered. The Lens looked a lot bigger than before. Whatever was going out or coming in once they finished would be massive.

It startled her to see the cross standing at the apex of the hill on which there had been a wedding eight weeks ago. The cross sent a shiver down her spine. She hoped there had been no crucifixions on Atlantis. The Government of Democracy forced her to watch one while she was at the Hague, and it sickened her. Crucifixion was the cruelest method of execution known to man, and you didn't have to be a priest to know evil created it.

They walked past the entrance to the new underground dorms and through a maze of sea cans stacked in what used to be the island's largest park. The wind blew loose garbage between the blackened trunks of burned trees. A sour smell lingered on the wind gusts, as if it someone had vomited, and the wind carried the scent of their distress.

At the back of the stacked sea cans, they came to a place where the earthquakes created a fissure on the island. The side of the fissure nearest the Main Building had buckled upwards fifteen feet in the air and left a small ledge behind it next to a gaping maw. All six of them fit on the ledge between the rock wall and the hole, but it was tight. The ledge was about six feet across. The upthrust wall prevented anyone from seeing the fissure or anything happening in the maw.

Someone had spiked a sturdy rope ladder into the rock near the lip of the ledge. Without warning, Sully swung his leg over the edge and started down the ladder.

"We're going into this thing?" Coventry said, not bothering to cover her expression.

"It's the only way we can talk," Heather said, slipping past Coventry to start her descent.

Coventry shrugged and started down behind Heather. The hole was dark, so she concentrated hard on her footing. She counted thirty rungs before her boots touched the ground.

Sully had lit a red lantern, which made the light easier on the eyes, and waved it until they were all standing around him.

Without a word, he turned and led them through a natural crevice in the rock. Five minutes later, they emerged in a tiny cavern.

The cave was oval shaped, and the brown walls were rough. Splinters of rock stood out from the walls, but they were dry. The cave was too far above the ocean for the earthquakes to disturb streams of water or cause condensation on the jagged walls. Still, the air smelled dank, as if it had once been underwater.

Sully activated a bioluminescent overhead light made of fungus, which gave the cave a soft, warm glow.

There were supplies everywhere. Cots enough for eight people, thermal containers of food, large jugs of water, and knapsacks of clothing were stored within the small space.

"What's all this?" Coventry said, reaching in to scratch under her cast. Mick had carried her bag down, which he leaned against a wall near the entrance.

The others sprawled out on the cots and gestured for her to join them. There were no chairs.

"This is the closest thing to a safe house we could make," Heather said. "The workers who found it condemned it as lodgings. The ground is too unstable to drill or form, so they declared it off limits. We secured the rope ladder at the top with explosive bolts. If worse comes to worse, we can drop the ladder and hide here. No one would know we were here if they didn't know where to look."

Coventry surveyed the cavern, and her forehead creased.

"What if you want to get back out?"

Mick flipped back a blanket, exposing a purple disk five feet wide.

"We found this in the ruins of the residences. It's an anti-gravity hover disk the rich kids played with before the Cataclysms. Someone on Atlantis owned one. It has a maximum altitude of one hundred feet, which is more than enough to get us back up. The only problem is the power supply. We have to sneak it up and recharge it every three months."

Coventry's frown deepened.

"So we can hide for three months and then we have to evacuate or be stuck down here?"

Sully chuckled.

"You Marines. You always go to the worst-case scenario. No, we stay down here for a few weeks, until our pursuers lose interest in where we went, then we hover up and reattach the ladder."

Coventry grinned; her face sheepish. Everything was shipshape, which she would've demanded from the two sailors. They'd planned for contingencies, which she should've expected from two retired SEALs.

"What's changed so badly since I've been gone that we need an escape hatch?"

Sully pulled his coat over his head and tossed it contemptuously against a nearby wall, where it caught and hung on an extruding piece of rock.

"Did you hear the eagle scream?"

It was warm in the cavern. Coventry removed her quilted outer jacket and laid it on a pile of knapsacks.

"Who didn't hear the eagle scream?" she said. "It's been weeks since it happened, but the world is still in an uproar. I watched holos of the two witnesses, who claim to be Moses and Elijah, preach day and night about the eagle being God's last warning. Repent, they said. Give your life to Jesus Christ. Be saved even in this dark hour."

Mick got up off his cot, shrugged out of his coat, and went to a crate of water bottles. He took out six and passed them to the rest of the group.

"The Beast and the False Prophet put out a video on the holo net," he said, "which claimed the so-called eagle was a drone used by followers of the false faith to spread their propaganda. They urged their worshippers to consider the eagle's message to be fake news, but the controversy hasn't died."

Heather cracked the seal on her bottle and took a long sip.

"Clean water is the new champagne. It's in such short supply," she said, with a sigh. "The controversy hasn't died because the followers of Christ won't let it die."

Coventry took a long sip from her bottle, then raised it in a salute to Mick. It felt good to be with her friends again after eight weeks of being surrounded by the enemies of God.

"What do you mean, Heather?"

"The 144,000 Jewish witnesses have spread throughout the globe and are preaching the same message as Moses and Elijah. We have access to the Dark Web and we're getting daily stats. The number of people rejecting the mark and placing their faith in Christ has grown astonishingly."

"So has the killing," Sully said, his voice sour. "Bounty hunters are finding horrible ways to torture and murder Christians for their faith. A bounty on the head of a Christian is high: fifty thousand bitcoins if the hunter brings one in alive to be crucified, twenty thousand bitcoins if they provide proof of death coupled with evidence their victim had been a Christian."

Coventry grimaced.

"It shouldn't be hard for them to prove their victim is a Christian," she said. "Most people have the mark now, so the identification criteria should be the easiest to satisfy. Just chop off the victim's arms and bring them in with a severed head. Identification problem solved."

Jeannie stood up and shrugged out of her pajama top. She bustled around the storage containers and came back with trays of Meals Ready to Eat.

"Great conversation before dinner. I don't know what they've been feeding you at the Hague, Cov, so this will either be better or worse than what you've been eating. The MRE is self-heating. Just press the red tab and move your hand away from it. Gave myself a nasty burn the other day when I wasn't mindful."

Coventry pressed the tab and waited for her tray to heat. When she pulled back the lid, the tray contained a brown substance the package claimed was beef, mashed potatoes, and peas. Coventry sniffed at the contents and recoiled. The meal smelled stale. She doubted farmers raised or grew any of it. From its looks, the food distributors 3D printed the meal from organic sludge. She brought a forkful to her mouth.

"Not bad," she said, lying. It tasted as bad as it

smelled. "This is better than what our brothers and sisters around the world are eating. For them, life has become a living hell. They scrounge for food, searching dumpsters and landfills for anything edible. They won't steal from the farms and orchards producing vegetables and fruit, so they wait for rejected or wilted products to be thrown away. A gathering of Christians will spend the day searching for food, clothing, utensils, and something with which to make a shelter, then share their finds with the rest of the group at night."

Mick looked at her with chagrin written on his face.

"I was just going to comment on how awful this tasted. Now I'm counting my blessings. Where did you hear this?"

Coventry swallowed against a lump in her throat, not being sure whether it was the food or the memory weaving its horror in her mind.

"They made me watch them interrogate a Christian they captured. After hours of torture, it's what he told them. Their group was always on the move, trying to stay away from mark-bearers as much as possible. Even if they could fake the mark, they wouldn't, because it proclaims worship to a false god and a denial of theirs. Being with mark-bearers is dangerous in the extreme; it begs for exposure. It was a miracle no one discovered me. I'll tell you the story in a second. How have things been on Atlantis?"

"Good, bad, and ugly," Payton said, scraping up the last of her meal. "Hart's gone to the dark side. Contradeum, or, I guess, Satan, visited here six weeks ago and brought new Mark Machines. He left in a fury when the machines wouldn't work. Hart left with him. He came back yesterday with a mark, an attitude, and an IT expert to solve the handshake problem between the Global Database and the machines."

"Pretty soon they're going to find my virus," Heather said in a soft voice.

"Virus?" Coventry said.

Heather bared her teeth, betraying a hint of nasty in her smile.

"As you know, back on November 2, Farouk Abdulhadi sent a pallet of Mark Machines into the ocean."

Coventry's mouth set into a stern line.

"Yeah, they arrested Farouk and charged him with treason after Hart reported him. They were taking him to the Hague for interrogation, and I insisted I go along for security reasons. I kept them from torturing him into a confession, but just. We avoided the treason charge, but they convicted him of dereliction of duty. An overbearing Judge sentenced him to six months in the hole, but he should be okay once he gets out. I left right after his sentencing."

"What happened to your arm?" Sully asked. "Professional curiosity."

Coventry lifted her arm and slapped it against the rock wall behind her back.

"Nothing at all. On the flight out, I noticed the crew all had the Mark of the Beast on their right wrists. We were flying to the world's justice center, and it made sense everyone there would have one. It wouldn't take any time at all for them to realize my wrists were bare. I 'tripped' on the hyper-jet and slammed my arm against a chair. They thought I fractured it and were so consumed by the accident reports they were going to file they never noticed I didn't have a mark."

"Why didn't the medic notice?" Sully asked.

"They didn't have one," Coventry said. "It seems the night before the medic consumed a lot of contraband booze and reminisced over the good old days. It cost me my best bottle of home brew, but it was worth it. The medic hadn't been drunk in a long time, so she missed her flight."

The others grinned at her ingenuity. After taking another sip of water to cover up the taste of her meal, Coventry continued her story.

"I had InstaPlast in my field pack, so I offered to patch myself up."

"What's InstaPlast?" Heather said.

"It's a gel that foams and expands when it's exposed to air," Sully explained. "When it hardens, it's as tough as ceramic armor. It keeps a soldier fighting with a broken bone; some versions have built-in topical anesthetics to reduce the pain. I'm surprised to hear it's part of the Marine Corps' field kit. I thought only Medics carried it."

Coventry allowed herself a slight smile. She shifted in her chair and tapped the cast.

"I guess the Corps is just better equipped than you froggies."

Sully acknowledged the good-natured dig by lifting a middle finger, which Jeannie slapped away with a glare.

"Before I plastered my arm," Coventry said, with a toothy grin at the rude gesture, "I taped a search-and-rescue beacon to my right wrist. Within a few minutes, I had a nice camouflage-colored cast around the base of my thumb, the bottom of my palm, and my forearm down to my elbow. Every time security screened me for the mark, they could detect the locator pinging as if it were searching for the Global Database, but couldn't read it through the cast. I told them I was waiting for surgery and had to leave the cast on until then. You wouldn't believe how long the waiting time is for surgery in the Netherlands."

Sully shook his head ruefully.

"Brilliant! I'm not sure I would've thought of it. It kept you safe for the last two months?"

A frown crossed the Marine officer's face.

"There were a couple of hairy moments. One security geek insisted they should be able to read and display the mark through the cast. He was going to bounce me up the line until I offered to cast his mark and he could see for himself."

Jeannie gasped and covered her mouth with one hand.

"How did you know the cast would block the mark signal?"

Coventry shook her head.

"I didn't. I prayed like crazy as I applied the InstaPlast the Lord would cover up his signal, too. Jesus was loving me extra hard that day; they couldn't read his mark through the cast. The rest of his security team turned on him like rabid wolves. They accused him of being a Christian and forging his mark because he had been so sure his equipment would read the mark through the plaster. He almost cut his arm off when he ripped a laser through the cast to prove them wrong. Security left me alone after word got around what the idiot had done."

"Will Farouk be okay?" Mick said. "He saved me, you know. I was going to attempt what he did, and I would've done it right under Wiesling's nose. I'd be up on treason charges right now if it weren't for Farouk."

Coventry took a deep breath and looked Mick in the eye.

"I won't lie to you, Mick. He's going to have a tough time. Farouk's never been a soldier. He's going to be under a lot of pressure to take the mark. Right now, he's in a stone cell getting one crappy meal a day, if that. If he takes the mark, his solitary confinement will be a tiny apartment with all the amenities: drugs, alcohol, decent food and sex. Their offers are going to be hard to refuse, and there's no one there to give him an opposing view. We need to pray for him."

"We need to pray for Marjatta, too," Mick said.

Coventry's eyebrows jerked upwards.

"Why are we praying for Marjatta?"

Payton explained Satan's visit, Marjatta's subjugation, and the surgery to remove her neural implants.

"After the surgery," Mick said, his voice echoing off the walls of the rock chamber, "I shared the gospel with her."

His statement rocked Coventry's head back. "No shi-, uh, kidding! How did she take it?"

Mick's eyes became bleak.

"Worse than I hoped she would. I thought finding the neural implant and removing it would move her soul towards Jesus. She was shocked to find out I was a Christian and looked like she wanted to vomit when I rolled out the gospel for her. I told her what was coming next, in terms of the Fifth Trumpet Judgment, and she put her hands over her ears. She said she wanted to think about what I'd said and I got out of there as fast as I could."

Heather put her arms around his shoulders, her face stiff.

"For the last six weeks, she's ignored all of us," Heather said, "and has gone out of her way to avoid Mick. She's gone back to functioning like she's still under the influence of the implant, which is smart. Satan probably has a spy hiding under every rock. They'll report back she's acting as he would expect her to act. The building's going up fast; she's been on the construction workers' backs hard."

Coventry drew in a long breath.

"She's looking for her own escape hatch." She gathered in the looks of the other five. "If she can get TTI running again, she can escape into the past with a god coin. Problem solved. She doesn't have to take the mark, or commit to faith, which would get her killed in this era in the most hideous and painful way possible."

"It's a terrible gamble," Payton said. "Heather and Mick are living proof we can retrieve people from the past. Marjatta would become a high value target. The government would task all of you with the mission to go back and get her."

Coventry nodded, then turned a sharp gaze on Heather.

"You started talking about a virus before I butted in."

The young Asian woman nodded and made an arcane gesture in the air. The others didn't know it, but she had traced the outline of the Ebola virus.

"I was never a rebellious child, but sometimes I wished I had it in me. When I was a kid, I thought of disrupting the internet as a hoax. I created a nasty little computer virus which doesn't allow devices to connect to the network. It's as if we tried to shake hands, but my hand was five inches above yours. When the Mark Machines took a swim, I knew it was inevitable the government would send others. I was programming TTI's new quantum computers back then. I planted my virus into our mainframe. The Mark Machines access the Global Database through a local server, which is our mainframe. The virus has been laying there, dormant, ever since. When someone activates the virus, it auto-propagates before self-immolation."

The others looked at each other and back at Heather.

"Dr. Wu," Coventry said, "I think you sometimes forget you're the smartest one in the room and we are not. Say what again?"

Heather laughed.

"When the Mark Machine tries to contact the Global Database, it activates the virus. The virus blocks the attempt by a Mark Machine to contact the Global Database, then it writes its code into another part of the primary storage unit."

She stopped to take a sip of water and grimaced at the taste.

"All we have are quantum computers. The storage units are molecular and there are a lot of them. The virus then kills itself at the location it intercepted the signal. It lies dormant in the secondary location until someone makes another attempt to contact the Global Database with a Mark Machine. Boom, it kills the handshake and the cycle repeats. They can't imprint a mark without the person's information from the Global Database, so the procedure stops before it has time to start. It's simple."

"Does it stop every attempt by any device to ping the Global Database?" Coventry asked.

"No," Heather said, and picked up two rocks from the bare earth at her feet. "Picture these two rocks as separate devices. Strike these rocks with metal and each gives off a tone characteristic of its composition, shape, structure, and density. Every device trying to access the global network not only has characteristics unique to itself but also has, of necessity, characteristics because of its species. A communicator will exhibit similar attributes to another communicator. A chrono will have similarities with another chrono. You see my point. The Mark Machines are in their own group; it's like they have similar DNA, as well as things making them unique."

Heather paused as the wrinkles on the foreheads of her friends deepened to various degrees.

"So," Jeannie said, rubbing her forehead as if she had a headache, "you wrote a code which will only react to Mark Machines and nothing else?"

"Yes!" Heather said, clapping her hands together. "You can't fix it. I programmed the virus to mutate every time it self-propagates, so its secondary characteristics are always different. You can't track and attack the virus by its primary characteristics because the code is based on the software used to create a quantum bubble to Antiquity. The secondary characteristics truly define it, and they change all the time."

Coventry nodded, mulling the ramifications of the computer virus over in her mind.

"Brilliant. Initially, they'll work the Mark Machines over to see if there's a flaw in the design. Once it tests foolproof, they'll check the equipment here. After they've checked the outgoing transmission equipment, they'll check the handshake between the two devices. Please tell me you didn't sign this thing."

The micro-expressions on Heather's face gave all the indicators the suggestion offended her.

"Of course not! I'm not in kindergarten. There's nothing on the virus capable of tracing it back to me. Except we don't have another Programmer on the island, so I become the primary suspect by default. I could've made it expire by mutating itself out of existence, but didn't do it. Once it's gone, the Mark Machines work just fine. If they find a way around it, I'm done. I won't take the mark, so it's the cross or some kind of escape for me."

The dread in Heather's last statement hung like a lead sheet in the air for several minutes. In their hearts, they knew they all might face the same choice someday. It was chilling.

"Lamek Davis, report to Administrator Korhonen at once. Lamek Davis," their chronos all chimed, making everyone jump.

"What's that all about?" Sully said, his eyes mapping Mick's face.

Mick shrugged, stood up, and stretched.

"Beats me, but I'd rather face whatever it is than be late to the party. The next time you see me, I might be down here for good."

Mick climbed up the rope ladder from the cave and felt trepidation making the climb with him. He pulled the quilted jacket up as close to his ears as he could before he made the long walk back to the main compound.

He hated being cold, and the afternoon had turned into early evening, bringing a fresh bite to the air.

The Administrator's office was not much more than a Quonset trailer the contractor had converted into her personal office until they finished the Main Building. It was a long rectangle with metal sides programmed to look like rich mahogany. The outer doors slid open after the panel near the door scanned his face.

Mick walked down the length of the trailer to the exterior of the office of the Administrator's personal assistant. He expected the assistant to greet him; instead, the door slid aside to reveal the short walk to Marjatta's door. Her door looked like it had been carved from rich, brown wood, but Mick knew it was also a holographic representation. No one built with wood anymore.

As Mick entered Marjatta's office, he felt a lot less blasé than his words in the cave had been. His heart pounded in his chest and his armpits were wet. Getting called into the C.O.'s office was rarely good news.

With some commanders, it meant you were getting kicked out of the military.

What he saw when he walked through her door shocked him. Hart sat in a chair opposite Marjatta and both their appearances had changed since the last time Mick was with them.

Hart was wearing a navy blue, tailored, very expensive suit. A tie with a kaleidoscope of multiple hues of blue stood out against a brilliant white shirt. It looked like he'd dropped about twenty pounds in the last six weeks, but he didn't look unhealthy. Whatever Hart was doing now, it was giving him a good life. Mick shifted his gaze to the mark sitting on Hart's right wrist. And a damned soul.

Marjatta's appearance was more shocking. She was sitting with her legs crossed on a plush leather chair behind a gunmetal gray steel desk dressed in a ridiculously short, tight-fitting skirt. Red high heels adorned her feet. The sleeveless red sweater covering her upper body pressed tightly against her chest and concealed nothing. The spicy smell of an expensive perfume hung in the air. Her makeup suggested she was a debutante ready for a night on the town.

She had a dreamy smile on her face while her body oozed sensuality. Mick felt his stomach lurch. They must have implanted her again. She was back to being the Marjatta Korhonen they knew when Satan controlled her mind.

After tearing his gaze away from his boss, Mick noticed the other man in the room. He wore a less expensive gray two-piece suit with a solid black tie and a white shirt. He was tall and thin; his features were long and had a sunken look. He looked like old depictions of a gravedigger, with the same pallid features.

Mick's first impression of him was that he was a degenerate slug. He never tore his beady brown eyes off Korhonen's body, his gaze roaming over her curves with a palpable hunger.

"Master Chief Davis, welcome," Marjatta said in a languid voice suggestive of impairment by alcohol or a drug. "You know Mr. Hart. The other gentleman is Dr. Archie Gallows. Dr. Gallows is an expert in Information Technology and comes to us to resolve our difficulties with the Mark Machines."

Mick nodded at the tall man with the creeping eyes. His name suited him, but he was not a gentleman.

"Dr. Gallows. I'm Master Chief Lamek Davis."

"Ah, yes, Davis," the man drawled, never taking his eyes off Marjatta. "I've heard much about you. A pleasure, I'm sure."

'Not for me,' Mick thought, while a brief fantasy played in his head of driving a knife through the leering man's heart. He turned his attention back to the Administrator of the Time Travel Initiative.

"You called for me, Administrator?"

Marjatta giggled like a schoolgirl. She reached into her desk, pulled out a bright red lipstick, and made a show of painting her lips while Gallows and Hart ogled her.

"So formal and direct, Master Chief. You really need to loosen up a bit. Maybe you need a diversion from your wife. I hear married life can be so confining. Look at you blush! You're so cute. Perhaps I'll order you to my quarters and see how it plays out. Would you like a drink, Mr. Davis?"

"No thank you," Mick said through gritted teeth. "It's been a long day, ma'am. Can we get to it, please?"

Marjatta let a throaty laugh escape and hooded her eyes. Everything she did seemed to send a jolt of electricity through the other two men in the room.

"So forceful. I like it! Very well. It seems our Mr. Hart has accepted an appointment as Chief Constable for the Government of Democracy, reporting directly to the Head Priest, Killian Hunter. As you know, our head of security died eight weeks ago. I was going to appoint Mr. Hart to the position, but now he has this much more important job. As a result, Mr. Davis, you are my new head of security."

Mick wasn't sure who was more stunned; himself or Hart.

"Wait a minute, you can't do that!" Hart said, spluttering saliva over his rotund chin.

Marjatta turned her dreamy smile on Hart.

"Why ever not, Chief Constable?"

Hart played his shifty eyes over Mick's face and frowned.

"You know I can't answer your question, Administrator. There are several people on this island who are the subject of an investigation. I cannot confirm or deny Mr. Davis is one of them. In the circumstances, it would be unwise to appoint him as head of security here."

Marjatta's face changed. Some of the dreaminess faded, and she injected a bite into her voice.

"Surely, Mr. Hart, you will not tell me how to run my organization?"

The question seemed to bring Hart up short. His mouth quivered as his brain tried to work up an answer.

"Appointing Davis, a possible criminal, to become the head of your security in Atlantis is stupid. It could be detrimental to your career. I'll have to take this up with higher authorities, Marjatta," Hart said.

"That's Administrator to you!" Marjatta snapped. "You *will* respect my office, Chief Constable. Take it up with whomever you wish. This is my enterprise and I'll run it as I see fit. Including making appointments. Is that clear?"

Hart visibly cowed under the harshness of her tone, but Gallows' lust seemed to deepen, judging by his face.

"Our apologies, Administrator," he said in a syrupy tone. "The Chief Constable didn't mean to offend, I'm sure."

Marjatta leaned back in her chair and stretched her arms above her head, straining her breasts against her sweater. The dreamy look returned to her features, and she smiled provocatively.

"Thank you, Dr. Gallows. I accept your apology on Mr. Hart's behalf. It's been a long day and I'm sure we could all use some rest. Why don't you gentlemen return to your VIP quarters and we can meet again in the morning? I need to have a few," she paused and licked her lips, making a show of running her small tongue over them, "words with my Chief of Security."

Gallows shot a glare at Mick, then nodded stiffly at Marjatta.

"Of course, Administrator," Gallows said with a pout. "I'd rather spend the evening with you getting to know each other better, but I accept your direction. Come, Chief Constable, let's retire for the night."

Gallows tugged on Hart's jacket and directed an envious glare at Mick again before the two men slunk out of the office.

Mick watched them go, took a deep breath, and returned his attention to Marjatta.

He wondered about the lengths he'd take to keep her hands off him.

"Now, Chief Davis, where were we? Ah, yes, exploring the depth of your relationship with your new bride. Not tonight, though. You need to get out of the hideous clothes you're wearing, take a shower, and change into something more suitable for your new station. Those pajamas are such a turnoff. In the meantime, come over to my side of the desk. I want to show you a picture I drew of the Supreme God of Heaven and Earth."

With reluctance, Mick went to her side of the desk and made sure he avoided looking at her exposed legs and tight clothing. Marjatta had cupped her hands around a piece of paper on her desk. Mick noted with interest none of the security cameras would pick up what she'd concealed. He expected to see Satan's depiction in whatever form Marjatta perceived him in her messed-up state.

When he looked at the paper, shock hit him like a hammer blow. The picture she drew was of Jesus Christ on the cross, a crown of thorns dripping blood on His agonized face. The Romans had nailed His wrists to the horizontal beam and had driven one spike through His feet, one overlapping the other, on the vertical beam. In the picture she drew, they had not yet pierced His side.

Under the picture, she'd written, 'For me and my salvation and the forgiveness of sin.'

Staggered, Mick pulled his gaze back to her eyes, which had a peaceful certainty about them he hadn't noticed before.

Marjatta put the picture to her lips and kissed it before scratching a corner of the paper. It flashed into flame and dissipated as fast, leaving a hint of smoke behind.

"Did you like my drawing?" Marjatta said, her voice a low purr as she arched her eyebrows at him seductively.

Mick nodded his head, still trying to get his mind wrapped around the contradiction of the picture he saw and how Marjatta was acting. The sudden appearance of a twinkle in her eyes calmed him down in an instant.

She'd made her choice. Marjatta Korhonen had pledged her soul to Jesus Christ, their Savior, the true God of Heaven and Earth. She had been acting a part to throw Hart and Gallows off.

It had convinced him.

Mick breathed a sigh of relief. She'd placed herself in grave jeopardy and now had to lead a double life.

For her, things were going to get tricky. For Mick and his group, everything was going to be okay.

Fate withdrew. There was nothing more to witness here, and she was called elsewhere.

It was enough to know that Lamek Davis was terribly wrong again.

His tribulations had just begun.

CHAPTER THE FIFTEENTH: SACRIFICE

February 14, 2100 AD, 4 ¼ years into the Tribulation, somewhere in the Amazon...

Someone was screaming.

It was a harsh, undulating screech, born of agony and bred by pain. The scream bounced off the walls and reverberated back into his ears, prodding him to a higher level of consciousness.

It took Mick Davis a second to realize he was the one screaming. He choked it off as his parched throat closed around the last note of the primeval howl. He struggled to open swollen eye sockets and fought the blurriness of his vision until he could focus on the man's face in front of him.

It was hideous.

Recognition pushed its way into the forefront of his brain. Erasmus Hart.

Erasmus Hart, whose life he'd once saved, was now his torturer.

Hart threw the cattle prod on the floor and slapped Mick. As soon as his hand connected, metallic flying creatures swarmed around Hart's body, stinging him. Hart fell to the ground, screaming and swatting at the creatures. When they finished stinging him, Hart rolled on his back and moaned, his body convulsing.

Hart's face had swelled to twice its size, and huge yellow green boils covered everything from his cheeks to his forehead. He looked like a monster out of an old horror holo. Hart rolled onto his stomach and struggled to his feet, glaring at Mick.

"Why don't they sting you, Davis? Huh? What's keeping you safe from those monsters?"

Mick wanted to smile, but his lips were cut and swollen. It was hard enough to breathe through them, much less crack a grin.

"It must be my pleasant disposition," he said to Hart. "Or maybe I'm not an ungrateful bastard like you."

Mick instantly regretted the insult as Hart drove a fist into his stomach, knocking the wind out of him. The second Hart struck the blow, the creatures once more swarmed him, stinging him as he backpedaled to the cell door. Hart yelled and flailed his arms, then screamed as the creatures stung him in a sensitive place he'd failed to protect with his hands.

The creatures backed off and Hart sunk to the cell floor.

"Davis, you traitor," Hart said with a ragged voice. "If I didn't have orders to keep you alive, you'd be rotting in the jungle. You're our only lead to two people now: your filthy wife and the barbarian you called your son. I can't kill you, but I'll make you pay for every time those creatures sting me."

Mick pulled in a short, staggering breath, getting air back into his lungs.

"We've been over this for six weeks, Hart. I don't know where to find Heather and Tul'ran. Don't you get it? No one's coming for me. You stupid, fat, dumbass. Every time you hit me or use the cattle prod on me, the demon locusts attack you. They've been stinging you since New Year's Eve. Why don't you just crawl into a hole and hide, you cockroach?"

Hart lurched to his feet and lunged at Mick, but drew back when the swarm converged on him. Mick could taste the hatred in the room on his blood-encrusted tongue.

"Chief Constable Hart, report to Rome at once!" Hart's chrono announced, causing him to jump.

Hart raised a puss-filled hand to his mouth.

"Affirmative. What do I do about the prisoner?"

"Leave him there for now. You are required on urgent business of the Supreme God of the Earth."

Hart put his mark on his right wrist up to his forehead.

"I hear and obey. Long live the Supreme God of the Earth."

Hart spit on Mick's bare feet and scurried out of the cell before the demon locusts could swarm him again.

Mick moaned and sank down against the rusted metal bracelets affixing him to the rough wooden prison wall.

He closed his eyes and dropped his chin to his chest.

"I don't know how much longer I can do this, Jesus," he said in a faint whisper. "I'm at the end of my strength, my will to live. You'll be coming for me soon. Where's Heather, Lord? I pray she's safe. Why did she abandon me?"

There was no answer. There was never an answer when he prayed.

Fatigued, bleeding from many slight cuts, his mind fogged by pain, Mick's thoughts took him back to Christmas Day…

Atlantis, December 25, 2099 AD… 52 days earlier
Christmas Day

Mick scanned the multiple readouts in the security displays, satisfied. His first act as the new TTI Head of Security was to order his staff to search for surveillance devices in the staff accommodations. To his surprise, there had been none. He called the specs up on his chrono, which projected them in the air in front of his face. The covert surveillance equipment had been in the blueprints. There would've been zero privacy if the contractors had installed them.

Mick spoke into the chronometer attached to his left wrist. The new devices combined timekeeper, computer, communicator, holo projector, and your best friend, Mike.

"Patch me through to the Construction Engineer."

A live holo appeared in front of his eyes of a beleaguered-looking older man.

"This is Reynolds," the gray-haired man said, testily. "I'm very busy, Mr. Davis. Can this wait?"

Mick cocked an eyebrow.

"It could, but it won't. Before you blow a gasket, Reynolds, I could've ordered you to come here in person instead of calling you on my chrono. Would you prefer to come here?"

"No," the other man said gruffly. "I wouldn't. My apologies, Mr. Davis. How can I help you?"

Mick didn't believe in beating around the bush.

"The plans for staff accommodations called for placing covert surveillance devices in their rooms. I just completed a security survey. Your crew installed none of them. This isn't a criticism. I, personally, deplore the idea of recording people in their homes. If this gets chased up the ladder without me knowing it, what should I tell the powers that be?"

The Construction Engineer's face relaxed.

"You'll tell them the truth. The crystals in the holo projectors were of such poor quality they wouldn't record anything, much less three-dimensional captures. Some devices didn't have crystals at all. We think black marketeers swapped out the good crystals for low-quality stones and, sometimes, rock salt. I made three requests for replacements and they told me each time our requisitions were so far under the pile they'd never see the light of day."

Mick dialed up a schematic of the covert holo camera. It was ovoid, smooth, and featureless. He made the image turn to look at every angle.

"This doesn't look easy to break into."

The Engineer shrugged.

"It's not as hard as it seems. You just need a lot of time."

Mick twisted his hand, and the schematic disappeared.

"If you say so. Sorry if I sounded doubtful. What use do the thieves make out of the stolen crystals?"

"Porn," the Engineer said bluntly. "To be specific, voyeurism porn. They plant the covert cameras in the homes of unsuspecting people, record their sex acts for three months, and then post the explicit videos on the Global Database for a fee of hundreds of bitcoins."

Mick felt his face stiffen.

"Isn't that illegal?"

The Engineer laughed harshly.

"Where have you been, sir? It's legal if you get paid a fee. If you post it at no charge, you face twenty lashes in a public whipping. If people pay you to watch the voyeuristic video you created, then the law presumes the people being recorded consented to it. It's sickening, but that's our world today."

Mick paid closer attention to the Engineer's face. The Engineer meant what he said, judging by his micro expressions. It bade well for a future conversation about the current state of his soul.

"Thanks, Reynolds. Excellent report. I'm putting you in for a dessert."

Reynold's face burst into an ear-to-ear grin.

"Thank you, sir! Desserts are so rare I can't remember the last time I had one! What am I getting if you don't mind me asking?"

Mick couldn't help but smile at the gruff man's response.

"Reclamation found a buried freezer in the last dig. It had a case of ice cream sandwich bars. You're among the first to get a bar."

The other man beamed.

"Outstanding! Thank you, sir."

Mick killed the connection and called up his notes. The chrono posted a holo pad in front of his face and Mick sent a message to the Commissary to give the Construction Engineer one dessert at the next mealtime.

He remembered when ice cream sandwiches were only a bitcoin per case. Now they were an indescribable luxury. My, how things had changed.

Mick clocked out for the night and went to their new quarters. Four inches of snow had fallen on Christmas Eve and through Christmas Day. It covered the earthquake debris in pillowy snow drifts and made everything look clean. The falling snow quieted the atmosphere and added a desperately sought peace to the night sky. Mick was too tough of a guy to use the term 'magical', but wouldn't have argued against it. It was cold, but somehow shuffling through the snow on Jesus's birthday made up for the chill.

The walk to their new quarters didn't take long. His promotion and Heather's station afforded them larger accommodation closer to the new Main Building, so they could entertain their friends. They now had room for a couch and two leather-clad loungers. Enough for seven people if you weren't too upset with being jammed together.

As soon as he entered their quarters, Mick saw the party had started without him.

Jeannie had made dresses for herself, Heather, and Payton. The material resembled the cloth the Commissary had ordered for curtains, but no one asked Mick to investigate where some of the fabric went, so he kept his nose out of it.

Sully and Coventry were in their dress uniforms; it was a miracle they'd recovered them from the debris after the global earthquake. Mick's uniforms were gone; he was stuck with the ugly bright-red regalia of his new station. True to Contradeum's ego, medals he never earned adorned both sides of his chest and gaudy gold epaulets sat on his shoulders. He considered it to be more of a clown suit than a uniform.

Sully was the first to notice him standing in the doorway.

"Hide your booze, everybody, the Emperor's here!"

Mick rolled his eyes and walked into the room. Heather danced up to him, her eyes sparkling. She handed him a glass of something alcoholic and then kissed him soundly on the lips. Mick grinned. The night held promises already.

"Honey, I'm home. What's for Christmas dinner?" he said.

Heather twirled away from him, gesturing toward the kitchen their new status merited.

"Turkey, mashed potatoes, stuffing, and steamed green beans," she said as she danced to the kitchen.

Mick followed her and inhaled deeply through his nose. It sure smelled like the real thing. The turkey didn't look 3D printed; it sat in the roaster in golden-brown splendor and the smells wafting from it were heavenly. The aroma was rich with the promise of crispy seasoned skin wrapped around moist meat. Saliva rushed into his mouth as he anticipated a taste lost to him since long before he joined TTI.

"Where did we get this?"

"I donated it." Marjatta stepped out of the bathroom, dressed far more demurely than the last time Mick saw her. She walked up to Mick and kissed him on the cheek. "Sorry about yesterday. I needed to throw Gallows and Hart off my scent. I don't need to tell you what they would've done if they found out I've put my trust and faith in Jesus. As for the turkey and fixings, Contradeum sent all Level 9 and 10 executives a turkey dinner to commemorate the day of his ascendancy to the throne of the world. We are to gather at 1800 hours to worship him in a live cast outside."

Mick lifted his eyes to the ceiling.

"He's replacing Christmas Day with a day of worship of himself. How like evil. Well, be sure to thank him after we've prayed to God the Father, the Son, and the Holy Spirit for this amazing bounty."

After grace, the seven of them dug into their dinner with gusto. Mick couldn't remember the last time he had fresh meat; each bite was ecstasy. The turkey melted on his tongue, and the mashed potatoes added a starchy essence to his taste buds. The green beans and stuffing made the dish complete. Not a scrap remained when they finished seconds and thirds.

Sully and Mick gathered the metal plates and utensils and set them in the sterilizing unit. The plates seemed so pristine; they didn't need washing.

"I'm so full," Payton moaned, as she leaned against Coventry's legs, who was sitting in one armchair. Payton stroked her belly. "Look, I have a food baby. I'm going to call him 'Crabs' because his momma has been so grouchy lately. Yup. Dr. Payton Dumont, the mother of Crabs."

The room filled with a roar of laughter. When it subsided, Mick looked at his chrono. They still had time before leaving for whatever Satan had dreamed up.

"Were Gallows and Hart in your face much today?" he said to Marjatta.

A look crossed her face.

"Not at all, which worries me. Gallows was in the computer room. Don't underestimate him by his scarecrow appearance. His previous identity was G the Deceiver on the Dark Web."

Heather's eyes widened, and the skin of her cheekbones tightened.

"No way! G the Deceiver is a legend! He used to encourage people to write viruses to challenge him, and he'd create counters. Fast. Incredibly fast. How did the government get their hands on him?"

Marjatta shrugged, then tossed back the last of her alcohol.

"Don't know. There are lots of rumors. Some say he tried to hack into the government's central bank account and got caught. They gave him the option of working for them or having both hands chopped off and tongue cut out so he couldn't code any longer. He's the only person who knows, and I'd have to bed him to get the answer. No way that's happening."

"G the Deceiver," Heather said in a soft whisper, "my poor baby virus doesn't stand a chance."

"What do you mean?" Mick said. "If you're trying to worry me, you win. How long do we have before he discovers the problem with the Mark Machines is a computer virus?"

Heather looked at him, the joy of the moment having fled from her eyes.

"Mick, he probably came in looking for a virus. It's the first place his mind would've gone. It'll take him a few days to find it, that's all."

"And when he finds it?" Mick said, his voice testy.

"Can he kill it?" Marjatta asked, putting one hand on Heather's arm.

Heather shook her head.

"The only way to kill it is to re-engineer it and make it attack itself. I made sure of it. But if he tries to re-engineer it, it will self-propagate wildly."

Payton blew out a breath of air, while her hands caressed her turkey-filled stomach.

"English, people, English."

"Hey," Jeannie said, laughing. "That's my line."

"That's funny, but I'm too stressed to laugh," Heather said. "What I mean is I programmed the virus, if attacked, to recreate itself to target multiple connections, not just those from Mark Machines. If it gets loose onto the global network, no one will access the Global Database from any device. It's going to create chaos, which will bring some heat on Atlantis."

Mick closed his eyes and considered the implications. Investigators would come and interrogate them; not all of them would be careful in how they conducted their questioning.

"We need a plan," he said, opening his eyes again.

"Yes," Heather said, wrapping her hands around Mick's arm. "But not tonight. It's Christmas Day. Let's not have the Antichrist ruin something the world celebrated for thousands of years. How about this? We can sing Christmas carols. I found some on the Dark Web."

Marjatta stiffened and shook her head once.

"Sorry, Heather, but no go. We can't let someone catch us singing a Christian carol. They'll have all of us on the cross by morning."

"Oh." Heather deflated. "I was having such a good time celebrating my first Christmas, I forgot."

Payton jerked her head up.

"This is your first Christmas?"

Heather nodded.

"My parents were Buddhists. They died in a car accident before I signed on with TTI. We never celebrated Christmas as a family, and I had no reason to until I became a Christian."

Jeannie stood up and pulled Heather into a long hug.

"Aw, *cariña*, I'm so sorry. We may not have a Christmas tree with all the decorations, or wrapped presents under it, but we have each other. Christmas is about celebrating Jesus with the people you love. You know how much we love you. *Feliz Navidad*."

The others swarmed Heather with hugs until they left her giggling through her tears.

"Mick is right," she said, after the others let her go. "We need a plan for when they find my virus."

Marjatta stood up and grabbed her red quilted

pants and jacket. After eyeing them distastefully, she put them on.

"We'll put one together. Right now, we need to get to the central square. It won't look good if I'm seen coming out of your quarters, and we'd better be there on time."

They dressed and left at staggered times. The square filled up with the island's residents, leaving the center bare. A raised circular panel sat in the middle of the square. Right at 1800 hours, a realistic giant hologram of Satan in Contradeum's body appeared. He clothed himself in a lavish metrosexual style, with gold-threaded and diamond-studded scarves wrapped around a pure white three-piece suit. Diamond earrings adorned his ears and someone had painted his face with blush and eye shadow.

He raised his hands.

"People of Earth, I greet you on this glorious occasion. I, the Supreme God of the Earth, appear to give my blessings. Today, we celebrate my ascension to godhead and my rule over this world. I've fed you, clothed you, sheltered you. I've rebuked the so-called god of the Christians, and no further harm has come to the world. See how I protect you. For those of you clinging to the foolish words of the two witnesses, I implore you to disregard them. They cannot help you. Only I, your Supreme God, am your breath, your heartbeat, your very existence."

A voiceover of people cheered as Contradeum's visage beamed. Then the image twisted. Static flew through the hologram, which changed from the leader's form into an image of thousands of monarch butterflies clinging to a tree. They spread their wings, and all took to the air at once. The people oohed and aahed as the butterflies swirled around the square before flying off in different directions.

Heather screamed and crumbled to the ground.

Sully dropped to his knees beside her.

"Heather, what's wrong?"

"It's my right side," she said, through grinding teeth. "I'm in excruciating pain."

Sully probed her abdomen and drew another scream from her. He lifted her up in his arms.

"What's going on?" Mick said, his eyes wide with alarm.

"Appendicitis. We have to get her into the OR right now. Jeannie, run ahead and prep for surgery. Mick, you need to stay here. I just saw a tall skinny guy flying out of the Main Building on a heading straight for Marjatta."

After an agonizing moment of indecision, Mick nodded.

"Okay, go." He grabbed Sully's shoulder. "Take good care of her, brother."

Sully held Mick's eyes.

"I have her, brother. She's been my sister since the two of you married. I'll protect her as if she was Kelci. You have my word. I'll take care of her, and you take care of our boss."

Mick stayed behind, chewing his lower lip bloody, as Sully ran to the Medical Wing with Heather in his arms. He walked to where Gallows was shouting and waving his arms at Marjatta. Hart was standing at Gallows' side, glaring at the Administrator.

"What's going on?" Mick asked in a soft voice.

"It's none of your concern!" Gallows snarled.

Mick put his body between Marjatta and Gallows, forcing the taller man to take a step back.

"It's my concern if you're yelling and threatening my boss with your body language. Before you get too full of yourself, Gallows, you should know I was a Navy SEAL. I've killed bigger men than you with a plastic spoon. So maybe calm your stuff down before I show you my training isn't as dated as you would like it to be."

Gallows eyes grew enormous.

"Are you threatening me?" he said, his voice still raised and a little shrill.

"Why yes," Mick said. "Yes, I am. How very astute of you. Now back off!"

The two stared into each other's eyes, then Gallows took a step back. Mick knew what Gallows saw in the depths of his eyes. A man who has killed had a menace to his gaze, which promised a painful death to anyone who wanted to try him.

"We shall speak of this later," Gallows said, backing away further.

"Yes," Marjatta said. "Let's talk in my office when you have your facts in order. Goodnight, gentlemen."

Gallows and Hart walked away in a huff. Mick could hear Marjatta trying to calm her breathing beside him.

"What was that all about?" Mick said, when the men had walked far enough away.

"They found the virus," Marjatta said. "Gallows tried to reverse engineer it and it mutated. Contradeum turning into butterflies was not part of the program. The virus spread to every device in the world and everyone saw the same thing. Contradeum apparently had a two-hour speech planned, bragging about his accomplishments and how beautiful the world was going to be. After he finished, we were supposed to fall on our faces and worship him. We've now lost all connection to the Global Database. There's going to be hell to pay."

Davis looked back to where Sully had disappeared into the falling snow with his bride.

"Do they know Heather designed it?"

Marjatta pulled the collars of her jacket higher as the frosty wind gusted.

"They didn't say."

Her chrono chimed in private mode and she pressed the hidden received implanted in her jawbone beneath her ear.

"Yes? What? When? Does it have to be now? I'll send Davis. You're already on the plane? Okay. I'll tell him, but you have some explaining to do when you get back."

Marjatta turned to Mick, her eyes shrouded with concern.

"Sully said Heather has blood poisoning because her appendix burst. He can't treat her here. They just boarded a hyper-jet for Walter Reed. They'll call when they get there."

Mick felt his face stiffen.

"I'm going to Walter Reed."

Marjatta shook her head sorrowfully.

"We only have one hyper-jet, Mick. C'mon, Heather's in expert hands. She's got Sully and Jeannie with her, and they'll report when they land."

Atlantis, December 31, 2099 AD

Except they didn't report that night or at all.

Global communications crashed. After an hour passed, well within the time the hyper-jet needed to get to Walter Reed Army Medical Center in Bethesda, Maryland, comms were still down.

Mick stayed in the security center for the rest of the night of Christmas Day, continuously pinging the aircraft and sending out messages. There was no response.

Mick was a wreck in the following days. When he wasn't eating or sleeping, he was in his office. He couldn't query the Global Database because Heather's virus, which Mick had taken to calling The Silencer, shut down every contact with it. Mick couldn't access imagery, intelligence, satellite feeds, or anything.

For a week he waited with building frustration for the government to get their act together and restore comms. His mind kept torturing him with 'what-ifs'.

What if Heather never made it to the hospital on time? What if their plane crashed? The statistics against a hyper-jet crashing were beyond conceivable. The anti-gravity engine wouldn't let it crash. But what if the engine failed for the first time in history? His mind tortured his waking hours and made it hard for him to sleep.

He sat in Marjatta's office on New Year's Eve and stared dully at the glass of amber liquid in his hands. He was beyond exhausted. Deep lines marred his face, and black shadows traced the underside of his eyelids.

At least Gallows and Hart had left. Within hours of the spread of the virus, a large government anti-grav plane landed on Atlantis and took those two back to Rome with them. There had been relative peace on the island for six days.

No sooner had the thought entered Mick's mind than a Security Tech burst into Marjatta's office, too excited to follow proper protocol.

"Administrator, Chief, the world is back online!"

Mick and Marjatta activated their chronos, which cycled up and announced a connection to the Global Database. He looked up into Marjatta's hopeful face.

"Maybe now we can get some answers," he said.

The two of them ran out of her office, but only got about ten feet from the door when a bright light blasted their eyes and an artificially enhanced voice assaulted their ears.

"Lamek Davis, this is Global Security. Get on your knees. Put your hands on your head. Don't move."

Mick complied, spewing profanities under his breath.

Six days of worry, stress, and fear, and now this?

Hart strutted out of the glare of the searchlight. He made a show of wrenching Mick's arms behind his back and cuffing him.

"Lamek Davis," he said, his voice consumed by gloating, "you're under arrest for treason. The Supreme God of the Earth has authorized me to arrest you and Dr. Wu on suspicions you are Christian conspirators and terrorists. You'll come with us. The Chief Priest wants the first crack at questioning you."

One guard shouted and pointed up into the night sky. High above, stars began to fall. In the middle, a bright golden star blazed its way to Earth, trailed by two lesser bright gold stars. The people gathering in the square were stunned by its majesty as it swept across the entire night sky. Hart had to yell at them and smack a few heads to get them focused on the task at hand.

The Global Security forces dragged Mick away as Marjatta stood frozen in her spot, stunned. After a moment, she made a hand gesture and Coventry faded in from the shadows.

"Two tactical teams," Marjatta said in a quiet voice. "They came in two hyper-jets. Make sure you're on one of them."

Coventry nodded, then paused as Marjatta grabbed her arm.

"Major, I'm giving you termination authorization. Your orders will be in your chrono before you get on the jet. Do whatever it takes. Just get Mick and Heather back."

Coventry withdrew her arm and saluted before she ran after the security team.

Marjatta could tell from their body language the security force had been scared out of their wits. The compound lights had come on and she could see them as they kept glancing around them into the sky. Some of the security forces kept pointing to the sky and arguing with their mates. Their panic surprised Marjatta.

Fate was not at all surprised by their panic.

Fear reigns when the stars fall.

In the Kingdom of Heaven, December 31, 2099 AD... three hours before Mick's arrest

"Abaddon, come forth."

The angel walked to the center of the sea of glass, where people and angels pressed shoulder to shoulder. He wore black leather armor, but the edges of his cloak were broad strips of pure gold. He dragged two long chains made of solid gold behind him. Each link had thousands of tiny hooks. His halo sat above a brilliant gold crown and into it were woven the outlines of the Daemonum Locuste, the demon locusts, soon to be unleashed on the world.

These were demons the size of a large human hand bound in the bottomless pit. They had back legs like horses, which ended in cloven hooves. Attached to their iron-plated chests were equally heavily muscled, fur covered arms. Their hands ended in long fingers with sharp claws. Their heads were human faces crammed with lion's teeth and pointed dark golden crowns rested on their long hair.

Instead of a horse's tail, each had scorpion tails filled with toxic venom. Thin metallic wings, which looked like dragonfly wings, stretched out from their backs.

These were creatures designed to torment the wicked, make them see the evil of their ways, and point their hearts towards Heaven. These creatures were about to be released into the world by the Creator of all things.

Jesus stood and walked to the edge of the stairs. He was resplendent in a white robe girded by a golden sash. His face glowed so brightly it appeared to be like the sun.

Jesus had the scroll, the title deed to the Earth, in His right hand. A hush fell over the multitudes before Him.

Abaddon kneeled before Jesus, spreading his enormous wings out wide. Jesus stared at the massive angel for long seconds, then raised His voice to Heaven.

"Let the trumpet of the fifth angel sound."

The fifth angel stepped forward. He had garbed himself in gunmetal gray and his trumpet was made of polished iron. When he blew a note from it, the sound was like a rush of dragonfly wings, but with a metallic ring. The eerie sound grew in volume until it spread through Heaven entire.

Jesus pulled a large brass key from his robes and walked down the stairs.

"Rise, Abaddon. Take from me this key. With it We appoint you the King of the Daemonum Locustae. Go as I have told you and do as I have commanded."

Abaddon slid the key into the sash at his waist and bowed deeply.

"Thy will be done on Earth as it is in Heaven."

In a blur, Abaddon turned and raced for the edge of Heaven, leaping over the edge as if he were a high diver. When his cloak flared out behind him, the gold inlay shone as bright as a torch. When he fell to the earth, it looked as if he was a star and the gold chains looked like two stars falling with him.

He orbited the Earth at an unfathomable speed until he found the entrance to the largest human-made hole in the world. It had been dug by China, which tried to research the secrets of the Earth.

With a depth of 40,230 feet, the Kola Superdeep Borehole in north-west Russia had been the world's deepest artificial hole, until the Chinese surpassed it by 5,000 feet.

In the physical dimension, the Chinese hole allowed scientists to study the internal structure and creation of the world. It provided valuable data for geoscience research. In the spiritual realm, it connected to a great deal more.

This location contained the bottomless pit. An iron gate, observable only through spiritual eyes, lay over the entrance to the pit. Abaddon took the key out of his sash and turned it in the lock. The fifteen-foot-thick doors slid aside with well-greased ease.

Abaddon gathered the two long chains and tossed them down the pit, keeping the leading edges wrapped around his massive left forearm. When he jerked on the chains, smoke billowed out of the pit as if from a deep explosion. The gold chains connected the physical realm to the spiritual realm, and the smoke belched into the air. It darkened the sun and the air surrounding the pit, pulsating as it spread the stench of rotting flesh into the atmosphere.

Abaddon drove his wings down and flung himself into the sky, dragging the chains behind him. Attached to the hooks on each link were millions of metallic-skinned demon locusts. Abaddon hovered in the air and addressed the intelligent creatures.

"I am your King. You will obey me or suffer harshly. Go into the world. You shall not harm any living thing, except for the humans who have not accepted Jesus as their Messiah. Even then, you shall not kill them, but you shall torment them with your stings, your poison, and your teeth for five months from this day."

Abaddon whipped the chains back and forth, and millions of demon locusts took to the sky in all directions. They flew through Inter-Dimensional Space, so within seconds they were everywhere on Earth.

Even on a small island called Atlantis.

Coventry watched the security team take Mick to the new Admin and Security Center. After a few minutes, they fanned out and started running to the staff's accommodations. Others spread out and moved on to the new semi-constructed TTI building.

If they were looking for Heather, they wouldn't find her. Coventry had been standing right behind Mick when Heather collapsed with appendicitis. She'd hung back when Mick confronted Hart and Gallows, covering his six. Coventry did her best work from the shadows.

Yup, they wouldn't find Dr. Wu on the island. Heather disappeared a week ago and no one on Atlantis knew where she was.

Their fruitless search gave her some time, though. Coventry slipped away to her quarters and opened a secret panel at the bottom of her closet. She'd stolen a Global Security Officer's uniform just for this contingency. It bore a high enough rank to give her access to the hyper-jet without enduring a bunch of questions.

The coverall was a little tight, but not so much as

to cause comment. It was winter, giving her an excuse to put long gloves under her quilted jacket and over where one would expect to see a mark. She would use the facilities on board the hyper-jet to re-plaster her arm over a location beacon.

Coventry stuffed her bugout bag with a few additional essentials, including a small sack of solid gold coins. The black market disdained the use of the mark for items bought and sold there. Too easy to track. Gold, especially for the illegal things Coventry intended to buy, was still the currency of choice.

She walked at a casual pace to the landing strip and returned a salute from the woman guarding the on-ramp to one of the hyper-jets. The security guard's salute was sloppy. No military training there. After eyeballing her rank, the guard let her on without examining her mark or asking for orders.

Coventry's mouth flattened as she made her way to the front of the plane.

The Government of Democracy, led by the Antichrist, had no state enemies, which meant a reduced prospect of warfare. Absent threats, professionalism and attention to duty faded. Everyone was just pretending to be a soldier now. Except for the Elite Guards, which the world knew at the Shock Troopers of the Supreme God. There were a lot of them, and they meant business.

The cockpit of the new battle planes was massive. It took so many people to fly a trooper carrier anti-gravity hyper-jet; the plane resembled a spaceship more than a fighter. As little as one person could pilot Atlantis's hyper-jet. Wherever it was now. Coventry hoped the location wasn't at the bottom of the Atlantic with Atlantis's ancient namesake.

There was no one in the troop cabin when she boarded. Coventry slipped into the facilities and wrapped her right wrist with InstaPlast. After the cast set, she ran her chrono over her wrist. It caught the ping of the beacon. She now had a perfect excuse for why her wrist could not display the Mark of the Beast. Grim lines touched her face. She'd die before she took that tattoo.

Satisfied, Coventry tucked her bag under her arm and when to the Control Center, taking a seat at the Life Support station. She knew no one else on the crew would staff the station unless their flight plan called for suborbital flight.

None of these planes had the same crew; each person came aboard expecting to fly a shift and then take four days off. They wouldn't even question why she was there.

Coventry slipped a comms device into her ear to monitor what the security squad was doing and waited. Her chrono vibrated, and she scanned her orders. When she finished reading them, Coventry deleted them from her device.

Marjatta had come through, true to her word. Coventry had orders to recover Davis and Wu and it didn't matter who she had to kill to get them. Her facial muscles stretched into the cold, stark grin she imagined the Angel of Death wore.

These were her kind of orders.

Global Security held Mick in his office, with his hands cuffed behind his back, while they searched for Heather.

Mick could've told them Heather was no longer on Atlantis, but held his tongue. Wherever his wife went, she'd need as much of a head start as he could give her. He owed Sully and Jeannie as much, too.

An hour later, Hart stormed into the office. He slapped Mick hard across the face. Mick felt the urge to kick Hart where men hated to be punted, but restrained himself.

"You're a pretty tough guy hitting me while I'm cuffed," he said, tasting the coppery bitterness of blood on his tongue. "Why don't you let me loose and try it again?"

Hart glared at him through bloodshot eyes.

"Where is she, Davis? My people have searched every square inch of this stinking rock. We just found out she boarded a hyper-jet a week ago. I had my people look through every database. There's no trace of the jet or Wu. Where'd your wife go?"

Mick's heart sank. Every hyper-jet had a transponder which pinged the Global Database from any location in the world. The jets never got lost. The transponder continuously sent a record of its location, accurate to within three feet. His worst fear just came true. The jet was gone.

Mick slumped against the desk and dropped his head to his chest. Grief overwhelmed him, while another part of his mind refused to accept what he'd just heard. They'd only had Christmas dinner a week ago.

A security officer ran in, babbling with excitement.

"Silence!" Hart yelled. "I can't make sense of what you're saying. Slow down and tell me what's going on!"

The security officer started hyperventilating. "It's. A cloud. Of something. It's coming this way and they're hostile."

Hart started swearing and grabbed Mick by the back of his uniform. He thrust Mick through the door and rushed him towards the landing pad.

As they were about to board the hyper-jet, Hart felt something land on his neck and he slapped it. Pain stabbed through his body as the demon locust drove its stinger into the soft flesh. He screamed. The other guards jumped as Hart screamed. Soon, they squealed and ran around in hysterics as the drone of metal wings filled the air. Each guard had a haze of metallic insects swarming around them.

Mick watched, amazed, as the mayhem spread throughout the island. One creature startled him when it landed on his chest. It looked up at him with intelligent eyes, then, of all things, smiled. It was an open-mouthed grin filled with jagged teeth and long fangs. Mick's heart skittered and missed a beat. The creature unfolded its wings and tore into the sky before finding Hart's exposed ankle in which to plunge its scorpion tail.

They eventually loaded the jet and took off. The locusts had almost disabled Hart's entire security force. Traveling at hypersonic speeds, it only took two hours to get to Rome. Moans and cursing filled the plane the entire trip.

Panic ensued when one of the security team pointed outside the window. Their escort was a tight group of Daemonum who had no trouble matching the jet's velocity.

When they landed in Rome, a cacophony of screams and wails shocked Mick. Tonight was supposed to be the Supreme God of the Earth's biggest party. He had commanded a worldwide orgy, and banned the use of clothing once all his adherents had found their way indoors. His government generously supplied food, alcohol, cocaine, heroin, ecstasy, and marijuana to every registered party. Strippers and prostitutes of both sexes were to have been the primary entertainment. The only requirement for a ticket was a mark and a promise to get intoxicated and take part in the orgy.

The government made sure they registered and supplied each party weeks earlier. When The Silencer killed access to the Global Database, people still went to the parties like lemmings following each other off a cliff. After the government reconnected everyone on New Year's Eve, the people took it as a sign for the upcoming year. It promised to be a new age of peace and prosperity.

It turned into a nightmare.

The locusts had no difficulty finding their way into buildings and discovered a plethora of exposed flesh to sting. The sound of torment was so loud it filtered onto the streets and into the night skies.

Hart dragged Mick through Global Security Headquarters while swatting at and cursing the locusts flinging themselves at him. They had a way of getting into the most tightly secured building.

He threw Mick through the doorway leading to the Chief Priest's office and fell to the floor, howling. It gave Mick a chance to look around. The office was opulent to the extreme.

They made every fixture out of solid gold. The carpet was thick and obviously expensive. The desk looked like someone carved it out of a rare wood and the chairs were all leather. A smell of new leather combined with a strange incense to give the room a surreal quality. It was the office of someone of eminent authority, indeed.

The Chief Priest entered as his acolytes frantically waved brooms to drive the locusts away from his body while being stung themselves. This was the highest paid and second most-powerful man in the world, and he swatted at the locusts like a naked man under a light at night trying to bat away mosquitoes.

Mick stood in the middle of the office, trying hard not to laugh. The eagle had prophesied woe, and this was woe, indeed.

He wouldn't have found it so funny if he knew the demon G'shnet'el indwelt Killian Hunter's body.

A guard punched Mick in the back hard enough to drop him to his knees. Mick bounced back up and delivered a roundhouse kick to the guard's face. When the other guards tried to jump Mick, dozens of Daemonum swarmed them, and they were soon all lying on the floor incapacitated, screaming and trying to slap away the angered locusts.

"Enough!" Hunter said, disgust dripping from his voice. Everyone stopped. Even the locusts paused at the sound of the Hell authority in his tone.

Hunter dropped into a plush leather chair and surveyed the room before freezing his dark eyes on Mick.

"Attack my guards again and I'll kill you, orders or no orders."

Mick stilled his facial muscles. They had orders to not kill him. This was interesting.

"Bite me," Mick said, his voice laced with irony. "What do you want, Hunter? I remember when you were a two-bit blogger who couldn't buy likes or fans. If you think I'm going to kneel to you, you've got another thing coming."

G'shnet'el drew Hunter's face into a mask which depicted the years he spent in the Abyss.

"I remember you to be a lot less cocky when my sword was about to cut your skull in half in Mesopotamia."

Mick couldn't keep a startled expression off his face. Hunter wasn't in Mesopotamia at any time Mick was there, and certainly not on the night he broke his ribs. He stared deeper into Hunter's eyes and suppressed a shudder. The eyes were the windows to the soul, and it looked like a demon lived in this one.

"You weren't in Mesopotamia, Hunter. You're too fat to transition. The lens would've busted if you'd stood on it."

Hunter rose with blinding speed and struck Mick hard across his face. A locust swooped in and stung the Chief Priest on his forehead just above his nose, and he fell back onto his chair, screeching.

Stars blurred Mick's vision and his ears rang. He worked his jaw to make sure Hunter hadn't broken it. He blinked back the tears which had sprung into his eyes and his vision cleared.

"Cheap shot, Hunter. Why don't you unleash me and let's do this like men?"

"Shut up!" Hunter snarled. "Just shut up!"

Mick could see the other men and women in the room were startled by Hunter losing his cool. Maybe the slap was worth it.

"Your wife messed things up for us, Davis. Tonight was going to be a great triumph for the Supreme God of the Earth. Her little computer virus jammed up our information operations and disrupted our new year celebrations. To say we're displeased is like saying the surface of the sun is a little warm. I'll make you a deal, Davis. Get the mark and tell us where your wife is hiding, and we'll forget about your insolence. I'll even let you keep your job on Atlantis. This offer is open for the next sixty seconds."

Tell us where your wife is hiding. Hope surged in Mick's chest. They'd didn't think Heather was dead, and they were still looking for her. Longing mixed with determination stiffened Mick's spine.

"I don't need sixty seconds, you smarmy pawn. Stick your offer where the sun doesn't shine. I won't take the mark, so do whatever you have to do."

Hunter stared at Mick, his breath coming in rough gasps, and hatred seething in his eyes.

"You Christians think you're so smart. Just a little suffering on Earth and then an eternity in Heaven. What price do you have to pay for your consolation? What price have you ever paid? Your Savior paid for it all, and you just needed to exercise a little faith. I'm going to give you the suffering you deserve, Davis. When my people finish with you, you'll not only tell me where I can find your wife, you'll beg me for death. You know what I'm going to do when I find Heather? Me and my men are going to rape her in front of you until she dies. Then we're going to burn out your eyes, so the last thing you see for the rest of your miserable life will be your wife's ravaged body rotting for days while you're chained to a wall. Hart!"

Hart scrambled forward and fell on his knees before Hunter.

"Yes, Your Excellency?"

"Take Davis to *La Prisión de los Fieles* in the Amazon. Torture him until he gives up Heather Wu's location. Then report back to me when you have it."

"You're wasting your time," Mick said, trying to keep his frantic emotions out of his voice. "I don't know where Heather is. She left Atlantis just as the comms died and I've had no contact since. I can't give you what I don't have. Even a moron like you should be able to figure that out."

Hunter glowered at him.

"Have it your way."

The demon-possessed man lunged off the chair and drew an energy pistol from his robes. He aimed it at Mick's face, then stopped.

A glowing sword passed in front of his eyes. Hunter's eyes followed the sword to the being who held it.

"E'thriel," he spat. "You traitor."

Everyone in the room had dropped to their knees, including Mick. The angel of the Lord's presence flooded the office with overwhelming power and purity. E'thriel's robes shone a brilliant white under his blue armor, and his halo glowed with intensity. His long blond hair framed a face both grim and intense.

"G'shnet'el, you fool. You knew the Father only permitted your master to sift this son of God to test his faith. He did not permit you to take his life."

The door to the office flew open and Satan burst into the room. He'd only taken two angry strides when a new light flashed into existence. This angel was just as tall as E'thriel, but commanded everyone's attention. He wore armor made of solid gold, and a massive sword hung from the end of his left fist. His energy passed over the room's occupants in waves and stopped Satan in a forward step.

"Michael," Satan said in a menacing tone. "How dare you show your face in my kingdom!"

"It's not your kingdom," the Archangel Michael retorted. "It never was. The Father has permitted you your time here, as the prophets and John the disciple foretold. You shall act according to the rules He set or you may not act at all. You know the Father only granted you permission to test the faith of Lamek Davis. The agreement did not extend to taking his life. You shall pay a price for your disobedience."

"It was that idiot, G'shnet'el!" Satan howled. "He's the one who tried to kill Davis! Punish him, not me."

Silence ensued as Michael seemed to listen to something far away. He nodded and sent a direct look into Satan's eyes.

"Leave."

There was a pause. To Mick, Satan seemed to struggle with the direct order, as if he wanted to challenge it. Then, without a word, the evil angel turned on his heel and walked away, slamming the door behind him.

The Archangel turned to the rest of the room.

"G'shnet'el, you tried to take the life of Tul'ran az Nostrom when he was in Antiquity, violating the Father's direct orders. You are plotting to kill him by using Lamek Davis as bait. Your defiance includes indwelling the body of the human you inhabit under false pretenses. Your time here is done. The Father has commanded you to appear before Him for judgment. Leave Killian Hunter's body."

Michael issued the last order casually, in a normal tone, as if he expected to be obeyed. He was. G'shnet'el slipped out of Hunter like a wraith and hovered in the air. As he opened his mouth to protest, Michael closed his right hand into a fist. The action immediately cut G'shnet'el's ability to speak.

"Remove him from this place and take him to the Judgment Seat," Michael told E'thriel, who was grinning from ear to ear.

"My pleasure," the young angel said, and skewered G'shnet'el's spirit form with his sword. The evil angel wailed silently, then disappeared with E'thriel in a flash of light.

Michael turned to Mick and the guards kneeling on the floor collapsed as they lost consciousness. He dropped to one knee and lifted Mick's chin with a massive hand.

"Lord Davis, I am the Archangel Michael. Satan has petitioned God for approval to sift your faith. For His reasons, which are unassailable, the Father granted the evil one permission. It would hardly be a test if we allowed you to keep a memory of this

371

encounter. I must remove from your mind all angelic involvement in this mess. Do you understand?"

Mick nodded, feeling numb. The prospect of being sifted terrified him. Maybe it was better if he didn't know his Savior agreed to test his faith. He hoped with all his heart he was up to the task.

"I understand, Archangel. I will do my best not to disappoint the Lord."

A smile flitted across the massive angel's face.

"I have great respect for you, Lord Davis. You will disappoint none of us. Close your eyes."

Mick opened his eyes, wondering why he was kneeling on the floor. Something had happened. Everyone but him and Hunter lay unconscious. Hunter was lying in front of his chair in the fetal position, sobbing.

Hart stood up shakily and scanned the room.

"What happened to the Chief Priest?"

Mick's head felt funny. He shook it, trying to clear the fuzzy edges. There was something important to remember, something about a test.

"I don't know. The last thing I remember was me asking him what he wanted. I think I passed out then."

Hart grunted.

"Doesn't matter. I have my orders. I hope you like prison, Davis. The Prison for the Faithful in the Amazon is a nasty place, and I'm going to make sure you experience every excruciating bit. We've been lodging Christian men there for a while. We can't seem to break them from their faith. I'll put you close to them so they can hear your screams."

February 14, 2100 AD, 4 ¼ years into the Tribulation, somewhere in the Amazon…

They didn't wait to get to the Amazon. As soon as the hyper-jet lifted into the sky, guards pinned Mick's legs while other guards beat him. As the guards hit Mick, the demon locusts stung them. The guards couldn't stop because Hart goaded them and threatened them with far worse. The beating continued until Mick passed out from the pain.

When they landed, the guards put a bag over his head and led him off the hyper-jet. Heat slapped him in the chest and flooded his lungs with humidity. Mick felt like he was drinking the air instead of breathing. He could smell wet vegetation, some of it bordering on rot. There was no question he was in the jungle.

They chained him in a small cell with a tiny window high on the back wall. It was hot and humid, with no ventilation from anywhere but the fetid corridor through the iron-barred cell door. His room barely accommodated a cot with a mattress and no pillows or bedding. The toilet was a hole in the floor and it stunk with stale urine and feces. Flies buzzed around the hole and landed on Davis when they were tired of laying their eggs in the manure.

His jailer's idea of food was a joke. They brought some slop in a pail every morning and they expected him to make it last the day. A separate bucket of water held a dank liquid; it was plentiful, but Mick drank as little of it as possible. He didn't have water purifiers, and he knew what foul water would do to his guts.

It was hard to sleep. The guards turned the lights

on and off at random times. Mick lost track of the time of day, and what day it was. To make it worse, the guards played loud, garish sounds Mick presumed were some kind of music. It pounded in his ears and often led to a headache.

Mick knew they were softening him up for interrogation. NavSpecWar had trained him to endure this kind of treatment without cracking. It was time to see if his training would pass the test.

For the first week, they threw cold water on him, screamed their questions in his ears, and beat him. The beatings were short, though; every time one of them assaulted Mick, demon locusts swarmed the attacker and sent the abuser to the infirmary. The locusts' actions strengthened Mick's resolve: he gave them only his name, rank, and serial number.

They changed tactics in the second week of January. The guards dragged a wooden bench into his cell resembling a seesaw. Mick's heart dove when he saw it. They were going to waterboard him.

Waterboarding is a horrific form of torture. The interrogator covers a detainee's face with a wet towel and drizzles water over it while the detainee lies in the feet up, head down position. Water splashed into the sinuses and lungs, making the detainee feel like he was drowning. At least it's how Mick felt as he fought to breathe.

After the fourth time they attempted waterboarding Mick, Hart slapped him across the face, then howled as a horde of demon locusts stung him. The other guards also fell to the cell floor, screaming and swatting at the locusts.

"Davis, you son of a bitch!" Hart yelled, after

panting on the floor. "Is this how you want to die? Why are you being so stupid? What has your god done for you? Has he saved you?"

They elevated the board as Mick coughed water out of his throat and sneezed fluids out of his sinuses.

"You don't get it, Hart," he said weakly. "You'll never get it. Maybe you had honor once, I don't know. I'd heard you were a good cop before TTI hired you. Look what's happened to you. How do you think you'll be able to understand me when your integrity is nothing but a pile of chicken dung?"

Hart lunged to his feet, his eyes burning white hot.

"Are you delusional, you stupid frog? You're the one strapped to the pine board coughing fluids out of your lungs." He dropped his voice into a more soothing tone. "We found a cow out here yesterday just wandering around. It had meat on its bones. Tonight, we're going to barbecue the cow right under your window. Real steak, Davis. We found a stash of Coronas in a cellar some druggie had kept. Beer and steaks, Davis, like your good old days in the Navy. Just give up. Deny Jesus as your Savior and acknowledge the Supreme God of the Earth as your deity. Then I make all this go away."

Coughs wracked Mick's throat and water spewed from a corner of his mouth. He lifted his head after his diaphragm spasms stopped.

"Man does not live by bread alone," he said. Then a ghost of a smile flickered on his face. "Or, in this case, T-bones alone."

Hart raised his fist, then backed away as a large

demon locust hovered menacingly in front of his face. Disgusted, Hart stomped out of the cell.

They roasted the beef in the open area outside his cell later in the night. Mick almost came unglued. He thought he was going to drown from the saliva coursing out of the corner of his mouth. He was a meat lover. Smelling barbecue and not having any was almost as bad as waterboarding.

His tormented mind flashed back to his days in BUD/S. He remembered lying in the cold Pacific surf, arm linked with fellow candidates, or Tadpoles, as they were called.

On the beach, the instructors sat around a large fire, drinking coffee, and laughing. Every once in a while, they'd yell out to the Tadpoles, taunting them with the promise of hot coffee and a hot meal if they'd just stop being so stubborn and leave the icy water for the comfort of the beach.

"One evolution at a time," Mick muttered to himself as the roasting beef mocked his growling stomach. "It's how we make it through. One evolution at a time."

In the third week, they brought in a sleep deprivation tank. They filled the tank with an oily liquid, which made Mick's body weightless. The tank was as dark as a grave and deprived him of his senses. He felt as if he were floating in a starless space. It should have been enough to break him, but Mick's counter-interrogation training had included hours in such a device. He withstood it, barely fighting panic and claustrophobia, but emerged with his lips sealed and mind intact.

Again and again, the interrogators altered

between demanding Heather's location and battering him to deny Jesus. Mick's mind wandered, and he lost focus, but nothing passed between his lips to satisfy them. His faith held. Barely, but it held.

Hart left during the fourth week, but his orders forced the guards to beat him as they deprived him of food and sleep. Mick lost weight. He struggled to keep a grip on his resolve. And his sanity. He could feel both slipping away every time he lay on his cell floor, shivering after being hosed with water or beaten by truncheons.

Then came February. Hart came into his cell and kicked Mick awake. As soon as he did so, locusts swarmed Hart and he scrambled away, cursing.

"Get up, Davis. You've had a nice vacation; it's time to answer some questions."

Two guards came in, threw him up against the wall, and put him in manacles. They beat him with rubber truncheons the first day, covering his body in bruises. It took many of them because every time someone hit him, Daemonum attacked the torturer in swarms.

That was two weeks ago. They tortured him with a cattle prod to every part of his body. He'd withstood it, but knew he was reaching the end of his strength and his will.

At the end of two weeks, Hart jerked Mick's head up by the hair and spit into his face. His matted hair and beard had grown out, and his faced itched like crazy from the stubble. Mick stunk of urine and feces, because they wouldn't take him off the wall for hours at a time. His frayed clothing hung off his body twenty pounds lighter. At night, he could count all his ribs when they allowed him to lie down.

Hart sneered at him.

"Happy Valentine's Day, Master Chief Lamek Davis. How do you feel pinned to the wall like a butterfly? Today's your last day to give us information or deny your useless god, you traitor. I'm leaving for Rome. When I come back, I'll have orders to crucify you on holo for the rest of the world to watch."

Mick didn't have the strength to respond. His mouth was dry and his tongue felt swollen.

"You've put up a good fight, Davis. Enough already. Give us your wife's location. She abandoned you, Davis. You told us yourself. She's not coming for you. What do you owe her? We need her to program the Transition Lens, and we won't stop looking for her."

Hart jerked Mick's head up and forced open one bloody eye.

"I told the Supreme God of the Earth about this great idea I had. Crucify Davis, I said, unless he denies his false god, but before you nail him to the cross, give his wife two hours to surrender. How much does she love you, Davis? Will she sacrifice herself to save your life? Or are you going to be the sacrificial lamb? Well?"

A tear leaked from Mick's eye. He knew what Heather would do. She would never let him go to the cross if there was a way to save him. He would gladly sacrifice himself for her, but couldn't stomach her becoming a pawn for Satan just to save his life.

Hart slammed Mick's head against the wall.

"Suit yourself, you dumb ape. When I come back,

I'm going to take great pleasure in driving the nails into your hands and feet. I don't care how much the locusts bite me. You know what we found out? They won't kill us. Oh, we feel like dying, but we can't die. They may sting the crap out of me for driving the nails into your hide, but it'll be worth it. Later, hero."

The cell door slammed shut, and Mick's head fell back onto his chest.

"Lord," he prayed silently and earnestly. "Please. Save Heather. Don't let her give herself up for me. I beg of you, remove me from this torment."

Tears leaked down his cheeks.

"Please, Lord Jesus, take me home. I've not always served you faithfully or well, but I'm ready to go home, if You'll have me."

His mind slipped into delirium. He was back with his squad again, in the middle of a mission. They were all there: Sully, Blinders, Mad Max, Dusty, the entire squad. Mick laughed as someone radio checked Gruesome's call sign. Gruesome was the most handsome SEAL anyone had ever seen, which is how he got his handle.

They were in a big fight somewhere. The mission was supposed to be in/out. He heard four explosions, one sounding right after the other. Good. They had air support. Air support was critical when a mission went FUBAR.

Another explosion rocked the building he was in, followed by two more in quick succession. This was bad. Someone called in fire support danger close. It irritated him they didn't warn him to take cover.

Automatic weapons fire? This delusion had taken him a long way back. He had barely been on his first

Team when they transitioned to energy weapons. That one, now, it sounded remarkably like a SAW, a Squad Automatic Weapon. Mick wanted to chuckle. If their Team had a SAW, someone else was having a bad day.

Dull, thudding explosions punctuated the sound of the automatic weapons fire. Flashbangs, his depleted mind told him. Essential in CQB. He tried to remember his mission; what were they assaulting? It had to be a compound of some sort. Maybe it was a rescue mission. He'd been in a lot of those.

Another tremendous explosion threw Mick against his restraints, and he shook his head, slowly regaining consciousness. Whatever just got hit, it happened for real and it was close. He shook his head, prodding his brain into wakefulness.

Mick heard the cell door open, and he moaned, but refused to lift his head. He almost hoped for more physical abuse. Torture would stop his heart and he wouldn't have to worry about Heather sacrificing herself to save his life. He uttered another prayer, raising his spirit voice in a shout to Heaven for his life to end.

Someone was advancing on him with a deliberate, heavy step. A hand lifted his chin, and Mick stared into a pair of warm, very concerned eyes. The voice spilling from the man's throat took Mick back into Antiquity. It was a voice he had cherished from the day he first heard it in Gilgesh, in Mesopotamia, in the long distant past. The voice meant peace, freedom, and healing. It was the voice he had longed to hear since they confined him in this hellish place.

"Your suffering is over. You are going home."

ABOUT THE AUTHOR

Dale lives in Cochrane, Alberta, Canada with his amazing and beautiful wife, and their bevy of furry children. When they are not practicing law, Dale and Anika enjoy collaborating on his novels.

When the Stars Fall is the fifth book in the series detailing the lives of Tul'ran and Erianne az Nostrom. The sixth book in the Tul'ran series, *Escape and Evade*, is well underway at the time of this publication.

The other four novels are available from Amazon in hardcover, paperback, and e-book formats. In their order in the series, they are:

The Ballad of Tul'ran the Sword
A Time, and Times, and Half a Time
Abandon Hope
Wolf's Den

Dale published this novel on the 40th anniversary as a practicing lawyer. If he's had any success in life, it's entirely because of a gracious, kind, and very loving God.

Manufactured by Amazon.ca
Acheson, AB

13302615R00226